"*Tangled Tides* includes a delicious romance that even the most dispassionate soul can't refuse. I absolutely adored Yara and her strength in all things, including love. And Treygan? I seriously want in on that merman action. Blue has never been so sexy. Hooper has created a believable underwater world that will leave readers wishing for a tail instead of legs."

Elana Johnson, author of *POSSESSION*

"I adored this tale of sea monsters and forbidden love. Full of deception, romance, and intrigue, *Tangled Tides* is a story best savored but impossible to put down."

PJ Hoover, author of *SOLSTICE*

"*Tangled Tides* is a delightful, smartly plotted tale of adventure, family secrets, and sizzling romance. I couldn't put it down!"

Rae Carson, author of *THE GIRL OF FIRE AND THORNS*

Published by Rhemalda Publishing
P.O. Box 2912
Wenatchee, WA 98801
http://www.rhemalda.com

Cover art by Melissa Williams
http://mwcoverdesign.blogspot.com/

Interior art by Alexandra Shostak
http://www.AlexandraShostak.com

ISBN   Paperback   978-1-936850-43-3
       ePUB   978-1-936850-44-0
       ePDF   978-1-936850-45-7

Library of Congress Control Number: 2011939822

Visit author Karen Amanda Hooper on the Web at
http://www.karenamandahooper.com

Acknowledgements

No woman is an island. That saying couldn't be truer about the creation of *Tangled Tides*. So many people contributed to making this novel a reality. I owe my eternal thanks to all of the following beloved folks:

My parents, for being the best mom and dad in this (or any other) world, and for instilling my steadfast belief that dreams really can come true. You gifted me with the ability to see magic and it led me to my greatest joy: telling fantastical stories.

Krista, my soul sister. Thank you for reigniting my love of fiction at the exact time I needed it, for chauffeuring me to my first writer convention, and for your instant faith that I would undoubtedly be published.

John, my Peter Pan. You helped me stay afloat while allowing me to drown in my writing, and you indulge my playful spirit with our escapes to Neverland. Thank you for loving such a complicated pixie.

Andrea, my twin Tinkerbell. Thank you for loving books, helping me name places in my story, and being a great friend.

Steve Graham for creating the music to the *Tangled Tides* trailer and helping me with all things website and computer related. You were one of my first readers and biggest supporters. I'll always consider you family.

Louise Geczy, my all-time favorite teacher who took my spark of passion for creative writing and fanned it into a roaring blaze. You told me that someday I would write a book; I'm sorry it took me so long to believe what you already knew.

My M-N-Ms. Megan, Natalie and Marie: my original writing group and my transcendental trinity.

Megan McBride, you make me dive deeper and bring the hidden details to the surface.

Natalie Bahm, you keep my romance in check and my characters loveable.

Marie Devers Jaskulka, you raise the writing bar while teaching me the rules and how to bend them.

You three are wiser and more powerful than the gorgon sisters. Thank you for supporting and guiding me every step of the way. I would be lost without you.

Sara McClung, my heaven-sent siren. You've been there through the good and bad, been my partner in mischief, and when my skies were stormy you parted the clouds and sent me sunshine.

Alexandra Shostak, my miraculous mermaid. You swam by my side offering me advice, reassurance and undying help and support while keeping me entertained with your own stories and singing me songs.

Rebecca Brown, for diving into my original draft back in 2009. You assured me I had a pearl then helped me buff it until it shined.

Michelle Davidson Argyle, for encouraging me to submit to Rhemalda. You pointed me down one of the best roads I've ever traveled and you've been an amazing supporter along the way.

Emmaline and the review team at Rhemalda. You read my story and believed it was worthy of publishing. How can I ever give adequate thanks for such a priceless gift?

Rhett. You tackled and mastered the feat of rushing *Tangled Tides* to publication yet never let the quality or end result be compromised.

Diane Dalton, my editor. While making my book cleaner and stronger you taught me how to forever be a better writer.

Melissa Williams, the creator of my magical cover. You are the queen of patience and accommodation, and a master at making my vision a reality.

Ron Schirmacher, for the beautiful designs on my blog and websites and answering my never-ending technical questions. You're a rock star.

My incredible blog peeps, many whom I now consider friends. Your support, comments, and encouragement have meant more to me than you'll ever know.

And last, but most certainly not least, to my readers. Sometimes it's hard to believe you're really out there. But for those who read *Tangled Tides*, imagine me reaching through these pages and hugging you. My gratitude is deeper than the oceans.

Dedication

For my Mother

Even when the waters are rough or dark,
you give me the faith and strength to
keep swimming toward the light.

Tangled Tides

The Sea Monster Memoirs

KAREN AMANDA HOOPER

Rhemalda Publishing

Mon-ster (noun)

1. a legendary animal combining features of animal and human form or having the forms of various animals in combination.

2. any animal or human **grotesquely** deviating from the normal shape, behavior, or character.

Gro-tesque (adjective)

1. odd or unnatural in shape, appearance, or character; fantastically ugly or absurd; bizarre.

2. fantastic in the shaping and combination of forms, as in decorative work combining incongruous human and animal figures with scrolls, foliage, etc.

The Storm

Yara

I needed to choose between the angel and the mermaid.

"Alright, ladies, which one of you are willing to sacrifice yourself?" I asked.

The angel's lips looked serious. The mermaid wore a mischievous smile.

Uncle Lloyd loved his hand-carved wall panels of mythical creatures, but the six-foot rectangular slabs of teak were the only things big and strong enough to protect the living room window. We used all the plywood we had as window coverings during the last hurricane. My uncle said he would replace it, but he must have forgotten. Poseidon was my first choice. He looked all tough, holding his trident high above his head, but the sea angel and mermaid were closest to the front door.

The wind howled outside. I said another prayer that my uncle would be safe. He was stuck on the mainland, but at least he had the shelter of a hospital, and hopefully they had given him his dialysis treatment.

I peered out the window to make sure the lighthouse was still shining strong. If any boaters were caught in this sudden storm they would see the steady beacon of light and take shelter here until it passed. They were my favorite kind of visitors. Sea dwellers always had such interesting and exciting stories to tell.

Mother Nature nudged me to choose between the wall panels by throwing a palm frond against the window. The fronds slapping against the glass made me jump. The downpour of rain sounded like pebbles pelting the roof and porch. Only one thing left to do.

I chose the mermaid.

She would have to take one for the team while the angel watched over me and the house.

After some serious struggling I lifted the heavy panel of wood off the wall. It thudded against the floor, missing my toes by a hair. I gripped the edge and began pushing it along the tile floor.

"Good grief, you're heavy," I grunted.

I needed to get the mermaid outside to block the window, but when I opened the front door the wind knocked me sideways. Thick, low-hanging clouds moved quickly, breaking apart then swirling together, forming constantly changing ink splotches in the sky. Rownan was out there somewhere, hopefully safe in the Keys. Part of me wished we could have been stormed in together, listening to the wind and rain while cuddling on the couch by candlelight.

No time to daydream, though. I had a home to protect. I slid the wooden panel a few more inches then stopped when it hit the doorsill.

"Come on," I groaned, leaning into it with all my weight. My flip-flops squeaked across the damp tile. My feet walked in place as I pushed, but the mermaid wouldn't budge. Between my groans and the wailing wind I thought I imagined a voice outside—until I heard it again.

"Would you like help with that?"

I jerked my head up to see a guy standing on the porch

wearing nothing but a pair of shorts, the wind whipping his long, dark hair around his face.

"Who are you? Where did—get in here!" I urged as a rumble of thunder shook the house.

He squeezed between the door and the mermaid panel, glancing at it as he smoothed back his wet hair.

I didn't see any boats arrive. Did I read the reservation log wrong? Did my uncle rent out one of the cottages this weekend?

"Are you a guest?" I asked.

His cobalt eyes met mine for the first time. He looked familiar, but I couldn't place him. Maybe his family vacationed here before. He looked about twenty, not much older than me.

"A guest?" he questioned.

"You're vacationing on the island, right?"

"No. I'm not." He nodded at the slab of wood beside us. "Any reason you're pushing that outside during a hurricane?"

"I need to get it on the porch to protect that." I pointed at the living room window. "More importantly, who are you and why are you here?"

He stepped close to me and I backed up against the wall, thinking he was about to touch me. Instead, he grabbed the top of the panel and rocked it up on one corner. His wet forearms, biceps and back muscles bulged and flexed as he maneuvered the panel over the doorsill and pushed it onto the porch.

I'm not sure why I stood there watching like a helpless mute. Maybe it was the shock of seeing someone else on the island, in my uncle's house, no less. The guy's shorts were soaked and hanging dangerously low on his hips. Rownan would so not approve of my gawking. By the time I snapped out of it, Mr. Mysterious had slid the panel in front of the window, blanketing the living room in darkness. He walked through the open doorway, backlit by storm clouds.

"My name is Treygan. Do you need help with anything else?"

How did this guy end up at Eden's Hammock during a hurricane? Should I be scared of him? If he wanted to hurt me or rob my uncle, he wouldn't help me with manual labor first, right?

"No, that's it," I replied. "Everything is boarded up." We just stood there looking at each other until I noticed the puddle forming at his feet. "Be right back."

I left him dripping in the entryway while I ran into the bathroom and grabbed a towel.

"Didn't you hear the hurricane warning?" I called over my shoulder. I raced back with the towel, but when I reached him I slipped on the wet tiles. He caught me by the arm and I blushed. I tried to cover my embarrassment by handing him the towel, but he just held it, not drying off or wrapping it around himself like I expected. He stood there silently.

"Um, you'll be safe here if you need a place to stay during the storm." I glanced around, pulling my damp hair into a ponytail and trying not to stare at his half-naked body. "If you need to, you could borrow some clothes from my—"

"Yara," he quietly interrupted.

I stiffened. I could've sworn his blue eyes darkened and teal lightning flashed around his pupils. "How do you know my name?"

"I need you to trust me." His voice was like a soothing rumble of thunder. "Let me take you someplace safe."

Again, teal lightning bolts streaked across his irises. I couldn't stop staring at them. My head felt hazy and disconnected from my neck, but I nodded.

He took my hands in his and I didn't resist. I should have, but I couldn't. His words stretched through the space between us like warm taffy. "If you want me to take you someplace safe, you have to say that's your wish."

I had no control of the words that came out of my mouth. My lips felt fuzzy as I spoke. "I wish for you to take me someplace safe."

4

An invisible ribbon that felt like velvet wrapped around us, pulling us close and tying us together. The house and everything in it fell away. We began floating through a mesmerizing silver fog.

Were we dancing? We glided and twirled in different directions. The steady beat of his heart pounded against mine. A scent of honey mixed with salty ocean air kissed my nose, evoking muddled memories from my childhood. Rain drops tickled my skin as the sound of howling winds and crashing waves grew louder yet more melodic. I held Treygan tighter, never wanting whatever this was to end.

Water caressed my legs, like I was sinking into a warm, inviting bath. I felt calm, peaceful, and safe. Treygan's tranquil voice echoed inside my cloud of euphoria.

"Take a deep breath," he whispered into my ear.

So I did.

day 1

I didn't know where I was. When I opened my eyes to a sea of aquamarine, I mentally processed the water surrounding me. I was underwater, yet not drowning. Breathing felt normal. Definitely a dream.

The slab of rock I was lying on jabbed into my back. Two dolphins spun around each other a few feet above me, stirring the water. Strands of my hair, the color of a Yellow Tang fish, floated around my face. Air bubbles drifted past me as I sat up.

Realizing I was naked from the waist up, I crossed my arms over my chest and looked down. What the crap? My boobs were still there—not that I had much curvage to brag about—but my skin was covered with shiny drawings of intricate twisting vines and symbols that looked like glowing tattoos. Sleeves of copper leaves crept up my arms, connecting with a maze of artwork that spread across my chest and ended just below my stomach. A golden tail lay stretched out in front of me where my legs should be. I dug my fingers into it, expecting the pain to wake me from my dream, but instead I felt slick scales dig under my nails. I touched my stomach and forearms, but my golden skin, if it was still called skin, no longer felt human— it was too satiny, too slippery. It reminded me of the time my uncle and I petted stingrays at the aquarium.

I bobbed my head back and forth, trying to figure out what my imagination had created. I looked up, down and side-to-side, but the water forced me to move in slow motion. Lack of sunlight indicated I was deep in the ocean, but somehow I could see clearly. Plants in vibrant shades of purple, green and yellow swayed back and forth. Coral in neon hues of pink, orange and blue stretched like crooked fingers, reaching for the fish swimming around them.

A ghostly pale merman with blue-black hair and the same color tail swam toward me. He slithered through the water like a menacing snake, stopping several inches from where I sat.

Do you know where you are? His words were clear, but his lips didn't move.

Did I just hear his thoughts? I wondered.

Yes, it's how we communicate. Again, his mouth stayed closed. His voice was only in my head. That could only happen in dreams. *Do you know where you are?*

My yellow hair floated around my face again. I pushed the strands away. *Yes, I'm in a crazy—yet kind of cool—dream.*

Dream?

This. I motioned to everything around us. *Imagining a world underwater where people are part fish.*

He blinked a few times, then his pale lips turned upward into an almost-smile. *I assure you, you are not dreaming. This,* he opened his hands to his sides, *is your new home.*

Memories of the storm came rushing back to me: pushing the mermaid panel through the house, the stranger in the low-hanging shorts, the feeling of being in a trance, Mr. Mysterious saying he would take me someplace safe.

My hands trembled. My breath came so fast I started to

hyperventilate—except I breathed in water, which should have been impossible. I felt lightheaded, like I might float away. The water surrounding me seemed to pulse with every rapid beat of my heart. I gripped the rock under me, trying to cling to something solid—something real.

"No!" I screamed, slamming my hands against the rock. But my yelling came out like muffled meowing, and trying to slam something underwater didn't have nearly the effect it did on land.

My boyfriend had told me horror stories about merfolk. He said they kidnapped humans and stole their memories, then used them as play toys. Over the past week he had been stuck on the topic, warning me to stay away from them. I thought it was his way of making fun of my uncle's obsessive art collection. Merfolk couldn't be real. People didn't live underwater!

I took a few deep breaths, proving without a doubt that I could breathe underwater. It wasn't a dream. This was actually happening. But accepting it as real would be insane. Had I gone insane? Could that be the explanation?

According to Rownan, merfolk were conniving and mean-spirited. The guy floating in front of me looked like he fit that description. Had I really been kidnapped and turned into a monster? If so, I wasn't going down without a fight.

Are you feeling alright? Creepy Guy asked.

Of course not! I'm a mermaid, and you're the finhole who kidnapped me.

His eyes widened. Maybe he thought he deserved more respect but, like my mother, I've never been good at controlling my temper.

What is a finhole? he asked.

An asshole, but custom-tailored for you.

He shook his head. *That doesn't even make anatomical sense.*

Whatever. Makes sense to me.

A school of orange fish swam by us. It concerned me that I could hear them humming a high pitched tune, but I had a hunch that many bizarre things existed in this world—a world I'd been brought to against my will. I ignored the fish and refocused on Creepy Guy.

Between his nearly-black eyes, corpselike skin and sharply angled chin, he looked like the Sea Devil of Death. I didn't know which emotion had more control over me: fear of being alone with this ghoulish, twice-my-size guy, or shocking disbelief that I was deep in the ocean, with a tail, having conversations through my mind.

Creepy Guy glanced to the east. What the—? How did I know which way was east? In every direction I saw nothing but turquoise water, colorful coral and plants, then more water. Nothing indicated which direction was which, but I felt like I had a built-in compass.

Your guardian will be here momentarily. Until then I suggest we refrain from communicating. He floated away from me.

I am eighteen. I don't need a guardian. I packed the thought with plenty of attitude, but he didn't flinch or respond. No way was some gothic-looking freak going to ignore me, or hand me over to some guardian. *Tell me how to get back to my island!*

Still no reply. I swam over to him, reaching up to poke his shoulder, but a rush of water churned around us and the current pushed me backward. When the bubbles cleared, a second merguy floated eye-to-eye with him.

The newcomer had blue hair that almost matched the water around us. His repulsive tail and fins were a shade lighter and iridescent. He looked colorful compared to the other guy. I swam forward and floated beside them, but neither turned to look at me.

Symbols, scrolls and designs similar to mine covered

their opalescent skin in shades of silver, black and blue. I blinked several times, trying to figure out if the artwork was shimmering or if the water created the illusion. Regardless, they looked like freaks. And I had become a freak too. My uncle could never see me like this.

My uncle. Dear God, what would I tell him? What would Uncle Lloyd think when he got home and found me missing? He'd spaz out! How long had I been under water? Hours? Days? Weeks? Stress was the last thing he needed in his condition. I had to find a way home.

Looking up, I watched the indigo merman swim away. His dark tail and hair snaked up and down as he faded into the distance. The other monster stared at me. He was the guy from the house—Treygan.

Hello, Yara. His eyes matched his Smurf-blue hair.

I crossed my arms over my plant-motif chest. Why had I trusted some stranger who appeared out of nowhere? Just because he was helpful and attractive? How stupid could I be? I felt like crying, if it was even possible to cry under water.

This guy—or whatever he was—wasn't worthy of my tears. I steeled myself and met his gaze again. *You did this to me. I trusted you, invited you into my uncle's home, and you put me in some kind of trance and kidnapped me.*

His head slowly turned from side-to-side. I couldn't tell if it was on purpose, or because of the water. Everything around me seemed to be in constant motion.

I didn't kidnap you. I saved you.

I slapped him. I couldn't stop myself. But slapping didn't work any better than slamming. I only brushed my hand against his cheek. He looked amused. Frustrated, I turned my back to him.

That was supposed to be a slap across your face! I mentally shouted. *How dare you bring me here? I didn't agree to this.*

I have loved ones who need me. They'll be worried. You can't just take someone from their home and—

His hand touched my shoulder.

I spun around to face him. *Don't touch me.*

He squinted, but didn't look away. *I wanted to make sure you were alright.*

Are you deaf? I just told you, I hate you for bringing me here. You had no right to do this to me.

Something about his chest caught my attention. Had his tattoos moved and changed color? I stared at them, expecting to see it again, but he waved his fingers in front of my eyes, breaking my focus.

I can't hear your thoughts if I can't see your eyes. If you thought something while your back was turned to me, then yes, I was deaf to it.

Oh. I didn't realize— I shut my eyes, trying to gather my thoughts without having them overheard by my new worst enemy. He *saved* me from the hurricane? I would have rather drowned, or suffered a fatal head wound from flying debris— anything but being taken from my home and turned into a fish.

My boyfriend hadn't been kidding. The evil mermonsters he warned me about were real. Why hadn't I listened to him?

Where was Rownan? Was he okay? Had the hurricane hit his town? We were supposed to go on vacation together to celebrate my birthday, but now he'd be disgusted by me. My eyes flew open. *I need to find my boyfriend.*

Your boyfriend? I didn't know you had a boyfriend.

You don't know anything about me!

He spun halfway around, then faced me again. *This boyfriend of yours, what is his name?*

None of your business.

His hands balled into fists. *How do you expect me to help you find him if I don't know his name?*

If I tell you, do you promise to take me back to Eden's Hammock? He's probably there, worried to death.

I promise to take you home.

Deal. His name is Rownan.

The chest thing happened again, and this time I got a good look at it. The skin around his tattoos changed from pearly white to dark silver. *Has this Rownan claimed the title of your boyfriend?*

My heart fluttered. We had fought over this issue. *He doesn't like labels.*

Of course he doesn't, Treygan scoffed.

You don't know him. Keep your snobby remarks to yourself.

Does he have spiky brown hair and a beard that matches it?

I lifted my chin. *He has a goatee, not a beard.*

Does he wear a long, white coat?

I looked away. Rownan's coat. I had never seen him without it, and never seen anything—or anyone—more gorgeous. He had such a cool style. It was one of the million attractive things about him. *Yes. How do you know him?*

Treygan's entire chest turned metallic gray and the tribal rope around his stone anchor tattoo definitely moved. *Rownan is a lying, cunning cheat—who happens to be my half-brother.*

 Yara repeated the words, *"He's lying,"* in various tones: certain, doubtful, questioning and back to certain. The sooner she mastered our form of communication, the better off we would both be.

Merfolk do not lie, I countered calmly.

Ha! That's a lie to cover up all your other lies! Merfolk are known for their evil tricks.

Delmar thought he had drained her of any sea creature

knowledge. However, it seemed she remembered being educated—or *mis*educated—about our kind.

Unraveling the intricate knots of Rownan's lies would take a while, so I made myself comfortable on a nearby boulder. When I looked up, Yara was rambling.

No way is that guy related to Rownan. No freakin' way. He really needs a haircut. How is he sitting underwater? This stupid way of life makes no sense—

Sitting is easy, I interrupted, gesturing at a large rock. *Why don't you try it?*

What? Hey, I didn't—some of my thoughts aren't meant for you to hear. Stay out of my head.

Look away if your words aren't meant for me. It isn't a difficult concept. I couldn't hide my annoyance. Transforming and educating humans was a daunting and never-ending task, and I had no time for it.

She eyed me from head to fins, her scowl softening a bit. *How can you live underwater and not be wrinkled like a prune?*

It's a sea creature thing: minimal effects of gravity, proper hydration, limited exposure to human pollutants, and other factors that could be compared to a fountain of youth.

She stared at me, a jumble of incoherent thoughts passing through her mind. For the briefest moment her eyes reminded me of autumn suns. Her long eyelashes fanned outward like amber rays of light. Then she squinted and returned to scowling.

How old are you? Twenty?

A few decades have passed since I was born.

A few decades puts you at thirty. That's a third of the way to ancient.

Ancient. She had no concept of what ancient meant. *Not in our world. Most of us live to be three-hundred years or so.*

Three-hundred! Why would anyone want to live that long?

We aren't considered old until about two-hundred and fifty.

13

We age differently than humans. I had promised the Violets not to participate in Yara's education without discussing it with her teacher first, but I wanted to suck this girl into my mind and show her the truth until her pretentious head exploded. *You have a lot to learn about the mer way of life.*

Apparently I had a lot to learn about human transformations. Her yellow hair and golden irises were perplexing. She should have started as a Red. Delmar assured me there had to be an explanation. He was on his way to update the elders, and soon we would have answers.

Yara continued to ramble. *I don't want to learn about this ridiculous way of life. I want to be human again. Take me back to my island.* She waved her hands above her head. *This is not my home and it never will be.*

Pissy—I believed that was the current slang word to describe her attitude. The pissy side of Yara was one I hadn't seen much of throughout the years. I didn't care for it at all. *If human life is so splendid then why did you spend so much of yours sitting on the beach, crying for hours on end and gazing at the ocean?*

She inhaled a mouthful of water. *You spied on me?*

Don't flatter yourself. I avoid going ashore whenever possible, and I have better things to do than stalk a human child.

I'm not a child! I'll be eighteen tomorrow!

My focus shot toward a turtle swimming in the distance. Yara didn't know today was her real birthday. Her mother was smarter than I had given her credit for. It reminded me that there were only eighteen sunsets left until the gateway to our realm could be unlocked. The reward was well worth putting up with this childish drama. I would do anything to return my people to safety, including keeping up my end of this wretched deal.

Our eyes met again. *Yara, I am well aware of your age. Reporters have been assigned to you for quite some time.*

Reporters? Numerous merfreaks have been spying on me?

Call my people freaks one more time and I will show you just how freaky I can be. I swam forward until our faces were inches apart. *If you think you hate me now, wait until you see me angry.*

I wanted to retract my words immediately. A lump bobbed in her throat as she watched my hallmarks swirl through my skin. Why was I letting this girl get me so riled up?

Yara rubbed her eyes. *Do your tattoos keep moving, or is the water making me hallucinate?*

I forced my thoughts to take a calmer tone. *They are called hallmarks. They represent our heritage and individual character traits. They also adjust according to our emotions.*

She glanced down at her own symbols and shook her head. *Back to my question. Who has been spying on me?*

Let's go meet some of the others, including the mermaid who reported your whereabouts to me. Rude thoughts continued to gush out of her. Civil conversation didn't appear to be an option, but maybe humor would help. *Shall I gather the seahorses for the long journey?*

She paused, glancing at the fish and plants around us. *You ride seahorses?*

I fought back a laugh. *If you believe that,* I nodded at the hallmark leaves covering her breasts, *you must also think the women wear seashell bikini tops.*

She folded her arms over her chest and floated away from me. *We had a deal. You said you'd take me to find Rownan. Or was that one of your merfolk lies?*

If I could have tied her to a sunken ship and left her there I would have. Who could have guessed she would transform into such a cantankerous brat? *Fine. We will find Rownan first.*

Then we would find Koraline. She had failed her assignment

miserably. How did we not know Rownan had been interacting with Yara? My serpent hallmark slithered down my back. Its silver eyes burned against my skin. *Yes, let's go find Rownan. My big brother might be surprised to see me.*

Rownan

Yara's house was all jacked up. Sections of the roof were missing, pieces of siding had come off, and lawn ornaments had blown around to random places. A garden gnome sticking out of the shed with his red boots in the air made me chuckle. I banged on the front door and discovered it was unlocked.

"Yara?" No answer.

After doing a sweep of the house and finding no trace of her, I stepped out onto the wraparound porch. The hurricane had given it one hell of a beating. Picking up a broken railing spindle, it occurred to me that playing Mr. Fix-It would be a good excuse for me to hang around and keep an eye on her. No need for the birthday vacation scam anymore.

I stared down the muddy road leading away from her house. Most likely, she had gone to Lloyd's place. Why she loved that old man I would never understand. They weren't even blood related.

"Rownan." Nixie's voice startled me.

"Nix, what are you doin' here?"

She flashed her sultry smile and leaned against the railing, flaunting her cleavage. Not that I minded—I'm loyal to my girl, but not blind.

"This storm was my doing," Nixie purred. "I wanted to appreciate the fruits of my *harrrd* labor."

Even with her sexy "r" rolling skills Nixie knew I would never give in to her flirting, but she couldn't help going through the motions. Sirens were hardwired to be seductive. I had a thing for redheads, so Nixie was hands-down my favorite eye candy.

"Your doin', huh?" I blew a crimson feather off of her neck. The satisfaction of mischief-making sparkled in her eyes and we both smiled. Then a realization hit me and I pulled back. "Why did you pick this Podunk island to bust up with a storm?"

Shrugging, she brushed the lingering feather from her bare shoulder. "Oh, I don't know, a certain handsome aqua stud might have asked me for a favor."

My blood ran ice cold. I tightened my grip on the spindle in my hand. "Nixie, no. Not Treygan."

She tucked a strand of hair behind her ear. "What's the big deal? Delmar had a gripe with some islander and Treygan asked me to give him a scare."

"Dammit, Nixie! Way to royally screw us!" I threw the spindle against the house and started pacing. This couldn't be happening. He used the storm as a cover and took her. So help me gods, I'd rip his fins off!

"Darling," Nixie cooed, "it was just a little hurricane. A Cat 2. Not even my best work."

I grabbed her by the shoulders, fighting the urge to shake her. "You're missing the point. He made you brew up that storm so he could take Yara."

She flinched and shrugged my hands off of her. "Yara? No, he said—"

"I don't care what he said! Tomorrow is her eighteenth birthday. He used you so he could kidnap her."

She tried to laugh, but doubt flashed in her ruby eyes. "No. He wouldn't have—he would've told me—we were just—"

"Ugggh, Nix, when are you gonna realize he's a manipulator?"

Her wings drooped low at her sides. "Treygan wouldn't lie to me."

"He twists the truth. It's as bad as lying."

It was Nixie's turn to pace. She walked so fast that her high-heeled boots didn't have time to sink into the mud. Her obsession with Treygan had cost me Yara. Every breath I took felt like inhaling dry ice. I cracked my knuckles over and over, trying to keep my hands from doing something I'd regret. If I didn't fear the wrath of Nixie's deranged sisters, I might have strangled her to death.

Treygan would pay for taking Yara. I didn't know how yet, but I would figure out a way.

Nixie screeched—a telltale sign of a pissed off siren—and our eyes locked. She looked as furious as I felt. Her wings extended high and wide behind her. "That bastard. Did he think he could deceive me and get away with it? Wait until I tell Otabia and Mariza."

Perfect. Let Treygan be the focus of the sirens' fury for a while. I had people to see and a plan to whip up—*pronto*. I hopped over the railing and pushed past her. "Send Mariza and Otabia my love."

She grabbed my arm in an iron grip and I gritted my teeth. Sirens were deceptively strong. I could already feel the bruise forming.

"Rownan, what are you going to do?"

"Try to shadow Treygan and get Yara away from him. They can't be far. Yara will be worried about Lloyd. She'll want to come back to check on him."

Nixie released my arm as her crimson wings flapped violently, lifting her into the sky. She gave one last nod and flew away.

I bolted for the water. Time was precious. They couldn't turn Yara until she was eighteen. I needed to find her and get her far away from any and all merfolk before her birthday tomorrow. If I screwed it up, we were all dead.

Yara

Relief set in once I saw the lighthouse poking through the nearly-endless blue of ocean and sky. Eden's Hammock was just up ahead. Home had never looked so good.

While we swam, I kept sticking my face in the water and inhaling. It was refreshing and tasted clean, like lemons. Breathing water made me feel better, which freaked me out a little. Since being turned into a freak of nature, the world seemed different above the surface. The air was humid and had the familiar saltwater smell, but it tasted dirty. Colors looked dull.

My swimming slowed as we reached the dock—what was left of it.

Treygan held onto the ladder with one hand. "Ladies first."

"I can't get out yet. My tail will disappear and I'll be naked, right?"

His blasé expression didn't change. "Yes."

"If you think I'm letting you see me naked, you've lost your waterlogged mind."

He dropped his hand back into the water. "Why are humans so embarrassed about being unclothed? It's the way you were born."

Just the thought of Treygan seeing me naked made my cheeks burn. "Umm, hello? Ever heard of modesty, or indecent exposure?"

He swam beneath the dock and seemed to search for something. "You're the one who demanded we go ashore. What do you suggest we do?" He glared at me.

"Get me some clothes!"

"There are none," he said through his teeth. "We usually keep a supply of garments stashed under piers, but the storm must have blown them away."

Clothes stashed under piers? He had to be kidding. "There's

no way. I've swam all around this island and under the piers. I've never seen any clothes anywhere."

"Merfolk have certain abilities that allow us to hide *many* things from humans."

I paddled closer to him. "You're telling me that you can make things invisible?"

He tilted his head to the side and winked, which I assumed was a cocky yes, but I didn't believe him. Rownan had warned me about merfreak lies, and I wasn't falling for this one.

"So, what are we supposed to do?" I asked, flooding my words with sarcasm. "Walk around the island naked?"

We both floated in silence, looking around and up at the sky like clothes might drop from the clouds. I bet his stupid magic merman powers couldn't make that happen.

Treygan spoke flatly. "We're not supposed to be here. You should be with your teacher, learning how to survive as a mermaid."

"How's it different from being human? I mean, besides the obvious."

"It's not my job to educate you."

"Not your job? You turned me into a fish. I'd say it's your job to answer every question I have."

His indifferent tone didn't waver. "You are not a fish, and I didn't turn you. Delmar did."

"Delmar? The scary Goth guy?" He shot me a mean look and mumbled something under his breath about interpretation. "You said you 'saved' me from the hurricane and took me underwater. So what, you couldn't go through with it? You had to ask that other guy to finish the job for you?"

He leaned back and closed his eyes, floating in the water with total ease. "I do not have the ability to turn anyone."

I hated that I was intrigued enough to ask more questions, but I couldn't help myself. "What do you mean?"

"Important matters such as transforming humans are

20

delegated by ranking. Only Indigos can complete that task without killing the person they are turning."

Rownan had mentioned a color ranking in the mer world. He said it established an order, but he never mentioned their color gave them special abilities. "Doesn't your order start with red?"

He perked up, surprised, and resumed treading water. "Yes. Red, Orange, Yellow, Green, Blue, Indigo and Violet."

"The rainbow? Seriously?" I wanted to gag at the sickening cheerfulness of it. "So, you're blue?" He nodded and smoothed down his wet hair. It wasn't until then that I noticed the color had changed again. "Your hair is darker. Like bluish-black. You look like you did during the storm."

"We are above water in human territory. I'm supposed to look 'normal,'" his fingers poked through the water, making air quotes. "Have you ever met a human with bright blue hair?"

"People dye their hair crazy colors," I snapped. You could pull off the punk look. Especially with your long hair and all your tattoo—er, hallmarks."

He lifted his arm above the water. As quickly as water dripped from his fingers, his markings vanished. His skin lost its pearly hue. He did look "normal." If he wasn't a mermonster, I might consider him attractive, maybe even bordering on hot. Maybe.

"Wow. That's too weird," I mumbled, shrugging my shoulders above the water. My leaf thingies disappeared and my skin looked ordinary again, but through the water I could see blurry hallmarks covering my shimmery chest. My hair, on the other hand, didn't go back to normal. I had always been a brunette like my parents. It was weird to see blonde hair floating around me.

"Why is my hair blonde, and why was it yellow underwater?" Again with the questions. Why couldn't I pretend not to give a crap about this stuff?

"I've been wondering the same thing. You should be a Red like every other new mer. You're an enigmatic Yamabuki."

"What did you call me?"

"Enigmatic."

"No, the yama word."

A cocky smile spread across his face. I wanted to smack it off of him. "Yamabuki."

"What's that?"

"Look it up."

What a prick. Why were the good-looking ones always such toolboxes? "If you're going to insult me, at least use words I understand."

"Why are you so defensive?"

"I'm not." He squinted, studying me like he was trying to read my mind, so I looked away. "Whatever. It's probably some merfreak thing. I don't care what it means. I'll find a way to be human again if it kills me."

"Do you have any idea how blessed you are?" Judging by the anger in his voice, he did want to kill me. "You're insulting our way of life without knowing anything about us."

"I know plenty about your kind."

"You only know what Rownan told you. He is not mer, therefore he doesn't know most of our secrets. Tell me, what do you think of his world? Does his way of life appeal to you?"

"His world is my world. We don't live underwater. We have legs and normal skin. We don't communicate through our minds." My voice got louder, but I couldn't control it. "We live in houses, wear clothes, listen to music, read books and drive boats. You know, *human* life!"

Treygan's forehead wrinkled and his mouth opened, but no words came out. Suddenly, Mr. Know-it-all didn't have much to say. He probably didn't know what movies or books were.

I had been gone less than a day and I already missed home. Would I ever help Uncle Lloyd in the garden again? Would we ever play another game of Scrabble together? Were my days of cuddling on the couch with Rownan gone for good? Would he ever kiss me again if he found out I had been turned into a mermaid?

"Rownan cares about me," I said. "He likes me for who I am, not what I am. He won't let this mermaid thing ruin our relationship."

Treygan arched an eyebrow. "Who are you trying to convince, me or yourself?"

I didn't have an answer. My comment replayed through my mind and I realized what a stupid, random thing I had said. Jeez, Yara, keep your big insecure mouth shut. Treygan stared at me so intently that I wondered what else he could see in me—or if he saw anything at all. Maybe he was just looking through me like my mother used to do. "I can't hear your thoughts anymore."

His eyes didn't even flicker. "We're not underwater."

"That's the only time it works?"

"Yes."

At least my thoughts were my own again. Thankfully, he hadn't heard that I considered him borderline hot. He already came off as too full of himself, jutting his chin out when I asked a question and constantly squeezing the bridge of his nose like I gave him a headache.

"You have a wide nose," I mumbled.

"You have a narrow mind," he shot back.

"Well, you could really use a haircut."

Another eyes-closed nose pinch. "If you tame your attitude, I'll cut my hair."

"Why are you so concerned with my personality?"

"Why are you so concerned with my appearance?"

I opened my mouth to deny giving a crap about his appearance, to tell him I didn't find him the least bit attractive, but the untrue words refused to come out.

Treygan

Finally, silence. I thought she would never shut up.

How could one soul be so important, yet so impossible? In the old days it would have been simple: drag Yara through the gateway, show her our world and she would never want to return to human life. Then again, if the gate was open, we wouldn't need her.

I floated at the edge of the drab dock, waiting for Rownan's radar to kick in so he'd make an appearance and I could get back to my mission. If all went well, we wouldn't step foot on land. Yara would be so furious she would beg me to take her away from Rownan.

"What do we do now?" she whined. "Float here all day waiting for clothes to magically appear?"

Her question made my skin prickle with irritation. Sarcasm was a lost art that Yara hadn't come close to mastering. "Rownan will be here shortly."

Her eyes bugged like a Black Moor Goldfish. "What?"

I didn't elaborate. Perhaps if I stopped answering her questions she would stop asking them.

"What do you mean, Rownan will be here? How could he possibly know where we are? He can't see me like this."

I heard my son-of-a-psycho half-brother approaching before I saw him. Better to ignore him until the last second. "He won't see you naked unless you get out of the water."

"You know what I mean. I'm a freakin' mermaid."

Rownan's boots stomping down the dock diverted her attention. I wondered how much she truly knew about him. How much did I even know about him anymore?

"Yara, baby!" he shouted. Baby. How nauseating.

"Oh, my God," she moaned under her breath. Her eyes

darted around the water. "Rownan, this isn't what it looks like. I—"

"I've been so worried about you," he interrupted.

Reluctantly, I turned my head to see my nemesis squatting at the edge of the dock. Our eyes met for the first time in over a decade. My jaw tightened, as did his.

He reached out for Yara. "Let's get you home."

"The storm—I—something horrible happened," she said, not taking his hand.

"It's all good. No worries," he assured her in a tone so fake it made my skin crawl.

She kept one arm pressed tightly to her chest while the other treaded water, then she shot me a smoldering glare. "He kidnapped me. I've been turned into a mermaid."

Rownan looked at me with shock and a hint of panic. Only a daft half-breed like him wouldn't have noticed the change in Yara's hair color, or her hallmarks and tail shimmering below the surface. He still believed her birthday was tomorrow. Chalk one up for keeping secrets.

Yara's bashful mumbling interrupted our brotherly stare-down. "I'm not wearing any clothes."

Rownan took off his coat, holding it open as it waved in the wind. "I won't look until you're covered. Sir, will you turn around while my girl gets out of the water?"

Sir? Really? Yara glanced at me and I did an about-face while her knight in furry armor pretended to rescue her. After some splashing and gasping from Yara, I turned back around.

"It was instant." She glanced from me to Rownan. "My legs, my arms. I feel normal again."

Rownan hugged her, blocking her face from my view while he sneered at me. They looked completely wrong together. Yara cloaked in white next to Rownan's black pants and t-shirt. Yin and yang, dark and light, cold and warm. Mr. Full-of-Lies and Miss Empty-of-Memories.

I cleared my throat loud enough to interrupt their phony sentimental moment and climbed out of the water.

"What are you doing!" Yara shrieked, shielding her eyes.

I brushed the water off my arms, torso and thighs. "You may be bashful and uptight, but that doesn't mean I have to be."

"Rownan, make him cover up," she ordered, keeping her back to me.

"Unfortunately," Rownan snarled, "I can't make him do anything."

"I'm not talking to either one of you until he covers up. I don't need to see his—you know."

"Have some manners, Treygan. Stand behind a tree or something."

Yara dropped her hands from her face and stepped closer to him. "You know this guy?"

Rownan didn't flinch. "Yes, babe, we know each other. I'm surprised he didn't tell you."

To spare all of us from more of Yara's shrieking, I moved behind a waist-high sago palm.

She cautiously peeked at me, then relaxed when she saw the lower half of my body hidden from view. "He said you two are brothers, but I thought he was lying."

"We are *half*-brothers," Rownan said, "but obviously not by choice. What else has he told you?"

Rownan appeared calm and collected, but I could imagine the panicked thoughts racing through his mind. How had I beaten him to the punch? How had I known today was Yara's real birthday? Had I exposed him? Had I told her his plan, his secrets?

Don't answer him, Yara. Unfortunately, we weren't in the water, so she couldn't hear my thoughts.

"He's told me lots of stuff," she said. "Most of it I don't believe."

Ooh, fantastic answer! I wanted to applaud, but instead I shrugged, letting Rownan imagine the worst.

He caressed her cheek and did a poor imitation of a man in love. "We can discuss it later, after we get you home."

I could have acted like a Neanderthal and dragged Yara back into the water, but I knew if I waited long enough, Rownan would dig himself into a hole even he couldn't claw his way out of. Not anymore. Things had changed.

He turned to me with a devious glimmer in his dark eyes. "Treygan, Nixie's on her way with clothes for you, so you should stay put."

My muscles tensed. "Nixie?" Why would she be coming?

He failed to suppress a grin. "We chatted earlier. She wants to discuss the storm with you."

Son of a bitch—literally. Well played, Rownan, well played. "Great," I said, as carefree as I could manage. "You two love birds go on ahead. I'll find you soon."

I expected a bratty remark from Yara, but instead she held Rownan's hand and they walked away without another word.

Thoughts of Nixie caused beads of sweat to form on my forehead. This would be difficult to smooth over. Nixie knew the grand plan, but this was a detour she hadn't seen coming. Sirens despised not knowing everything.

I hadn't lied. Nixie would already know that. Delmar really had quarreled with one of the islanders—a few of them, actually—but I had used Nixie in a roundabout way and she wouldn't let that go unpunished. Hopefully, she hadn't told her sisters what I had done.

"Treygan, you beautiful bastard!" Nixie shouted over the fluttering of her wings.

"Nixie, my favorite garnet goddess!"

"Don't try to sweet-talk me. I know what you—" her red eyes looked me up and down, lingering at my crotch. She landed in front of me, almost on top of me. "Mmm, I do love it when you're in human form, especially *raw* human form."

I bowed politely. "Rumor has it you brought me clothes."

She licked her strawberry lips and pressed against me. Her wings folded backward, covering the bag strapped to her back.

"Clothes? I don't have any clothes," she said innocently, twirling around. "But I could strip out of mine if you'd like." Her talon-like fingers ran along the hook-and-eye closures of her corset top.

"Nix, hand over the bag, please."

She grabbed hold of my wrists and pushed herself against me, whispering against my neck. "You want it? Then take it off me."

"I can't. Your wings are in the way."

A hollow snapping sound echoed behind her as her wings disappeared. The gust of air blew her hair into my face. Locks of shimmering red faded to a human shade of auburn. I slid the bag straps down her arms while she evaluated me with rust-brown eyes. They were much less intimidating in her human state.

"You tricked me, Treygan."

"I did not trick you. Delmar did have a problem with those men. He and I are grateful to you for the storm. You did wonderful work."

Unzipping the bag, I found a pair of tan shorts with more pockets than one person could possibly need and put them on. I held up a blue t-shirt with a red and yellow triangle on the front. The letter S in the middle of the symbol was cracked and fading. "What's the S for?"

"Slimeball." She zipped up my shorts. "This is all backward, you know. Usually I'm *un*dressing someone."

I pulled the Slimeball shirt over my head. "Thank you, Nixie, for everything. You're a life saver."

She twirled a strand of hair around her finger. "Are you referring to the clothes, the storm, or the fact that I unwittingly provided you with a distraction while you stole that over-hyped human and turned her into one of your kind?"

I could've added a few more items to her list. "Take your pick."

In a blur of red she threw me to the ground so hard it knocked the wind out of me. She straddled me and sat down.

"You choose, Treygan. Share a song, or I tell my sisters what you did."

I closed my eyes, debating which would hurt less, the wrath of Otabia and Mariza, or Nixie taking a part of my soul. A few minutes of pain and my debt to Nixie would be paid. Who knew what the outcome would be if Mariza and Otabia got involved. They knew how to hit where it hurt, and they knew I'd endure any amount of torture to protect my people. Nixie was offering me a reprieve.

"This is very gracious of you," I replied.

"Gracious if you choose correctly."

"My decision was made before I asked you to conjure up the hurricane. I had a feeling you would find out about Yara, and I knew the consequences. What I didn't know was if you would let me choose the memory."

Her eyes glistened with hunger. "You anticipated sharing yourself with me?"

"Payment for the prize."

She squeezed her thighs tighter and pinned down my arms. Rocks dug into my back. "You are a fool for thinking your idea will work. You and your brother are both fools."

"Yes, stupidity runs in our blood." Stupidity and evil.

"It's not the blood you share that makes you fools. That cold blood is your only saving grace. You should stop fighting your heritage and embrace it."

Rage coursed through my veins as I reared against her, but on land sirens were stronger than mer. I barely budged her. How dare she bring my father into this? She knew I despised that part of me. She leaned so close I could smell her metallic breath. "Mmm, yes, struggle, my love. It makes this dance more exciting."

Gray clouds above me became thicker, dropping from the sky and stretching around us like a web. Lightning flashed, sending an electrical current buzzing through my muscles. The change in weather meant Nixie was becoming ravenous. We needed to get it over with.

"Do it, Nix. If you want to enjoy yourself, take the memory I chose for you."

She bit her bottom lip. "If it's not a juicy one, my thirst won't be quenched and the process will take much longer."

"Trust me, it's as juicy as it gets."

She gave one powerful lurch forward. Her body arched as her wings exploded from her back and spread out behind her. The red in her irises returned. Her hair shimmered around her narrow face while she sang a melodic siren song.

I rolled my eyes. "That isn't necessary with me."

"It will hurt more because you're in human form," she warned, but there was pleasure in her voice. Sirens fed on pain—emotional and physical.

The water's edge was several yards away. I could've begged her to do it in the water so it wouldn't hurt as much. Then I reminded myself that the pain would be nothing compared to what awaited me on the Triple Eighteen. Might as well get used to it.

"More pleasure for you, my garnet goddess. Have your way with me."

Her mouth closed over mine and I forced myself to think of the memory I had tried so hard to bury. Bringing it to the surface, I focused on the last time I had seen my grandmother's sapphire eyes, and the fear in them as she died—gruesomely and needlessly—because of me. Just like my mother.

Nixie's teeth sank into my bottom lip. I clawed at the muddy ground as my back bowed, plowing my shoulders deeper into the earth. The pain forced me to tense so rigidly I thought I would snap in half. Nixie moaned in ecstasy while she devoured a pivotal moment of my life—removing it from my mind and soul forever.

Rownan

How could I possibly act normal when my world was crash-and-burning? Suspecting Treygan had kidnapped Yara was one thing. Actually facing the reality of her as a mermaid had my head all jacked up. How much did she remember about me, or us, or any of her past?

Treygan screwed up everything. Years of planning, wasted. I had lost her. My heart, my soul, the love of my life—we would never have our happily ever after. There had to be a way to fix it. True love always triumphs. Isn't that what fairytales preached?

To add to the misery of my current hell, it had to be nearing ninety degrees outside. The ocean breeze wasn't helping my internal temperature. My blood felt like it might start boiling any second.

Yara ran her hands over the fur of my coat. "I've never felt anything so soft against my skin." Her voice sounded silkier than the layers of fine, white hair she was petting. Her mer traits were already developing. "It's incredible."

I faked a smile. "You look incredible in it."

She stopped walking and squeezed my hand. "You don't have to pretend you're okay with this. I know you're not, and neither am I."

I pushed a damp, blonde lock of hair over her shoulder. Waves of repulsion shot through my arm, but I stopped myself from cringing. "I did like you better as a brunette."

She pressed my palm against her cheek and sighed. "Me too."

How long would it be before she realized my touch didn't feel the same? Could the bond we shared be strong enough to keep her crushing on me? The answer terrified me.

"Jesus, Rownan! What happened to your arms?"

I forgot she would be able to see my scars. Playing dumb would be my best option. "What are you talking about? They've always been like that."

She held my hands in hers, studying the faded lines on the insides of my arms and the bruise from Nixie. "There's like a hundred. What happened to you?"

"Clumsy kid. Lots of accidents."

"How did I never notice them before?"

"You're a mermaid now. Your sight has enhanced. I can barely see them." That sounded good, even to me. Totally believable.

Her new fluid voice went all soft and weak. "Are you grossed out by me?"

I wanted to say yes. I wanted to scream it. "Baby, no, of course not. Have you seen yourself? You're glowing."

"Ugh. I don't want to glow. I don't want to be a mermaid."

I didn't want her to be a mermaid either. I wanted a rewind button so I could go back and do it all kinds of different. I would keep her locked in my arms, surround us with an army, and do whatever it took to keep the merfolk from getting anywhere near her. Why hadn't I done that in the first place? My piece of shit brother had ruined my last chance at having love in my life. "Treygan will pay for this. I promise."

"Yeah, about that, why didn't you tell me you had a half-brother who was a merman? Kind of an important detail considering how much you hate their kind, don't you think?"

"Their kind? You mean *your* kind." I waited for her to respond, but she only gave me the evil eye. At least in human form her eyes were the same light brown they used to be. "I didn't tell you because we don't associate. We share blood, that doesn't mean we share anything else."

"Same mother or father?"

"Father."

"I don't understand. How can you be human if he's a merfreak?"

Sweat dripped down my neck and back. "Long story. I'll explain after we get you home and into some clothes. You must be burning up in that coat."

She fanned herself. "It is hot under here. How can you wear this thing all the time?"

"My blood runs cooler than most." But not without my coat. I would have to think through every word I said from now on—unless I came clean. What would happen if I told her the truth?

"Treygan said I haven't even been gone a full day. Have you checked on Uncle Lloyd? Is he home yet? He got stuck on the mainland during the hurricane. I'm worried about him."

"Haven't seen him."

"Is my house damaged?"

"Definite windburn and water spoilage, but nothing I can't repair. Less than three weeks and you'll forget all of this happened."

Her head drooped and she kicked a shell along the ground. "I'll never forget this. It's like I'm stuck in a nightmare."

"I hear ya." My worst imaginable nightmare had come true. I put my arm around her shoulder and pretended we were a happy, normal couple. Yeah, right. It made me nauseous, but at least I had contact with my coat again.

She stiffened when she saw the house. "The roof! The porch. It's—look at it."

"It can be fixed."

"The house is the least of my worries. We need to check on Uncle Lloyd."

We kept walking past her property. Her eyes lit up when she saw the old man's place. "His is fine! Look!" Same old buttercup-colored dollhouse with gag-me-green shutters and a garden so full of flowers a clan of faeries should have been living in it. You would think after his wife died he would've made an effort to make it look more manly.

"Come on!" Yara's barrel-you-over spirit hadn't changed. She took off running, but I was hella burning up, and running would've made it worse.

"You go ahead," I shouted. "I'll catch up."

Nobody was around so I pulled out a seagarette and lit up. I held my breath for the rest of the walk, letting the ice-cold smoke fill my lungs and cool my insides.

Four minutes later I stood at Lloyd's doorstep and exhaled a cloud of silver smoke. Smoking made me feel somewhat better, but I would have to make sure this wasn't a long visit. Treygan would be right behind us. Yara needed to hear the truth from me. He would take way too much pleasure in telling her my secret. I couldn't figure out why he hadn't told her already. Sneaky, self-centered fish—they always had an ulterior motive.

I took one more drag from my seagarette, put it out on the porch railing, and saved the rest for later. Then I wiped the frost from my lips and debated whether or not to knock on Bastard Lloyd's door.

Uncle Lloyd was already home. He had removed all the boards from the windows and was polishing the re-hung mermaid portrait. He looked great. Not a scratch on him or the house. After exchanging our usual greetings, I insisted he sit in his leather armchair and relax.

"You had your dialysis treatment, right?"

34

He grunted, which meant yes and he had hated it.

I sat on the ottoman at his feet and gave his knee a squeeze. "You feeling okay?"

"Some hours are better than others." He picked up a picture of his wife, Liora, from the side table and polished the frame.

Liora had passed away before I ever arrived at Eden's Hammock, but that was before he became so sick. Without me around, he would have no one to take care of him. I guiltily looked away from him.

My life was here with Uncle Lloyd, not underwater. I watched an orange and black fish swim around his aquarium—three-hundred gallons of tropical reef, smack-dab in the middle of his living room. Little did he know a real version awaited me just outside his door. How could I tell him I had been turned into a supposedly mythical creature? The very thought of it seemed so insane.

He scratched his flaking forearms and I grabbed the bottle of cocoa butter from the coffee table. Treatments dried out his skin, and he was awful at taking care of himself.

"It's amazing how your place didn't get hit." I rubbed lotion into his arms and hands. "Did you see my house? It's in shambles."

He waved me away and wiped off the excess lotion with the bottom of his shirt. "Storms are finicky things. The sisters of nature must have kept my house out of their path of destruction."

Storms. One of the few things my mother had loved, and one of the only things we had in common. "Do you think my mom would have cared what happened to our house?"

"My guess would be no. But I do think she would have enjoyed the storm. Nature's fury dancing on our little island would have made her smile."

"My mother never smiled."

He studied me all fatherly-like and mussed up my hair. "Once upon a time she smiled a lot."

The only memories I had of my mother were of her sad and crying, or her mumbling—in a drunken, catatonic state—that she wished I was never born. If she had never had me, maybe she would've been the happy, goodhearted person my uncle spoke of so fondly.

She died when I was eight, so Uncle Lloyd took me in. He was the only person in my life I truly loved and trusted. I could still remember moving into his house. My room had periwinkle walls and white lace curtains. The dresser and headboard looked like dollhouse furniture—not that I knew what dolls were at the time. He said it was my new home, and that he and I were family.

"The kind who takes care of each other," he said.

He held me when I cried, made me love-cooked meals, and tucked me in at night. All of those things were strange and new to me, things my mother had never done. One night Uncle Lloyd gave me a stuffed teddy bear, but I didn't know what to do with it.

"You just love it," he told me.

"Love?"

He sighed and shook his head. He did that a lot the first year of us living together. As I got older and learned about the world beyond our little island, I discovered many interpretations of childhood, family, and love. But my uncle's definition of love—the one he told me while I held my first teddy bear in my hands—was my favorite. "It's when you care about someone so much you would risk everything to keep them safe."

We never kept things from each other, but this mermaid craziness would have to be an exception. He would be safer not knowing, and part of loving him meant keeping him safe.

"Decided to try being a blonde?" Uncle Lloyd asked.

I froze. I had forgotten about my hair. He had been gone a couple days. I could say I had dyed it before the storm. Easy peasy. "I d-d-d—"

Crap! Why couldn't I speak?

He saved me from my stuttering spell. "Didn't think I would notice? I must say, you look beautiful."

His compliment made me smile, but the knock at the door made me smile even bigger. "That's Rownan. We're gonna do damage control on the house, but I'll be back in the morning."

I kissed Uncle Lloyd's cheek, and he grunted as I left the room. He didn't think Rownan was good enough for me. Truth be told, in his opinion, no man would ever be good enough.

Rownan swooped me into his arms and carried me up the steps to my house. Things felt off between us, but what could I expect after being transformed into a half-fish?

"Is this what it'll be like on our wedding day?" I teased.

He rolled his eyes and nodded at the front door. "Open that and you'll get it."

I turned the handle and pushed the door, which was much harder to open than usual. The floors were covered with an inch of water. "Aw, crud."

"I didn't want you walking through it in your bare feet. I'm not ready to see you with fins yet."

Me with fins. How could he say it so casually? What would happen if we went swimming and he saw my tail? I bet he wouldn't act so nonchalant after that freak show.

"Believe me, it's not pretty." Looking down at my feet, I saw the hem of his white coat was caked with mud. Add another item to the long list of reasons why he should dump me. "Ugh, I ruined your coat! I'm so sorry."

"No biggie."

"Yeah, right. I'm sure it costs a fortune to have this dry-cleaned."

He carried me up the stairs to my room without saying another word and set me down on my bed. "You should get dressed. We need to talk."

"Okay." A lump formed in my throat as he walked out of the room. Would he break up with me over this? Of course he would. Why would someone like Rownan keep a half-fish as his girlfriend?

I changed into my favorite sundress, hoping it would give me a shred of confidence, and then called him back into the room.

He looked relieved when I handed him his coat. Even though the house was stifling, he slipped his arms into the heavy sleeves and instantly relaxed. "Yara, I need to tell you something."

This was it. I was going to lose him because a cocky finhole had turned me into a freak of nature.

"Sit down." He pulled out the chair to my vanity table.

"No, thanks, I'd rather stand." Even if I couldn't be strong on the inside, I could fake it on the outside. Never let them see you vulnerable. One of the few useful lessons my mother taught me.

"There's a lot you don't know about me. Stuff I couldn't tell you before. Now that you've been turned, you have to know. Things will change between us and—I don't know how to say this."

Then don't say it, I mentally begged. *Stay with me even if I am a monster.* "Just say it."

"I'm a selkie."

Not even remotely close to what I expected. "A what?"

"Selkie."

Silky, silky, silky. The familiar sound ricocheted around my brain like I should know what it meant, but no definite answer or image came to mind. "Repeating the word doesn't explain what it means."

"Selkies are … we're sea creatures who can shape-shift into humans. In the water we're half seal."

I fought back a laugh. "Is this your way of making fun of me?"

His jaw muscles rippled as he rubbed his hand over his goatee. "No. I swear it's the truth."

My mind went blank. I stared at him, unblinking..

"Yara?"

"You're telling me you're like a merman, but instead of being part fish, you're part seal?" He nodded. "There's no such thing."

He stood up taller and lowered his chin. "I assure you there is. Many such things."

I shook my head involuntarily. He had to be kidding. Never in all my home schooling, or all the stories told to me by vacationers and boaters, had I ever heard or read about a creature like that.

He took my hand and put it against his fur coat. "This coat is like a skin to me; it helps my blood stay cold. Selkies are meant to live in cold temperatures. Without our coats and some other preservers, we'd die—especially here in this warm climate."

"We?"

"My kind."

My fingers gripped the soft, white hairs. How had I never questioned why he wore a fur coat in the hot Florida weather? Why didn't everyone who saw him question it? "There are more people like you?"

"Of course." He said it all snarky, like *I* was the strange one for not being savvy about secret seal people.

"For weeks you've been telling me how much you hate merfolk. Now you're telling me you're just like them?"

"We're nothing like merfolk. You and I are very different, but that doesn't change the way I feel about you."

My mind raced. Did this mean we could be together? We were both some sort of half water, half land weirdos. Would this bring us closer, or drive us further apart? Rownan had never taken me to his house, never introduced me to his family or friends. The mysterious thing had seemed cool at the time, but now I understood why he was so secretive. "Do you really live in Key West?"

"Yes, I didn't lie about that."

"What else *did* you lie about?" My legs felt wobbly and my heart pounded so hard I could feel it in my throat, but Rownan didn't seem rattled at all.

"You never asked me if I was a selkie."

"I didn't know such a thing existed! Why would I ask you about it?"

"If I told you, what would you have done? Freaked out? Never spoken to me again?"

He was right. I probably would've run away screaming if he told me he was a—"Selkie," I whispered, trying to lodge the strange, new word into my vocabulary.

"We're extraordinary creatures if you keep an open mind about us. Please don't shut me out because of this. You have no idea how important you are to me."

Yesterday hearing Rownan say something so sweet would have sent me floating into the clouds. He never talked to me that way. Today his words sent a chill through me. Shock. My body must be reacting so strangely because of shock.

He was the same as before. Dark chocolate hair, goatee to match, and thin lips that curved downward into a sexy pout. His strong hands still looked like they could snap someone into pieces, contrasted by his big, puppy-dog eyes. His irises were so dark they almost blended with his pupils; two black, full moons floating in almond-shaped skies. He did resemble a seal, but he also resembled his half-brother.

I pictured Treygan's eyes. They were the same shape as Rownan's, but Treygan possessed blue moons—rare, unusual, blue moons. *Stop it, Yara. No more thinking about Treygan.*

"I'd never shut you out, Rownan. We're meant to—we're—" Why couldn't I say it out loud? A week ago I had started telling him we were meant to be together. It was my line. It always made him smile.

"I know, baby. You don't have to say it."

Warmth spread over my skin, but it had nothing to do with Rownan. My mind felt like it was physically stretching out the bedroom window and down into the front yard.

"Treygan's here," I announced suddenly. How did I know that? It was like I could sense him approaching the house, but how? Were merpeople psychic? Too many new things were being thrown at me at once. I felt dizzy.

Rownan glanced at the window. "Be careful with him. He'll try to turn us against each other."

I had never seen Rownan scared before, but now fear practically oozed from his sweaty forehead. Did he really think Treygan could come between us? I wanted us to get back to normal, but with these new revelations, I didn't know what normal was anymore. "He could never turn me against you."

"Promise me that will always be true."

To stop the room from spinning, I focused on his pale lips framed by his goatee. "I promise. Why can't Treygan just leave me alone?"

His coat slid out of my fingers as he stepped backward. "I hate to say this, but you need him right now. He'll have to teach you to survive as one of them."

"Whatever he has to teach me, he can do it with you here. I don't want to be alone with him."

41

"You're one of his kind. He'll look out for you. Just remember your promise."

I slid my hands inside his coat, wrapping my arms around his waist and burying my face against his chest. He smelled different, like saltwater and smoky mint, but I tried to ignore it. My legs felt stronger and my head felt clearer. "Don't leave me."

"You have to go with him, but I'll be fixing up the house and trying to figure a way out of this mess."

"Row," I looked up at him. "Do you think there's a way for me to turn into a selkie?"

His ebony eyes seemed to glisten. "Legit? You would do that?"

"I'd rather be part seal than part fish."

"You did look hella cool in my coat." He kissed my forehead and turned away.

I pulled him closer, but something still felt off. "I want a goodbye kiss."

Our lips met and I waited for the familiar tingle to rush through me. Strangely, I felt nothing. We went through all the motions, his hand gliding up the back of my neck and his tongue making perfect circles around mine. So where was my tingly feeling? I opened my eyes and pulled away. My lips felt cold and tasted salty.

"I'll find you soon," he said. "Put on your boots before you go downstairs. I'm still not ready for your fin premiere."

We walked together down the stairs, our kiss on instant replay in my mind. Why was that kiss so bad? Were things already changing between us?

I was careful not to splash water on my legs as we made our way to the front door. Treygan sat on the porch steps—wearing clothes, thank God. He didn't move a muscle as Rownan walked past him.

"Why didn't you tell me?" I huffed once Rownan was out of ear shot.

Treygan didn't turn around. His blue t-shirt stretched against his rounded shoulders. "Tell you what?"

"That Rownan is a selkie."

"It wasn't my place to tell you. Besides, you wouldn't have believed me."

"You're probably right." He stood up and turned to face me. I sneered at his t-shirt. "Ironic, don't you think?"

"What?" he asked. "That you don't believe what I tell you? Yes, ironic indeed."

"No. It's ironic that you—the villain—are wearing a Superman shirt."

"Superman?" He looked down at his chest. "I thought the S stood for Slimeball."

"In your case it does. And why would my not believing you be ironic?"

"Because merfolk can't lie."

I had been distracted by the t-shirt, but now my eyes were drawn to his swollen bottom lip. "What happened to your mouth?"

He lifted his hand and wiped away a drop of blood where a bruise was forming. "Strangest thing, a bird bit me and wouldn't let go."

Fish, seals, and attacking birds. If only I lived in the desert, maybe my life wouldn't be so bizarre.

Treygan

She seemed to believe me. Nixie being part bird was the truth. Sure, she was a much bigger and sexier bird than Yara would picture, but a bird nonetheless. If she believed an absurd story about a bird pecking at my lip, then she must have experienced our inability to lie firsthand.

"Really?" she asked. "We can't lie at all? To anyone?"

"It isn't part of mer nature."

"People decide their nature. If they want to lie, they lie."

"That might be true for humans, but there are different rules for being mer. Same with selkies." I wanted to retract my last three words. I had set myself up for another round of twenty questions.

"What rules do selkies have?"

"You should ask Rownan about that. I wouldn't want to misinform you." I wanted to tell her about their aberrant lifestyle, especially since Rownan had filled her head with falsehoods about merfolk, but it wasn't my place.

The pink and purple sky meant the day was ebbing like the tides. My part in Yara's transformation process was taking much too long. The crops hadn't been picked today, and I had missed appointments with four of my people. I hoped they would find C-weed from someone else to sustain them until I returned. With such a meager amount of plants drying in the sun, supply would be short for the next couple days. I needed to hand Yara over to her teacher so I could get on with my duties.

"When I was upstairs," Yara said, "I knew you were approaching the house, even though I couldn't see you coming. What's that about?"

"You'll sense when other mer are near. You'll also sense humans, but it's a very different feeling."

My head ached from exhaustion. I pulled my last joint out of my waterproof armband and debated whether or not to smoke it. My loyal side wanted to save it for someone in more desperate need than me, but my throbbing head and aching limbs insisted I light it. Snapping my lighter shut, I inhaled and watched the sparkling smoke dance around me.

"Perfect," Yara moaned.

"Beg your pardon?"

"You smoke weed."

How did she know about C-weed? "Yes. Speaking of, we need to return to the ocean. People are counting on me for their supply."

She leaned against the porch post and crossed her arms, making no move to leave. "Even more appropriate. You're a dealer."

"Why do you sound so disgusted?"

"Is that your job as a Blue? To deal weed?"

"It's my duty as Treygan. I'm the only merperson who can access the plants."

"Oh, of course." She mockingly bowed. "You're like the kingpin of the mer world."

I took another puff and blew smoke in her direction, hoping she might inhale some. "Kingfin? What is that?"

"King*pin*, not fin. Forget it. I'm tired of explaining things to you." She walked back into the house.

I snickered. *She* was tired of explaining things to *me*? Surely she was joking. I stayed outside the doorway, assessing the water on the floor.

She turned around and looked me up and down. "Aw jeez, are we like vampires or something? Do you have to be invited in?"

"No," I laughed. "However, I do have manners. It's polite to wait for an invitation."

She almost smiled. "Whatever. Come in." For the first time since she awoke from her transformation, the tension seemed to ease between us. "You should laugh more. It makes you less monsterish."

I took one last drag from my joint, put it out on the doorframe, brushed away the ashes and replaced it in my armband. I stepped aside to clear a path. Flexing my fingers and reaching my hands in front of me, I guided all of the water across the floor and out the doorway. Within fifteen seconds the house was no longer flooded.

"Holy crap!" Yara yelled, her eyes wide with astonishment. "How'd you do that?"

I had forgotten how impressive our abilities might seem to someone who had never seen them. "Controlling water is one of our gifts."

"Teach me how to do it."

"Not now, Yara. We need to get back."

She flopped her hands at her sides. "Something finally seems cool about being mer, and you won't show me how to do it?"

I had to admit that part of me wanted to show off, but there was my promise to the Violets. I couldn't interfere in Yara's learning process. "You don't possess the ability to control water yet. Let's get you back in the ocean so you can strengthen your mer traits."

"Please, Treygan, I'm exhausted and I want to sleep—here, in my house. Not underwater."

Daylight was fading with each passing minute. She needed to get to a resting pool. "Sleep isn't necessary for you anymore."

"Don't tell me you people don't sleep," she said, taking her boots off. "You have to rest at some point."

"Rest, yes, but not sleep. Only one half of our brain rests at a time. The other half stays conscious. We're similar to dolphins that way."

Her nose crinkled as she rubbed her eyes. "How do you dream if you never sleep?"

"We have ambitions and goals. We don't need sleep for that."

"Not those kinds of dreams. Dreams like flying through candy-filled skies, or being a beautiful princess. You know, amazing, unexplainable things that stay with you after you wake up."

"I'm not fond of sweets, and why would I want to be a princess?" I asked, following her into the living room.

"Oh, shut up. You know what I mean." She flipped a light switch but nothing happened. The storm must have caused a power outage.

"We can daydream, but even that seems like a waste of valuable time."

"Forget it. We are obviously way too different to understand each other." She stretched out on the sofa, resting her head on a pillow and yawning. "My body feels weak."

I should have insisted she smoke. How could I have been so careless? "Why didn't you say that before? You need weed."

She crinkled her nose again. "I'm not a stoner."

I went rigid. Did she know what I was? No, she couldn't possibly. She had to mean something else. "What's a stoner?"

Her mouth twisted into a sneer. "Um, a drug addict. Man, what rock have you been living under?" She propped herself up on one elbow. "That weed you smoke, we call it drugs here in Humanville. It's illegal and kills brain cells."

We couldn't be talking about the same thing. "C-weed does not kill brain cells. And it would be useless to humans. Eventually, you will have to smoke it—unless you're suicidal." And if that was the case, I had a different proposition for her.

She rummaged through the coffee table drawers. "You smoke seaweed? Gross."

"Not regular ocean seaweed. It's a plant that grows in the Catacombs—where the gateway to our realm is." It looked like I would be partly educating Yara whether I wanted to or not. "Souls entombed in the Catacombs act as a conduit between this realm and ours. A new type of plant started growing there. We had the Violets examine it, and they discovered its purpose."

"Violets?" she asked, setting two candles on the table.

I pulled out my lighter and lit them. A strong scent of vanilla wafted through the air. "Violets are the wisest of our kind. They discovered that if we smoke the plants, we stay healthy. If not, we get sick. We would all be dead by now if the lost souls hadn't graced us with C-weed."

"Let me get this straight. This weed grows in an underwater graveyard, and you all smoke it? Eww! How sick and twisted is that?"

"C-weed has to be taken from the Catacombs and dried in the sun. The spirits of the lost souls seep through the plants growing on the tombs, supplying us with our realm's energy. Because C-weed grows in Earth's ocean water and dries in the Earth's sun, it provides us with a life force that lets us survive here for longer than we could otherwise."

Candle flames flickered between us, causing shadows to dance along the walls. Yara should know the rest of the story.

About all the people who died rushing to swim through the gate before it was sealed. How their stone statues form an ominous labyrinth along the ocean floor, reminding us of the consequences of broken promises. But none of our kind should have to live with such a depressing image. Every day I was grateful to be the only merperson who had to wander the Catacombs' eerie pathways.

"Sounds creepy," she mumbled, curling into a ball.

I couldn't deny it, so I remained silent and watched her eyelids drift closed. She looked peaceful—such a change from earlier. After her breathing became slow and steady I thought about carrying her back to the ocean, but instead I covered her with a quilt like Lloyd used to do when Yara was a child. I would make up for the missed harvesting time tomorrow night.

Yara should be granted one last night of sleep. Once her transformation was complete, she would never sleep again. She had been through so much in her short life, and over the next few weeks she'd be burdened with an enormous responsibility. The future of our kind depended on her. And we only had seventeen sunsets left to teach her how to do her part.

Rownan

Jack Frost's was infested with the regular crowd. Walking through the door, I inhaled the minty smoke filling the bar. The drastic temperature drop was a comfort I had taken for granted over the years. Air conditioning was pumped in to make the bar twenty-eight degrees Fahrenheit. It wasn't anything like authentic cold weather, but it beat being outside in the heat.

When the bar first opened humans swarmed our turf, but the novelty wore off as more ice bars cropped up around the world. Little did they know our bar wasn't some Eskimo gimmick—it was a key to selkie survival. With bar tops, tables, walls and chairs made of ice, it almost felt like home.

Nah, scratch that. It felt nothing like home. And now that Yara was a mermaid we might never see home again.

I slumped onto one of the ice thrones.

"What'll it be, hon?" Dina shouted over the music. She absently twirled her leather wristband. "Stiff, or stiffer?"

"Stiffest. The nightmare has begun."

She narrowed her eyes quizzically and scurried off to the bar. Jack's bushy brows lifted when she told him my order. He poured a tall glass of Siku vodka and made his way across the room. Jack didn't come out from behind the bar often, but only hours had passed since my last drink and I needed another. That hadn't happened in years.

He handed me the glass. "Hey, son, Dina said you've had a bad day."

A god-awful metal rock song blasted over the sound system.

"Bad is an understatement," I shouted before slamming my drink in one gulp. The combination of alcohol and glacier water slid down my throat. An arctic chill traveled through my chest, along my arms, and extended to my fingertips. Body-freeze beat brain-freeze any day, but it still wasn't enough to numb me. "They won. They turned her."

Jack signaled to Dina who slithered gracefully from behind the bar. Her black fingernails gripped the clear bottle of Siku as she poured us both a shot. Jack studied his drink in silence until the song ended. When a new song blared through the speakers he held up his glass. "A toast."

"To what?" I asked, reluctantly lifting my drink.

"To there bein' more than one way to skin a fish!" He swirled his vodka in circles and sniffed it like it was some fancy wine.

"You know something I don't?"

He wiped his mouth with the back of his hand and smiled, flashing the gap between his front teeth. "I'm the oldest selkie this side of the worlds. I know who's hiding skeletons in their closet and who has an Achilles heel. Give me a seagarette and let's talk outside where I can hear myself scheme."

"First I need a real drink."

He winked as he stood up. "I'll have Dina bring it out. Got a fresh donation this afternoon."

Out in the back alleyway, under a buzzing streetlight, Jack and I smoked while we discussed the situation. Yara's transformation couldn't be undone, but everything could still play out in our favor. We had time to convince her that we were the better side. She didn't have to live with the merfolk or play by their rules once she learned how to survive. She could choose us over them.

"It could get messy," Jack said, "but in the end it would be worth it, right?"

I sat on my chopper, considering his uncivilized plan. "I'll do whatever it takes to be with her again."

"This ain't about just you and her. It's about all of us."

"You know what I meant."

Dina opened the door and stepped in front of my handlebars, passing me a frosty mug. "Here, hon. It's been on ice since it came in. She says it's full of passion and—"

"Dina!" I flicked my seagarette at her. "I told you, don't ever tell me anything about the donor."

"Sorry, I thought maybe—"

"Back inside, Dina," Jack ordered.

She shut the door without argument and I gulped down the blood, trying not to wonder who it belonged to. Whoever the donor was, Dina hadn't lied. Rapture coursed through me. I ached to devour someone—body and soul—but knew it would pass in a few minutes.

"Damn," I grunted, wiping my mouth. "Somebody had a good time last night."

Jack smacked me on the shoulder. "That's half the fun of donating to you. We can anonymously gift you with highlights of our lives."

"I'm grateful for it, but it's nothing compared to—well, you know."

"Soon that will all change. You two will be able to share your souls with each other and forget all about this donor business."

"I hope so. For hours I've been walking around thinking I've lost my soul mate forever." I punched the seat of my bike. "Treygan's a meddling prick. Just like our good-for-nothing father."

Jack stomped out his seagarette with the heel of his boot and tossed the empty vodka bottle in the dumpster. "Forget about him. We'll get Yara to side with us. Love will triumph."

Right. That's what fairytales claimed, but from where I stood, everything just got a hundred times harder—and messier—for the love gang.

day 2

Before I opened my eyes, I sensed someone watching me. Somewhere between half-asleep and almost-awake, it gradually came back to me. The hurricane, my tail, those tattoo thingies, the coldness in Rownan's kiss and—

My eyes flew open and there he was. Treygan.

"What a massive waste of time," he said. "Ten hours have passed since you closed your eyes. Do you know how much we could have accomplished in ten hours?"

I sat up and pulled my blanket over my arms. Sunlight beamed through the living room window. "It's called sleeping, jackass. Ten hours is an acceptable amount of time." I could have slept for another two or three. "You didn't sleep at all?"

"I told you, Yamabuki, I don't sleep."

"Stop calling me that."

"You can call me freak, kingpin, slimeball and jackass, but I can't call you Yamabuki?"

I made a mental note to stop calling him names. "What do you do at night if you don't sleep?"

"Work." He sounded awake and alert, but dark circles cradled his eyes.

"All night?"

"Yes, and it still isn't enough time."

So Treygan was a workaholic. No surprise there. I could totally see him having a never-ending need to feel important. "If you didn't go to work last night, what did you do?"

"Sat here, waiting for you to finish sleeping."

He looked even stiffer than usual, like he really had sat in the rocking chair for ten hours. "You sat there all night watching me sleep? Are you one of those deranged stalker types?" Dang it. Again with the name-calling.

"May I request you refrain from insulting me or any of our people today? I am running low on patience and might not have the restraint I had yesterday."

"Restraint?" I leaned forward. "Are you threatening me?"

"You will know if I threaten you. There will be no question about it."

"I don't like your tone."

"I don't like wasting an entire day and night here on land accomplishing nothing while our people are getting sick. I'm behind in my work, and you have a lot to learn in the next few days. We have to go." He stood up and walked to the door.

"When can I come back?"

"You may not want to come back."

"Oh, I'll want to come back," I picked at the hardened pools of candle wax on the coffee table. "You're delusional if you think I'm going to spend the rest of my life underwater."

"You'll be able to come and go as often as you like once your initiation is complete. That will take a few sunsets."

"Sunsets? I'll be gone a few days?"

"Yes."

"I need to see my uncle before we go."

"Your uncle?"

"You know, the man whose house you stole me from."

He tilted his head back like he just remembered something.

"Right, of course. But please hurry. You're part of a much larger family now. Some of them are suffering because we've been ashore too long."

Some of *them* are suffering? My uncle's kidneys could shut down at any moment. I needed to be on the island looking after him. Instead, I had to go live like a fish. I followed Treygan out on the front porch. He kept his face to the sky, eyes closed, as I summoned up conviction for my next argument.

"First off, none of you merpeople are my family. My family is my uncle—that's it. Secondly, don't blame your insufficient drug supply on me. Your people are suffering because you turned me against my will."

He didn't move or open his eyes. "Go say goodbye to Lloyd. If you aren't back in twenty minutes, I will come get you."

"Don't you go anywhere near him."

He turned and looked at me. I expected his eyes to be piercing and angry, but he looked calm and indifferent. "Be back in twenty minutes and I won't have to."

"Ugh! I h—I hay—"

"What? Hate me? You don't know me well enough to hate me. Now go."

The walk to Uncle Lloyd's was a daily routine, but today it felt strange. Trees and shrubs had been blown over by the hurricane. Flooding shifted the sand and dirt along the roadways and made hills and barriers where none had been before. Uncle Lloyd's house hadn't been damaged, but it looked different. Maybe it was the sun rising behind it, or the reflection off the ocean yards away from his porch, but the house appeared to be surrounded by a shimmering bubble.

The thought of explaining everything to him made my stomach hurt. The truth was unbelievable, but according to Treygan I couldn't lie. What could I possibly tell him? *Hey,*

Uncle Lloyd, this is Treygan the merman. He turned me into the Little Mermaid and I'm going to live under the sea for a few days. Hold down the fort while I'm gone. Yeah, that would go over well.

I knocked on the door and stepped inside. "Morning," I called.

Uncle Lloyd came down the stairs with his usual laid-back grin and a limp that made my heart ache. "Happy birthday, sweetie."

My birthday. I had almost forgotten. "Thanks! I'm officially an adult. You can evict me from the house whenever you like."

"I would never."

As I followed him into the kitchen, I tried to memorize every detail about him just in case I ended up being gone longer than Treygan said. All things considered, he looked pretty good for being in his sixties. He still had a head of thick, white hair. Most of his muscles had gone flabby over the years, and he walked with a limp because the dialysis made his legs cramp and his joints ache, but he kept a positive attitude. He always wore yellow. Whether it was bright, tropical shirts, Capri pants, or his garden gloves, almost every memory I had of him involved a garment in some shade of yellow. Uncle Lloyd was my own personal sunshine, even during the dark times.

He grabbed a cake box out of the refrigerator and set it on the table. Opening a kitchen drawer, he pulled out two packages wrapped in pink and green paper. One was flat and rectangular. The other was small and square.

"You didn't have to get me anything. You already give me too much." I recited the same line every year before I tore open my gifts, and every year he smiled and watched in silence. I opened the flat one first. A manila envelope felt like it held papers of some sort.

"What's this? A million dollar recording contract?" I

puckered my lips and turned my chin over one shoulder—my best pose for an album cover.

"Unfortunately, no. However, your voice *has* sounded more velvety these last couple days. Maybe this adulthood thing is making you rock star worthy."

"Really? I sound different?" I tried to focus on the typed document in front of me to calm my nerves. My hair turning blonde, my voice changing; surely Uncle Lloyd would start getting suspicious of— "Oh, my God!" I blurted out, finally comprehending the words on the paper. "This is a deed to mom's house with my name on it."

"It's your home now. Free and clear."

This, along with a million other reasons, is why Uncle Lloyd was my superhero. "This is—it's way too much. I can't accept—"

"Yara, we both know my days are numbered. I haven't enjoyed forcing you to grow up so fast, but I need to make sure you'll be taken care of when I'm gone."

"You promised not to say things like that. They'll find a donor soon."

"Alright, then." He folded his hands in front of him. "How about stating the obvious? You earned the right to own that house a long time ago. You haven't exactly had a normal childhood, kiddo."

He had a point. My mother never cooked, cleaned, or did laundry. In fact, she never did much of anything. Some days she didn't get out of bed because she was too tired. She had a weak heart, which up until Uncle Lloyd set the story straight, I thought was my fault. Every night I would go to her room to say goodnight, and she would tell me that my father and I made her heart sick. I didn't remember much about my father. He died when I was three, but back then he and I were an imaginary team. Together, we made my mother sick.

After she was gone, my uncle explained that her weak

heart was a medical condition. She was also heartsick—very different from a diseased heart—over my father's death and the fact that she couldn't give me a better life. I still questioned if his take was an accurate one.

For the first few years after I moved in with Uncle Lloyd, I visited my old house every day, hoping my mother would magically reappear. When I turned thirteen my uncle let me stay the weekends by myself whenever I wanted. At sixteen he let me live there alone full-time, as long as I checked in with him every day. It was our secret, and if anyone asked I had to say I lived with him. No one ever asked.

Now that I was eighteen it didn't have to be a secret anymore. A new secret took its place. One we couldn't share. I had to keep the truth from the man who had never kept anything from me. I would come back in a few days and pretend nothing had changed. Uncle Lloyd would never have to know about this mermaid thing, and we could return to our normal routine.

"Thank you," I said. "This means a lot to me."

I remembered Treygan's threat to come get me if I took too long, and my pulse quickened. I didn't want him showing up and having to explain him to Uncle Lloyd. My hands shook as I hurriedly unwrapped the next present.

It was a pendant made from a grayish-colored stone. Veins of deep red snaked through its polished surface.

"Thank you, I love it," I said in a rush, despising Treygan for making me hurry through my birthday.

Uncle Lloyd laughed in his deep, full-bellied way. "You haven't seen the best part. Open it. It's a locket."

Inside the cracked stone I found a photo of my mother and father. They looked young and happy. I examined my father closely because he was sort of a stranger to me. "Oh," is all I managed to say.

"You don't like it?"

"I'd rather have a picture of you."

"Yara, they're your parents. They gave you life. Treasure their memory always."

I closed the locket, rubbing my thumb over the smooth surface. "What kind of rock is this?"

"It's an old sea stone. Protects those who keep it close to their heart."

I hated having to leave him. What if he got worse while I was gone? Or what if—I couldn't think about losing him. It would be a life without sunshine. I held the necklace out to him. "Will you help me put it on?"

Uncle Lloyd secured the clasp while I held my hair up. The stone hung low against my chest and felt cool on my skin. When I turned around to thank him I got a titanic head rush and swayed forward.

"Easy there." He held onto my shoulders. "You alright?"

I squeezed my eyes shut repeatedly, trying to blink the dizziness away. "Yeah, sorry—minor dizzy spell." Except it wasn't minor. Shades of blue and red flashed across my vision and my limbs felt like gummy worms. Treygan said we'd get sick if we were away from the water too long. If this is what he meant, and weed could cure it, bring on the smoke fest.

"Maybe you should sit down," Uncle Lloyd said.

"I'm fine. I just haven't eaten since—jeez, I didn't eat at all yesterday or today." How had I forgotten to eat? My stomach never growled once. No hunger pains or anything. If merfolk didn't eat, I'd be pissed off. I loved food and didn't want to give it up just because I had been turned part fish.

"Your blood sugar must be plummeting. How 'bout some cake?"

I forced a smile. "Birthday cake?"

"The best kind." He sliced two pieces and put them on plates.

"What? No birthday song?" I teased, still feeling lightheaded.

"You're the singer, not me. I didn't want to torture you on your special day." He was right. Singing was not one of his talents. Things like gardening, wood carving and repairing boats were what he did best.

I stuck my fork into my first bite of cake, hoping I'd be able to taste it. If I didn't get hungry anymore, had I also lost my sense of taste? Moist, dark chocolate cake with buttercream icing slid onto my tongue. Sugary decadence exploded in my mouth, more intense than ever.

"Mmmm," I moaned with pleasure. "This is the best thing I've ever tasted!" I definitely hadn't lost my sense of taste. If anything, it was amplified—or exceptionally great cake. I wasn't sure.

"Glad you like it. I ordered it from a mom-and-pop bakery in the Keys. Locals rave about how good their stuff is."

"They ain't lying. In-freakin-credible."

"Glad I listened to the recommendations." He smirked while I shoveled more chocolaty goodness into my mouth.

I couldn't believe how fast I finished. I fought the urge to lick my plate clean. "May I have another slice?"

He pushed the box across the table. "Help yourself. And relax, would ya? You look like you're about to rush out the door."

Guilt is a funny thing. Uneasiness coated my stomach, totally killing my appetite. The remaining cake read *Happy Birth Yara* in pink icing. We had eaten the "*day*." Fitting, because a few short minutes were all I had left with my uncle.

"Uncle Lloyd, I have to go somewhere for a few days."

The wrinkles around his eyes deepened and multiplied as he slid his fork out of his mouth. A bit of frosting clung to his bottom lip. "The birthday getaway?"

"Kind of."

"Well, enjoy yourself, but be careful."

That was it? No more questions? "Don't you want details?"

"You're more responsible than most adults I know. I trust you."

"Wow. Okay." All that worrying for nothing. My allotted twenty minutes were almost up. "I hate to eat and run, but I have to get going."

"I understand." He pushed back his seat, chair legs squeaking across the tile floor. He didn't seem worried at all. "Both boats held up well during the storm. You're welcome to take either one."

The boats. Right. He would definitely question where I went if I didn't take a boat. Had Treygan considered that in his ridiculous plan? "Guess I'll take mine. Better gas mileage," I added nervously.

He kissed the top of my head and set our plates in the sink. "You've outgrown Eden's Hammock. It's a big, fantastic world out there, kiddo. Go explore it."

I didn't want to explore. I wanted to stay here and take care of him, but he seemed anxious for me to leave. How long had he felt this way? What if something happened to me? What if I never came back from Mermaid World? Wouldn't he miss me? The thought of never seeing Uncle Lloyd or Eden's Hammock again made my eyes burn as I fought back tears. "You're going to take good care of yourself while I'm gone, right?" He nodded. "Say you promise."

"I promise." His promises were worth more than gold.

My throat tightened and my new necklace felt like it was suffocating me. I reached up to adjust it, but the stone was so warm that I clenched it in my hand, pressing the heat into my palm.

Suddenly, another feeling rushed through me. Comfort or safety, followed by a flash of a forgotten childhood memory: Treygan's blue eyes staring into mine as I coughed up water from my burning lungs. The image was so clear.

How could I have forgotten?

He had cradled me in his arms while I stared up at a black, starry sky. He looked younger, unafraid, caring. His warm fingers wiped away the tears running down my cheeks. Then he swam so fast, carrying me through the cold water. He kept promising me everything would be okay, that I was safe. He was so … different.

I sprang up and gave Uncle Lloyd a quick hug. "I have to go! I love you."

"I love you too," he shouted as the front door slammed shut behind me.

I took off running toward my house. I couldn't get back to Treygan fast enough.

 Treygan

Eden's Hammock had seen its share of death and despair. It contained more secrets than the gorgon grotto. The ominous energy in Yara's house—though years old—made my head spin, so I retreated to the porch for fresh air.

We practically collided with each other. "Yara, what's wrong?"

Struggling to catch her breath, she managed to gasp out, "It was you." She bent forward, bracing her hands on her knees. "Why didn't you tell me?"

"What are you talking about?"

"That night …." More panting and bobbing her head. "You … saved my life."

I said nothing. Merfolk cannot lie, but we always have the option to remain silent. She couldn't be referring to *that* night. She couldn't remember. I had made sure of it.

When her breathing steadied, she stood straight. "Why?"

"Why what?"

"A million whys! Why didn't you say anything? Why did you let me call you all those names and be so mean to you? And why didn't I remember you saving my life until a few minutes ago?" She stepped closer and I held my breath. "The night my mother died, you saved me from drowning. It was you, wasn't it?"

I couldn't claim that I didn't know what she was referring to. Not one sunset had gone by when I didn't think of *that night*. How could she remember it? I froze that memory minutes after it happened.

"Answer me," she pleaded.

She seemed vulnerable, like the girl I rescued ten years ago, except now she looked even more fragile. What happened to that bratty know-it-all who stormed out of the house earlier? She had returned looking like an angel, begging me for answers I never thought I would have to give.

"Treygan?" Our eyes locked. As much as I wanted to look away from her, I couldn't. No one ever had such an emotional pull on me. I had never been more thankful that I wasn't underwater. If she could hear the thoughts running through my head about our past and her history, it would further complicate an already complex situation.

My voice came out hoarse. "We need to get back."

She grabbed my wrists. "Please, tell me the truth. It was you, right?"

Tears glistened in her eyes. The thought of her crying made my chest constrict with pain. Great gods, was I having a heart attack?

Her grip tightened. "Please, tell me I'm not crazy. The night my mother died, I remember putting her in the boat, jumping in the water and swimming for what felt like forever, but then everything goes gray. I've never been able to remember what happened after that. But a few minutes ago it all came back to me. I remember. *You* were the one who saved me. Right?"

My heart pounded so hard that the floorboards under us should have been vibrating. "You said it out loud. That means it's true."

She let go of me, but didn't move away. "Why didn't you say anything?"

My wrists tingled where her fingers had been. I rubbed at them, trying to get the sensation to go away. "It didn't seem important."

"Didn't seem important? I almost died! You saved me and carried me back to shore." Her eyes darted out over the yard as if watching the memory play out in front of her. "You carried me here, took me in the house and wrapped me in blankets. Uncle Lloyd came in and—wait, do you know my uncle?"

My head throbbed again. I turned away and unzipped my armband, desperately needing to smoke.

Yara stood so close to me I could feel her body heat against my back. "I remember the two of you talking," she half whispered. "You told him I shouldn't remember anything about you."

I couldn't turn around. I couldn't face her. I knew how intrusive it felt to have someone steal a song from you. Freezing one was a similar violation of the soul. It had seemed like the right thing to do at the time, but if she remembered what I had done, she would see me as the worst kind of thief.

Yara's fingers tugged at the bottom of my shirt. "You held my face in your hands, your eyes turned silver and …."

Somehow I found the courage to turn around. She had gone pale. Her legs wobbled, so I held onto her. "Yara, you're getting too weak. We need to get you back underwater."

"You were inside my head. My veins felt like they were filling with ice, and then you … oh, my God." She barely got her last words out before fainting in my arms.

"Forgive me," I whispered into her hair, carrying her limp body down the steps and into the water—to her new home.

The Violets had educated me on what needed to be done, but never once had they advised me on what to do if she passed out and didn't wake up once we were in the water. I had waited too long. I should have known better. Why hadn't I insisted we go back sooner?

Regardless of how fast I swam to Paragon Castle, it felt like an eternity. Yara's eyes weren't opening. Her pulse was weak. What if she never woke up? I would never forgive myself. I had vowed to keep her safe. Everything we worked so hard for, gone because of my carelessness.

The guards saw me approaching and moved to the side. My tail couldn't propel me forward fast enough. Each turn and climb through the sea-glass corridors felt longer than ever before. Turning at full speed into the gathering hall, a rush of water blew past me as I halted in front of the Violets.

I bowed my head and extended my sight so they could both hear me. *She fainted on land. She was out of the water for over twelve hours. A memory I froze ten years ago returned to her and—*

Treygan, Caspian interrupted calmly. Indrea smiled and laid her hand on top of his.

Yes, elders?

Caspian swam toward me, placed his hand on Yara's forehead and closed his eyes. When he opened them I heard the faint murmur of his secondary thoughts being pushed away. *She will be fine. A bit more rest is all she requires.*

I nodded with relief.

We will have another guardian take Yara to Koraline's, Indrea said. *She needs to be in a resting pool.*

I can take her.

Caspian gingerly took her from my arms. *You have other essential matters to attend to. Go harvest the Catacombs.*

It's daytime, I argued.

You will have to ask for an exception. Many are in desperate need of C-weed.

I stared at Yara, unconscious in Caspian's arms, then closed my eyes so they couldn't hear my thoughts. The pain in my chest, the tingling in my wrists when she touched me, they were warning signs. I could not become emotionally involved with Yara. More importantly, she couldn't grow fond of me. That would be a catastrophe.

Caspian touched my shoulder. *Do not worry yourself with Yara's health.*

I beg your pardon, Caspian, but Yara's wellbeing is my responsibility.

Indrea's eyes flashed purple as she sent tranquil waves over me. For the first time in days, my muscles relaxed. *You've done well, Treygan,* she said. *Let the rest of us do what we can to help ease the burden placed upon you. You are only one merman—and a fine one at that. Do as Caspian said. Return when the weed supply is back in balance.*

As you wish, Indrea. Thank you, Caspian.

They both nodded.

I glanced at Yara one more time before swimming out of the hall. She was in the hands of merfolk who would take exceptional care of her. No matter how badly I wanted to stay, I had to leave her. My unexpected feelings for her meant I needed to stay away from her until the Triple Eighteen.

Rownan

In the Catacombs, almost no life existed. A few plants grew out of concrete statues. That was it. No fish or sea creatures swam through the labyrinth, no coral flourished, not one snail crept across the ocean floor. Nada.

For the first few years, the eerie tombs and lack of color creeped me out. I had the same reoccurring nightmare about being trapped in a deserted blue and gray void. Massive concrete eyes stared at me, never blinking. Their screams and cries for help made the ocean boil until my skin and tail fur melted off. Several times I woke up screaming. Back then the fear of dying—or worse, being alone forever—overwhelmed me.

Maybe it still did.

Picking weed from the tombs gave me too much time to think. I hated it. Hated the job, hated the Catacombs, hated that I'd known and loved most of the souls entombed in the cold stone. Swimming around statues of dead friends and family while picking weeds, had to be the worst job in the worlds. But it was my job, and it wasn't like I could up and quit. Treygan and I were the only two souls who could swim into the Catacombs, and he sure as hell wouldn't give my kind the plants they needed.

When the water around me began to vibrate, I knew it was him. Treygan never entered the Catacombs during my shift. In all the years we had been harvesting, neither of us had ever reneged on our agreement.

He swam around my mother's tomb, biceps flexed and shoulders hunched, guarded and vigilant. The uptight bastard would never change. I floated behind a selkie statue, keeping my claws out of sight behind the stone wall of what had been her flowing hair. Treygan and I had no reason to fight—yet— but better to be safe than snapped in half.

Treygan, we've been avoiding each other for over a decade. Seeing you two days in a row is making me nauseous.

Those ugly, blue eyes of his narrowed, but he kept calm. *I need to harvest our crops.*

It's daytime. This place is off limits to you.

He glided closer. *I'm requesting an exception. Our supply*

is running dangerously low. Yesterday I couldn't work because I granted Yara time to stay on land so she could see you.

He still had an eerie way of not moving whatsoever. Under water everyone bobbed or floated back and forth a bit, even when we tried to keep still. Not Treygan. When he was intent on something, no part of him—with the exception of his hair—swayed even an inch.

No one asked you to do that, I said.

She asked me to do that. He spiraled sideways, circling one of his people's tombs and examining the plant growth. *You were her first concern when she awoke. You've done a good job of convincing her you care about her.*

She's important to me.

She's not important in the way you've made her believe.

My flippers tensed with the urge to propel myself forward. My claws extended. In one swipe I could tear through his skin and rip his heart out so he'd never speak to Yara again. But that swipe would never reach him. He was faster than any merman in history. *I can't help how she interprets our relationship.*

The charade is over, Rownan. She's immune to being mysted. You can't control her thoughts or feelings anymore.

That's my concern, not yours.

Treygan squared his shoulders and his fists curled tight. *She's one of us now. Stay away from her.*

I swam forward, floating face-to-face with him. *Just because you turned her doesn't mean she'll side with you. She has free will to choose, and we'll make sure she chooses to side with us selkies.*

His hand was around my throat in an instant. *Are you asking for a war?*

I grasped his forearm, sinking my claws into his skin. Small clouds of blood floated between us, dissipating into the water. I wanted to tear through his muscles and tendons just to prove I could, but I held back. I knew what Treygan was and wasn't capable of. *Merfolk wouldn't survive a war with us.*

He squeezed my throat tighter. *Things have changed. We will fight for her.*

You're forgetting selkies are darker by nature. We'll go to extremes your kind never would. You *might play dirty, but your people won't.* Thank the gods for not needing air to breathe, because Treygan's grip was crushing my windpipe. It hurt like hell, but I refused to show it.

The stakes have never been this high. We'll do whatever it takes. He looked so determined. I had almost forgotten that side of my brother.

I will say, that was a sneaky move turning Yara first. How did you know today wasn't her real birthday?

He let go of me, glancing away for a second before he answered. *Inside source.*

Mother or father?

None of your business, he replied.

With one quick arch backward I maneuvered away from him, putting more water between us. *How did you do it? We all believed her birthday was today. Hell, she believes it's today. You must've planned this ages ago.*

I don't take the future of my people lightly. I did what needed to be done.

I tried not to sneer, but failed. *You really believe she'll think your numbskull method of opening the gate is the right one? She's not a pushover. She has her mother's fiery spirit—when her mother still had one. Yara won't just do what you tell her to.*

Treygan advanced on me. *We will make her see it's the right thing to do.*

We floated eye to eye again, both stiff and unwavering. The outstretched stone hand of a mermaid covered with swaying weeds was the only thing between us. *I assure you, Treygan, when Yara arrives at the gateway it will be with me, and the right thing will be done.*

Don't bet your life on it, brother.

At the reminder of the blood we shared, I retracted my claws, but it didn't calm my agitation. *I will bet all of our lives on it. And don't call me brother.*

That's another difference between us, Rownan. I would never bet the lives of my people.

Jack and I had a meeting scheduled, and all this chitchat with Mr. Shit-for-Brains made my craving for a drink unbearable. *Pick your plants. I'm done here.*

I swam past him, brushing my fingers along my mother's tomb and making sure her water lily was secure in its place. Even though her eyes were coarse, lifeless rock, I knew her spirit watched over me. *Rest in peace, Mom. I promise to win this one in your honor.*

day 3

Yara

Again, I woke up underwater with no clue where I was.

When I was a kid, I would lie in the bathtub and try to open my eyes underwater. Everything looked blurry and sounds were muffled. Now I could see wooden ceiling beams above me with crystal clarity and hear every word of *What a Wonderful World* being sung by a female voice in the distance. I sat up and glanced around at the shallow water. My golden tail flopped down in front of me, making a splash. An indoor pool?

The room was small with bamboo walls. Skylights let in plenty of sunlight. Wild flowers grew everywhere: up the walls, around the ceiling beams, in huge seashells acting as planters. How had I ended up here? And who was singing in the next room?

"Hello?" I called out.

The singing stopped and footsteps approached the open French doors. A round face framed by bright green pigtails peeked around the doorway. "You're awake!"

"Uh, who are you, and how did I get here?"

She stepped into full view and my mouth dropped open. She wore a tank top and denim skirt, but the rest of her skin—with the exception of her shiny face—was covered with hallmarks. Beneath the intricate artwork her skin had a satin sheen to it. I knew she was a mermaid. Not by her looks, but by the internal sensory system Treygan mentioned.

She licked a spoon clean and stuck it in the yogurt container she was holding. "I'm Koraline, and you're in my resting pool, in my house."

"But you're a mermaid, and not in the water, so how—?"

She flashed a grin of obnoxiously white teeth. "This place is harbored, meaning I can be on land and retain my mer traits. Except the tail, of course. It wouldn't be much fun to drag myself around from room to room."

Where was Treygan? Why had he left me here with a stranger? He still needed to explain himself. I rubbed my arms like I was cold, even though the temperature was comfortable. "Could I maybe borrow some clothes so I can get out of here?"

"Sure."

She disappeared from the doorway and I examined my skin. The plant motif hallmarks were back, and I looked like I had applied way too much glistening bronzer. Reaching into the water, I ran my fingers over my tail and cringed at the rough, scaly texture. "Gross."

"What's gross?" Green-haired gal asked, walking into the room with a towel and clothes.

I tried to say "nothing," but the words wouldn't come out. This unable to lie stuff was no joke. "Just talking to myself."

She held out the towel, but I had no idea how to get out of a pool without my legs. "How do I get out of here?"

"Pull yourself onto the ledge and swing your tail up."

It was so bizarre to hear someone say that and accept it as reality, but I scooted to the edge of the pool and did what she said. Just like at the dock, my tail instantly changed into legs—

hallmark covered legs—when I pulled them out of the water. I stuck my feet back in and they were pale yellow fins. I pulled them out again and I had ten toes, shimmery and covered with vine artwork. I lowered them in and yanked them out as fast as I could, trying to see if my fins would appear out of the water. But the transformation happened quicker than I could move.

Koraline giggled above me. "Neat, huh?"

Neat wasn't the word I would use, but it was sort of fascinating. I glanced up at her and back at my legs before taking the towel from her and standing up. While wrapping the towel around me, I looked down and noticed my locket was missing.

"What happened to my necklace?"

"What necklace?"

It had felt so heavy thumping against my chest as I ran from Uncle Lloyd's back to Treygan, but I couldn't remember if it had been around my neck when I reached him. Had I lost it already? Great. That gift lasted a long time. "Never mind. Where is Treygan?"

"He went to work."

"You mean to sell weed?"

"Sell it? Sweetums, you have so much to learn about how things work in our world."

Sweetums? Was she serious? "I don't want to know how things work. As soon as possible, I'm going home and pretending this mermaid thing never happened."

"But being mer is so much better than human life. Some people would give anything to be one of us."

"Yeah, well, I'm not one of them."

"Delmar mentioned you weren't keen on the idea. I couldn't believe that was possible, but here you are, dissing a beautiful existence you know nothing about."

"Beautiful? Having a tail one second and legs the next?

Skin and tattoos that look like something out of a science fiction novel? None of that is my idea of beautiful."

She shoveled more yogurt into her mouth and tapped the spoon against her bottom lip. "'Never did an eye see the sun unless it had first become sun-like, and never can the soul have vision of the First Beauty unless itself be beautiful.'"

"What?"

"Plotinus," she said. I stared at her blankly. "Great ancient philosopher. Don't tell me you've never heard of him."

"No."

"Looks like I'll have to teach you the basics. Come on, I'll show you around first."

Before I could argue she walked into the other room, leaving me with no choice but to follow.

The rest of the house looked normal: living room, kitchen, even a regular bathroom. The entire place had a pastel, nautical theme, and every shelf was filled with books.

"What do you think?" she asked.

"Nice, but where are we?"

She headed for the front door. "Sorry, I almost forgot the best part." She swung open the peach-colored door and we stepped onto a small porch made of rope and wood.

My breath caught in my throat. I had never seen anything like it. Her house was one of many thatch-roofed cottages scattered on rolling green hills. All the homes looked like they were made from natural materials that blended into the surrounding tropical foliage. Some were connected by streams. Gushing waterfalls, flowing waterways and chirping birds created a surreal soundtrack for the lush stage surrounding us.

"Welcome to our 'hood'," she said. "You're looking at the harbored island of Solis. Home to about a hundred merfolk, it's inaccessible to humans, undetectable on any radar or satellite, and invisible to the naked eye."

"How is that possible?" I marveled. The twinkling,

emerald mountains made the sky's cerulean blue look dull in comparison.

"After we realized we'd be stuck here for a long time, the Violets cast a protective spell over the island. If humans discovered this place we would become their next big experimental study. Merfolk are supposed to be a myth, ya know?"

I wished they were a myth. "What do you mean by stuck here?"

"The gateway between our realm and this one was sealed years ago. We had no way of getting back home, so we were forced to adjust."

"This world isn't your home?"

"Gosh, no. This place is so lackluster compared to Rathe. Our people visited here so they could interact with humans, visit the cities and experience new things. This world was like a playground to us, but we never stayed more than a few days at a time. Then the gate was sealed, and we've been trapped here ever since."

"Rathe? That's an awful name. It sounds sinister."

"You couldn't be more wrong. Rathe means a place of blooming and ripening." She ran her pale hands over the porch railing. "We miss our realm—especially our loved ones there. It's awful not knowing if they're okay."

"Can't you call or send a letter or something?"

She didn't laugh at what in hindsight sounded like a ridiculous question. "No. We have no way of communicating with them."

"Will the gate ever open again?"

She bit her lip. Her white teeth against the lime green reminded me of a Granny Smith apple slice. "We really, really hope so."

In a weird way, I felt like I could relate. Many times I wondered if my parents were okay on the other side—a side I had no access to. It was a lonely feeling. "Why is the gate sealed?"

"The simple answer is that a promise to the gorgons wasn't kept, so they concocted a dreadful curse and sealed off the gateway until we could figure out a way to repay them."

Answers only led to more questions. "Gorgons are real?"

"Ever heard of Medusa?"

"Sure. One of the three daughters of Phorcys and Ceto. Breathtakingly beautiful, but turned into a monster." She was one of the prized wood panels that hung in my uncle's house.

"Nice. At least you know more than 'she had snakes for hair.' Medusa was horribly misunderstood, but if it weren't for her, none of us would exist. She played a major part in the creation of most other sea creatures. Did you know that?"

My answer must have been written on my face, because she continued before I could speak.

"Many think of gorgons as our temperamental gods. That's a matter of opinion, but they are undeniably powerful. They used to watch over us, but after Medusa was killed they couldn't anymore. Thank goodness, because if they get angry they can make our lives hell. They're not very forgiving."

"They sound like monsters."

She playfully bumped her shoulder against mine. "We're all monsters."

"Speak for yourself."

"Well, like all monsters, gorgons still have a soul and feelings. *Beauty*, my favorite poem, was written by Medusa's great-great-granddaughter. She's a gorgon—obviously—but she inherited Medusa's passion and positivity. 'Beauty is sometimes hidden under a veil of tragedy.' I read those words every morning. They give me hope."

"Hope for what?"

Koraline stared at a waterfall in the distance. Her eyes dimmed with a contagious sadness. "For a world where it isn't us against them, a place where all of us can coexist peacefully again. But more than anything it reminds me to love. Screw the rules, damn the consequences, and just love. Love until it kills you, because there's nothing better worth dying for."

We both stayed quiet, listening to the birds and water surrounding us. Then she shot me a sideways glance like she expected me to say something.

"Love. Got it," I offered, hoping that would appease her.

"Oh! I almost forgot." She glided down the steps to the lawn and sang a wordless song. When a similar tune answered in the distance, she turned around and stuck her hands in the pockets of her skirt. "Kai will be here soon. She's a messenger. I'll send her to tell Treygan you're okay."

"I need to talk to him in person."

"You *need* to start your education."

Why was everyone so insistent about that? "Hey, do you know what a Yamapuku is?"

"You mean Yamabuki?"

"Whatever."

"Sure. It's a gold Koi fish. Why?"

"Treygan kept calling me that."

She pursed her lips together, holding back a laugh.

"What's so funny?"

"They are the most, um, what's a good word for them—*adamant* kind of fish."

"You mean stubborn."

"To-*may*-to, to-*mah*-to. He probably called you that because of your yellowish coloring and meant it as a compliment."

"Probably not," I grumbled to myself. "What do the colors mean?"

"Reds are students. Oranges are messengers. Yellows are teachers, but you, sweetums, are an anomaly. You should have begun as a Red like every other merfolk."

"What about green?" I asked, looking at her pigtails and lime-tinted lips.

"I'm a reporter. However, I've been asked to teach you

since I'm a rank above you. The Violets worried if you were taught by another Yellow, you might not give them the respect they deserve. Plus, they know I love to teach. Or learn. I just adore knowledge."

"Treygan said he's my guardian. Is that what Blues do? Guard humans?"

"Heck, no!" she huffed, as if I had said something offensive. "They guard everything sacred to us, especially the Violets and the castle."

Castle. Of course, there had to be a castle. Why wouldn't there be a castle in this fairytale land? "Why do the Violets need to be guarded? Wait, why do *I* need to be guarded?"

"We'll get to that part. I've prepared a couple lessons to get us started. You'll have to learn History and Popular Mechanics first."

"Koraline, I don't mean to be difficult," *or stubborn*, I thought, "but I don't plan on being part of this world. I just need to learn how to survive on land and pass for human around my uncle."

She tugged on the ends of her hair and opened her mouth to say something, but then we both sensed someone coming.

A tawny-skinned girl swam up the stream toward us. Her crinkly, orange hair reminded me of Cheetos

"Our Yara is awake! Hello, Miss Yara!" The young girl waved excitedly. "I am Kai. 'Tis an honor to meet you."

I waved back half-heartedly and walked down the steps. Koraline leaned down to talk to her and they exchanged a few words.

"See you soon, Miss Yara," Kai shouted before diving beneath the water.

"That was quick." I watched the blur of orange swim away from us. "Where is she off to in such a hurry?"

"To report to Treygan," Koraline said. "He wanted to know when you were awake."

Without hesitating, I dove into the water to follow her. I needed to see Treygan and refused to let Koraline tell me no.

 **Treygan** Delmar and I hurled packages of C-weed onto the shore.

"She can't be that bad," he insisted.

"You're right. She's only impossible ninety-five percent of the time."

"She's the key that unlocks the door to our world, Treygan." Delmar almost said something else, but the others approached.

Pango was a great physical asset when it came to hard labor, but he was also the most notorious gossip in all the waterways of the worlds. His green curls broke through the water, followed by Merrick's floppy, yellow bangs.

"Gentlemen." I nodded.

Pango spit a mouthful of water at me and flicked me with his tail. "Don't gentle man me. You two sped ahead so you could discuss our newest Goldilocks. You better share some juicy porridge with Papa Bear."

"Pango, there isn't that much to tell."

Merrick rolled his eyes. "Even I'm declaring sharkshit on that one."

"Yes," Pango agreed, untying the rope around his shoulders to release his bags of weed. "You two hijacked the girl during a hurricane and changed her against her will. This is the most interesting initiation to date. Start dishing it out. Too hot, too cold, we're not picky bears. Just give us something scrumptious."

Delmar shot me a look of caution.

My guess was Merrick didn't care to hear details. He and Pango were polar opposites—one of the many reasons they were perfect together—but we all knew Pango wouldn't drop the issue until he received some sort of update. We had a few hours of work left to do and I didn't want to listen to Pango whine or beg the entire time. I had been harvesting most of yesterday, all night, and half of today. The lack of rest made me irritable.

"You'll be disappointed, Pango," I said. "She abhors us."

He finished heaving the last of his packages onto the rocks and turned to help Merrick. "Us? All merfolk?"

"Yes."

Throwing his head back, he let out a theatrical laugh. "She hasn't met *me* yet. No one could ever abhor me. I'm too loveable." Merrick chuckled and Pango punched him on the shoulder. "It's true and you know it."

"I didn't argue," Merrick said before diving underwater for a bag that slipped off his ropes.

Pango watched him swim away before probing further. "Whom has she met so far to establish this abhorrence? Just you and Dr. Doomsday?" He flicked his head in Delmar's direction.

"Hey!" Delmar shouted over his shoulder, climbing the rocky ledge onto land.

"Delmar, darling, you know I love you, but let's tell it like it is. You are a bit intimidating with your dark hair and ghostly complexion. That raspy voice of yours probably convinced her she had met the Grim Reaper of the sea."

Merrick glided back through the water. "What have I missed?"

Delmar finished buttoning his shorts and opened his arms wide. His indigo hallmarks glimmered in the sunlight. "I have been named the Grim Reaper of the sea."

Pango clapped and Merrick snorted a laugh. "Only if Daddy Death is a closet die-hard romantic who wouldn't hurt a shrimp."

We all climbed out of the water and grabbed shorts from

the shed. Pango reached for a pair of sneakers and I raised my brow at him.

"What? I got a pedicure yesterday. Sand is a great exfoliate, but it's murder on the polish."

For being six-feet-five-inches and the most muscular merman around, Pango was exceptionally feminine at times. Merrick was a saint for putting up with his high-maintenance lifestyle.

"Lace them up and get to work," I grunted. "We're way behind."

Pango bowed dramatically. "Yes, master."

I shot him a look that said *don't*, but he just laughed and tied his shoes.

We were hanging the last bag of plants to dry when I sensed the girls approaching. "You have got to be kidding," I groaned, turning to look out at the ocean. I expected one, not three.

"What?" Delmar asked, squeezing excess water from several leaves, but then he also sensed them. "Oh. Never mind."

"Good, glittery gumdrops, we have visitors!" Pango sang. "But horrors, I'm not equipped to make a proper first impression. Why don't we keep designer apparel on this island in case of emergencies?"

Merrick patted Pango's stomach. "You look great. She'll drool once she sees your washboard abs."

Pango sighed. "I hate it when my perfect body is the first thing people see. I'm more than just a pretty face, ya know?"

My plan was to stay away from Yara until we began our training together, but here she was, showing up where I worked. I threw my garden shears so they struck the ground a few inches from Pango's shoe. "She shouldn't be here."

Pango squealed and jogged in place. "You heathen! I could've lost one of my little piggies."

"Pango, cool it for a minute," Delmar ordered.

I made my way to the water's edge followed by Delmar, Pango and Merrick. Kai was first to reach us, with Koraline and Yara close behind.

"At least we know she's awake," Delmar murmured.

"What is she doing here?" I shouted to Kai and Koraline.

"My apologies, Mister Treygan." Kai lowered her guilty eyes.

Koraline reached the rock wall at my feet. "She insisted. She wouldn't let Kai leave without her, and I wasn't about to let you yell at Kai for it."

"It's your job to tell her no, Koraline."

Yara waved her arms above her head. "Hellooo? I'm right here. How about taking it up with me?"

I shifted my annoyed gaze back to Koraline. She put her hands up protectively. "You know what she's like. There's no stopping a Yamabuki."

Yara glared at me. Of course she had already asked Koraline about that.

Pango peeked over my shoulder. "Hello, Yara. I'm Pango. Enraptured to meet you."

Her eyes widened. No doubt wondering why such a huge man spoke in such a prissy manner.

"This is Merrick," Pango continued, resting his hand on Merrick's shoulder, "the most handsome merman of all the oceans. But don't start fantasizing, because he's spoken for." After kissing Merrick's cheek, Pango motioned at Delmar. "And word on the water is you've already been acquainted with Delmar."

"Nice to meet all of you." Yara's pleasantry shocked me, but people couldn't resist Pango's good nature. I had never met anyone who didn't like him.

"I'd like to speak to Yara in private," I announced. Kai and Koraline swam toward the beach.

"Meet you merry maidens over there," Pango sang as he and the other men walked away.

Yara swam up to the rocks and I knelt down. "What are you doing here?"

"I pass out and you dump me at some stranger's house?" she practically hissed at me.

"Yara, I wish you would stop being so difficult."

"You mean like a *stubborn* Yamabuki?"

I ignored her indignant tone. "For your own safety, there are rules you must follow and things you need to learn. I don't have time to argue with you every step of the way. There aren't enough hours between sunsets for me to complete my work *and* educate you. Koraline will answer any questions you have."

"You saved my life when I was eight years old. I don't want to hear about that from Koraline, I want to hear it from you!"

Childlike innocence flashed in her eyes again, even as she tried to put authority behind her words. What answer could I give that would satisfy her? The whole truth was far too complicated. "Many merfolk have rescued drowning humans. As I said, we have highly attuned senses when it comes to knowing when humans are near. I was in the right place at the right time." None of it was a lie.

"My uncle told me a fisherman found me."

I tried not to smile. "Well, I can be a fish-or-man."

She rolled her eyes. "I know there's more to it than that. What are you hiding from me?"

"Listen, I have work to do. Once I've caught up on cycling the crops, I'll meet with you and we can discuss it further."

She crossed her arms, pouting with her typical disgruntlement.

"Yara." I pulled my hair back so she could see the sincerity in my eyes. "A Yamabuki is the most steadfast of all Koi fish. According to legend, the Yamabuki is the only one to succeed at swimming up the River of Suffering and climbing into the mist of the Eternal Falls where it transformed into a powerful dragon. Not because of stubbornness, but because of determination, bravery and spirit."

She blinked rapidly. Her glare softened with each flutter of her lashes.

I stood up and shouted, "Kai, Koraline, please take Yara back to Solis."

As I walked away I was tempted to look over my shoulder and see why she wasn't arguing or asking more questions, but I resisted.

Not looking back at her was astoundingly difficult.

~Sunset 3

Koraline and Kai swam on either side of me. Yamabuki. Steadfast. Brave. Did Treygan really see me that way? My uncle said similar things about me, even when I was a kid. I already missed my uncle. I missed Rownan too. This new existence was a lot to take in.

The scenery during our swim to and from Weed Island was breathtaking. The tropical fish, the sea turtles, the coral and plant life: it was a never-ending aquarium. We swam high above an old sunken plane. On land, it would have looked big and majestic, but the deteriorating heap of aluminum on the sandy ocean floor looked so small and disregarded.

At one point Koraline heard the engines of a cruise ship nearby, so we dove deeper, keeping far from its path. Three dolphins spun around us, clicking and whistling as one pushed a large leaf with its nose. The air bubbles they left behind tickled my skin. I kept hoping to see a selkie, assuming they'd look a lot like us except half seal, but no seals were anywhere to be found.

I reached over and touched Koraline's shoulder. *Koraline, can we talk?*

Sure. She made a short yipping sound and Kai looked over at us. Koraline pointed upward and we all swam to the surface.

"Sorry," I said, bobbing up and down with the gentle waves, "but this couldn't wait. I hope you two don't think I'm fussy and stubborn like Treygan does."

They stared at me, their chins dipping in and out of the water.

"Oh, Miss Yara." Kai's eyes had been orange underwater, but now they were hazel and her hair was strawberry blonde. "Fussing don't bother me. I'm used to it. My sisters and brothers fuss and shout too. You remind me of home."

So they *did* think I was fussy and stubborn. Way to make a first impression, Yara.

Koraline smiled at Kai and nodded to me. "Go ahead. What did you want to talk about?"

"Do either of you know where the selkies live?" I asked.

Koraline's jaw practically fell into the water. "I didn't realize you knew about selkies yet."

"My boyfriend is a selkie."

"Boyfriend?" Koraline gasped. "How did I not know you had a boyfriend?"

"Wait, were you one of the Reporters Treygan sent to spy on me?"

"Well, I—" she fidgeted with her starfish necklace. "Yes, but I only checked on you once in a while. To be honest, I sort of slacked off these past few months. I figured I knew enough about you that I didn't need to keep a close eye on you. Plus, you seemed really suspicious whenever I came around. I thought I had blown my cover."

"You and I met before? I don't remember seeing you on the island."

She pursed her lips and glanced at Kai. "Um, well—"

Kai interrupted. "Many times new merfolk forget things when they are turned."

"Hmph, well, I'm sorry I don't remember. I've seen so many tourists over the years. Anyway," I continued, "I don't exactly know where my boyfriend lives, but I need to find him. Do selkies live together like we do?"

Kai shook her head. "No, ma'am, but they spend a lot of time at the frosty bar."

"Frosty bar. Will you take me there?"

"No way," Koraline chimed in. "Not a good idea. We need to get you back to Solis."

I drifted closer to her. "Koraline, do you know what it's like to love someone?"

She hesitated and her cheeks went pink. "Of course. I love my family very much."

"Exactly. My boyfriend is one of the only two people I care about in this whole world. Please, imagine if you wanted to talk to someone you loved and nobody would take you to see them."

Koraline fiddled with her necklace again.

"Miss Koraline." Kai reached over and held Koraline's hand. "If Miss Yara needs love and her boyfriend has it for her, how can we say no?"

Koraline sighed, tugged on one of her dirty blonde pigtails, and sighed again. "Fine, we'll go to Jack Frost's. But if your boyfriend isn't there then it's back to Solis. And if he is there, you can stay an hour at most."

"Oh, thank you, Koraline!" I squealed, splashing water as I hugged her. "What about clothes?"

"We keep clothes hidden under many piers," Kai replied. "There will be no problem finding something for you, Miss Yara."

"Why do you call everyone Mister or Miss?" I asked. "You don't look much younger than us."

"I'm from the Ketokys tribe. We have different customs. Anyone better off than me is Miss or Mister."

"Better off? I'm no better off than you."

"You are Yellow. I recently became Orange. You swim higher than me."

I shook my head in confusion, but Kai just smiled and grabbed my hand. "Come, Miss Yara. We will find your selkie sweetheart."

Koraline didn't look too happy, but the three of us dove beneath the water and swam toward Jack Frost's.

We stood outside, looking through the windows at everyone in the bar.

I watched Rownan sip his drink at a table in the corner. "He's the one in the white coat."

Koraline grunted, "Of course he is," and turned away.

"No," Kai said, "Cursed White Coat has a beard."

Cursed? Cursed with good looks, maybe. "It's a goatee," I corrected. "I love how rugged it makes him look."

"Miss Yara, he is a scruffy face. Scruffy face means a selkie is married."

"What?" I laughed. "He's not married."

"I cannot lie. Scruffy face on a selkie man means he has a mate."

I whipped around, glancing between Kai and Koraline. Neither of them looked like they were kidding. "No, he would've told me."

Koraline kicked a rock across the parking lot. "Yara, do you know much about Rownan?"

"Of course. We've been together for weeks. He tells me everything."

Kai snorted. "He tells you what you want to hear. Most of what the icy ones say is lacking truth."

"Did he tell you why his coat is white?" Koraline asked. "Why he has the *only* white coat in a sea full of dark selkies?"

"No, but—" I glanced at Rownan again. Why did I know so little about him? My hands felt shaky. I clenched the sides of my sundress and took a deep breath. "Come on, we're going in."

"No, no." Kai stepped back. "Our kind is not welcome in frosty place."

"Fine. I'll go in by myself."

"Wait." Koraline grabbed my arm. "You can't walk in there blind. I wouldn't dare go with you, but it's my job to prepare you." She exhaled, eyeing the bar's tinted windows. "The place is freezing. Everyone in there is a selkie. They all know who and what you are. I don't know what happened between you and Rownan, but I'm guessing it was all an act."

My breath shot out of my lungs like someone had punched me in the stomach. "An act? Why would you say that?"

"Because they wanted you to be one of them, but Treygan got to you first. When you were human, Rownan had the ability to myst you, control your mind, make you think or feel whatever he wanted. He can't do that anymore. You need to figure out if your feelings for him are real or if he forced you to be attracted to him."

I felt dizzy. Rownan had brainwashed me? I replayed every conversation, every touch, every kiss, every thought or feeling I had about him. None of it had been real? That seemed impossible. He would never play me like that. Would he?

Even in the dim lighting of the parking lot I could see pity and sincerity in Koraline's green eyes. "I'm sorry. I know it's not easy to hear."

After standing there speechless for a minute, I smoothed down my dress and glanced at the door. "I can find my way back to the island if you don't feel like waiting. I might be a long time."

Kai put her hands behind her back and bowed her head. "You are brave to go in there."

Koraline shrugged. "'You will never do anything in this world without courage. It is the greatest quality of the mind next to honor.'"

"Plato?" Kai asked.

"Aristotle," Koraline corrected.

I thanked them both for helping me and opened the bar's front door.

A blast of arctic air made me shiver. Almost every head turned to stare at me with dark, hostile eyes. I inhaled a deep, icy breath and stepped inside.

Rownan

Years of sitting in Jack Frost's most of the night had made me immune to looking at the door every time someone came in. But even after doing six shots and nursing my fourth pint, I couldn't ignore the silence that fell over the bar.

Yara walked toward me, surveying everyone. They were checking her out with equal skepticism. I jumped to my feet and wrapped my coat around her.

"Holy iceberg, it's cold in here," She gasped through chattering teeth.

"I know. Let's get you back outside."

"No." She shivered. "I n-n-need to talk to you."

"Baby, you're freezing. Let's go to my house and talk."

She nodded, pulling my coat around her. I pushed the door open and held my hand up in a *screw you* wave to anyone—meaning everyone—watching us.

"My God." She stumbled off the curb, practically running away from the bar. "You all even look similar: the dark hair and eyes, the scars, all those fur coats. How do people not notice?"

"You never noticed it."

"I never saw so many of you gathered in one place before."

"Humans don't come around here much. And if they do, well, they don't remember much by the time they leave."

She held my coat open. "Why is yours the only white one?"

"Because I'm so pure and innocent?"

"Rownan."

"It's because my father was a rare breed." I climbed onto my chopper. "Lame story, trust me."

Her mouth hung half-open. "You drive a motorcycle?"

"Hop on."

"Umm." She eyed my bike like it was a rabid dog.

"I won't let anything happen to you. You're irreplaceable to me." With that reassurance, she climbed on and wrapped her arms around my waist. "Hang on!" I yelled, cranking the engine to life. Her grip tightened.

Two days with merfolk and she came back to *me*. Jack was right. She might take our side after all.

We pulled into my driveway. I had barely shut the engine off before she leapt from her seat and started pacing. Something was obviously bothering her.

"What's going on in that pretty head of yours?" I asked.

She spun around and got up in my face. Her frizzy hair resembled a rat's nest. "Are you married?"

Shit. I should have known this would come up. Since I couldn't myst my way out of the tough questions anymore, honesty was my best option. "Yes."

Her fists slammed into my chest. "Go to hell!"

"Wait." I held her hands, expecting her to pull away, but she only stared at me, unblinking, just like the eyes that haunted my dreams. "It was a long time ago. She's ... on the other side."

"I—wait. What?" Her angry glare changed to something resembling ruefulness. "I'm ... so sorry."

I shuffled my feet. The other side meant something different to humans. I knew that, but it was my way of telling the truth without telling the whole truth.

She wrapped her arms around me and rested her head on my shoulder. "I had no idea."

Whatever went on between us the past few months, regardless of how fake, this moment felt genuine. I hadn't mysted her into seeing me as charming or attractive. Whatever she was feeling, it was real. I wrapped my arms around her.

"Hang on." She pulled back to look at me. "If it was a long time ago, how old are you?"

"Much older than you." I ran my thumb along her jaw bone. "Let's go inside and I'll explain."

My house was nothing spectacular. Yara studied the few pieces of furniture like they were a museum display. She peeked into an empty bedroom. "Where's all your stuff?"

"I don't need much."

"Obviously," she mumbled. "Do you sleep on the couch?"

"No." I gestured to the back deck. "I crash outside. Wanna see?"

We hadn't made it all the way through the sliding glass doors when she gasped, "Oh, how cozy!" She walked over to the circular mattress and felt the slick cover. "It's cold."

"It's a selkie thing."

"Why don't you sleep inside?"

"The moon isn't inside."

She threw her head back, saw the half-moon above us and smiled at me. "You love the moon that much, or is it another selkie thing?"

"Second guess. Sit down and I'll dish details." I gathered my dirty t-shirts from an unfrosted patio chair, but she climbed into bed and waved me over.

"Lie down and tell me."

Goosebumps rippled up her legs, so I lifted her feet and adjusted my coat under her. "Keep your skin off the mattress or you'll freeze." I crawled beside her and lay back, putting my hands behind my head to avoid holding her. As much as I claimed I was okay with it, the mermaid thing was repulsive.

Her much-too-warm head settled on my chest. I took that as my cue to start. "Do you know where we came from yet—the realm where merfolk and selkies are supposed to live?"

"Sort of. I don't know the details, but I know everyone is trapped here."

"Right, and we're all struggling to survive. Selkies need a cold climate."

"You told me that. But you're warm-blooded, right?"

"Laws of Earth species don't apply to sea creatures from our realm. We don't exist the way Earth's cold or warm-blooded animals do. We have some features of seals, and some of humans, but not all of them. We were created using different rules. We sleep in the moonlight to soak up this world's cold energy."

"Sounds complicated."

"It is to an outsider. Over time it will make sense."

"So why do you stay in Florida? Why not go north?"

"We can't be too far from the gate. That's where the plants grow that keep us from getting sick. We need a fresh supply daily."

"Treygan said his C-weed does that for his people."

"Your people," I reminded her, but she didn't tense like I expected. "Nah, you misunderstood him. They have the sun, we have the moon—hot and cold. Plants help. His C-weed is how they absorb energy from our realm. It lives in the plants they smoke and helps with the physical pain and weakness. We have something similar—seagarettes."

"Cigarettes help you feel better?"

"*Sea*garettes. There's a difference. Did dickhead tell you where his weed comes from?"

"Yeah, some creepy graveyard underwater."

"It's not creepy, it's tragic."

She sat up. "I'm sorry. You're mad."

"I'm not mad, but don't call it creepy."

"Maybe this is what I need—to know more about this graveyard where magical weed and tobacco grows."

I took a breath of humid air and fought back a cough. *They* were supposed to educate her, but it seemed I was stuck doing all the work, as usual.

"That's opening up one hell of a Pandora's Box." I pulled a seag out of my wristband and lit up. Yara watched the smoke dance through the darkness with a new understanding.

I hadn't talked about this night in eighteen years, but she needed to know. I blew a ring of smoke above us. "Her name is Vienna."

"Who?"

"My wife."

"Oh." She cocked her head to the side. "Hold on, you said *is.*"

"Right."

She looked like she wanted to say something, but I continued. "Did they tell you when and why the gate to our world closed?"

"No."

What would be their reason for waiting? Would telling her benefit our side, or help theirs? I've never been good at strategic planning. That was Jack's department. I figured I should stick with the honesty tactic. "The day that changed everything was eighteen years ago. The gorgons were pissed because—wait, do you know about the gorgons yet?"

"Kind of."

Figures. "Okay, here comes the crash course, because I'm exhausted and it's not my job to teach you this stuff, but your merfoes are doing a piss-poor job. So, the gorgons were lied to. Broken promises, a debt never paid to them, blahdy blah.

They delivered a message to members of each group; us, your freaks, and the sirens."

"Sirens?"

"You don't know about the sirens? What the hell have they been teaching you?"

"I haven't exactly been the most cooperative student."

"Well, I'll be damned if I'm going to do their job for them. Ask them about sirens later. They aren't a crucial part to this story anyway."

She nodded as if to say *okay, get on with it*, so I kept explaining.

"The message spread like an oil spill through the waterways. Whoever didn't make it through the gate by sunset on a certain day would be trapped in this world until the debt to the gorgons was paid. Rumor had it that wouldn't be possible for eighteen years. None of us could imagine being in this world for more than a week without going back to our realm. Years would be a death sentence. So everyone fled to the gate. Thing is, we were spread out all over this world. Some of my kind were in Antarctica and Alaska. The smart ones figured out ways to hop a plane then swim from Florida. Others didn't get back quick enough. It was a catastrophe. Like hearing your planet is about to be A-bombed and there's nothing you can do to stop it."

"That's horrible," Yara offered meekly.

"Horrible isn't the word. Imagine thinking everyone you knew was about to die a slow and painful death over the next few weeks."

She rubbed her forehead, but didn't say anything.

"Vienna and I were near Boston. We got back here as fast as we could. When we got within a half a mile of the gate it was … chaos." My chest ached remembering the terror of that day. "Merfolk and selkies rushed in by the dozens. Every pair of eyes I scanned was screaming, trying to figure out who had gone through and who hadn't. Many of them were yelling out loud." I paused. "Have you heard the sounds your kind make underwater yet?"

"We talk through our minds."

"So do we, but we have an underwater dialect too. To hear that many sea creatures screaming underwater …." I shivered. "I'll never forget it."

"Why were they screaming?"

"Everyone was worried about their families, friends, anyone they cared about—desperate to know if they were safe on the other side, or still making their way to the gate. Many were panicking, crying, debating whether to swim through or wait.

"My cousin almost rushed past us, but I grabbed him, and asked if he had seen my mother. The look on his face told the truth before his thoughts formed. He said they'd been together off the coast of Maine. They left together, but she and his kids got tired near the end.

"He had his son and daughter, one collapsed in each arm. He said he couldn't carry my mother and his kids. He tried, but—" I shrugged and closed my eyes. "He apologized for being weak. Said he'd never forgive himself for leaving her behind. They were his children. Of course he had to put them first. I assured him he made the right choice and I would go back for her.

"He and Vienna both told me there wasn't enough time. My mom had been so close to where we were. If I had known, I could've carried her. We all would've made it in time." I took another drag. As if smoking could make me feel better. "I couldn't leave her behind."

My heart raced like I was living the moment all over again. I rubbed my lips, remembering Vienna's cool mouth against mine. "I kissed Vienna and promised her I would make it back before the gate closed, then I pushed her through.

"I searched the mob swimming past me, hoping to see my

mom. For miles I swam the opposite direction of everyone else. Swimming against the flow of traffic wasn't easy, but I finally saw her and locked my arm around her waist.

"Her scream was so intense I thought my mind might shatter. She thought I would've already been through the gate. She kept crying, telling me the sunlight was almost gone, that I should've gone without her. She was so exhausted she went limp in my arms. I never swam so hard or fast in my life. We blew past people. I couldn't feel my tail or arms, but I kept going, racing for our lives."

Yara had stopped breathing. I didn't want her to see me upset, so I turned away and stared at the moon.

"The gate came into view. We were seconds away from it. Then the gorgon kinfolk appeared. Five of them formed a line and forbid anyone to cross. Some obeyed, but most of us ignored them. We were too close to give up.

"At first I thought my eyes were playing tricks on me. All the selkies and merfolk around me slowed to a turtle's pace. Treygan and his grandmother were just ahead of us, but his grandmother looked strange. She had lost her color. Everyone had lost their color—except me and Treygan.

"He was a Green back then. The only other trace of color in a sea of blue and gray. I couldn't understand why there was so much gray. That's when I realized my mother felt hard, like stone. I looked down to make sure she was okay, but her eyes were rock. Just like the rest of her. Like everyone. All those bodies. Everyone who crossed the gorgons' line had been turned to stone—everyone but me and Treygan."

I waited for Yara to ask why or how we survived, but she only looked at me with glassy eyes and wiped a tear from my cheek.

"I'm so sorry," she whispered.

Part of me wanted to explain all of it to her. She had the biggest heart of anyone I had ever met. Too human for her own good, but that weakness would be they key to convincing her of what she needed to do. What if she accepted her fate, understood the sacrifice and opened the gate? I couldn't hit her with everything at once. She'd learn who and what she was soon enough, and she'd need time to accept it.

"I'm exhausted, Yara. I need to rest."

She curled up against me, adjusting her position several times. In my soul stirred memories of our realm and my love for Vienna. In my bed lay the reason for the curse, and the key to opening the gateway home.

Yara was the only one who could make my life whole again.

 No matter how I adjusted, snuggling against Rownan felt uncomfortable. Like lying on a cold, hard, rubber matt. He didn't smell good either. A mix of saltwater, mint and—pennies, or something else I couldn't put my finger on.

He lied about so many things, that he was nineteen, and that his parents lived in California. What really irritated me, even though it confirmed he must have a heart, was that he never told me about Vienna. Sure, that would have meant explaining why he looked like a teenager at age thirty or whatever—and that he was a selkie—but still, he should've told me. His wife might be alive in some other world, waiting for him. Why had he spent the last few weeks chasing after me and telling me how much I meant to him?

"Row, was it all an act?"

His only reply was long, deep breaths.

I sat up, frustrated, and glanced down at him. Sound asleep.

He lied—a lot—but for some reason I still cared about him. Nothing about him seemed attractive anymore. I had no—and I mean no—desire to kiss Rownan or sleep beside him. I had no desire to sleep at all, so I got up and walked inside the house.

His place couldn't have felt less like a home. No decorations, hardly any furniture, stark, white tile floors and countertops—minimalist would be an understatement.

I headed for the kitchen and opened the fridge: three glass bottles of tomato juice, fish fillets, and cans of sardines. Gross. I grabbed the juice and looked for a cup, but the cupboards were all empty. I swigged a huge gulp straight from the bottle.

Shock made me spit it out. Definitely not tomato juice.

Rownan's coat, my dress and the countertop were covered with the red stuff. I couldn't find anything to clean up my mess, so I used my skirt to wipe it all up.

I brought the bottle to my lips again and took a smaller sip so I could figure out what kind of juice it was. Closing my eyes, I tried to pinpoint the ingredients. Instead of sensing hints of fruits and vegetables, a surge of happiness rushed through me. I giggled uncontrollably with no idea why. After taking another sip it happened again. Maybe it was some kind of amazing alcohol that instantly got me giggly drunk. Sip after sip, I stood in Rownan's kitchen, laughing hysterically and hanging onto the counter to stay upright.

When the bottle was empty, I headed back outside to tell Rownan that I must be drunk. I paused in the doorway. Much to my surprise, I could walk straight and I felt fine—better than I had in a long time.

Rownan hadn't moved a muscle. One arm was still clasped behind his head while the other dangled off the mattress, holding a burnt out seagarette. He looked so innocent sleeping there under the moon.

I was there when my mother died, but he had watched dozens die. I couldn't imagine that kind of horror. All those people racing for their lives, screaming underwater. How did he and Treygan survive it? Why didn't they turn to stone?

Gazing up at the moon, I wondered how much more there

was to this otherworldly magical existence. I covered Rownan with his coat and left.

A kiss goodbye didn't cross my mind until I was walking down the street. I had never left Rownan without kissing him, but my urges and feelings were changing rapidly. I didn't know whether to fight the changes or embrace them.

A white heron perched atop a streetlight spread its wings above me. It let out a deep, guttural groan and craned its neck. The street seemed creepy with no trace of anyone but me and the bird.

I looked over my shoulder a few times, but never saw anything other than shadows. When I heard a faint laugh coming from an alleyway I took off running to the ocean, eager to get away from something—or someone—I felt watching me.

The feeling of being followed stayed with me until I reached the water. Still wearing my dress, I dove in. Before the bubbles even settled Koraline appeared in front of me. Of course. She had probably been watching me all night.

Her green pigtails floated on either side of her head.

Hello, Yara.

Hi.

We've wasted too much time, she thought sternly. *We're returning to Solis.*

Okay.

She looked startled. Maybe she expected me to put up a fight, but I wanted to go back. I wanted answers. I wanted to understand what I was, and what it would mean for my future. And to tell Treygan I was sorry for what he went though.

Koraline and I swam side by side while I marveled at my ability to see. As a human I had been swimming at night plenty of times. Back then, even in the shallow parts of the ocean, I couldn't see anything. Now I could see clearly. Things were a tad darker and colors had a neon hue to them like an arcade game. But I could see in the middle of nowhere with no sunlight.

Exhaustion crept over me and my speed decreased. Koraline drifted ahead, then turned back when I stopped swimming.

Are you okay? she asked.

Can we rest for a minute?

She looked around. *We aren't in the best resting place. This is a high-risk zone for predators.*

Predators? I scanned the area, expecting to see a giant squid. *I figured we would be safe in the water because—* Well, crap. Why would I assume that? Why would I assume anything about this way of life?

Because? she prompted.

Because I'm an idiot and don't know anything about being a mermaid, or what I should be afraid of.

I would like to change that if you would stay put and let me educate you.

I nodded in agreement. I wanted to ask her some questions right then, but she broke eye contact, squinting at something behind me. Her head turned from side-to-side, pigtails gliding against her cheeks with each swing. Then her eyes met mine and her usual confidence changed to alarm.

Yara, are you bleeding anywhere?

Bleeding? No. Why?

She grabbed my forearm, dragging me beside her much faster than we had been swimming earlier. I wanted to ask what was wrong, but she stayed focused ahead. Why would she ask if I was bleeding? Did I look injured?

Something big moved in my peripheral vision. I tried to catch a glimpse of it, but we were swimming too fast. Then another big something loomed in front of us. Koraline dove deeper, pulling me with her. This time I saw it. I wished I hadn't.

Inches separated us from the white belly of a shark. I swallowed a mouthful of water, gasping with fear.

Predators. Bleeding. Sharks. Oh, God.

I pumped my tale with all my strength, trying to help us swim faster. Koraline looked over her shoulder. I followed her gaze. Another shark swam just yards behind us.

This isn't normal, she mentally shouted. Even with terror consuming me, I noticed her skin had taken on a purplish hue. *They don't stalk like this unless they smell blood.*

What do we do?

Her eyes were wide. A stream of unintelligible chatter poured out of her. It was like listening to a cassette tape on fast forward. She yanked me upward and the tip of my fins brushed against a shark's head. He flailed his tail and snapped his teeth at me.

Keeping a death-grip on my arm, Koraline grabbed my chin with her other hand. *We have to fight,* she insisted.

What!

We're crazy strong underwater. Hit them on the snout and all around their eyes. As hard as you can. Destroy their receptors. Hit them over and over and keep swimming away after you do. You'll know when they can't detect you anymore.

No! I can't. I'm too scared.

You have to, Yara.

My eyes bulged at the massive bull shark swimming up behind her. Its razor-sharp teeth looked like a splintered picket fence. Koraline let go of me and spun around to face it. I watched, paralyzed, as she raised her purple arms above her head and smashed them down in front of her.

She flipped herself over like she was about to ride on the shark's back. She kept swinging, punch after punch, while he thrashed in every direction. How was she moving so fast? I couldn't do it. I couldn't fight like her. I was so scared I couldn't move.

Something butted against my back, shoving me forward. I turned to face a giant, creepy eye belonging to a tiger shark. I thought the other sharks were big. I was wrong. This shark was *huge*.

This is it. I'm going to be eaten alive by sharks.

Koraline rushed toward me, but so did the shark's rows of teeth. I swung at the tiger, nailing him in the side of his head.

Good girl! Koraline cheered in the seconds our eyes met. *Keep hitting!*

Adrenaline made me brave. I cocked my arm back and hit him again while Koraline grabbed the snout of the bull coming up behind her.

My arms moved so fast. I couldn't believe I was holding my own against a shark. *We've got this,* I thought, smashing my fist into his face non-stop.

I felt a tearing pain and a faint cloud of red flowed past me.

No. Please no.

The tiger had nicked me in the shoulder. I still swung violently, but more sharks swam toward us. I swam away, dipping and weaving. The trail of blood following me was causing a feeding frenzy.

Koraline dove down to the reef below us. She returned with a long piece of coral in her hand. She lunged at the nearest shark, stabbing his side. Blood burst into the water as she ripped the gash open. She shoved the bleeding bull at the approaching crowd of sharks.

Now look who's for dinner, she thought while smiling at me.

We turned to see another shark coming at us. Koraline swung at him, but I swam up and away. Sharks collided with each other, snapping and flailing their tails, tearing apart the one Koraline wounded.

Another shark swam up behind Koraline, but she was busy fighting the first one. She couldn't see the second one coming.

I tried racing down to her, but everything happened so fast. He opened his mouth, baring his teeth. I screamed out loud, trying to warn her, but she turned the wrong way. She turned to look at me.

Red exploded through the water around her. A wall of bubbles rushed up in front of me.

I saw a blur of familiar blue.

More red.

Then all the sharks were gone.

And so was I.

 **Treygan**

The first two shattered into pieces.

At times, no matter how much I practice, I can't control the gorgon side of me. Seeing Koraline in the jaws of a shark was one of those times. It was also one of the few times in my life that I was grateful for being able to turn living things to stone. The rest of the sharks were sinking statues within seconds. At least I didn't blow up all of them.

Koraline was unconscious, but she had a pulse. I lifted her tail, wincing at the sight of it. Her fins were gone. The tattered end of her tail hung in ragged, bleeding strips.

I took a calming breath. My focus needed to be pinpoint accurate to seal the wounds without making them worse. My serpent hallmark stopped burning against my back. Icy calm took over.

Hairlines, Treygan. I told myself. *Thin as a strand of hair.* I sealed off each wound with painstaking precision, careful not to make the stone too deep, wide, or heavier than necessary, creating stone stitches that could be removed later by a Violet. She stopped bleeding. At least there was that.

Pango and Merrick would be here any minute. Her brother shouldn't see her like this, but there was no avoiding it. I held her tight, monitoring her slow heartbeat as I sped through the water.

Pango's eyes didn't meet mine. They didn't need to. When he saw Koraline he let out a bloodcurdling scream that would be heard through the ocean for miles. Merrick and I didn't try to stop him or assure him it would be okay. We couldn't. We knew how bad it was.

Pango gently took his sister from my arms. His loud, low, heartbreaking cries echoed through the water. A severely scarred manatee circled us, sympathizing with Pango's pain. Any underwater creature within hearing range would understand the sorrow in his voice. It was a universal language down here, more powerful than human words could ever be.

Merrick tore his eyes away from Pango to look at me. *Treygan, thank you. We would have been too late. I'm sorry you had to use your—*

I still may have been too late, I interrupted. *Take her to Indrea and Caspian. Go!*

Merrick took Pango's face in his hands. Koraline hung limp in her brother's arms between them. Then in a cloud of bubbles they were gone, swimming as fast as they could to Paragon Castle.

The second explosion of red had been the wrong shade for blood. I recognized the blur of ruby wings. Nixie had dived in and swiped Yara away like a bird catching a fish. Yara might have been saved from the sharks, but what would the sirens do with her?

I swam off in the other direction, to Sybarites Nest, praying Nixie had gotten to Yara in time. And that I could get to Yara before Otabia and Mariza did.

The climb up the sirens' cliffs didn't bother me. I would rather make the rigorous trek than give one of them the satisfaction of carrying me. The problem was, once I reached the top of the cliffs, their nest sat atop trees which were impossible to climb.

"Nixie!" I shouted up into the dark.

A chorus of moans came from the elaborate tree house above me, followed by a loud fluttering of wings. Otabia flew out of a window and joined me on the ground.

"Treygannn," she hissed, running her curled, black fingernails across my chest, and down my back as she circled me. She kept her ebony wings extended, forming a wall of black silk that blocked the moonlight. She was the showiest of the sisters, but the most sensible—as sirens go.

"Evening, Otabia."

She ran her tongue from the base of my spine to the nape of my neck. Why sirens bothered with me was a mystery. I never reacted to their advances. "Delectable. Your serpent mark tastes of fury and death." With one smooth leap into the air she repositioned herself in front of me. Her jet-black bangs framed her piercing eyes as her pupils enlarged and shrunk repeatedly.

"Otabia, you have a new hairstyle. It suits you."

She licked her lips with typical siren thirst. "You killed recently. I can smell it on you. Who did you kill, Treygan? You reek of it, and it's driving me insane with passion."

"Sharks. Not exciting in the least." I wanted to ask about Yara, but I had to wait. Angering a siren is never a good idea, so I let her continue leading the conversation. Asking a siren about another woman never ended well.

"Sharks. Bleh." She stuck her dark tongue out and waved her hands between our faces. "You are here to see Nixie?"

This was why Otabia was easy to deal with. She never took long to get down to business. She was the oldest of the sisters, therefore she didn't get quite as consumed by lust. She flirted, and we both knew what she wanted, but she could multi-task.

"I saw Nixie swimming where the sharks attacked. She wasn't harmed was she?" Yara was my concern, but I had to give the impression that a siren's wellbeing took first priority.

"Nixie is fine. Come." She wrapped her arms around my waist. "We've been expecting you." We soared upward into the nest.

Otabia sat me down at the edge of their sunken living room. Burning torches embedded in the tree branches throughout the room created an almost romantic glow. Sirens have an affinity with fire, so the mild flames meant the sisters were calm—for the moment.

The smell of beer, lust and blood hovered in the air. I could only imagine the things that took place in their nest on a regular basis.

A human man was curled up in the fetal position, trembling in a dim corner. Black feathers lingered in his hair. One clung to his forehead above his bulging, terrified eyes. Otabia's latest catch. If sirens don't kill their victims, they remove the memory of their encounter before returning them. That extraction of the last hours from a human's soul was like dessert after the meal for a siren. Otabia hadn't had dessert yet, and the man watched all of us like we were a scene from a horror movie.

Mariza and Nixie lay in a heap of velvet blankets and pillows covering the floor. Yara was passed out between them. Nixie stopped licking Yara's shoulder when I arrived, but Mariza continued sucking at the wound, trying to extract every possible drop of blood. Nixie might be younger, but she had more control than her older sister. Mariza never knew when to stop.

I wanted to jump in and snatch Yara away from them, but that would cause a scene and make Mariza want her even more. It might make all of them thirst for her. Sirens want what they can't have, and they love a good fight.

"Riza, the girl is dry and unconscious. Stop looking desperate in front of our company," Otabia ordered.

Mariza lifted her chocolate-colored lips and grinned. "Welcome, Trey-Trey." Her brown eyes glazed over when she looked at Yara again. "Just a little more. She tastes divine."

Nixie shoved Mariza backward into a pile of pillows. "You're a lush! You finished off three islanders during the hurricane. All by yourself! Leave some for the rest of us."

Stray brown feathers floated through the air as Mariza crawled toward me. She flipped onto her back, letting her wavy hair spread over my feet. "How could I resist?" she moaned. "Those men were flaunting their songs in my face. Swaying to and fro, acting like morons while liquor flooded their veins. One deep-rooted fear after another poured out of them, begging to be consumed."

"You killed them, Riza," Otabia scolded. "Sucked the life out of them. You have no self-control."

When I was a child my grandmother used to say, "B for brunette and baneful. Stay away from the brunette." The man in the corner cried as he watched Mariza—the most dangerous of the sisters—rub her cheek along the top of my foot.

"Part of me knew I should stop, but I couldn't," Mariza elaborated. "They were so delicious. Such horror in their souls. You wouldn't believe the heinous things they had done in their short lives, some of the crimes they performed as a team. I've never tasted anything so dark and rich, blending together so sinfully. I should have drained them slower. Drawn it out."

"Get off of Treygan," Nixie demanded.

The jealousy in Nixie's voice caused Mariza's eyes to light up. The torches around the room burned brighter in response. Mariza threw her arms behind my knees and I fell to the floor in front of her.

"Trey-Trey, you should repay my red-headed twit of a

sister for rescuing that bland creature over there. Let Nixie have her way with you. I promise you will enjoy it."

Pulling away from the grasp of a siren is next to impossible, so I chose a different tactic. Smoothing Mariza's hair from her face, I sweetly replied, "We both know how dangerous it would be if Nixie got involved with me."

Mariza flew backward, tousling her hair. "Pathetic excuse, merman! You never live! Don't you want to devour someone?" Her wings burst to her sides, creating shadows that stretched to the edges of the room. The human pressed himself against the wall, crying louder. Mariza twitched furiously—a sure sign of over-excitement. "Take him, Nixie! Otabia and I will hold him down."

Nixie leapt through the air. Her wings rustled as she crouched in front of me, facing her sister. "Flighty fool! He could kill us all."

"He cannot!" Mariza shrieked, charging at Nixie to get to me.

Nixie's wings flew open, wrapping back and around me protectively. She pushed Mariza away. "He can! Have you forgotten petrification works on anyone in this realm? We may be immune to his blood, but his gaze could still turn us to stone! When he spirals into uncontrolled rapture, will it be worth it? Would you enjoy becoming a statue for the rest of eternity?"

Her words stung. I couldn't forget or change what I was, but hearing it spoken out loud never ceased to bring back the shame.

"He is adamant about not using his gorgon sight," Mariza hissed. "He will control himself."

Otabia shrieked from behind me, outside the cocoon of Nixie's wings. "He used his power minutes ago to kill numerous sharks. Petrified at least five, from what I tasted. His soul is battling itself. Part of him would love to continue the killing streak."

"Now do you wish to seduce him?" Nixie clicked her tongue several times. Her wings resumed their natural position. The torches returned to a slow, steady burn.

Otabia's nails dug into my neck as she whispered in my ear. "Take the mermaid and leave our nest. I do not like to see my sisters argue. And while you appear to be in control, I don't trust you."

Without hesitation, I stepped around Nixie and gathered Yara in my arms. Her eyelids fluttered briefly. The wound didn't look as bad as I imagined. The Violets would be able to heal her. Koraline, on the other hand—

I pushed the worry from my mind. Otabia placed her hands under my arms and carried me and Yara out the window. As we flew away from the nest, Mariza's siren song echoed through the night sky, followed by the man's terror-stricken screaming. It sent a chill through me, and I held Yara tighter against me. Her warmth could have melted the iciest of souls.

Even after we splashed into the ocean and Treygan started swimming, I waited to open my eyes in case Otabia watched from the sky. Nixie must have been able to see through the water when she dove in to rescue me, so her sister might have that ability too.

Being carried like I was a helpless baby should have pissed me off. Instead, I was all too aware of how strong Treygan's arms were. He kept a firm grip on me as his body arched up and down, over and over, propelling us forward. My skin tingled every time it rubbed up against his. It had to be a mer thing.

After opening my eyes, I reached up and touched his shoulder.

You're safe, he assured me. *You were attacked by sharks, but we're on our way to get you healed.*

First things first. *Where's Koraline? Is she okay?*

She's with the Violets. She was severely injured.

No! She was fighting. She— I felt sick. I recalled the look in Koraline's eyes after I yelled out to her. The next thing I knew I was swinging into a dark sky.

The red siren—Nixie—she said Koraline would be okay. I begged her to go back and get her, but she promised she'd be fine.

A siren's word means nothing. Wait, you spoke to Nixie?

She saved me from the sharks. She told me where she was taking me. She said I had to act unconscious. No matter what I heard, I had to keep my eyes closed and try not to feel scared. She seemed nice, in a bizarre sort of way.

His nostrils flared. *Did you think she was nice when she sucked blood from your wounds?*

She warned me about that before she took me to the tree house. She wanted her sisters to think I was passed out. She said to focus on the pain of my wounds and try to ignore anything else, which wasn't hard. My shoulder feels like it's been run through a meat grinder.

I didn't know which was more disturbing, two bird-women licking and sucking at my shoulder, or the awful, animal-like sounds of that man. The tree house—or nest, or whatever— was a house of horrors.

She shouldn't have taken you there, Treygan said. *It wasn't safe. Don't trust the sirens. Don't trust anyone except other merfolk.*

Not even gorgons?

His bicep flexed against my skin, but his face remained unchanged. *Especially gorgons.*

But you're part gorgon, right?

His eyes bolted away from mine and he focused straight ahead. Underwater communication had its flaws. No eye contact, no more conversation.

I tried wiggling out of his arms, but pain shot through my shoulder. Dull and achy pain, but it still packed a wallop. Treygan didn't let go of me. If anything, he held on tighter. Deep down I was happy to stop resisting. Everything felt like it hit me at once: the confusion of this new life, Rownan's lies, the fear and adrenaline of the shark attack, the disturbing experience with the sirens, the shock of hearing Treygan could turn things—and people—to stone.

What else was he capable of? If he was part gorgon, then he had just warned me to never trust him. But he was definitely part merman, and mermen can't lie, so could I trust Treygan or not?

He looked down at me again. *May I ask you something?*

Sure.

Are you in love with Rownan?

I had already asked myself the same question. *No. He lied to me. How could I be in love with him if I can't trust him? I'm not sure I even know what being in love means, but I'm pretty sure trust is a big part of it.*

Treygan squinted. *I wasn't born with the romance gene, but I'm certain you're right about the trust part.*

Our speed increased, and I was too tired to keep holding my head up against the constant current. Reluctantly, I rested my head against Treygan's chest and closed my eyes, trying to ignore the fact that he felt so comfortable.

Breaking through the surface, I saw the tall bordering cliffs of Solis. Treygan released me and I floated to his side. His foot brushed up against my tail. His foot?

"What the—?" I tried to see through the water, but the hallmarks on his chest were the last visible part of him. "Do you have legs right now?"

"Yes," he said nonchalantly.

"How is that possible?"

"Unlike the folklore, we *do* control if we have legs or a tail."

"No. I tried at Koraline's house to keep my tail outside of the water, but it changed instantly."

"You haven't mastered your abilities yet. It will come in time."

"Seriously?" I'd have no problem going back to Eden's Hammock and living a human life. I could even swim with legs.

"I told you. We're amazing creatures. Would you like assistance out of the water?"

"Um." I looked up at the towering rocks above us. No way would I be able to climb them. My shoulder throbbed just thinking about it. "I think I will *need* assistance. That doesn't look like an easy route."

"My pleasure."

He grasped my uninjured arm. With a swooping motion of his free hand, the water beneath us rose up and carried us into the air. The churning wave sounded like a hundred ice cube trays cracking as it hardened, forming a translucent bridge that stretched out in front of us, connecting to land.

"Wow," I gasped, looking down in awe as we walked across. "It's like wet glass."

Once we were on actual solid ground he lowered his arm. The bridge went soft and fell splashing into the ocean below. I stood at the edge of the rocks, looking down and gaping. "You'll teach me how to do that, right?"

His lips twitched at the corners like he wanted to smile. "If you behave, yes, I'll teach you how to do that."

"Deal."

I squeezed water out of my dress and tried not to gawk at his chiseled body. I was curious to see if his hallmarks covered *every* part of him, but I couldn't lift my gaze from the scrolling artwork on my own feet. He must have noticed my nervous fidgeting.

"I apologize for not having clothes on. We can follow this trail to the nearby stream. Once we're in the water—"

"Treygan, its fine."

His eyes drifted downward and lingered at the low-cut neckline of my dress. I stepped back and crossed my arms over my chest. "Exactly what are you staring at?"

"Your emotions."

"What?"

"I'm trying to figure out what orange means."

Looking down, I gasped. "Why is my skin orange?"

"Your mer traits are developing. Our skin changes color when we feel strong emotions."

"Oh, dandy. We're real-life mood rings." Koraline's skin had turned purple when she fought the sharks. Did purple mean scared?

"So?" Treygan urged.

"So what?"

"Will you tell me what orange means?"

"Don't you know what it means?"

"Colors vary from person to person. What were you feeling when you turned orange?"

I wanted to say offended or insulted, but I couldn't. It was more like embarrassed, but also flattered and excited, like my skin ached to be against Treygan's again. Every time he touched me it felt like a million dragonflies fluttering along my skin. If he knew that, I'd be humiliated. "I plead the fifth."

"What?"

"The right to remain silent. I choose not to answer."

I scanned the moonlit mountains around us, trying to think about anything but the fervent sensations Treygan caused inside of me.

The silence didn't last long. "We should get you into

a resting pool," he said. "I'll send for a Violet to heal your shoulder. In the meantime, Koraline will have supplies at her house to treat it."

How could I be so self-centered? Koraline was attacked by sharks! Treygan should be the last thing on my mind. I turned to face him again. "How badly was she injured?"

"Severely. She may have lost too much blood. They ate her fins away entirely."

I threw up. It was pure water, but I buckled over and wretched, making awful, mortifying sounds. Treygan pulled my hair back, keeping it away from my face. A few more stomach spasms passed, but nothing else came up. I stood up, silently wishing it had been me instead of Koraline.

"Gross. Sorry," I mumbled, convinced I would die from humiliation.

The quizzical tilt of his head combined with the moonlight reflecting in his eyes almost made him look concerned. Between his hallmarks his glistening skin lightened. Speculating what the silvery shade might mean caused my heart to hammer in my chest. I looked up at the starry sky and squeezed water out of my dress again. This *must* be a mer thing. I *could not* be attracted to Treygan.

"You're bleeding." He stepped closer and examined my shoulder. "Let's get it taken care of. A stream to the village is just around that bend."

Blood made me queasy so I didn't look at it, but I felt the warmth trickling down my arm. We walked side by side as he guided us along a pathway.

"Too bad the sirens aren't around," I joked. "They could clean this up for me."

"Don't let them drink from you again. If they ever attempt to make you drink blood, refuse it. No matter what they say or promise."

"Ew, I would never drink blood. That's disgusting."

"Glad to hear you feel that way. Now that you've seen it firsthand, you might as well know that selkies are also blood drinkers."

The beginning of a laugh escaped my lips. Surely he was kidding. Then I froze. My legs went numb and I stopped walking, remembering the mystery juice at Rownan's house. No. It couldn't have been. I would've known if I had been drinking blood.

Events of the night clicked into place, one after another: the red liquid, spilling it all over myself, wiping the counter clean with my dress, Koraline asking if I was bleeding, the frenzied sharks, and my last glance at Koraline's wide, green eyes.

"Oh, my God, Koraline," I blurted out, clutching my stomach. Treygan had walked ahead, but he turned and made his way back to me. "I'll never forgive myself."

His voice softened. "You're not to blame."

He could say that because he didn't know yet. But I *was* to blame. I should have never left to find Rownan. I should have stayed and let Koraline teach me what I needed to know. She would still be safe. I would have never drunk— My stomach flipped over just thinking about it. An entire container. Almost a gallon of it.

"Treygan." I glanced apprehensively at my wound. The blood didn't make me queasy. It should have, but it didn't. When my mouth watered it confirmed my fear. I swallowed hard. "What would happen if I did drink blood?"

By the look on his face you would have thought I had ripped his heart out.

day 4

Rownan

Morning shed a new light on things. I gawked at the empty bottle sitting in the sink. It had to mean something, but what? Merfolk didn't drink blood. They were repulsed by it.

I searched the trash can for any sign she had just spilled the blood and cleaned it up. I found nothing. She drank our blood. A lot of selkie blood.

This wasn't in any of the rule books. This went against the natural order of things. What if the instinct to live like us—to be one of us—ran deeper than we thought?

"This could change everything," I said, slapping my hands against the counter. What would Treygan do when he found out his precious mermaid had become a blood guzzler? I grabbed my coat and the keys to my bike and flew out the door. This newsflash had to be broadcasted as soon as possible.

Jack Frost's wasn't open yet, so I used my key and let myself in the back door.

"Jack?" I shouted. No answer.

Jack was like a father to me, but I couldn't predict his roaming patterns. If he was in the water, I could guess where to find him. If he was in human form, he could be in any female's bed anywhere in the Keys.

I made my way down the hidden corridor and slid open the door to the walk-in freezer. Steel screeching against the floor and the smell of wet animal hair triggered the memory of the man who had died here.

A human patron found our hiding place once, years ago. If humans knew we were selkies and that we sometimes kept our skins hidden in the bar's freezer, they would probably steal them. Without our seal skin we couldn't return to the ocean—much less to Rathe. We had to make sure a siren drained the trespasser of every memory he had of the bar. The problem was we asked Mariza to do it.

After his death we made sure the myst on the freezer was ironclad. No human had come close to this room since. Regardless of what merfolk believe about selkies, we don't like watching others die needlessly.

Jack's black seal skin hung in its place. He was on land somewhere, but there wasn't enough time to look for him. I needed to go to the Catacombs and start working.

I heard the sound of footsteps approaching and my claws shot out reflexively.

Dina walked into the freezer and laughed at me. "Easy, killer. It's only me."

"She drank our blood," I blurted out, itching to tell someone.

She hung her wet coat on her appointed hook. "Who did?"

"Yara."

Dina's head snapped around so fast her wet hair sprayed droplets across my face. "Legit?"

I nodded.

"What does that mean?"

"I don't know. That's why I need to talk to Jack."

She pulled a seagarette out of her wristband, tapping it against the top of her hand. "Did she enjoy it?"

"Must have. She downed an entire bottle."

A grin spread across her face. Dina would be wondering the same thing as me. Did this mean Yara was meant to take our side? *Be* on our side?

"Jack thought this would happen," she said. "Genes have major influence. You should tell her the truth about her father. Imagine how much stronger that would make our case."

Many times I had wanted Yara to know her father had been a selkie, but if her own parents kept it a secret, what right did I have to tell her? "Vyron made it very clear that none of us could tell her anything about selkies."

"Only until she turned eighteen."

"The eighteen stipulation was her mom's idea. If Vyron had his way, Yara would never know about any of us."

"Screw Vyron! He broke his promise. Did he care when the gorgons sealed the gate? No! He abandoned us. Tell his mongrel child what she really is. Maybe she has daddy issues and she'll come running to us," she pouted and continued in a baby voice, "hoping we'll give her the love and acceptance she never had as a child."

"Dina, stop it. The girl's been through enough."

She rocked on her heels, scanning the seal skins and frozen goods surrounding us. "Would it matter, though?" she asked, suddenly thoughtful. "Surely the merfolk will tell her what needs to be done to open the gate—their interpretation and ours. Even if she prefers our way of existence, she wouldn't give up her life for us."

"Maybe not for *only* us," Jack said, startling me. He was so light on his feet that I hadn't heard him approach. A seag bobbed between his chapped lips. "But she'll have a hard time condemning both species to this world for eternity. That's a lot of lives to ruin."

Jack had a way of finding a solution to every problem. His casual lean against the doorway made me relax.

"You know, don't you?" I asked. His smile revealed the gap in his teeth. "How'd you hear about it already?"

"Ran into Nixie. You know how she likes to gossip."

"How did she know?" Dina asked.

Jack tossed his seagarette on the floor and smashed it with his boot. "Who cares? It's true, right? Yara drank from you?"

"Nah. She drank a donor container from my fridge."

"Did she enjoy it?"

"No idea. I was asleep. She probably didn't know what it was."

Dina laughed. "If she drank the whole thing then she must have loved it. We've got her, fellas. She's as good as addicted."

Jack shook his head. I knew what he was thinking before he said it. "She needs to drink from you, Rownan. Direct from the tap. *Then* she'll be addicted."

Jack knew I refused to drink directly from anyone, or vice versa. Everyone knew. "It would crush Vienna if I shared myself with someone else."

"You're the only one she would ever consider drinking from. If you don't do this, you may never see Vienna again. Yara needs to bond with you. Really bond. It's our one sure shot."

Dina voiced the concern I didn't want to say out loud. "Jack, if she drinks from him, she'll consume his gorgon blood. Look at what that did to Vienna. What if it works against us?"

Jack and I glared at each other, but for different reasons. I wanted to curse him to hell for making me do this. He wanted to knock me upside my head for being so vulnerable. As if I had any say in who or what my father was.

"Why couldn't you have gotten Treygan's power?" Jack grunted.

At that comment I left the room. As part gorgon I inherited the ability to shadow other gorgons, dial in on their location, watch over them and sometimes see through their eyes. The first time Vienna drank my blood she developed the same ability. We were connected, always able to find each other, until the gate closed.

"You have to do it," Jack called out behind me.

I kept walking, but he was right. Soon Yara would crave blood again, and when that time came, she would have to drink mine.

 We had been at it for hours. Yara and I were mentally drained from the ongoing Q and A session, but she wanted to learn more.

"Okay." Yara looked up from her history book. "Let me get this straight. Medusa was turned into a gorgon because she shacked up with Poseidon in Athena's temple. She was banished to live in a cold, dark, secluded grotto along with her two sisters, Stheno and Euryale. All of them could turn living things to stone."

"Right."

"Poseidon was immune to the petrifying thing because he was a god, so he secretly visited Medusa and continued the affair—even though she was a hideous monster."

I nodded. "He still saw her as beautiful. Blinded by love, I suppose."

Yara shook her head in disbelief. Her fingertips glided across the page. "Okay, so then he created a siren for each of the gorgons; bird women who could travel through water or fly to the heavens to find Poseidon or relay messages for the sisters. But the sirens hated the grotto, so they hardly ever returned." She flipped a few pages back, then forward, scanning chapters she had read several times. "Then Medusa and Poseidon had kids, and Stheno and Euryale were jealous and wanted their own, but couldn't have any because of the petrifying issue, right?"

"Right. Plus, what man would go into the grotto to have sex with a hideous monster?"

Yara blushed and tucked her hair behind her ears. "That's why Medusa asked Poseidon to create the selkies. So she and her sisters had creature children that loved the cold and darkness and would stay in the grotto."

I sat back in my chair, impressed by how much she absorbed so quickly. "Until the grotto couldn't hold all of them, then Poseidon created an ocean to harbor them."

Yara scanned over the pages again. "But the sisters got bored with the dark selkies, so they asked for children who liked to play and sing. Poseidon created merfolk, modeling them after fish and dolphins. But they needed sunlight and warmth, so he created a whole different realm for them?"

"Not exactly. We all live in Rathe. Think of our separate halves as different countries. The grotto sits in the middle, directly on the border of our light and dark territories."

"And Medusa is the one who requested selkies and merfolk be able to travel to the human realm and explore land?"

"Yes, because the original sea creatures grew bored and restless. The sisters arranged it so they had to return to Rathe regularly or they would die. They didn't want them disappearing for long bouts like the sirens."

Yara glanced down at her book again. "Is that why the gorgons had the all-seeing mirror in the grotto? So they could watch over their children wherever they were?"

"You're a fast learner."

"Who is more powerful, the gorgon sisters or Poseidon?"

"Hmm, well, Poseidon pretty much gave Medusa and her sisters whatever they wanted. That included the ability to create rules, gift abilities, and control the gateway between the realms. When Medusa was killed by Perseus, the other sisters lost most of their power."

Yara's eyes widened. "Stheno and Euryale aren't still alive, are they?"

"They are. Medusa was the only mortal of the three."

She studied the drawings of the gorgons on the page in front of her; their heads full of snakes, claws for hands, huge fangs, serpent-like tails, and pinwheels of fire and ice for eyes. A small shiver ran through her and she snapped the book closed, placing it back in its case.

"Why is every book kept in glass?" she asked.

"They're waterproof so we can store them underwater, and they're charmed so that if a human found them they'd appear to be chunks of useless concrete."

One nod. From observing her the past several hours I learned her single, firm nod meant she was accepting truths, saving them to memory, not questioning my words anymore— definite progress.

She pushed a book and plate of food away from her and stretched her arms over her head. "My shoulder feels a lot better."

"The Violets are amazing healers." One of the Violets, Prynne, had been waiting at the house when we arrived. She nursed Yara's shoulder right away, and confirmed her injury wasn't severe.

Yara picked at the bandage on her arm. "I still don't get the whole drinking blood thing."

Explaining the siren and selkies' blood-drinking habits had been daunting, but Yara seemed genuinely disgusted by it and agreed to fight future cravings. I blamed myself for her drinking blood. I should have warned her right away. Moving forward, my job would be to make sure no selkies—especially Rownan—came anywhere near her.

I pulled a book over to me and thumbed through the pages. "Here." I spun it around and slid it toward her. "Left page, second paragraph."

Yara read out loud in a voice that sounded like harp music. "The gorgon sisters longed to return to the human realm. However, the curse had sentenced them to solitude. Therefore the three united together and devised a plan.

"The sirens were summoned and offered seductive beauty and the power to control the weather if they agreed to a proposition. The sirens would seduce mortals, a give and take of body and soul, including drinking the life force from the veins of their prey. They would then return to the gorgon sisters and regurgitate the blood, allowing Stheno and Euryale to consume it. Thus they could relive the encounter as their own.

"As time passed, many selkfolk envied this system. They begged the gorgons to allow them to drink the stolen blood. Medusa refused. As a compromise, she gifted the selkfolk with the ability to share their souls by allowing another to drink directly from their veins.

"The bloodshed of the original selkfolk was horrific for several moons. Many died because they had no self-control and drained one another of all life. Once the selkfolk had their habit under control, they boasted of their superior ability.

"This did not please the merfolk. They believed they were equally entitled to pleasure as the selkfolk. The merfolk went to Medusa and requested the same gift. Medusa, still heartbroken over the loss of so many selk, refused to lose any of her mer in the same careless manner. Thus she and her sisters conjured up a new gift."

Yara cracked her neck from side-to-side and rubbed her temples. What would she think of the next part of our history?

"No blood would be necessary for the mer to share themselves. Medusa and her sisters resented their inability to gaze into the eyes of another with great emotion. Thus they chose sight as the manner in which merfolk would share their souls with one another."

Yara glanced up from the page and caught me watching her, but I couldn't look away.

"Pretty gross," she murmured. "Sirens regurgitating blood and people drinking it."

"Not people, gorgons," I corrected. "Birds regurgitate. It's part of their nature."

"Still. Gross."

"Agreed."

As if defending itself, a heron spread its large wings just outside the window. Yara and I both turned to look at it.

"No offense," Yara said, "but this house is depressing without Koraline here. Can we take a break? I'm itching to be back in the water and sunshine."

That was a good sign. She should gravitate toward sunlight and water, though it baffled me that she wasn't curious about the ability to share our souls with each other. "Of course, but only floating. No swimming. Your shoulder needs to heal."

We walked to the stream in silence and waded in.

Yara scanned the cottages around us. "All merfolk live here on the island?"

"We all have homes here. Solis is protected from discovery by humans."

"Koraline told me that part. I didn't know if all merfolk lived here, or just some. I hardly ever see anyone else."

At least she wasn't calling us freaks anymore. "Sadly, there aren't that many of us. One hundred and twelve are here in this realm. You make one hundred and thirteen. Most spend days at a time away from here. They like to explore or interact with humans, but this is a safe haven for whenever they return."

"How many, you know, didn't make it? How many are in the Catacombs?" Splotches of red spread across her chest. Her red must mean sadness.

"Thirty-one," I answered somberly.

Her eyes widened as crimson swirls snaked across her shoulders. "I'm sorry."

How much had Rownan told her? Was Yara apologizing because she didn't know what else to say, or did she know about her parents' broken promise and blamed herself? "The actions of others sometimes affect our destiny. No one blames you."

She looked thoroughly confused.

So Rownan hadn't told her *she* was the reason for the gate closing. Good. I felt she should hear it from one of us.

"Treygan, the night you saved me, what did you do to me? Why didn't I remember you for all these years?"

How could I explain it to her? We were finally making progress. I didn't want to scare her by telling her part of *me* was as awful as she originally suspected. The last thing we needed was her running back to the selkies. It was bad enough she drank blood at all. If Rownan offered to let her drink from him she might not be able to resist, and then he would have the upper hand. Jack had unexplainable manipulative power over his kind. The stronger her selkie connection, the better chance Jack would have at controlling her actions too. "It's complicated."

"My entire life has been complicated. I can handle it."

"This is an exceptional level of complicated."

"Is it because you're part gorgon?"

My people never brought up this topic. They knew I hated that side of me. Many of my own kind feared my gorgon side and stayed away from me because of it. Why didn't Yara?

"If you don't tell me, I'll swim back to Eden's Hammock and ask my uncle."

Her uncle. They weren't even related. "Lloyd and you seem very close."

"He's been like a dad to me. My father died when I was four. My mom and I moved to Eden's Hammock and Lloyd sort of looked after us. I remember the first time I met him. At least, I think it was the first time." She flicked the water with her fingers. "Guess you don't want to hear about my childhood."

"No, I don't."

Her face scrunched up in a sour expression. "You don't have to be a jerk about it."

"Much of human sharing feels superficial to me. It's a lot of talking and very little listening."

With a swat of her hand she splashed water in my face. "Okay, I get it. I won't tell you any of my lame stories."

"You're not letting me finish. This is the lack of listening I'm referring to."

"Sorry. Go ahead."

"Merfolk share in a deeper way than talking—more intimate." Bonding with one of us was crucial to her siding with us, but her first experience was supposed to be with Koraline. Not me. I had to back-pedal. "But I would never ask you to share yourself that way with me."

"More intimate?"

"The mer sight you read about. Sharing your soul."

"Wait, what?" She cocked her head to the side, reminding me of the Golden Retriever Lloyd once kept as a pet.

"You can share pieces of your life with other merfolk—if you choose to. You take them into your soul and they relive a memory as you."

"You're joking."

"You just read about it. Did you think our history books were a joke?"

"I thought it meant how we communicate underwater. The eye-contact mind-speech thing."

"No. Sharing songs—memories—is very different from that."

"You're telling me that you could relive one of my memories as if you were me? Like flashback to my childhood without me having to tell you about it?"

"Without verbally telling me about it, yes. Your soul would tell the tale."

Her head jerked backward like she had been punched. "That's unbelievable."

"It's our way of sharing ourselves." The Violets' warning not to do anything without their permission rang through my conscience. "But it's extremely personal. You and I shouldn't engage in that practice."

She grabbed my hand and pulled us closer together in the stream. "Oh no, I have to try it now so I can see if you're telling the truth."

"How many times do I have to explain this to you? We can't lie."

"Sorry, I keep forgetting."

Our bodies were too close. The gentle current of the stream caused her hair and tail to brush against me several times. The sensation of bubbles under my skin returned.

"Tell me how it works," she pleaded.

"You concentrate on the memory you want to share with me, then—"

"No, you share with me first."

Alarms went off in my head. Not allowed! Not until the Triple Eighteen! "Your first time should be with Koraline."

"Koraline isn't here. And who knows how long she'll be recovering?"

I had seen the damage. Koraline might never recover. If

that was the case, wouldn't I be the next logical choice for Yara to bond with? I had already started her education. She felt more comfortable with me than any other merfolk. Maybe I could use this opportunity to make her comfortable with the others and give her a glimpse of our realm at the same time. Surely, that could only help matters.

"Fine," I agreed. "You think Delmar is scary, correct?"

"I wouldn't want to meet him in a dark alley."

"Well, then. I'd like to prove otherwise. Are you ready?"

She let go of my hand and drifted backward. "I don't know. What do I have to do? And once I'm there, how do I get out of it?"

"You stare into my eyes. Most of us feel a tug in our chests. You'll feel like you're being pulled into my body, but you won't actually go anywhere. You'll see, hear and feel what I felt when I lived that moment. When I end the memory you might feel a push. Or, if you want to end the experience early, think of an object back here—in this time and space."

She glanced around. "Like what?"

"Like a particular flower, a rock, anything, and then concentrate on its details."

She studied me intensely for a moment. "Okay. I'm ready. I think. I'm sorta scared."

I tried to comfort her by smiling. The new experience would be incredible for her, and I was surprised at how happy it made me that her first time would be with me. "Don't be scared. I chose a good memory."

Treygan and I stared at each other. My whole body tingled, even my tail and fins. For a split second silver clouds passed over his eyes. Then I felt the tug in my chest and everything went bright blue and silent.

I was Treygan, sitting beside Delmar on the rocks of a shoreline of violet sand and gazing out at the water. My tail—Treygan's tail—was sage green, but each shining scale looked as if it was outlined in chrome. Delmar was a Yellow. His hair was blond and shorter, but he looked the same age as his present day self. A rainbow-colored sun beat down on us as our tails splashed in the surf.

"Will you be singing today?" Delmar asked with a grin.

As Treygan, I watched water sprites sparkle below the surface. "Of course. I'm your best man."

Delmar skipped a sapphire shell across the water. "You're like a brother to me, Treygan. I marry my true love today, but that doesn't mean our bond weakens."

"Kimber is first in your heart. I'm happy to step down from my post."

Delmar shook his head. "Love knows no rank. I love you and Kimber differently, but I would lay down my life for either of you in a heartbeat."

"You would lay down your life for any of our kind."

"I'd like to think that's true, but now that I have Kimber, my priorities are shifting. I would do anything to spare her from pain and suffering. Her happiness means everything to me."

I smiled, even though part of me felt sad and lonely. "All the more reason to get you to the grotto on time. Kimber already worries too much."

"Race?" Delmar asked.

"I won't let you win just because it's your wedding day."

Delmar waved his hand and a large wave crested up out of the water and pulled us deep into the surf. He clutched my forearm and grinned at me underwater. *Stop stalling and race.*

He darted off, but I floated in place, watching him swim

away. A water sprite flitted around my head like a glowing, miniature tornado. She stuck tiny bunches of kelp in my hair, skidded to a stop and sat on the tip of my nose.

Her tinny voice sounded like coins dropping in an empty fountain. *You always give him a head start.*

I winked at her. *Today I'll give him an even longer one.*

I felt a steady push against my chest and opened my eyes to see Treygan turning away. For a moment I was disoriented. Switching so fast from *being* Green Treygan—living and feeling as if I was really him—to seeing Blue Treygan in front of me left me dizzy.

"Treygan, that—that was incredible! I was you! I didn't have any thoughts of my own. Your thoughts were my thoughts. Your feelings were my feelings. I wasn't scared or confused. I was whatever you were. You were peaceful, then sad, then … so happy."

He dipped his head back into the water, wetting his long hair and rubbing his hands over his face. "Do you still think Delmar is a bad guy?"

"I—well, no. But where were we? Or where were you? Everything was so beautiful. That beach had lavender sand and the sky swirled with colors I've never seen before."

"We were in Rathe."

I thought Eden's Hammock or Solis was paradise, but the other realm trumped them by a landslide. No wonder everyone wanted to return home. And I felt awful for judging Delmar so harshly. Was he here without his wife, or were he and Kimber living together in this world?

"Did you let him win?" I asked.

"What?"

"The race."

He squinted into the sun and his shoulders bounced with silent laughter. "Maybe someday I'll let you see how it ended."

"Why did you push me out? I could've stayed there forever. The water sprites were gorgeous. You didn't feel that way about them, though. You felt so indifferent, like they were as common as a fly. I didn't even have an opinion about them until I came back here. Or got inside me—or—I'm still confused about how that was possible."

"Many things about our existence are considered magic or impossible to humans. It seems normal to me because I was born mer. You'll become used to our way of life over time."

Maybe being a mermaid wasn't so bad after all. I searched the stream around me for any sign of flying lights. "How come I haven't seen any sprites yet?"

"They were the first to die off after the gates closed. None survived on this side."

"That's horrible." My chest turned a splotchy red. Had Treygan realized red meant I was sad, or did he even notice the color change? "Some are alive in the other realm, right? They aren't extinct, are they?"

"We have no way of knowing what's happened in Rathe. Not until the gate opens."

"Why did the gorgons seal it off? Koraline said someone broke a promise, but what could've been so bad that they shut so many of you out of your own world?"

His lips parted like he wanted to answer, but then he silently dipped straight down into the water. His long blue strands danced in every direction. He popped back up and slicked his hair back. "Let's get back to your story about the first time you met Lloyd."

He had become a pro at dodging my questions, but I let him win this one. "It's dull compared to your memory. You don't want to hear it."

"You're right. I don't want to hear it." He swam so close

that his breath warmed my face. "I want you to share it with me."

Reading his facial expressions was like trying to read a book written in a foreign language. Did the way he slowly batted his wet eyelashes mean he cared?

"Okay." I took a jittery breath. "How do I do this?"

He stared at me and raised his hands, touching my neck with his fingertips. The tingling started again. "Try to remember a detail that stood out. A place, smell, something you felt—whatever triggers that memory for you."

I closed my eyes, trying to ignore the delicious heat Treygan's touch sent through me. I focused on the day my mom and I moved to Eden's Hammock.

"Yarrraaa," Treygan stretched out my name playfully. "It won't work if your eyes are closed."

I felt like an idiot. "Oh, right. Sorry."

When I opened my eyes, he looked at me in *that* way again. The same way he did after I finished reading out loud earlier. All I could think about was the moment at Koraline's kitchen table when I had an overwhelming urge to kiss him.

My muscles had been achy from sitting and reading so long, but when I looked at Treygan, the pain disappeared. Instead, I craved him in a way I had never felt before. I wanted his hands on my skin again, wanted to know what kissing him would be like. Did he have a girlfriend, or a wife, or some lost love on the other side? And if he didn't, could he ever see me that way, think of me as attractive, or want to kiss me?

Days ago I despised him for turning me. I thought I hated him, but now—

No! I mentally yelled at myself, snapping back into the present. I needed to stop daydreaming—especially about Treygan.

I concentrated on a childhood memory to share with him. I stared into his blue eyes as I recalled the feel of sand between my toes, the smell of the baby powder my mother wore, and the peeling cherry nail polish on my mother's fingernails.

Then I transported to a different time and place.

Walking the sandy road between Uncle Lloyd's house and ours, my mother towered above me, her sandals dangling from two fingers. With every step she took, her red shoes swung back and forth, each time almost hitting me in the chest. I watched her so intently that I didn't notice we were standing in front of a yellow house until a man's deep voice said hello.

"We've moved in," my mother said gruffly. I peered through the fence at all the colorful flowers in the man's yard.

"Cleo, if you need anything, absolutely anything," the man said, "I'm here for you and Yara."

At the sound of my name, I peeked around a bush of bright purple flowers and looked at him. His tan feet were huge and his toes were covered with fuzzy, white hair. A green garden hose hung from one of his hands. The other hand, covered by a yellow gardening glove, waved at me. I waved back and stepped through an arched trellis onto a sidewalk that matched the color of the man's hair. Several worms crawled along the pathway, so I stopped and pointed at them.

"Lot a worms," I said in my high-pitched toddler voice.

"Well, little one," he said, "when the waterin' starts, they tend to want to cross the sidewalk."

"Why?" It was the textbook reply of most four-year-olds when an adult attempted to answer questions.

He looked around his yard while he thought about his answer. "Many reasons, I suppose. The sun may burn too bright and they'll dry up, or a bird may fly over and take them for—" Maybe he thought it wasn't his place to explain the food chain to such a young and impressionable child, because he stopped himself before saying the real answer. "For a change of scenery."

"Seen-or-ee?" I repeated, trying to save the new word to my limited vocabulary.

He bent down and picked up a worm from the sidewalk, then gently set it in the grass.

I giggled, arching my back and throwing my arms open wide. "Why you do that?"

"Sometimes creatures need help getting to the other side," he answered with a wink.

I squatted down and grabbed a slippery worm between my fingers, marveling at how slimy it felt and watching it wiggle back and forth. Then I set it in the grass, looked up at the man's yellow glove, then at his wrinkled face, and smiled. He smiled back, so I stood up, went to the next worm, and repeated the process, each time getting a brighter-than-sunshine smile from the big, friendly man.

"Yara, we've bothered this man enough." My mother grabbed my hand and pulled me away from the two remaining worms that needed help.

"Oh, it's no bother, Cleo," he said.

"Still, sorry for all of this." My mother dragged me along, stumbling behind her. I kept looking back over my shoulder, worried about the worms. The man bent down, then stood up again and held his yellow-gloved thumb up at me. Even at four years old I knew that meant okay—that the worms were okay. The man in yellow would always make everything okay.

I pictured the cluster of freckles on Treygan's cheek that reminded me of the Canis Major constellation. Instantly, I was back in the present moment, floating in the stream on Solis Island, birds tweeting from nearby trees, water trickling as it flowed past me and Treygan.

"How did I do?" I asked.

I wasn't sure if I had mentally brought him back with me, or pushed him out, or whatever I was supposed to do to end the memory, because he just stared, not blinking and not saying anything.

"Treygan?"

"No," he murmured.

"No, what?" Had I done it wrong?

"The answer is no," he said a little louder, finally blinking.

"What are you talking about? You didn't see my uncle's garden and the worms?"

"I saw the worms, but—" He swam in a slow circle until his back was to me and gripped the grass on the bank. "The first memory you shared, in Koraline's kitchen. You wondered if I had a girlfriend or someone on the other side. The answer is no. I've never had anyone like that."

My heart catapulted into my throat. I wanted to sink below the water and drown. He lived *that* memory as me too? He felt what I felt? Knew my thoughts about him? Knew I wanted to kiss him? I couldn't breathe. I was beyond humiliated.

"And no," he continued in a stony voice, his tensed back turning forest green, his serpent hallmark darkening. "You shouldn't want to kiss me or know everything about me."

I was too embarrassed to say anything, so I focused on the water flowing past me. Hearing my thoughts would have been bad enough, but he felt my emotions. He knew how giddy he made me. The feeling wasn't mutual. I had never felt so exposed—or so stupid.

A blur of bright green appeared upstream. It got bigger and closer until the huge merman I met at the weed island poked his head through the water.

"Hello, Yara," he said, water dripping from his green curls and eyelashes.

"Hi." I couldn't remember his name. Pamby, or Plato, or something.

At some point during my trance of humiliation, Treygan had turned around. His skin had returned to its normal color. His forehead wrinkled and his chin lowered when he asked, "Pango, how is she?"

Pango! That was his name. He drifted toward Treygan. Without a word he wrapped his huge arms around him and they floated there, silently hugging. The urge to vomit returned. Did their hug mean Koraline was dead?

Pango said something, but I couldn't hear him over the gurgling stream. I could see Treygan's face though. His wrinkles and tension fell away.

"Is Koraline okay?" I asked.

Pango faced me again. His emerald eyes were glassy. "She's still unconscious, but her vitals have improved. The Violets think she might pull through."

I exhaled so loudly it surprised me. How long had I been holding my breath?

Pango glanced back and forth between me and Treygan. "They're holding a healing vigil tonight after sunset. The Oranges in the area have been sent to spread the word since most folk weren't arriving until tomorrow."

"We'll be there." Treygan squeezed Pango's bronze shoulder. I nodded, trying not to stare at his hallmarks. He was so big that every marking looked gigantic.

"Indrea ordered me to rest for a few hours," Pango sighed, "so I'll be on my way, but I wanted to thank you again, Treygan. I owe you."

Treygan unzipped the his armband and pulled out two joints. "You owe me nothing. Go rest."

Pango took the joints, zipped them away in his armband, and dove beneath the water. He was so different from the bubbly, flamboyant guy I had met yesterday. It seemed like the life had been sucked out of him.

"Is he close to Koraline?" I asked.

Treygan stared downstream where Pango had disappeared. "She's his only sibling."

Being bit by a shark felt like nothing compared to the guilt that ripped through me. Pango could lose his sister because of *me*. My stomach knotted. I couldn't swallow. He hadn't said goodbye to me when he left. He must know the attack was my fault.

Koraline was unconscious somewhere and clinging to life, Pango hated me, and now that Treygan knew how I felt about him he probably wished he could ditch me again. Just when I started to give in and embrace the mer world, I was quickly becoming an outcast.

"Well." Treygan pulled a lighter from his armband and lit a joint. "Change of plans. We won't have as much time as I thought to prepare for the ceremony. We'll have to start now."

"What ceremony?" I asked as he passed me the C-weed. Earlier this morning at Koraline's house I had coughed like crazy the first time I tried to smoke. Hopefully this time I would look less like a dork. I took a few short puffs.

"The Welcoming Ceremony," Treygan explained. "Tomorrow at sunrise every merfolk in this world will gather to welcome you as one of our kind. We celebrate in your honor until sunset."

I coughed so hard I thought I might hack up a rib. Treygan smacked me on the back, pointed at the water in front of me and told me to drink. I dipped down, sipping from the stream until I stopped coughing enough to reply. "I don't deserve a celebration."

"Oh, but you do." His blue eyelashes batted as he smiled. "It's a required step of your transformation."

My chest was on fire, my throat stung, and my head

swirled. I had never been good in crowds. Even visiting towns like Key West gave me anxiety because of all the people and commotion. A hundred merfolk were gathering to meet me? The urge to run or swim away again was overwhelming.

"No worries. They will all adore you," he assured me.

They didn't matter. There was only one merman in the world I wished would adore me—and he didn't want me to know anything about him.

Sunset 4

Rownan

I couldn't believe I was swimming to Paragon Castle, but I needed to see Yara. If any of the merfolk—especially Treygan—found out she drank blood, they would try to keep her away from me. If they didn't know yet, then I needed to see her again before anyone found out.

Nixie said the mer were gathering tonight for some kind of healing gig for Koraline. With any luck, I would find the one merman who might agree to let me talk to her. Maybe he had been promoted to a Blue by now. If he was on guard duty I could talk to him without drawing a lot of attention.

Keeping my distance, I made a lap around the perimeter of the castle. More Blues hovered outside than I expected, but I didn't see him anywhere. Even a few Indigos stood guard. I watched all the Greens too, just in case he hadn't advanced over the years.

A conch horn wailed through the waters, announcing the start of a ceremony. I hovered behind a reef, watching a few Blues and Indigos leave their posts and swim inside. The waters around me vibrated so strongly the hairs on my tail stood up. I turned around, expecting to see someone. A ten foot manta ray soared past my head, looping through the water. I would never get tired of watching the massive, winged-like creatures fly through the seas.

A hand grabbed my elbow, spinning me around.

What are you doing here, Rownan?

Delmar, damn! No wonder I couldn't find you! Look at you, you're an Indigo.

His face stayed stern and serious. *Why are you here?*

Come on, not even a hello, how ya been? I haven't seen you in years. Is that any way to treat an old friend?

We used to be friends. Not anymore.

Well, I squeezed his shoulder. *I hope that can change after we're back in Rathe.* He glanced down at my hand and shrugged it away. So much for playing the friends card. *How did you move up two ranks while Treygan stayed a Blue?*

He remained a Blue by choice. Now, why are you here?

By choice. Of course. I should've known. *I just wanted to see Yara for a few minutes.*

Ha! Delmar's lip lifted in a sneer.

Del, whether or not you and Treygan believe it, she means a lot to me. We got pretty close these past few weeks. I want to make sure she's okay.

She's fine.

Man, relax. I raised my hands so he could see my claws weren't out. *I'm not here to cause trouble. I just wanted to check on Yara.*

Rownan, this is a sacred night. You can't be here. Tomorrow is Yara's day of welcoming. Once that's over, you can see her. That is, if she wants to see you. Until then, don't let me catch you within a mile of this castle or Solis. Agreed?

I looked away from him.

He didn't know about her drinking blood or he would never agree to let me see her tomorrow. An entire night and day meant a lot of time for Yara or someone else to figure it out. Her first time cravings would start soon. Someone would recognize the behavior and know what it meant, even if she didn't. And if she didn't quench her thirst during her first cravings, she would survive the worst of it. She would have better control over future urges. She might be strong enough to resist drinking again altogether. Especially since her first drink was secondhand.

I needed to see her tonight. But with the healing thing going on, and their pointless celebration tomorrow, the place would be swarming with merfolk. All eyes watching their prized inductee. Jack would have to figure out another way for me to get to Yara. Until then I had to let Delmar think I was fine with waiting. If he suspected something, they would never leave her side. Then we would really be screwed.

Okay. I extended my hand. *Enjoy the celebration tomorrow. I'll say a prayer for Koraline.*

His dark eyes narrowed, but he shook my hand. *Thanks. Now get out of here.*

I swam away hoping I had played it cool enough, but when I looked back Delmar swam through the castle entrance faster than I had ever seen him move. He only moved fast for two reasons. He wasn't racing my dickhead brother, so that meant he was on his way to protect someone. Damn it.

 Treygan

We floated outside the doors to the gathering hall with about thirty other merfolk. Each person who came forward to meet Yara was friendly, welcoming, and happy to see her, but her unease continued to grow.

I feel like I can't breathe, she said, massaging her throat.

Once we enter the hall you'll feel more relaxed. Indrea fills it with calming energy in preparation for the ceremony.

Right, sure. She rolled her neck around. *They need to hurry up. I might have a nervous breakdown.*

Just then the sea-glass doors swung open. Others swam into the hall.

I rested my hand on the small of Yara's back. *Remember what I taught you about adjusting your vision?* She nodded. *It's time to do it.*

Her lashes flickered. After one hard squint she smiled. *I did it! It's so dark I can hardly see you.*

Good. I'll lead you in.

We hadn't made it two feet into the hall before Yara stopped swimming. I glanced back, but she was floating in place, staring up at the tall, arched ceilings in awe. For a minute I let her observe the hundreds of glowing jellyfish above us. They slowly bobbed through the water, opening and closing, most with long tentacles that dangled like ribbons. Gossamer bells of the sea, illuminated by their blue and white fluorescent lights.

I momentarily established eye contact with her. *If you listen closely, they make a soft ringing sound.*

She lifted her astonished gaze again.

Some of the most exquisite parts of our traditions had become taken for granted over time. It felt good to stop and appreciate the spectacle above me. A minute later I floated directly above Yara, blocking her view. *We need to get our lanterns and take our positions.*

This is incredible!

I watched her with fascination. I had never been part of a new merfolk transformation. Seeing her reaction to things for the first time was like watching a child. She had barely seen a glimmer of how incredible her new life would be. *Come, the ceremony will begin soon.*

When we approached the circle, two Reds handed each of us a lantern. I thanked them and led Yara to our places. Yara tried moving to my other side, but I guided her back between me and Pango.

Stay between us, I explained. *You should be next to folk you're comfortable around.*

Maybe you should be next to Pango. I could stand between you and Kai.

Kai's place is on the other side of the circle. You're where you need to be.

She glanced at Pango and he hugged her, but she looked uncomfortable. I hoped she wasn't still feeling guilty about the shark attack or assuming Pango blamed her. He didn't know about the blood incident yet, but his take on it would be the same as mine. It was an accident. Plain and simple.

The gathering hall was even calmer than I expected. Indrea had done an excellent job.

Still nervous? I asked Yara after pulling her focus away from her lantern.

Um, no, but why are these fish glowing? She glanced at the three fish swimming inside the glass globe, each radiating a different color: pink, yellow and orange.

It's called bioluminescence. It means living light. We each carry a lantern as a symbol of light and healing energy for Koraline. I glanced at my own lantern. The fish emitted a blue, green and white glow.

She tapped my arm. *How do they light up?*

Some have cells called photophores, others have a bacteria or protein inside of them that— Caspian blew the conch horn. Three drawn-out notes announced the beginning of the ceremony. *Just watch and listen,* I told Yara. *You haven't yet learned the songs we'll be singing, but you'll feel the power of them.*

Okay.

Caspian, Indrea, and the other five Violets hovered above the castle floor and linked hands around a raised stone slab in the middle of the hall. They began singing the song of *Clearing*, creating a scared place for Koraline to rest. Sixel, one of the Indigos, swam through the doorway with Koraline in his arms. Her mangled tail and other injuries were covered with flowers. I looked around Yara at Pango, knowing the flowers must have been his doing. The thoughts running through his mind made me grin.

Her hair should be in pigtails. I told them pigtails tied with daisies. Like it's such a difficult task.

Yara reached for my hand when she saw Koraline, but she missed and her fingers scraped the side of my tail. It felt as if a million water sprites flitted along my skin. I tried to ignore the sensation and block my schoolboy thoughts before making eye contact with her.

My God, she looks awful, Yara said shakily.

Focus on the positive. She's alive. Yara's chest turned red. A curtain of rainbow light fell over her eyes. I thought she was tearing up, but it was hard to be certain underwater. I touched her shoulder. *Sadness won't help her. Only positive thoughts.*

We watched Koraline being placed in the center of the circle. The Violets continued singing, growing louder as they reached the section where the rest of us would join in.

With the first note of the group singing, Yara raised her head and her mouth fell open in surprise. Hearing one merman or mermaid sing could take your breath away. Hearing all of us sing together—well, someone once proclaimed we must be the souls who taught angels how to sing.

The opening song, *Connecting*, strengthened the bond between everyone in the hall and prepared us for the other songs. As we sang, Yara observed everyone in the circle. Most folks' hallmarks were changing colors, moving or shimmering, but it was difficult to see in the dim lighting.

Indrea motioned to Pango and he moved toward the table,

swimming above the Violets before dipping down into the middle of the circle to hover face-to-face with his sister.

He placed two fingers over his heart, then over his eyes. Finally he reached out and placed them on Koraline's closed eyelids.

What were those hand gestures? Yara asked me.

It meant, his heart, his soul, he shares with her, I explained.

Pango sang the first few notes of the song, *Love*. The rest of us joined him.

When we finished, Pango returned to his place in the circle.

Yara rubbed her rainbow-hazed eyes. *They're happy tears. I promise.*

We're underwater. No need to wipe them away. Though if you direct your tears at Koraline, your emotions will carry through the water and bathe her in love—or whatever it is you're feeling,

Really? Is that part of our ability to control water?

Tears are water. You should start small.

She smiled her biggest grin to date. *I'm not crying anymore. But it's good to know for next time.*

The yellow blur of Merrick swimming toward Koraline momentarily distracted me, then I refocused on Yara. *You'll be the last to go, so follow what everyone else does.*

I'll be the last to go where? She almost sounded concerned, but as calm and love-filled as the hall was, it was impossible for her to reach any level of anxiety or fear.

Just watch.

Merrick hovered over Koraline, two fingers resting on her eyes as he led the song of *Healing*. Yara watched Merrick swim back to his place beside Pango while everyone continued singing. The mermaid next to him swam forward, floated above Koraline, put two fingers over her heart, and completed the pledge before returning to the circle. The next merman went and the ritual repeated over and over.

I was eager to hear Yara's reaction, but she wouldn't face me. She stared ahead, focused on every merman or mermaid swimming above the stone table as they pledged their hearts and souls to share with Koraline.

And then I saw them.

Pango's lantern on the other side of Yara's face offered just enough glow to backlight her rainbow tears. A few iridescent droplets left her eyes and glided toward Koraline, blending with the volumes of water surrounding us. But in that split second in which her tears were visible, I watched Yara control water for the first time.

When it was my turn I glided forward, lantern in hand, and floated above Koraline. I scanned the faces of the Violets surrounding us, but none of them appeared worried. My eyes met Indrea's.

You will not harm her, she assured me.

Koraline looked better already. The golden hue had returned to her cheeks and her puncture wounds were starting to heal.

I pressed two fingers on my chest. *My heart.*

I placed them over my eyes. *My soul.*

After resting my fingertips on her eyelids, my sadness intensified, so I sealed my eyes shut to be safe. *I share with you.*

As the singing continued, I returned to my place beside Yara. She swam forward, not hesitating whatsoever, and completed the final pledge of the circle. When she returned, we smiled at each other. In that brief moment, even with everyone singing around us, I felt like we were the only two souls in the worlds.

The last round of *Healing* grew louder, and that's when I heard Yara sing for the first time. She was absolutely the most angelic singer I had ever heard. Even others near us in the circle stole glances at her. Unfortunately, the song ended, and when it did Yara looked at me.

She said, *That was the most beautiful thing I've ever experienced.*

You are the most beautiful thing I've ever experienced. The thought came out before I could look away. Through the glow of jellyfish and lanterns, I saw her cheeks flush. Blue swirled across her chest, expanding to her shoulders.

Embarrassed, I pretended to focus on the last part of the ceremony. I released the door latch of my lantern and my three fish swam free into the water. Yara followed my lead and released hers. Fish flooded the hall, glowing in fluorescent colors, as everyone emptied their lanterns.

Indrea sang the final notes that concluded the vigil, and folk began swimming out of the hall. Thankfully, Kai approached us and initiated a conversation with Yara.

How could I have said something like that to her? Knowing how she feels about me, and knowing she and I could never be together. I wanted to apologize, but how do you tell someone you're sorry for calling them beautiful?

Pango and Merrick were thanking the Violets, so I waited patiently for Yara and Kai to finish their conversation or include me in it. But then I saw Delmar hovering by the entrance, so I excused myself.

In spite of the dim lighting, I could clearly see the perturbed look on Delmar's face. That look meant trouble lurked nearby, and I already knew that trouble's name was Rownan.

Yara

Pango floated there, chatting and sharing stories with me, Merrick and Kai. He was laughing and joking, acting like his sister wasn't fighting for her life a few feet away from us.

I couldn't take it anymore. I confessed to Pango. I told him about me running off, spilling blood all over myself, causing the shark attack, and how guilty and horrible I felt. I must have apologized twenty times. He wasn't angry, and he insisted I stop blaming myself.

He lifted my chin and winked at me. *Don't you worry, my sister will pull through. She's a spunky little sprite.* He hugged me, then he and Merrick said goodbye and returned to the Violets and Koraline.

Kai's hands closed over one of mine. *I must go, Miss Yara. So much to do for the celebration at sunrise.*

Okay. See you tomorrow.

She kissed me on the cheek and swam away with a Green and Blue who had dark skin like hers.

The hall had nearly emptied. Delmar and Treygan floated on the other side of the room, both looking solemn. They'd been that way for at least ten minutes. I watched them, waiting for Treygan to remember I existed, but Delmar's black eyes found me first.

For a few seconds we just stared at each other. He wasn't thinking anything, at least not that I could hear, but I might have been too far away to hear his thoughts. He didn't scare me anymore. Not since Treygan had shared that memory of him with me.

Delmar cocked his pale, pointy jaw to the side and returned his attention to Treygan. They laughed at the same time, gripped each other by the hand and leaned forward in an almost-hug. Treygan looked up and waved me over.

Hi, Delmar, I thought, when I reached the two of them.

Happy Welcoming Day Eve, Yara. He smiled. *Big day for you tomorrow.*

So they tell me. I shot Treygan a sideways glance but when I looked at Delmar again he was swimming behind me. I only caught the end of what Treygan said to him.

—you. Only a sun.

What about a sun? I asked.

Treygan shook his head. *We should go. You need your rest.*
Delmar floated at my side. *Kimber is looking forward to meeting you. We'll see you in the morning. Sweet night, Yara.*

His wife was in this world with him. Good. That made me happy. *I look forward to meeting her too.*

Treygan was eerily quiet on the way back to Koraline's.

Once we were in her living room I tried breaking the awkward silence. "It feels kind of weird staying at Koraline's house without her here."

"I'm sorry. My place isn't ideal for guests. Plus, she would want you to stay here. That was the plan. Koraline is a stick-to-the-plan kind of girl."

My stomach flipped with guilt. The ceremony tonight gave me hope that she would survive, but I would never forgive myself for being the reason she almost—and could still possibly—die.

"What were you and Delmar saying about the sun or whatever?" I asked.

He walked around the room, looking out the back door and every window. "The hallmark on your back. The sun represents you being mer. Everyone's looks different."

Like an idiot, I tried looking over my shoulder to see it. "Oh."

I had studied the symbols and artwork on Pango, Merrick and Kai tonight, mainly to keep my focus on something other than Treygan. I didn't want them hearing my thoughts about him. I glanced at Treygan's blue hair and all of his blue, black and silver hallmarks, and fought back a laugh.

His eyebrows lifted. "Did I miss something?"

Kai had told me about one mermaid who couldn't come to the vigil because she was stuck granting a wish to a human, which led to Pango explaining further. "Just remembering something Pango said."

"Do tell."

I kept a close-lipped smile, fighting back the visual of the blue genie from the Disney movie, *Aladdin*. "He explained the duties of blue merfolk."

Treygan stood up straight. Any trace of a smile disappeared. He didn't say anything, so I continued.

"He said if a Blue is discovered by a human, they have to grant the human a wish before returning home."

"It's a stupid rule. We're fighting to have it nullified."

Pango warned me that Blues were sensitive about it. Most stayed away from populated areas to avoid running into humans. They referred to it as the genie complex. Everyone tried to get through blue rank as fast as possible. Treygan definitely seemed touchy about it in an unbearably cute way.

Maybe I could use this knowledge in my favor. "Well, you're my Blue guardian, so you have to grant me a wish."

His chin jutted forward in one of his cocky know-it-all grins. "We grant wishes to *humans*. You're no longer human."

"But you didn't grant me a wish when I was a kid, or when you showed up at my house during the hurricane."

"Oh, but I did. The times when you were a kid you don't remember, but I most certainly did. And during the hurricane you specifically said you wished for me to take you some place safe."

"But you had me in some kind of trance. You made me wish for that."

"No, I made you feel comforted and told you that you had to wish it if you wanted me to take you someplace safe. I didn't force you to wish for anything."

Figures. The loopholes always seemed to work against me. "Don't you want to know what I would wish for right now?"

"I'm fairly certain I know."

"Oh, yeah? What would I wish for?"

"To not be a mermaid?"

"No."

My heart beat so hard I could feel it between my ears. I could do this. I could say it. I struggled to say the words louder than a whisper. "I would wish for you to kiss me."

His eyes met mine and I struggled to breathe. Neither one of us moved. Deep wrinkles appeared around his eyes. Then he looked away and stared at the floor.

God, why was I such an idiot? What was I thinking saying that to him? To Treygan, who had never dated anyone and admitted he wasn't romantic. I huffed out loud and tried to play it off.

"I was only—" Crap. I couldn't say the word kidding out loud. "I didn't really mean—" Nope, that would be a lie too. "This is so embarrassing," I moaned, covering my face with my hands.

I never heard his footsteps—probably because my heart was hammering too loudly. His hand touching mine startled me into looking up. There he was, only a couple inches away, staring at me with those hypnotic, cobalt eyes. He placed my hand against his chest, raised his other hand to my cheek, and ran his thumb along my lips. His heart pounded against my palm as glorious pins and needles pricked and teased the deepest parts of me.

"You are such a mystery to me," he whispered.

I exhaled shakily. "I've never felt like this before. Is this a mer thing or ... is it you?"

His eyes darted around, studying my face. Then he stared at me so intensely I was sure he could see every secret inside of me. "I don't know, but it wouldn't be fair to wander down a dead-end road."

Dead-end road? He started to pull his hand away but I held

it against my face, pressing my cheek against his palm. "I don't care how it ends. Kiss me, Treygan. Please."

He closed his eyes, rested his forehead on mine, and we pressed against each other. I fought to lift my lips to meet his, but he kept his mouth beyond my reach, even as his breath warmed my chin.

"Yara, I care about how it ends. I refuse to break your heart."

"My heart can handle it." It felt like a lie. The thought of being hurt or left by him seemed painful, but I said it out loud, so it must be true. Besides, we had no idea how it would end, or if it would ever end.

He pulled away, ran his hands through his long hair, and turned his back to me. My face felt so cold without his warmth against me. I asked him to kiss me—twice—and he said no. How much more pitiful could I look?

"You may think you want this, Yara, but you don't. I'm protecting you."

"Get out."

He turned and gaped at me. "What?"

I clenched my teeth together, fighting back my humiliation. "I said get out."

His confused expression turned to concern or hurt, I couldn't be sure which, but it didn't matter. He stepped toward me, but I took two steps back. "Yara, I didn't mean—"

"Get out! The longer you stand there, the more pathetic I feel. Just leave me alone and pretend this never happened." I ran for the bathroom before the last words were out of my mouth. I slammed the door, leaned against it and slid to the floor, hugging my knees and feeling like a total loser.

How could I ever face him again? He didn't feel the same about me. He probably couldn't see me as anything except a girl who had dated his brother. He hated Rownan. He would never consider being with someone who had kissed his worst enemy. How could I have been so stupid? My attraction to Rownan wasn't even real! Even when I was mysted my feelings were nothing compared to how I felt for Treygan. Every time he looked at me, or spoke, or I heard someone talk about him, I felt—

"Yara," Treygan called out, his voice muffled by the door between us.

"Go away!" I burried my face in my arms.

The sound of him sliding down the other side of the door made me lift my head. I pictured us sitting there, back-to-back, with nothing but a slab of wood separating us. His voice sounded closer. "Do you have any idea how badly I want to kiss you?"

I sucked in a stifled breath. "What?"

"I want to kiss you. I've wanted to kiss you since we collided on your front porch. But you have to trust me when I tell you it's ... we shouldn't. You could get hurt, and I vowed to protect you, not harm you."

I turned around and reached for the door knob, but stopped. "Explain."

"What?"

"You've said I shouldn't want to kiss you, so it has to be true. But you're saying you *want* to kiss me too. So explain. Why does this have to be so complicated?"

"Can you open the door?"

"Not until you explain." I leaned closer, not wanting to miss anything he said. I barely heard him sigh.

"I'm half gorgon."

"I already know that."

"Most gorgons can turn living things to stone."

"Know that too." Did he think I hadn't been paying attention?

"If my emotions get too intense, I lose control of my ability. Accidents happen." His voice was quieter, but I heard every word. I had to process it for a second, then I crawled onto my knees and leaned closer to the door.

"You mean you could accidentally turn me to stone?"

I heard one soft thud, like he had banged his head against the door. "Yes."

I was glad he couldn't see me. I must have looked terrified. "But …." I knew he had turned the sharks to stone, and I got the impression he could do the same thing to people, but this was crazy. He couldn't kiss anyone without possibly killing them? "How do you know that? Maybe it's only when you're angry."

He stayed silent. The longer I sat there, staring at the crystal doorknob and imagining him sitting on the other side, the more I didn't want to hear his answer. Then I realized. "Oh. It happened before, didn't it?"

"Once," he said. "I was practically a child. My first kiss was with one of my best friends."

The hurt in his voice sent a tremor through me. I couldn't take it anymore. I opened the door and he rocked backward, but caught himself and scooted over. I crawled beside him and laid my hand on his knee.

"What happened?" I whispered.

He dug his thumbnail into the floorboards. "She felt it happen and pushed me away. The kiss only lasted seconds, but her lips and part of her tongue turned to stone. I thought petrifying only happened through sight. I figured she would be fine. But it can be sight, saliva, or blood."

I didn't know what to say. I imagined being that girl. Could she talk? Could she open her mouth? Who would ever want to be with someone who had stone lips? She would never be able to feel another kiss again.

"With her it was just a silly kids' game," Treygan continued. "What I feel for you is … I can't bear to think of what I might do to you."

I nodded, staring at the floor. "But Rownan is part gorgon and—" I didn't want to remind Treygan that I had kissed the brother he hated. I tried to forget it every day. "He never turned me to stone."

"He didn't inherit that ability. His gorgon trait is that he can shadow other gorgons. Much less violent than what I'm cursed with."

My heart ached. For him, for me, for some girl I didn't know who had been sentenced to a lonely life with a mouth of stone.

He stared ahead at the wall. "You'll meet her tomorrow. I should tell you who she is now, so you're not blindsided."

"Okay."

He turned to face me. His eyes looked bluer than ever. "She is Kimber, Delmar's wife."

day 5

Treygan Sitting outside of Koraline's resting pool until midnight had been draining, but I had to watch over Yara. I didn't want to leave her to harvest the crops, but I had no choice. Even though she was in capable hands, I rushed through my work so I could return to her.

Delmar was on the couch reading when I returned. He didn't even look up at me, so I snatched the book out of his hands. "Why aren't you guarding the pool room?" I asked, louder than I intended.

"Shh." He propped his feet up on the ottoman. "I am guarding her. You might feel the need to hover outside the door, but I'm confident the extra few feet won't make a difference if someone tries to break in."

I glanced at the closed French doors. "Has she asked about me?"

"Hasn't stirred once. If I didn't know better, I would think she was asleep. She'll never know you left. Don't worry, Prince Charming,"

"Don't," I warned, handing his book back to him.

"Don't what?" He leaned forward. "You think I don't see it? You're in love with her."

"I don't know what love is. I've never even been on a date."

"Sharkshit. You love so selflessly it's nauseating at times. Me, Kimber, Koraline. Hell, some days you even love Pango and Merrick. You've loved Yara since she was a child. Except now it's different. You're *in* love with her. And she's in love with you, but you're too scared to do anything about it."

"*In* love. Like it's a pool you dive into. What if I turn the person I love to stone and she sinks to the bottom? Wouldn't it be safer to stay out of the water?"

He chuckled. "No, it's always safer in the water. Always."

"Thirteen sunsets, Delmar. That's all I have. It wouldn't be fair to her."

"Thirteen is more than twelve or none. Shouldn't she have a say in whether it is or isn't enough time?"

I flopped down on the couch beside him. "She asked me to kiss her last night. I can't even kiss her."

"Well," he said, with a cheeky grin, "I can tell you from experience there are other ways to show love. Kissing isn't everything."

"You and Kimber are different," I sighed. "And that's not the main issue. It would be greedy of me to act on my feelings, knowing I have to leave her behind."

He spun his book in his hands, staring at it. "Reconsider your feelings on love, Treygan. As wonderful as our realm is, it's not the best thing in creation. Love is." He turned to face me. "Believe me, you'll never know how amazing life can be until you allow yourself to fall in love."

I walked over to the resting room, looking through the glass at Yara. She floated peacefully in the dark water. Moonlight shone through the high windows, illuminating her skin and hair. "She takes my breath away."

"Good. Enjoy it." Delmar opened the front door. "You've been breathing steadily for far too long."

With a quiet click of the latch he was gone, on his way home to see Kimber and get ready for the big day. Soon the sun would rise. There wasn't enough time for me to rest, but there was one thing I wanted to do before Yara woke. I headed for Koraline's kitchen and searched through the drawers for scissors.

"I can't lie around anymore," Yara said, pushing open the glass doors. "I'm too nervous about—"

She stopped abruptly in front of the kitchen table and stared at me. I sat back in my chair, rubbing the back of my neck.

"You cut your hair," she gasped.

"I wanted to look shipshape for your special day."

She walked toward me, staring at my head. "I just got used to it being long."

"So you don't like it?" I felt like a fool. I grabbed my glass of juice and stood up.

"No, I—" She touched my chest and looked up at me. "You look so ... young."

"Is that good or bad?"

"It's good, but," she bit her lip, "it's not even. I could fix it for you, if you want. I've been cutting my uncle's hair for years."

"We don't have much time. We need to leave soon."

"Where are the scissors?"

"In the bathroom."

By the time she came back with a towel and scissors she was laughing.

"What's funny?" I asked.

"You're such a guy. You didn't even attempt to clean up your mess in there."

I moved past her. "Damn, I came out to get a drink and forgot."

She caught my arm and pushed me back down in the chair. "Sit. You'll have more hair to sweep up when I'm through. You can clean while I'm getting ready."

She wrapped a towel around my neck and ran her fingers through my hair. I closed my eyes, amazed at how good it felt. I wanted to wrap my arms around her, pull her onto my lap, anything to get her closer to me, but instead I slid my hands under my legs.

She pulled two pieces of hair taught against my chin and bent down, evaluating me. "I may have to go a little shorter to make it even."

"Fine."

"Treygan." She looked at me longingly. "If we *could* kiss, I would definitely be kissing you right now."

My fingers flexed under my thighs. I wanted her to know I felt the same way, but it wouldn't be fair. I leaned back and my hair slid out of her fingers. "Pango and Merrick will be here soon."

Her brow wrinkled. She stood up straight and moved behind my chair. "Right."

She tilted my head forward and began snipping. The only sound after that was the scraping of stainless steel blades as she attempted to fix the mess I had made. Areas of my chest and arms were bright white and silver, but it almost blended with my regular coloring. Hopefully she hadn't noticed how excited and happy she made me.

As soon as Pango and Merrick arrived, Yara's questions began. What should she wear? What would she have to do all day? Did she have to talk to people? And on and on.

I stood by silently, amused that Pango would be her new

teacher. Given Koraline's condition, he volunteered to take over his sister's job. I assumed the Violets agreed so he would have something to take his mind off of his sister, and it seemed to be working.

Several pearl hairpins bobbed between his lips as he mumbled, "Yara, my shimmering sunbeam." He secured more hair to the top of her head and took the pins out of his mouth. "Leave it to me. I will be your personal Sir Gawain today."

"My who?" Yara asked.

"Sir Gawain. One of King Arthur's knights. The exemplar of chivalry."

"I've only heard of Sir Lancelot."

"Yes, well." Pango gave her a hand mirror and leaned down in front of her. "We all know who is playing Lancelot, don't we?"

Her eyes met mine in the reflection of the mirror and she blushed. Pango looked over her shoulder at me and winked.

"Yara should get dressed," Merrick interjected. "We're already late."

"Fashionably late." Pango took the mirror from Yara. "Go, my lady, to the boudoir! Your gown awaits." He paddled her butt with the mirror and she giggled as she went to Koraline's bedroom. Pango looked at me and pumped his eyebrows twice before following her.

Merrick mouthed the words, *what are you doing?*

"I don't know." Others were noticing our attraction to each other and that couldn't be good, but I wasn't sure if I could stay away from Yara. Maybe it was the close call with the sharks. I felt guilty for not being there to protect her. Or maybe Delmar was right. Could I be falling in love with her?

We stood there, listening to Yara and Pango talk and laugh in the other room. I was certain Merrick was literally biting his tongue, wanting to remind me a relationship with Yara would be impossible—as if I wasn't aware of it every time I blinked.

"Gentlemen," Pango announced, standing so tall that his green curls brushed the arch of the hallway. "May I present the pertinacious, catechizing, yet somehow enchanting Lady Yara."

She walked out, and I swallowed my breath. Her dress accented every curve of her body. The plunging neckline and her hair pulled back made me wish we were alone so I could kiss every inch of her exposed skin.

My own thoughts forced me back to reality. And then what? Turn her to stone? What was wrong with me? I never had urges like this.

Yara curtsied and Merrick told her how lovely she looked. All three of them fixed their gazes on me.

"You look nice," I said, trying to sound casual.

Pango threw his hands up. "I doozied her up from head to toe, and you can't come up with something better than she looks *nice*?"

Yara ignored Pango and thanked me.

"I have something for you." I reached into my pocket and pulled out her armband, custom made to match her copper hallmarks. "In case you haven't noticed, every merfolk wears one, and today you're official."

She lifted her arm. "Will you put it on?"

I wrapped it around the top of her silky arm and our eyes met. "There's a gift inside for you."

"Thank you," she smirked and rolled her eyes.

I wanted to tell her there were more than just joints in the pouch, but Merrick cleared his throat and opened the front door, so we all filtered out.

Pango and Yara walked ahead of me and Merrick. I admired the way Yara's hips shifted as she walked, the few loose tendrils bouncing against the nape of her neck, and the way her skin glowed under the sun hallmark between her shoulder blades. She was stunning, but I wouldn't be able to think of her that way for the rest of the day. If the Violets suspected my feelings or overheard my thoughts, it would cause problems.

Today I would have to put on an award winning show of indifference for Yara—which, given the circumstances, seemed impossible.

Yara

I had never worn a gown in my life. Each step I took, I feared I would trip and fall on the draping bottom, landing face-down in mud and ruining the dress forever. Treygan would have the perfect view, and once again I would be humiliated.

Pango said my turquoise and yellow gown represented water and the sun, but why couldn't a comfy, short sundress represent the sun? I had never seen the guys wearing shirts before, so this was obviously a dressy occasion, but they looked comfortable in their khaki shorts and linen button-downs. I wanted to be comfortable too.

When I glanced up from carefully placing my feet, I saw merfolk walking over a nearby hill toward the faint humming of voices and activity. The sun wasn't up yet, and it made me more nervous, hiking through the dawn to who-knows-where to gather with a bunch of strangers.

Pango held my hand when we got closer. "You ready?"

His soft hand felt huge closed over mine. It made me wish for Treygan's lean, rough fingers entwined with mine instead. I looked back at Treygan.

"Take a calming breath," he said.

Pango and I rounded the hill which opened up into a massive valley with a lake in the center. When I saw all the people I wanted to run in the other direction. Treygan said there would be just over a hundred of them, but to me it looked like a million.

The mob of people gathered around the lake had skin in varying shades of white, silver, copper, or gold. Their hair represented every color of the rainbow. Some sat on blankets, others stood around talking. Several kids ran around laughing, chasing each other or tossing beach balls in the air.

"Miss Yara!" Kai shouted. She was at least fifty yards away, waving vigorously while a red-haired toddler pulled on her other arm.

More than a few heads turned in my direction. The crowd quieted as more people looked. Silence fell as everyone stopped moving. They were all watching *me*. I squeezed Pango's hand so hard I thought it might break, but he didn't flinch.

"Am I supposed to do something?" I asked Pango, trying not to move my lips.

"Just wave."

My fingers barely flexed open before I shook my hand back and forth. As if on command, everyone broke into applause. Terrified, I glanced up at Pango, but he laughed and brushed his knuckle against my cheek. "We'll sit over there. It's the best view."

I glanced over my shoulder again, but Treygan had disappeared. I scanned the people around us, searching for him, but Pango kept pulling me along, so I concentrated on not tripping on my dress.

Merrick spread a blanket over the grass. Most people had returned to their conversations and sat down facing the lake. Blues or Indigos were spaced around the perimeter every few feet. They stood watching the sky and each other like they were waiting to dive into the water at the same time.

"This is crazy," I murmured to Pango. "All these people are here just because I've been turned into a mermaid?"

"Yes, twinkle bug. You're quite the celebrity in the world

of sea monsters. And wait until they find out you and Treygan are falling in love. The paparazzi will have a field day!"

"What! Falling in love?"

"Oh, please. Have you seen how giddy you are around him? Have you seen the way he looks at you, and protects you like you're his precious jewel?"

"He's doing his job as my guardian." I looked for Treygan again and found him standing in the distance.

"No, seriously." Pango adjusted one of the pins in my hair. "I'm asking if anyone has showed you yet? Because if not, I'll take you into my pretty head right now and let you watch the magic the rest of us see. It's better than any reality TV show the human world has come up with."

A high, whistling sound cut through the air, interrupting our conversation. Delmar pointed across the lake. Treygan stood a few feet away from him, squinting in the same direction. I looked at where Delmar pointed and saw the top of the sun peeking over the horizon.

A man blew into a conch shell and the sound echoed over the lake. The crowd fell silent again. Someone started singing a song I hadn't heard before, then all the Blues and Indigos joined in. On one particular note they all opened their hands at their sides, and for a minute—when the singing stopped—I thought we were being hit by an earthquake.

The still surface of the lake trembled. Then the water rippled outward toward the shore, creating a giant cyclone-shaped hole. The reflection of the rising sun melted into the lake, creating a swirling pool of orange, but in the center was empty darkness. I leaned forward, half expecting the large funnel to suck us all in, until a glint of ivory sparkled in the center of it. Something was rising out of the water.

Pango leaned against my shoulder. "Paragon Castle, in a fanciful light."

The highest turret rose in front of us, then another, and

another, followed by the rest of the huge palace. Underwater I hadn't appreciated the exquisiteness of the castle. The exterior shimmered like mother-of-pearl. The windows and doors made of different colored sea glass reflected beams of rainbows across the lake. As it continued to emerge, towering high above us, water dripped from its roofs and walls like a giant god rising out of a bath.

I realized I had been holding my breath and let it out. "It's gorgeous."

"Yes, it is," Pango sighed, holding hands with me and Merrick.

As the castle finished settling on the lake, I watched Treygan. He and the others circling the perimeter were in the same stance: arms low at their sides, fingers stretched wide, focusing fiercely on the water.

"Are they lifting it?" I asked Pango.

"Merfolk are up here and down below, working together and controlling the water to make it rise. Next they'll create a plate of hardened water beneath it so it remains above the surface for the rest of your celebration."

How freaking cool. "They do this for every new merfolk?"

"What can I say? We love a reason to celebrate."

I looked around at the crowd. Most people watched with a smile, but some hardly paid attention. To me, a glistening castle rising out of a lake was the most unbelievable thing I had ever seen, but most merfolk almost looked bored.

Merrick leaned over Pango's lap and winked at me. "Wait until you see the parties we throw in our realm."

That explained it. As spectacular as this seemed to me, it was probably tame compared to what these people were used to. But how could anything be better than this?

My focus landed on Treygan and my question was answered. He would make anything better. Even from a distance I could see the muscles in his forearms, taut and flexing. The guy could lift castles into the air. Eat your heart out, Cinderella.

The main doors to the castle opened and Indrea and Caspian walked out first, followed by the other Violets. Like the rest of the crowd, they were dressed in fancy clothes. I was thankful Koraline had planned ahead and picked out an appropriate dress for me.

"Caspian and Indrea are like the king and queen of the Violets?" I asked.

Pango chuckled. "Not according to them, but we all think of them that way."

"Why?"

He plucked at the grass by his feet. "Do you know about the day the gates closed, yet?"

I nodded sadly.

He twisted a blade of grass between his giant fingers. "None of the Violets were in this world when the gorgons sent word about the curse. Violets, Indigos and Blues rarely left our realm. When Caspian and Indrea realized how many merfolk would be trapped here, they chose to be trapped with us. While everyone else rushed through the gates to get home, those two were leaving Rathe behind, volunteering to help us survive." Tears pooled in his eyes and Merrick rubbed his shoulder. "Can you imagine?" Pango fanned himself and sniffed. "Such selflessness. They are two of my biggest heroes."

I stared at Caspian and Indrea with a new respect. Not that I didn't think highly of them before, but wow. They gave up a world they loved for the unknown. Rownan said everyone assumed those trapped here would die. They knew they might die, but they did it anyway.

I could only dream of being that brave.

Caspian began a speech, welcoming everyone and thanking them for traveling to be here. When I glanced at Treygan again he was watching me. I sat up straight, taken aback by his attention. I gave a timid wave but he looked away, focusing on Indrea as she spoke.

Then I heard my name.

I didn't catch why Indrea said my name, but she stopped talking and everyone stared at me.

I reached for Pango's hand, but he pushed on my back. "Go," he urged. "Indrea requested that you join them."

My hands shook. Not excessively, but enough to make me fumble with my skirt when I stood up. The grassy distance between me and the castle was only twenty feet or so, but my legs were trembling. I would trip or pass out from fear, I just knew it. I had the undivided attention of way too many people.

"Yara, please, come join us," Indrea said, loudly but pleasantly.

I couldn't walk. Pango pushed the back of my calf, but fear had anchored my feet to the ground. Birds chirped, people shuffled around on their blankets, children giggled and whispered.

Treygan appeared at my side. He lifted his elbow, offering me his arm. I clung to it like a lifeline.

"Deep breath," he whispered to me, flashing a grin at Indrea. "Perhaps Yara was confused about how to reach the castle. Delmar, Sixel, the bridge please."

The quiet didn't feel so deafening with Treygan beside me. People seemed to relax and move around again. Delmar and another Indigo were positioned in front of the castle entrance. A span of water separated them and the Violets. They both made a simple hand gesture and water rippled upward, forming a transparent bridge.

Treygan placed his free hand over both of mine. My nails dug into his arm, but I couldn't loosen my grip.

"Shall we?" he asked, taking a step forward. Somehow I uprooted my feet from the ground and walked beside him.

With each step I felt a fraction better, knowing Treygan wouldn't let me fall. But when we reached the bridge he lowered his arm.

"This part you have to do alone," he said softly.

I glanced at the bridge, then at the Violets. They were all smiles on the other side. The bridge wasn't long, but it had no railing. That, combined with the fact I could see through it, convinced me I would fall off into the water.

Delmar made an ushering motion, urging me to cross.

I mentally repeated Treygan's words, *deep breath, deep breath*, but my legs were rooted in place again. Then Treygan's breath warmed my ear. "The sooner you get over *there*, the sooner you can come back *here*, with me."

That's all it took. I walked forward, my skin tingling. Whatever the Violets wanted me for, I hoped they would hurry up. I wanted to be back by Treygan's side as soon as possible.

Each Violet hugged me like they had known me all my life. One of them brought out a chair made of wood and stone. Caspian laid a shimmering fabric across the seat and Indrea invited me to sit down.

Pango mentioned I would have to sit for a long time while each person gave me a token that represented their wishes for me and my future. I figured it would be later in the day, but after I sat down and looked out at the grassy bank of the lake I saw a line of people forming. Treygan wasn't one of them.

Caspian went first, handing me the largest pearl I had ever seen. "Yara, my wish for you is eternal joy."

"Thank you." I paused way too long before remembering my line. "I wish you the same."

He kissed my hand and walked away. Thank goodness Pango had told me what to say. Otherwise, I would've had no idea how to respond.

Indrea placed her fingers on my shoulder. "You may place it in the bowl now."

"What?" I glanced up at her and the glass bowl she held. Pango hadn't mentioned a bowl.

"You accept each wish with fresh hands."

"Oh, right." I placed the pearl in the bowl and it rolled around, making a smooth, hissing sound.

"No need to worry." Indrea smiled. "They are yours to keep in the end."

A stocky Violet with chubby fingers handed me a pearl, smaller than the one Caspian gave me, but eggplant-colored and very pretty. "I wish you excessive, heartfelt laughter."

"Thank you." I contagiously smiled at his chubby-cheeked grin. "I wish you the same." I admired the pearl again before placing it in the bowl.

The next mermaid approached shyly.

We went on like that for a long time. Almost everyone gave me a pearl of some kind. Big, small, perfectly round, oval, black, silver, champagne and every color or variety I could imagine. By the twentieth one or so, I started asking each person where they found it and what kind of pearl it was. That led to them sharing the story of why they chose it or what it meant to them, which made each pearl and person even more special to me.

Pango gave me a baroque abalone, the most unusually-shaped of any pearls I received. The blue-green coloring reminded me of a peacock feather. He explained it was rare and abstract, like he and I were. After kissing my hand he stepped aside.

That's when I saw Kimber for the first time.

Delmar stood behind her, his arms wrapped around her curvy waist. Her sparkling eyes matched her curly, sky-blue hair. Her skin was as pale as Delmar's, but her hallmarks were silver, and while he wore a huge grin, Kimber had a closed-lipped mouth of stone.

"Yara, this is Kimber," Delmar announced, a hundred times

happier than I had ever seen him. His skin and hallmarks had a yellowish hue. "The love of my life."

Kimber stepped forward. Her eyes were smiling, but her lips didn't move, of course. She handed me a teardrop-shaped pearl that was a lustrous mix of silver and blue. Then she handed me a small note card. Inside it read:

Dearest Yara,

My wish for you is that you always follow your heart. No matter the risk.

With love,
Kimber

I stood up and hugged her. "Thank you, Kimber. I wish the same for you."

She squeezed me tighter and Delmar chuckled. "She has that effect on me too. But move it along, your fans are waiting."

I sat back down, watching her walk away and stand beside Pango. Sections of her skin were streaked with purple. I wondered what emotion that meant for her. Delmar placed a black pearl in my hand and I startled, realizing I hadn't placed Kimber's pearl in the bowl yet.

"It's all right." He closed my fingers around both pearls. "We're a package deal." He crouched down in front of me, still holding my fist in his hand. "Yara, my wish is that you see deep inside of a person, past any insecurities, walls, or stony exterior, because it's the heart and soul that truly matter."

How could I have ever thought the sweet, sentimental man in front of me was scary?

"Thank you, Delmar." My voice cracked. "I wish you the same." I felt ridiculous saying it. He had already looked past Kimber's stony exterior. I had never seen two people so visibly in love with each other.

The line of people continued behind him. A few people gave me gemstones, but they also had great stories about why they chose the one they did. I felt connected to every single soul.

Over a hundred merfolk later, the gift giving ended. Indrea told me the bowl would be kept safe in the castle and delivered to me tonight. I almost argued that it couldn't be over.

One merman hadn't been in line.

Treygan hadn't given me a gift or wished me anything. Before I could speak up, Indrea announced the beginning of breakfast. Everyone cheered and Caspian offered me his arm to walk across the bridge.

No one waited on the other side.

All throughout the pancake and French toast breakfast I searched for any sign of Treygan, but he was MIA.

Afterward, Pango escorted me around telling me about the activities, events and customs. They had foot races, swimming races, sand sculpture contests, a synchronized swimming show, live music, face painting—the list went on and on.

The surfing contests were impressive, especially since several Indigos and Blues stood on land creating unnaturally high and crazy-shaped waves for contestants to ride. Merrick participated and pulled off astonishing tricks on his board, but so did Kai and most of her tribe.

Then there were the jet-ski races. Pango ran the event, so I asked Merrick where so many jet-skis came from. He just grinned and said Solis was full of hidden surprises.

"Merfolk like to play," Delmar added, stripping off his shirt and handing it to Kimber. "We have quite the toy collection." He kissed Kimber's forehead, then ran down the beach and jumped on a jet ski.

Watching Kimber and Delmar being all sweet and romantic with each other all day made me miss Treygan even more.

I had seen fleeting glimpses of him throughout the day—carrying trays of food to the lunch buffet, lifting a child into a chair to have her face painted, handing out joints to grateful people—but there was always too much space and so many people between us. A few times our eyes met, but he would turn away or someone would talk to me. By the time I looked up, he would be gone again.

Even with all the people around me—some I now considered friends—I felt abandoned. Why did Treygan make that comment before I crossed the bridge if he didn't plan on spending any time with me today? Had I done something wrong?

Dinner at sunset was a sit-down event. Tiki torches burned around tables covered with richly-colored fabrics. Elaborate floral arrangements decorated the center of each table. Drinks were served in coconut shells, and the food looked and smelled delicious.

"Wow, they outdid themselves, huh?" I said to Kimber who sat beside me. She nodded and I sipped my drink. "Mmm, what is this?"

Pango sat on the other side of me and raised his coconut shell cup. "Guava champagne. Isn't it dee-lish?"

Everyone raised their coconuts and toasted. It wasn't until Kimber set hers down without drinking that it hit me. My cup banged loudly against my plate as I turned to her. "You can't—gosh, all day I never thought about—" How do you politely ask someone about their inability to eat or drink?

Kimber's kind eyes squinted and she gave a little shrug, as if to say *it's okay.* She touched my hand, then leaned over and squeezed Delmar's shoulder. He and Sixel were talking, but Delmar held up one finger to his Indigo friend and looked at Kimber. She made a few quick hand gestures.

"Sure," Delmar said. He smiled at me. "Don't worry, Yara. She eats and drinks. Quite the lush, actually, and hopelessly addicted to sweets."

Kimber rolled her eyes and shook her head.

"But how?" I asked.

"She has a G-tube in her stomach," Delmar said, as if it were the most normal thing in the world.

Rudely, my gaze drifted to Kimber's stomach as if I expected a tube to be sticking out of her dress. "You never get to taste anything?" She shook her head. "I'm so sorry." She shook her head faster and waved her hands.

"Don't be sorry," Delmar said. "Kimber dislikes being pitied."

I covered my food with my napkin. "We can't sit around here eating and drinking while Kimber can't enjoy it."

Delmar wrapped his arm around her shoulder. She bowed her head, keeping her ice-blue eyes on me. Delmar seemed to voice her thoughts. "She has lived this way for decades. She hardly remembers what anything tastes like, so she doesn't miss it. We snuck home an hour ago and she had her meal, so eat, drink. Enjoy yourself."

I tried not to look at her with pity, but I couldn't imagine what her life must be like. No food, no drinks, no talking. "Oh, my gosh," I moaned, dropping my head into my hands. "I'm such a horrible person."

Kimber pulled my hands away from my face and raised her eyebrows questioningly.

"All day it never occurred to me that you and I could talk if we went underwater. I would love to sit down—or swim down—and get to know you better."

Her eyes lit up and she nodded vigorously. The stone lips on her pale face weren't exactly expressionless. They were in a permanent, subtle pout, the ends slightly curved upward. That must have been how they were when Treygan kissed her—almost smiling.

Kimber was living proof of what could happen to me if I acted on my desires for Treygan. What would she tell me if she knew how I felt about him? Stay away from him? Don't get too close? I downed the last of my champagne and tried not to think about it.

A merman took the stage and made an announcement about lost and found items, then cued the band to start playing. Everyone finished their dinner while the sun faded below the hills. I couldn't eat. My appetite was non-existent. Why had Treygan stayed away from me all day? Thinking about all the possible reasons made my stomach hurt.

As I pushed my dessert around my plate I glanced around at the tables of colorful merfolk, searching for him. Finally, four dimly lit tables away, I saw him. He sat with his arms crossed over his chest, watching me.

I didn't mean to, but I glanced at Kimber and bit my lip. It wasn't until he bowed his head, got up from the table, and walked away from the party that I realized my thoughtless action.

"Kimber, since you aren't drinking that," I gestured at her champagne, "would you mind?"

She handed me her cup and Pango laughed. "Cheers to Yara overcoming her shyness!"

I downed the whole cup and stared at the dark hill where Treygan had disappeared.

Rownan

I hadn't been to a moondezvous party in ages. Jack and his second in command, Eve, threw one every weekend, but I always stayed away. They got too crazy, and it felt wrong partying without Vienna. But I had to attend tonight, and the vibe was already toying with me.

175

Jack mysted some rich human into letting him throw the gig at her mansion while she was out of town. Eve chose a South Beach-chic theme. Illuminated water lilies floated in a glowing green pool. She went overboard with lights: round white paper lanterns strung through the air, backlit ice sculptures, frosted orbs sitting around the patio. Even the wine and martini glasses had lights in the stems.

The D.J. had been throwing down wicked mixes all night. People danced everywhere. Merfolk might be gifted with singing, but no living soul could dance as well as a selkie. I loved watching my people showboat. My stomach kept knotting with excitement and guilt. I missed dancing with Vienna. She would've loved this party.

Dina slid into my chair with me. "Looks like the moon, huh?"

"What?" I grunted, pushing her legs off my lap.

"This chair. It's big, white, and circular. Like the moon."

"Feels like I'm sitting in an egg."

"Cheer up, grump. Come dance with me."

I had been bobbing my head to the beats all night. Dancing would relieve some of my tension, but Dina was into that raver glow stick crap that drove me nuts. "I'm waiting for Nixie."

"Like Nixie won't make it known the second she arrives." She tugged at my earring. "We could sneak off to a cabana and let you get a practice session in before Yara gets here."

"I don't need practice. *She* will be drinking from *me*."

Dina grabbed an ice cube from her glass and rubbed it along her neck and chest. There was nothing sexual about it, it was just a humid night. All of us would have much rather been at Jack Frost's, but we wanted this party to feel welcoming to Yara, not freeze her to death. "You do realize the second she drinks blood from you, you'll want to devour her, right?"

"There's only one soul I'll ever want to devour."

She tossed what was left of her ice cube at me. "I'm getting in the pool. Eve frosted it. It feels amazing."

I gave her a nod and watched her prance away in her black bikini. She had great legs, but Vienna's were ten times better.

A winged shadow swept across the pool. I looked up to see Nixie fluttering to the ground near one of the cabanas. I jumped to my feet, but Jack was five steps ahead of me. He held back a white curtain while Nixie ducked behind it with Yara passed out in her arms.

"Don't you question me," Nixie hissed at Jack as I entered the cabana. "It took so long because there were a hundred merfolk hovering around."

"What happened?" I sat beside Yara on the lounger. "Why is she unconscious?"

"She's not unconscious," Nixie snapped. She lowered her voice to a whisper. "I had to make her stop kicking and screaming. You have no idea how close we came to being caught by Delmar. He was watching her like a greedy hawk."

"Did anyone see you?" Jack asked.

Nixie's wings fluttered. "No."

Yara stirred and made a low, moaning sound.

"Shh, it's okay, baby." I pushed loose strands of hair from her face.

Nixie morphed into human form. The gust from her wings disappearing blew the curtain walls of the cabana outward.

"Rownan?" Yara mumbled, squinting with confusion.

"Hey." I squeezed her arm. How the hell could I explain how she ended up here? Jack never mentioned this part of the plan, and I was a fool for not asking.

"Look at you, party girl," Nixie interrupted, pushing me out of the way. "Finally awake, huh?"

"What?" Yara rubbed her eyes. "Where am I? Where did you come from?"

"Oh, don't tell me you don't remember?" Nixie ran her red nails along the inside of Yara's forearm. "My sisters and I came to your celebration to offer our congratulations, but you had slipped away and no one knew where you were. When I found you," Nixie lowered her voice and sounded sad, "you were all alone and crying about Treygan. Not to mention hammered on champagne."

"I was?" Yara asked.

Her lips were red and swollen. I glanced at Jack, realizing Nixie had sucked the memory of being kidnapped from Solis from her mind. Jack just shrugged.

"You were," Nixie reassured her. "I told you Rownan was throwing you a party and you begged me to bring you here. That champagne must have hit you hard, because you passed out while we were flying."

"Flying?" Yara sat up and looked around. "But ... I don't remember. Did I—what did—does Pango know where I am?"

"Of course," Nixie cooed, curling up beside Yara. "He made me promise to have you home by sunrise."

No way would Yara buy that garbage. She looked confused and disoriented, but eventually she would realize Nixie was feeding her a bunch of B.S.

"You threw me a party?" Yara asked me, blinking several times.

"Don't you hear the music and all the people?" Jack pulled back the white fabric that separated us from the rest of the pool area. "They're all here for you."

"Aww," Yara squeaked. "Look how pretty."

I followed her gaze. All of my kind dancing in and around the illuminated pool did look impressive.

Dina entered with a glowing glass in her hand. "Hi, Yara, I'm Dina. It's so nice to finally meet you." Jack took the drink from her and passed it to Yara.

"Drink up," Nixie said.

Yara sipped what looked like a martini, but I suspected it

might contain more than vodka. Was there a secret meeting about how this thing would go down, and I wasn't invited?

"Jack, will you show me the way to the bar?" Nixie asked.

"Certainly." Jack assisted her out of the lounger. "We should let Rownan and Yara catch up." He slapped my shoulder as he and the girls ducked out of the cabana.

Yara patted the cushion beside her. "Sit."

I took a seat at the foot of the lounger.

"Good seal," Yara barked, then giggled and took another sip. "Nixie's right, you're drunk."

"Oh, please." She leaned back and pressed her bare feet against my stomach. "Only a few glasses of champagne."

"A few? You've never had a drop of alcohol in your life." I tried taking the glowing martini from her, but she held it above her head, splashing it on her gown and laughing.

"My party. My rules."

"Hmph, you think so?"

She nodded like a bobble-head doll. She was kind of cute in her intoxicated state—much less uptight and not nearly as chatty.

"Love this music." She tapped her foot against my ribs.

"We can dance if you want."

"But my head's all spinny."

The past few weeks of us as a couple—or whatever we were—had been an act, but the comfort between us was real. Out of habit, I took her foot in my hand and massaged up to her calf. She let out a sigh and went limp.

"You did eat, right? Alcohol hits you hard if there's no food in your system."

"Mmm, I had pancakes."

"Pancakes?" It was nearing eleven o'clock at night. Merfolk would never serve pancakes at a welcoming dinner. "Are you telling me the last time you ate was at breakfast?"

She giggled. "Looong day."

"Hell, Yara, you need to eat. I'll grab you some food." I stood but she sat forward and clung onto my arm.

"Don't leave me too." She sounded like she might be on the verge of crying.

"Too?" I sat back down. "Who else left you?"

"Treygan," she said through pouty lips. "He can't kiss me. I think he hates me. He didn't even give me a wish."

What in the world was she rambling about? Treygan couldn't kiss anyone. I eased her back against the cushion. "Treygan isn't worth getting upset over. And I would never leave you, but you do need food. Be back in two minutes."

A cheeseburger, half a dozen *hors d'oeuvres*, three glasses of water and seven songs later, we were on the dance floor, sweating out whatever alcohol was left in Yara's system. Being surrounded by forty dancing selkies made her awkward, off-beat moves look that much worse.

"You're a horrible dancer," I shouted into her ear, trying not to get head-butted while she jerked back and forth.

"I know, but I can sing." She lifted her elbows up and down in a wretched version of a chicken dance.

I wiped the sweat off my face and looked at the pool. People kept jumping in to cool off before climbing out to dance again. Others danced in the water.

"Go," Yara insisted. "This heat must be killing you."

"I'd invite you to come, but the water is thirty-four degrees."

"And I'm sure all these selkies would love my mermaid tail flapping around their pool."

I kissed her sweaty hand. "Go dance with Dina while I'm gone."

"I want to rest. I'm not feeling so great."

Nixie had filled me in on Yara's condition when she took

her from the island. She watched Yara drink non-stop for two hours after dinner. When Yara slipped away to the bathroom, Nix found her huddled by the toilet, sweating and clammy. Nix couldn't tell if it was from drinking too much or the first sign of cravings.

"What's wrong?" I asked her.

"Just need a breather," she said, turning away.

Twenty minutes later when I walked into the cabana, Yara was curled up on the lounger. Dina dabbed her face with a wet towel.

"I promise it will," Dina whispered to her.

"No," Yara moaned.

I sat beside them. "What's going on?"

Dina pulled her hair back into a ponytail and shook her head. "She's started craving, but she refuses to drink blood."

My eyes widened. Could she be any less subtle about it?

"Simmer down," Dina continued. "She knows she drank blood at your house. She and Treygan discussed it and she promised to never drink again."

Damn it. That would make convincing her to drink from me nearly impossible.

"Yara," I said softly, rubbing her leg. "It gets worse. You'll have to drink to stop the pain. The sooner you do it, the less you'll have to suffer."

"No," Yara argued, flipping over to face me. "The pain will stop. If I get through this without drinking, then I'll never want to drink again."

"Ha! Who told you that?" Dina asked.

"Treygan."

"How would he know how it works?" Dina snarled.

Dina and I both knew Treygan had experienced cravings firsthand when we were kids.

"Trust me," Dina lied, "the pain doesn't stop, and you'll always crave another drink." From behind Yara's back she winked at me and tossed the wet towel in my lap. "I'm not hanging around to watch you wither in pain, but I will give you an easy way to make it stop."

In true selkie style, Dina grabbed me so fast I didn't have time to react. She dug one of her claws into my forearm and tore open a long gash. Blood flowed instantly.

Yara looked frenzied. She licked her lips, but turned away. "Get it away from me!"

I covered the gash with the towel and curled up behind her, wrapping my non-bleeding arm around her waist.

"I'm sorry," I whispered. I hated seeing her in such agony. "I should've warned you what was in my fridge. You shouldn't be going through this."

"I feel like I'm gonna puke," she groaned.

"I know, but you won't." I pulled her wet hair off of her face. She was already trembling. Treygan couldn't have told her everything or she wouldn't have agreed to stay at our party. She wouldn't be speaking to me, much less allowing me or Dina to take care of her. But he had discussed our blood habits with her. Did *she* figure out she drank blood, or did one of the other merfreaks? "Did the first time make you sick?"

She shook her head. "It made me laugh."

"Then why are you so against drinking again?"

"Because it's disgusting."

"What's so disgusting about it? It's our way of sharing ourselves with each other."

She looked over her shoulder at me, almost shivering. "You *drink blood*."

"You eat food."

Her teeth were chattering. "What's that g-got to do with anything?"

"You eat to survive. Food provides you with energy. I've

seen you eat hamburgers and steak. Are you denying there
was ever blood in that meat? That you absorb the life force of
the animal that died so you can stay nourished?"

She gaped at me with dilated pupils.

"What we do isn't nearly as bad," I continued. "We share.
We don't kill or eat each other. We share blood to make others
stronger, healthier, happier, or to feel loved. Our soul's energy
carries through our blood the same way merfolks' does by
sight. We're no worse than you, just different."

Her eyes flickered to the towel on my arm. A dark red patch
seeped through it. Thirst shined in her eyes, but she shook
her head. "No. I'm a mermaid, not a selkie." She brought her
knees to her chest, wrapping her arms around them. "If I drink
again I'll have to drink forever."

Not forever, I thought. The Triple Eighteen was less than
two weeks away—a reminder that I couldn't take no for an
answer.

"Selkie instincts are in your blood. You'll always have
cravings." This was it. I had to tell her. I wasn't sure if she
heard me, so I put my lips against her ear. "Yara, your father
was a selkie."

Her head snapped around so fast that her chin nailed me in
the forehead. "Liar."

"I swear on my life, it's true."

Yara's whimpering and chattering teeth were her only
reply.

"He was brave and strong," I said quietly. "I had nothing
but respect for him."

Tears welled in her eyes. "Y-y-you knew my dad?"

"Yes. Before he turned human and moved away."

For a second she looked like she was about to ask
something, but then her chest jerked forward and she gasped.
"Owww! W-w-what was that?"

"What was what?"

"It felt like s-someone electrocuted me."

"It gets worse. Please, let me help you." I slid the towel off my arm and squeezed the wound so fresh blood surfaced. "You can't fight your genes. Seeing you like this kills me."

She wiped at her lips and rubbed the dark circles under her eyes. Her hands shook uncontrollably. "You s-s-swear on V-V-Vienna's soul that my father was a s-selkie?"

"I swear." I lifted my arm. After a long moment of staring she took it in her hands, pulling my bloody gash closer to her mouth and swallowing hard. She leaned forward.

The music stopped and a loud crash outside startled her. Someone shouted her name.

"God dammit!" I jumped up from my seat. We kept this party location top secret. How did he find us? When I walked out of the cabana and saw Treygan surrounded by forty angry selkies, I covered my bleeding arm and cursed under my breath.

Talk about the worst possible timing.

 Once I saw Rownan step out of the cabana I didn't need to ask where Yara was. I pushed my way through the crowd, but Jack grabbed my arm before I reached my son-of-a-psycho brother.

"This party is invitation only," Jack said.

I glared at his hand. "Take it off of me before I turn it to stone." He let go instantly. I could feel and hear the crowd gathering behind me. "Tell your minions to back off."

Rownan stepped closer to me. "Your threats don't work on me, Treygan."

"I'll petrify Jack in your place."

"You wouldn't," he snarled.

"Try me."

"She wants to be here. She's free to make her own decisions."

"Then why did you send Nixie to kidnap her?" I shouldered my way past him and into the cabana.

Yara was balled up in a lounge chair, dripping sweat and shaking.

"How bad is it?" I asked, kneeling in front of her.

"M-my d-dad was a s-s-selkie?"

I took a deep breath. "I'm sorry. I wanted to tell you."

Her bloodshot eyes wouldn't focus, and her blotchy cheeks weren't just from being sick. She was crying. Her shaking worsened.

"I'm getting you out of here." I started to gather her in my arms.

"No! I w-want blood. It's who I am."

"No, it's not." I held her face in my hands. "*You* decide who you are. I don't give a damn who your father was. We make our own choices, and you can fight this. If you drink from one of them, they win."

"W-w-win w-what?"

"I should have told you everything sooner, and I promise I'll explain, but I have to get you away from here. Please, trust me."

"Y-y-you left me."

"I had to keep my distance from you today. I'll explain that too, but you're getting worse. We need to go."

The selkies jabbered outside. The longer we stayed here, the more time they would have to come up with a plan to stop me, but I refused to leave here without Yara. I didn't want to petrify anyone, but I would to save Yara. Her eyes opened and closed slowly, then she sat up, looking like it took every ounce of strength she had. I leaned down to pick her up but she limply pushed me away again.

"I can w-walk. Not help-l-l-less."

She was in no condition to stand, but I let her try anyway.

When her knees gave out I caught her and lifted her into my arms. "I know you're not helpless, but now is not the time to be stubborn." I pushed through the slit in the white curtains and stepped into a sea of drunken selkies.

Rownan lifted his bleeding cut toward Yara's face. "Last chance."

I wanted to rip his arm out of its socket. She buried her face against my chest.

"Get out of the way," I ordered, flashing a warning glare at Jack.

He stepped aside and the rest of the selkies cleared a path. Just as I reached the iron gate, Rownan put his hand on my shoulder. "Wait, Treygan."

"Rownan, I swear to—"

"Stop and listen, dickhead. She's sick. She needs blood. If it has to be mer blood, then so be it." His claws shot out, ready to strike my skin, but I jumped back.

"Have you lost your beastly mind? I turn living things to stone! Who knows what would happen if she drank my blood?"

His shocked expression proved he really was a clueless idiot. "Oh," Moron uttered, pulling his claws back.

Yara moaned again. I shook my head in disgust and walked through the gate, hoping Rownan felt as guilty and barbaric as he looked.

We reached the ocean and I swam to a secluded, private pier. Yara's shivering calmed down once we were in the water, but I knew the worst was still to come.

"How long ago did it start?" I asked.

Her eyes stayed closed and her head bobbed forward. Judging by her weakness, I would have guessed twelve hours, but she had only been missing for four.

"Almost an hour," she murmured.

That didn't make sense. Her symptoms should have been milder if she had only been craving for an hour. I thought her reaction might be weaker because she didn't drink directly from a selkie, but instead her symptoms were progressing faster than normal.

There were no signs of humans nearby, but I wanted to be safe. This would take a while, and we couldn't risk someone seeing us. I stayed in human form, but Yara's yellow tail glistening under the surface would be easily visible. I paddled us over to the shallow, sloped area under the pier where it was darkest. Plowing my feet into the sand to anchor us, I sat down and pulled her onto my lap, trying to keep everything but her head submerged.

Her eyes fluttered open. Her voice was weak. "Did you know him too?"

"Who?"

"My father."

"I knew *of* him."

Her eyelids drifted closed again. "Is it over?"

"Is what over?"

"The cravings."

"I don't think so. Usually there's a period where it feels like an electric current is roaring through your veins."

"I already felt that." Her hand floated up and rested limply on my chest.

"You did?" She nodded—barely. "How long did it last?"

"A second."

I leaned her head against my chest so she couldn't see the worry on my face. In a perfect world she would never have to feel the electrical burning, in a fair world the second of pain she felt would be the only one she would have to endure. But we didn't live in a perfect or fair world.

She needed to hear part of her story before the real wave of electric shocks hit. Mainly because she deserved to know, but also because she thought I had abandoned her. I needed to regain her trust, but now wasn't the time to explain why I had to stay away from her.

"Would you like to hear a story about your parents?"

Her chin glided against my chest as she nodded.

"Your father, Vyron, was a highly respected selkie. Five years before you were born, he fell in love with your mother. Here comes another fact people have kept hidden from you." I looked down at the top of her head and took a breath. "Your mother was a siren."

She slowly pulled back and stared up at me with quivering eyes.

"For years they lived as a taboo couple. Your father wanted her as his mate and he wanted children, but sirens can't reproduce. Only one sea monster had ever successfully become human, but it was proof it could be done. Your mother went to Stheno and Euryale, the original gorgon sisters, and begged for her and your father to be turned human so they could have children."

"And they agreed," Yara muttered.

"They made a deal. Vyron and Cleo's first born—you—had to be given to the gorgon sisters. Then your parents were free to have as many other children as they wished."

"But … why did they want me? I don't understand."

I caressed her face, hating that I had to be the one to tell her all of this. "Medusa was the only mortal sister. When she was murdered, the sisters lost a lot of their power because they no longer had a third in their trinity. Stheno and Euryale wanted that power back, but Medusa's replacement needed to have human and monster blood like she did. You fit the requirement, and you would be too young to put up a fight."

"They wanted me to be a gorgon?"

"Yes, part of the cursed trinity. Meaning you would take Medusa's place and never be able to leave the sunless grotto."

She shuddered. "That's why we moved away."

A snowy white heron landed in the water practically on top of Yara. I splashed it away. The bird's S-curved neck extended toward me. It squawked in my face before flying up onto the pier.

"Your parents loved you, Yara. The sea monster-turned-human I told you about, he helped your father put a binding spell on you. No sea creature could turn you until you were eighteen. Your dad figured by that age you could decide for yourself if you wanted that life or power, and you would be able to fight if you didn't want that dark existence. He took you away from here in case the sisters figured out a way to break the spell."

"I'm eighteen now. Will they come for me?" Her trembling became steadier. I needed to tell her the rest before she became too weak, or in too much pain to comprehend it.

"No. When your parents fled, the gorgons were furious and sealed the gate. On the Triple Eighteen—your true eighteenth birthday, which in the sea creature world means eighteen years and eighteen days, we have one chance to offer the sisters a replacement for Medusa. If by the end of the eighteenth hour—sunset—no one has offered themselves, then the gate will be locked eternally."

Her pupils were huge, black suns. "*I'm* the reason the gate closed?"

"Not you, your parents."

Her body jerked and she let out a whimper. "The electric thing is back." Diamond tears ran down her cheeks. "That's why you stayed away from me. You knew I would be a gorgon soon."

"That's not why." Her hair was a disheveled mess. I started removing the hairpins Pango had twisted it up with, letting her long locks fall into the water.

She cried harder, shaking violently. "I'll do it. Everyone can go home."

"No. Your mother arranged for you to be turned into a

mermaid to protect you. You're a monster of the sun now. Your soul wouldn't survive in their cold, dark grotto."

She gripped my arm tightly as another shock surged through her. "It hurts!"

Her skin stretched taut over her tensed muscles. Soon the pain wouldn't be waves, it would be steady and unbearable. She continued crying, trying to catch her breath. "Why did you turn me?"

"I vowed to your mother that I would."

"But I could've opened the gate."

"We figured out another way." I dipped her head back into the water and ran my fingers through her wet hair. "Someone else meets the requirements. They volunteered to take your place."

The heron landed near us again. Yara's face twisted in pain. Her teeth chattered so hard I thought they would break. She started mumbling broken sentences about her mother.

"The cravings will be excruciating soon," I said. "We're going away for a while. I don't know how long I can last, but we'll relive some of my memories. You'll be conscious through my soul, so you shouldn't feel your own physical pain."

"Will that w-w-work?"

Gods, I hoped so. "We're about to find out. Don't think about anything here. I'm going to try and keep us in a different time until the cravings stop."

She let out a gut-wrenching scream as her skin rippled with pain. I hoped no humans were nearby to hear her. I placed my hand on her cheek. "Open your eyes, Yara. Let me take you someplace safe."

Her teary eyes met mine. I made certain to keep my emotions under control as we spiraled away to another time and place. I silently prayed I could keep us gone long enough—preferably forever.

day 6

Treygan was right. The pain and cravings stopped seconds after the teal and silver clouds blew across his eyes.

There were too many wonderful memories to keep track of. I must have stayed in his mind for hours until a gentle push forced me out of Treygan's soul and into a bright fog.

I had returned to my own mind and body.

The first thing I saw was Treygan's sunlit face. His cobalt eyes looked exhausted. His blue-black hair was dry and spiked up in different directions. Yesterday I thought I had cut it too short, but he looked stunning. The sun was shining in the sky high above the water. It must have been nearing noon.

"Hi," I said, gazing into his tired eyes.

"Welcome back."

He had me cradled against him, but when I began to move he let go and scooted back. I floated in the water, losing physical contact with him, and I hated how it felt.

"It worked." I ran my fingers along the sandy floor beneath me. I felt strong and healthy. No shivering, no nausea, no overwhelming thirst for blood, no electrical shocks. "I don't remember feeling anything after the soul sharing thingy started—except what you were feeling. Which were mostly happy memories."

"Good." He wiggled his feet free from the sand and swam past me into deeper water.

"You must have kept me there for hours."

"I wanted to make sure all your cravings had passed."

Before Treygan took me away, every minute of sickness felt like forever. The pain was worse than anything I had ever felt. I kept seeing and hearing my mother. I thought for sure I was dying.

Cringing at the thought of how awful the night had been, I swam after Treygan. How much suffering had he saved me from by sharing his soul with me for so long? Did it hurt him or make him sick? "You're quiet. Are you okay?"

"I'm fine. We need to go back to Solis. Everyone will be worried about us."

"Wait." I grabbed his arm. "I want to know more about my parents. You said my mother was a siren. So at some point she lived like Nixie and her sisters?" He nodded. "Did they know her? Did *you* know her?"

"Yes and yes."

"She could fly? And lived in your realm?"

"Sirens prefer this realm. They thrive on taking human songs. Like her sisters, she spent the majority of her time here, with humans. And then with your father."

"Wait. So the sirens are—or were—my mother's sisters?"

"Mariza and Otabia were. Nixie took your mother's place in the trio after your mother turned human. There must always be three of them."

"What do you mean by take human songs?"

"One of the original purposes of a siren was to deliver human memories to the gorgon sisters. They can only experience life outside of the grotto through the sirens. The sirens have to take the memories entirely from a human's soul, otherwise it wouldn't hold up through two transfers—human to siren, siren to gorgon."

"Those poor people. Memories just get stolen from them?"

"Yes, but they don't remember them being taken. They never know they had them, so they don't miss them."

"What if someone brings up an event or conversation they had and the person doesn't remember it? Wouldn't they figure it out then?"

"Humans have terrible memories. They don't use a fraction of the brainpower they are given. They would dismiss the void and use their common line about getting old or shrug it off to forgetfulness."

"My mother stole memories from people," I repeated. "How awful."

"She had to. It's that nature thing I told you about. We can't fight the laws of creation. It would be like telling a human to never eat or drink anything. They wouldn't live a week without nourishment."

"Still, I'd be furious if someone took a memory from me."

His eyebrow arched. He looked everywhere except my face. Water lapped against his neck and shoulders. Such a peaceful sound, but I sensed something unspoken looming between us.

"Treygan, what aren't you telling me?"

"What did you say the other day? I plead the fifth?"

"Uh-uh. That's my line. You're hiding something from me. Start talking."

He pinched the bridge of his nose. "Do you remember Nixie taking you from the party?"

"No, but she said I was drunk."

"Mm-hmm. I might believe that, except you have a fresh bite mark on your lip."

I ran my fingers along the raised scab. "That's why it hurts."

"See, you don't remember her taking it from you."

"No, not at all."

"That one is gone forever, but it's probably for the best." He swam closer to me. "Don't be angry, but many of your memories were taken. The turning process, whether it be monster to human or vice versa, requires temporarily draining most of the life force out of a soul so it can be filled with whatever species they're becoming. For us that means our memories, for the selkies it's blood. The sirens require both. No one is ever completely drained of what and who they are originally. That would be fatal."

"But Delmar turned me, and I still have my human memories."

"Right now you have very few. Like I said, if Delmar drained you of all of them you would have died. Some of your strongest memories will return over time. Only a siren could completely take them from your soul."

I thought hard. I had memories of Uncle Lloyd. I only had a few of my mother, but she died when I was eight, so how much could I possibly remember? "No, I remember lots of stuff."

"Think about it. How many events or conversations of your human life can you remember? Considering you've been alive for eighteen years, shouldn't you have many more? It feels like a lot because you don't remember the ones you're missing, or know they existed."

"That's—no. I remember everything. I showed you that memory of the first time I met my uncle. I remember you showing up at my house in the storm, and the night you saved me from drowning."

"Delmar left your strongest memories, your earliest, and the most recent. He couldn't touch the last several weeks of your life. Otherwise you might wake up not remembering anyone, or why you care about them, where you live, who you are, the basics. Some memories your soul clings to for survival. He leaves those."

"How does he know which ones to leave?"

"He said they're colored differently, like he sees them through a sepia-toned lens, so he passes over them."

"This is crazy. I know I remember everything. Maybe Delmar didn't erase much."

"I would love for that to be true, but if so, you wouldn't have survived the transformation. Changing from human to monster takes a toll on the soul and body. We can test your theory, though. Three years ago a hurricane hit near Eden's Hammock. Do you remember it?"

"What was its name?"

"Otabia called it *The Dryad*. Sirens name storms after legends or fairytales, but humans attach names to them that we don't pay attention to."

"I don't remember storms unless they were serious."

"Serious?" he huffed. "How's this for serious. You were helping Lloyd board up windows and you slipped off the porch roof. You broke your left arm and needed twelve stitches in your elbow." He lifted my hand out of the water and bent back my forearm so I could see a faded, white scar. "You and your uncle stayed at Mercy Hospital in Miami for two nights until the storm passed. Do you remember any of that?"

"No, but ...." I couldn't believe it. How did I not know about the scar on my elbow? How could I forget staying at a hospital? "How do you know about all of that?"

"I'm your guardian, Yara. It's my job to keep you safe. Though there were times—like the arm-breaking incident—I did a pretty poor job." He looked away, but I reached for him, wanting to assure him he had done a great job. He raised his chin and our eyes met. "I've been your guardian for fourteen years."

"You—what? Fourteen years! You've been watching over me since I was four? And I never saw you?"

"You saw me on several occasions. Most of the time I had reporters check on you. I'm sure it's a bit unsettling, but over the next several years most of your memories should return."

"Years? I need to sit down." This was way too much for me to process while treading water. I swam to the beach. Treygan followed without argument.

We approached the shallow slope of sand and Treygan stood up. Tan shorts hung low off his hips. I glanced down at my gown and tail. Any other time I got out of the water, I crawled up a ladder, or lifted myself onto rocks or land where my legs had time to appear before standing. This beach thing had me stumped.

Treygan looked down at me. "You'll need your legs."

"Thanks for stating the obvious, but you haven't taught me how to change while I'm in the water."

"Right. Sorry. Concentrate on how your legs feel, imagine the space between them, the bones, bending your toes. They'll change."

He made it sound so simple. I pulled my skirt up and stared through the water at my tail lying beside me, trying to imagine the feel of everything human. All I felt was sand and my dress brushing against my scales with the ebb and flow of waves.

"Not working," I groaned.

He sat down beside me. "You're not focusing on what you want to feel."

"I am. It's just not working. Maybe that ability hasn't formed yet."

"It has. You must not want your legs badly enough."

"I do! I'm trying."

"First, sit more humanlike. You should have your legs in front of you, not to the side." As soon as I adjusted my tail he reached his hand through the water and rested it where my knees would've been. "Feel good?"

"I guess."

His eyes squinted because of the bright sunlight behind me. He leaned forward, either to get closer to me or to use me for shade I wasn't sure which. He pushed my dress up higher and lifted his hand so it hovered an inch from my hip and upper tail. "Skin is more sensitive. In five seconds I'm going to set my hand down. Do you want to feel my fingers on your scales, or the skin of your thigh?"

I couldn't answer. The raspiness in his voice combined with the thought of his hand on my thigh left me speechless. He kept his eyes locked with mine, waiting for my answer, but then my tail turned into legs and no words were needed. His warm fingers pressed against my skin.

I wanted him to kiss me so badly I thought I might explode. My toes curled when he rubbed my thigh. His hand moved firmly down to my knee then back up again. I swallowed the warm air between us and put my arms around his neck, wanting to pull him on top of me. Instead, he stayed solidly upright. He slid his hand up my hip and around my waist and hooked his other hand under my arm, rising out of the water effortlessly with me attached. My skirt dropped to my feet.

"There, see how easy that was?" he said gruffly.

I lifted my face to look at him. Why, oh why did I have to fall for the guy who could turn me to stone? I leaned in and pressed my lips against his neck. He tasted like saltwater taffy. For a second he tried to pull back, but I kept a firm grip and kissed him again. He let out a deep breath and pressed himself against me.

"Mmm, yes, so easy," I whispered, moving my kisses down his chest.

I started running my fingers through his hair but his hands closed over mine. He pulled back, pushing my hands to my sides.

"Enough," he said. "We can't do this. As incredible as that felt, it's wrong and unfair to you."

"How is it not fair to me? I want to be with you, Treygan. We can find ways around the kissing thing."

"It's not just that. We wouldn't even have two weeks together. The Triple Eighteen is days away. We shouldn't start something knowing how fast the end is approaching."

"The end? You said I didn't have to live with the gorgons. You said someone volunteered to take my place."

He clutched my hand to his chest. He stood so straight that his shoulders seemed to double in width. I could see my reflection in his eyes. "Yes. That someone was me."

 **Treygan** "You?" She gawked. "No. Last night you said I wouldn't survive in the grotto because I was a mermaid. You're a merman."

"A merman with gorgon blood and genes," I explained, taking a seat on the beach.

Yara kicked up sand as she paced in front of me. "You said I was chosen because I was born human. Your mother was a mermaid, and your father a gorgon. There's nothing human about you. You don't meet the requirements."

"My father was the gorgon who turned human I told you about. A gorgon and mermaid could never be together—never mate. His physical passion would have turned my mother to stone. But he loved her, so he found a way for them to be together. He turned human, and they had me, which makes me part human."

"Even though your father turned human, you still inherited parts of his gorgon qualities. How is that possible?"

"I told you. When a soul is turned, part of who they originally were stays with them. Their children carry on that bloodline." Even I heard the shame in my voice. There was no hiding the fact I was an abomination. "No matter how twisted or unnatural it may be."

Yara sat beside me and linked her arm through mine. "You were created this way for a reason. Nothing in this universe is by accident. What did Koraline's poem say? Beauty is hidden under a veil of tragedy?"

"Beauty? Yara, I can't kiss you. I can never have a wife or children because if my emotions get too strong I turn people to stone. I've known my fate my entire life. I killed my own mother seconds after she gave birth to me." My voice cracked. "It was the first and only time we saw each other. She gave me life and I robbed her of hers. My father lost his soul mate because of me. How could any of that ever be beautiful?"

Yara looked away.

When you're raised amongst sea creatures, the legends are a part of you. Our kind knew my story. They knew about my father. Many mourned the loss of my Violet mother. Every mer parent warned their children not to get too close to me. No mermaid could ever consider me as a possible mate. But all of this was new to Yara. If seeing Kimber hadn't scared her away, this confession would.

"You were an infant," Yara said softy. "You had no control over what you felt, or what happened. You have to forgive yourself for the past. What does your father say about it?"

"I don't talk to him."

"Why?"

"I killed his wife. He's reminded of that loss every time he looks at me."

"She was your mother, Treygan. You both suffered a loss. You should be there for each other."

I stared out over the ocean. The stone wall I had tried to build around my heart felt like it might be cracking. "He would also be losing me in a few days. It's better that we're not close."

Yara didn't say anything. She brushed her fingers up and down my arm, sending a rush of bubbles through my skin. It felt too good.

"Why are you doing this?" I asked.

"Doing what?"

"Staying. Getting close to me. You know what I am and what I'm capable of. You should be running away."

"You saved my life when I was eight. You volunteered to take my place with the gorgons. I've seen and felt the love you have for Delmar, Kimber, Pango and all the people in your memories. *That* proves who you are and what you're capable of." She cuddled up against me, resting her head on my shoulder.

I wanted to wrap my arms around her, but giving in to our feelings would only make our task more difficult. Breathing in the scent of her hair was unavoidable. "You always smell like apple blossoms."

She glanced up at me and smiled. "I've never smelled an apple blossom. Do they smell good?"

"If we had more time I would take you to climb apple trees, so you could know what you smell like."

She kissed my shoulder. "You taste like saltwater taffy. But your smell is like—I don't know. It's what I imagine heaven smells like."

I laughed hard. "My gods, is this the kind of cheesy stuff couples say to each other?"

Yara laughed too. "I guess so. Are we a couple?"

More cracks splintered the wall around my heart. My thoughts spilled out of me uncontrollably. "All I want to do is protect you, hold you, and show you how much I care about you. Those thoughts and words feel so foreign to me, but they're always there. I'm constantly fighting the urge to say them to you. I want to promise you forever, but I can't. At sunset on the Triple Eighteen I will leave to live in the grotto. Forever."

Yara spun around and positioned herself in front of me, kneeling between my legs. "It's time for you to tell me. What will happen on the Triple Eighteen? The specifics."

I took a deep breath. "I have to sacrifice myself completely to the gorgons. All trace of me being mer has to be removed from my soul. I have to be ready and willing to fully become a gorgon."

Her fingers tapped against my knees while she tried to figure out what it meant. "We share souls through our memories, so is it like what Delmar did to me? Someone has to take your memories from you?"

"Yes."

She scrunched up her face, looking repulsed. "And Delmar agreed to do that?"

"Delmar can't do it. It's different than what he did to you."

"How is it different?"

"It must be a total sacrifice. My memories and my soul must be consumed entirely."

She cringed. "Like what the sirens do?"

"Sort of, except to take every bit of mer *and* human life force from me it has to be someone with mer and human blood, and also siren blood so they can remove my songs forever." I swallowed down the bitter taste in my mouth. "Because of your unique genes, you are the only soul who can do it."

Her head jerked backward. "Me? They want *me* to take your memories from you?"

"By sunset of the Triple Eighteen, you have to drain me of my songs. All of them."

"I would never do that!"

"Yara, the Violets spent years interpreting the spell. The only way to open the gates is for a total sacrifice of the soul. I willingly give mine, and the gate opens."

"But, I don't even know how. You *share* your memories with me. I have no idea how to take them from you."

"You have your mother's siren blood in you. The Violets think it will happen naturally once you start. You'll get absorbed, it will become addicting and you'll keep taking more. We've been preparing for this for years. We'll coach you through the process."

"No. Find someone else."

"There is no one else. You are the mixed blood mentioned in the poem. You were the soul originally promised, and the only one they'll allow at the gate. The only reason I can get near it is because I have gorgon blood in me. I meet the requirements for taking Medusa's place—human and monster blood. You are the only soul who can go to the gate and drain me. It has to be you."

"Without your memories, you'll be … empty. If I take them all, then you would have no soul left. Won't you—"

"Die? In a way, yes. Until the gorgons make me whole again. My soul will be transformed into whatever they need me to be."

"No! You have decades of memories. The other realm, your people, weddings, your parents, your friends, me, us."

"Do you think I want to remember those things? I'll be taking Medusa's place in the trinity. I won't ever be able to leave the grotto. I'll never see the sun again unless it's through a secondhand experience delivered by the sirens. I won't be able to talk to you. I won't even be able to see you unless I use their mirror to watch over you like a spying god. Do you know how hard it would be to miss you, or ache to be near you and not be able to do anything about it? I *want* to forget who I am, and how good my life has been. You'll be helping me by erasing it all. I couldn't do it any other way."

She rubbed her hands over her face. "I hate this. I hate that anyone has to live in the grotto. Of all people, why does it have to be you? How am I supposed to live with myself, knowing you exist in some awful, cold, dark place? That you went there because of me. That it's supposed to be *me* down there and not you."

"As long as you absorb all my memories, I won't suffer. I won't remember being mer or living this life."

"But I'll suffer!" Tears formed in her eyes, shimmering with every color of the rainbow. "I'll live my whole life loving you and missing you, knowing you have no idea I exist."

A lump formed in my throat. I stared at her tiny hands, wanting so badly to hold them. "I know. I hate myself for hurting you this way, but I had no other choice."

"You did! You should've never turned me. I could have lived with the gorgons."

"I promised your mother. She thought this through, Yara. The gorgons wouldn't have drained you to turn you into one of them. Who knows how painful the transformation would have been? Plus, you would have gone to the grotto with all your human memories and feelings. You would always know what a horrible existence you were sentenced to. I promised her I wouldn't let that happen."

I couldn't fight it anymore. My hands linked with hers. "I can protect you and open the gate. For fourteen years that's been my mission. I wanted to do this, and I made the right choice. What I didn't know is that we would fall for each other. If I would've known that, I may have done things differently, but I can't change the past. This is the only way it can play out."

She jumped to her feet, pacing again. "We can run away. It's a huge world, they'll never find us."

"You're thinking in terms of you and me. This is infinitely bigger than us. So many merfolk have been suffering for the last eighteen years, clinging to hope and believing that you and I will be the key to returning to a world they love."

"But—"

"There is no but." I stood up and held her shoulders.

"You've seen how beautiful our realm is. Our people have loved ones on the other side. Some of the children born here have never even seen Rathe. Are you willing to let so many people never see their home again just so I can retain my memories?"

"Y-y-ye—" She struggled to get the word out.

"No, Yara. The answer is no. Deep down you know that."

Just then we heard shouting in the distance. Kai waded through the surf.

"Miss Yara, Mister Treygan," Kai yelled. "We have been searching for you for hours."

"What's wrong?" I called to her.

"I do not know, but all messengers were sent to find you. Mister Caspian has ordered you to return to Solis immediately."

My pulse quickened. Yara must have seen the worry on my face.

"What do you think it is?" she asked.

"I'm not sure, but something horrible must have happened for Caspian to give that kind of order."

"Koraline," she gasped, and ran into the surf.

I followed, but if my instincts were correct it had nothing to do with Koraline and everything to do with my bastard brother and his slimy selkies.

 **Rownan** I had never seen Paragon Castle above water, but I was grateful to be in human form with normal communication. Jack and Caspian did most of the talking, and if we were underwater I may have missed some parts.

Indrea glared at me from across the table most of the morning. Her purple eyes unnerved me. I had never spent much time around a Violet. All the other colors I could handle, but Caspian and Indrea gave off a disturbing mind-reader vibe. No one had ever mentioned any merfolk could read minds out of the water, but maybe it was one of their protected secrets.

For the past two hours I had randomly been thinking outrageous comments to see if Indrea would flinch: *Your husband's hair looks like purple cabbage. Yara is a blood guzzler. There's a bomb in this castle!*

There was no bomb, but I figured she couldn't ignore that one. Her brow didn't furrow, her nose didn't twitch. No indication whatsoever that she heard me.

Jack shifted in his chair. "I don't see why *we* need to wait around for the two of them to show up."

Caspian kept his hands folded in front of him. "If your accusations are true, we may need to reevaluate our plan. Nothing seems to be unfolding as we had hoped on our end."

"That's because your plan was bullshit from the start," Jack grunted.

Caspian stood up and leaned stiff-armed over the table. Indrea placed her hand on his. I cracked my knuckles, ready to fight on Jack's behalf. After a long staring contest between him and Jack, Caspian sat down.

"Look," Jack said. "The gate needs to be opened. I don't care if Medusa rises from the dead and chains the girl to the grotto. Me and my people just want to go home. You do have the same goal, right?"

"Of course," Caspian answered.

"Then let's not let these love birds screw it up for the rest of us."

Caspian opened his mouth and I thought we were about to suffer through another speech about Treygan's loyalty, how he would never be so irresponsible, blahdy blah, but footsteps in the hallway caught everyone's attention. Two Indigos entered first, Yara and Treygan followed. The shock on their faces when they saw us sitting at the table with their untouchable Violets was priceless.

"What's going on here?" Treygan asked.

"Treygan, Yara, please sit," Caspian ordered.

Treygan pulled out a chair for Yara. She sat down, but couldn't peel her confused eyes away from me.

"I prefer to stand," Treygan said.

"Jack," Caspian began, "would you please tell Treygan and Yara why you are here?"

Jack kicked his boots up, resting them on the table. "This harebrained plan of yours has always seemed like a surefire failure, but after I saw you two at our party last night, there ain't no way we believe you'll go through with it."

Treygan stood tall, speaking only to Caspian and Indrea. "We are going through with it."

Indrea leaned forward. "Jack and Rownan seem to think the two of you," she waved a finger at him and Yara, "are falling in love with each other."

Yara whipped her head around to look at me. "You have no right to discuss my personal life with anyone!"

Jack slammed his feet to the floor. "*You* haven't been part of this long enough to grasp how important you are to our world. We'll discuss you whenever we please, and we'll do whatever it takes to make sure you don't blow our one shot at opening the gate."

"Enough," Indrea interrupted. "Yara, you know what you have to do on the Triple Eighteen, and you are willing to do it, correct?"

Yara lowered her eyes.

"She won't do it," I said. "I know her better than any of you. I've seen how Treygan looks at her. He won't do his part, either."

Treygan bolted toward me, but Jack jumped up and stopped him. Treygan's gaze stayed locked on mine over Jack's shoulder. "You have no idea what I'm capable of," Treygan snarled through clenched teeth. "How dare you come here and question my loyalty!"

All we needed was to plant the seeds of doubt in the minds of the Violets. I had never seen Treygan look at any girl the way he looked at Yara. He wouldn't be able to lie about it. "So prove me wrong. Tell us you aren't falling in love with Yara. That you don't care the days are numbered until you have to forget she exists."

His skin looked like it was bruising right before our eyes. Shades of blue, gray and green swirled around his hallmarks. Sadness, anger and shame all surfacing for the Violets to see.

"Treygan," Caspian said firmly.

Scattered clouds of red deepened against Yara's golden skin. I hadn't known her as a mermaid long enough to know what it meant, but I assumed it was sadness.

Treygan faced Caspian and Indrea. "We will do whatever it takes to open the gate."

"Good," Jack said. "I'm sure Yara sees our plan is the logical one, now that she's a blood guzzler."

"What?" Indrea gasped.

Treygan grabbed the back of Yara's chair. The muscles in his neck and arms rippled. He hadn't told the Violets about Yara's blood-drinking incident. If he hid something that major, what else would they suspect him of keeping from them?

"Yara drank my blood," I said.

The stone chair broke into pieces under Treygan's grip. "That's a lie! She did drink selkie blood, but not directly from you."

"And you kept this information from us?" Caspian asked him accusingly.

"I explained it to her. I explained the cravings, that she would have to fight them and never drink again. She endured the withdrawal." He sounded desperate and guilty. "Examine her. She has no moon hallmark. The coldness isn't a part of her."

Yara looked terrified. I wondered if she had ever seen the power of Treygan's temper. Crumbling chairs was child's play for him.

"That's not the point," Indrea chided. "You kept it hidden from us, along with your feelings for Yara. Pango said he hasn't even had a chance to teach her how to share memories. None of this is very promising to the success of our plan."

"But I do know how to share memories!" Yara exclaimed.

"Yara," Treygan said. "Please hush."

"Why should she hush?" Indrea asked. "Let her speak."

Treygan and Yara exchanged a glance that said something, but I couldn't tell what. Yara hesitated but then faced Indrea. "Treygan and I have shared memories several times."

Indrea and Caspian's eyes widened. Treygan dropped his head in his hands. This just kept getting better.

Caspian walked over to him. "*You* shared a memory with her? *You* were her first? Did we not forbid that very thing? That bond is stronger than any other! Do you realize what you have done?"

Yara stood. "He didn't do anything wrong. I made him teach me. He tried to tell—"

"Yara, stop," Treygan said. "I apologize, Caspian. She hated our kind. Hated what she had become. Koraline was clinging to life with minimal hope of recovery. Yara needed to understand more about us, and to connect with one of our kind."

"Yes, but not you!" Caspian roared. "Anyone but you, Treygan. Good oceans and heavens, you've made it impossible for us to believe you two will proceed with our plan."

"No!" Treygan grabbed Caspian's arm. "We will, I swear it. You know how strong my loyalty is."

"*Your* loyalty, yes, but your actions have set up an

impossible task for Yara." Caspian glanced at Yara who stood watching nervously. "She couldn't possibly do what will be asked of her."

Treygan tried speaking softly so no one else would hear. But Jack and I were close enough. "Please, let me explain it to her. I will make her understand. She'll do it."

Caspian studied him for a moment and turned to Yara. "Are you in love with Treygan?"

Her eyes darted toward Treygan then back at Caspian. "I prefer not to answer."

Caspian folded his hands in front of him. "I will ask you one more time, Yara. If you choose not to answer, I will arrange it so this will be the last time you see Treygan. Ever."

She swallowed hard, panic flashed in her eyes.

"Are you in love with Treygan?" Caspian asked again.

Yara bowed her head and closed her eyes. "Yes."

Jack smacked me on the back. A dull pain surged across my chest, but I didn't understand why. I didn't love Yara. What did I care if she fell for Treygan?

"Indrea, a word in private." Caspian motioned to the doorway. She rose and they left the room together.

Treygan stared at Yara. She kept her head down, but Treygan lifted her face.

"Why is it such a horrible thing for me to love you?" she asked. "Why are they acting like we committed a crime?"

Jack had the nerve to speak. "Because Treygan is—"

"Shut up, Jack!" Treygan turned on him with fury burning in his eyes. "Why are you still here? You accomplished your goal. Go back to your filthy bar."

"Listen, you worthless—"

I stood between them. "Jack, stop. He's right. We're no longer needed here."

"You were never needed here," Treygan hissed.

Caspian and Indrea came back into the room with four

Indigos. None of them were Delmar, which wasn't a good sign. Treygan knew it too. He stepped in front of Yara, putting his arms out protectively like he could shield her from what was about to happen.

Caspian stepped forward. "You and Yara will be separated until the morning of the Triple Eighteen."

"No!" Treygan argued.

"Yes," Caspian insisted. "Pango will continue her education, and you *will* stay away from her."

"You can't do this!" Yara shouted, trying to move around Treygan.

"We can, Yara, and it must be done. This isn't your fault. Treygan committed careless actions which have serious consequences. We are taking this step to protect you."

"Treygan protects me! He's my guardian—the one who saved my life. He would never do anything to hurt me."

Treygan's expression became stony. I couldn't decipher it.

He slowly turned to look at Yara. He bent his knees so they were eye to eye and cradled her face in his hands. "Yara, listen to me. They're right."

"No," she whimpered, shaking her head. "You didn't do anything wrong. We shouldn't be apart."

"We have to be."

"They can't order us to stay away from each other!"

"I'm agreeing to it," he said somberly. "I've done too much damage as it is."

"No!"

"Enough," Caspian announced. "Treygan, go to my private quarters."

Treygan ran his thumb down Yara's cheek. "Goodbye, Yamabuki."

"No!" She clutched his hands.

It pained even me to watch him pull free of her and walk

out. She started to go after him, but two Indigos held her back. She kicked and struggled while shouting Treygan's name.

I should've been ecstatic. We did what we came to do. But as much as I disagreed with the merfolk's plan, and as sure as I was that Yara had to be sacrificed for our future, I felt sick. Jack wore a satisfied grin.

"Yara, calm down," Indrea pleaded. "Causing a scene will not help the situation."

"You're soulless monsters!" Yara yelled. "All of you!"

Indrea smoothed down her dress and lifted her chin high, but she looked hurt. "Take her to the library," she told the Indigos. "I will be there momentarily."

They dragged Yara out of the room as she screamed over her shoulder, "Rownan, how could you? I would have never done this to you and Vienna! Never!"

If I hadn't been feeling guilty before, that did the job. I slumped into my chair, feeling weak and nauseous.

Her screaming faded down the hallway.

Caspian turned to me and Jack. "As much as I hate to say this, we may have to reevaluate our plan. We will spend a few days monitoring the situation, then meet with you at the end of the week to consult. If it truly seems Yara isn't able to follow through with our plan," Caspian hung his head, "we will turn her over to you."

Jack smiled and reached his hand out to shake Caspian's.

Caspian put his hands behind his back. "We have no alternative. It does not mean we agree with it, or that we will ever forgive ourselves for letting it come to this."

Indrea gave one nod of agreement, and then a purple tear ran down her cheek.

Treygan

The sun had traversed the sky four times since they had separated me from Yara.

Pango and Merrick had been ordered to stop helping with the crops. Two other greens were assigned to take their place. The Violets worried Pango would deliver messages between me and Yara. Delmar had been allowed to stay on duty, but since he spent his days with me he wasn't allowed within fifty feet of Yara.

We had finished hanging the plants for the day, so the two Greens said goodbye as Delmar and I put the tools in the shed.

"You're miserable," Delmar observed.

He knew what happened at the meeting with the Violets, and I told him I never wanted to discuss it again.

"Beyond miserable," he continued. "I've never seen you like this."

I coiled the hanging line and shoved it onto a shelf.

"Treygan, what can I do?"

"Make sure all the bags have been picked up outside."

He rested his hand on my shoulder. "That's not what I meant. What can I do to help you and Yara?"

"There is no me and Yara."

"Knock it off. This is me you're talking to. It's tearing you apart being away from her."

"It's for the best."

"That's sharkshit."

"What do you suggest I do, Del? Disobey the Violets, fight my way into Pango's house, and demand he and Merrick jeopardize their rank by letting me see her?"

"Stellar plan. Do it."

I rolled my eyes. "It's not rational."

"Love is not rational. You have a limited number of days left with her. Pango and Merrick will do whatever they can to help you. They saw what I saw. You, for the first time ever, in love and deliriously happy—even when you were trying to hide it. You have to fight for that."

I sat down on the bench, exhausted by my own emptiness. "I should have stayed away. I made it a million times harder on her."

"That girl loves you. Even after seeing Kimber and realizing what you're capable of at your worst, she watched you with a sparkle in her eye that any fool could see was unconditional love. You think Yara cares about what happens a week from now? She's dying inside because she can't be with you."

"She's tough as a seawall. She'll be fine."

He sat beside me. "Pango said she doesn't eat. She doesn't talk, smile or laugh at his jokes. She doesn't swim or go out in the sunlight. She's not fine. Neither of you are fine."

Hearing about Yara torturing herself made my stomach twist in knots. "She's smoking, right?"

"No. Pango said her only saving grace is that she spends a lot of time in his resting pool, but she only does it so she can be alone. She asked to visit Lloyd, and when the Violets agreed she didn't show a hint of excitement or happiness."

"Not even when she saw him?"

"He wasn't home."

I stood up and leaned against the shed's doorframe, watching the last trace of sun disappear over the water. "What do I do? Which path will hurt her less?"

"What do *you* want to do? For once in your life, Treygan, do what's best for you. Don't act out of guilt about your mother or your grandmother. Don't do it for your people, for honor, or for Rathe. Do it for *you*. You've earned it."

"Earned it? What have I earned? I vowed to protect Yara. I promised her mother I would keep her safe from a future of misery. I've broken that vow. I singlehandedly made her more miserable than she's ever been."

He stood beside me. "She's miserable because she can't be with you."

"Does she know yet? Has Pango told her the selkies' plan?"

Delmar's cheeks puffed out as he exhaled loudly. "He wanted to wait until she showed some improvement. She's too emotionally unstable. He's worried telling her will push her over the edge. The Violets agree."

I nodded.

"Treygan, the Violets are wavering in their faith. In two days, if Yara isn't ready and willing to do her part, then …." Delmar's skin streaked with shades of green. He rarely showed sadness.

"What? Then what?"

"They'll turn her over to the selkies."

"No! How could they agree to that? It's barbaric!"

"They don't know what else to do. They're distraught over it."

My heart pounded. All of my hallmarks snaked around my body. My skin deepened to dark gray. "They can't do this!"

"You tell me what you want to do, and I'll stop at nothing to make it happen."

"I need to see her. I have to make her understand our way is best."

"When?"

"Now."

"Give me a few hours. I need to find out which guards are at Pango's and call in favors. I don't want us fighting any of our people if we don't have to. You might lose control."

"No. I mean, of course." I couldn't think straight. Yara's life was on the line and I had to wait hours before I could do anything to protect her. "Delmar, the selkies can't come near her. I don't care if we have to run away until the Triple Eighteen."

"I'll work on getting a place for you to hide out, just in case it comes to that."

I hugged him. "You're risking everything by helping me. I can't thank you enough."

"You want to thank me?" He clutched my shoulders. "Love her, Treygan. And let her love you. Remember Koraline's motto: Love until it kills you, because there's nothing better worth dying for."

The sickness made my connection to my mother stronger.

I couldn't tell Pango. I wanted to, but he would think I was nuts if I told him I was making myself sick so I could see my mother's ghost again. Let him assume I was torturing myself because of depression. No one would believe me if I told the truth. No one except Uncle Lloyd.

I kept hoping I would see my mother again like I did at the pier. She looked like a white orb of light, but I knew it was her. She tried to tell me something, but I had been in too much pain to understand her.

Two days ago, the memory of another time I saw her ghost had returned to me. Years ago when I was sick with pneumonia, I had seen her at the hospital. I told Uncle Lloyd and he said I wasn't crazy. He believed guardian angels hung around to help us and communicating with spirits was possible. Maybe my mother could help me and Treygan.

Pango refused to tell me the selkies' plan until I started eating. All he would say was that it wouldn't work. My mother had been a siren, connected to the gorgons. What if she knew something the rest of us didn't? What if she could help?

Pango's resting pool was more secluded than Koraline's. He and Merrick weren't within hearing range, so I shut the door to the room. Rain clouds had covered the moon. No light shined through the window. I sat at the edge of the pool and dipped my feet into the cool, liquid darkness.

My head had been pounding for days. My stomach hurt so badly from hunger it made me nauseous. My muscles trembled from fatigue. But if my mother had the answers I needed, then it would be worth the suffering.

"Mom," I whispered. "Are you here?" I kept very still, squinting into the black water, watching for any flash or floating light, waiting for my skin to start prickling from her energy. Then I saw something. At first it looked like a white rock shimmering at the bottom of the pool, except I knew the rock liner was made of black and brown stones. I leaned closer, blinking through the tightness behind my eyes and trying to ignore the headache. I focused on the white blur in the water.

The cloudy spot was growing bigger, floating toward me, pulsing and flexing. The foggy outline of a face appeared. I felt so weak I could hardly keep my head up, but I leaned even closer, my face inches from the water, my fingers gripping the edge of the pool.

My mother's voice rippled through my aching head.

I felt like I had cotton balls stuffed in my ears. Most of her words were a faint stream of murmuring I couldn't understand, but I caught a few of them.

Truth ... secret ... visit ... sirens ... blood ... die.

"Die?" That one word snapped me from my concentration. "Who dies?"

The cloud shrunk away. The whispering stopped.

"Mom, please don't go."

A white bird crashed against the window above me. It threw itself against the glass, over and over. The loud noise made my head feel like it was cracking open. Sharp pains shot through my temples.

I reached out to where the light had disappeared and fell forward, splashing into the water. I was too weak to swim. My eyes drifted closed as I sank to the bottom of the pool, reaching for my mother and for a way to save Treygan, but never finding either.

I never actually passed out.

My body went numb and my mind was hazy while everything happened around me, but I remembered bits and pieces: Pango pulling me out of the pool, being wrapped in towels, and then sinking into a bed. At one point I saw Merrick, his lips moving above me, but I couldn't hear him. I remember smelling rubbing alcohol, a sting in my arm, then, eventually, the wood ceiling beams came into focus.

I stared at the beams for a long time, thinking I needed to move my body or do something, anything, but I couldn't. I couldn't keep my eyes open, but I never fell asleep.

For a long time my world consisted of nothing but the inside of my eyelids. I hadn't noticed they had a shimmery, golden hue. I couldn't recall what I saw when I closed my eyes as a human, but it wasn't all bright and sparkly.

I forced my eyes open and stared at the ceiling beams again. Then I stared at the back of my eyelids.

Ceiling beams.

Eyelids.

Over and over, until it changed: ceiling beams, eyelids, Pango.

I kept my eyes open and he smiled.

"There she is. Welcome back to Oz, Diva Dorothy. We've missed you."

My stomach didn't hurt anymore. I sat up and my muscles didn't feel like wet noodles. Pango stuffed pillows behind me. I was lying in his bed with a catheter in my arm. An IV fluid bag hung from the trident floor lamp beside me.

I felt much better.

Crap.

"It's a good thing you're a mermaid," Pango teased. "Otherwise you would have drowned in that pool. You're supposed to rest face up, ya know? Face down gives you saggy skin."

"Yara, how do you feel?" Merrick asked, sitting on the other side of me.

"Better." They had ruined it. I had made notable progress with making myself sick and contacting my mother, and they had ruined it by pumping me full of miracle juice.

Pango rested his hand on mine. "Please tell me you aren't on a suicide mission. Self-pity is so not in style."

"I'm not suicidal."

"Then why did you let yourself get that sick? Between you and my sister, my fragile heart can't take any more."

"I'm sorry, Pango." He deserved to know the truth. We only had a week left. If I explained everything he might understand and we could try again. "It was the only way I could ...." I looked into his emerald eyes and took a breath. "Communicate with my mother."

The bed bounced as Pango and Merrick both sat up straight. "Come again," Pango said.

"The night Nixie took me to Rownan's party I got sick—*really* sick—and I saw my mother. I think she's been trying to tell me something. Right before I fell into the pool she said someone might die. I think she has the answers, but I have to be sick to talk to her."

Merrick's bulging eyes resembled lemons. "You do know how crazy that sounds, right?"

"Are you kidding me? We're half fish. We control water, talk through our minds and relive each other's memories, and communicating with spirits is crazy?"

Pango massaged his temples. "What else did she say?"

Merrick jumped up. "Pang, you don't actually believe this?"

"Yara's right. Why shouldn't it be possible considering how magical the rest of our existence is?" Pango laid his hand on top of mine. "Go on, what else did Mommy dearest say?"

I went over the words in my mind. *Visit ... siren ... blood.* "I think she wants me to visit the sirens."

"No way," Merrick said. "Not happening."

I tried to push the covers off of me, but the catheter in my arm tugged at my skin. "Think about it. The explanation on how to open the gate came in the form of a poem, and merfolk and selkies interpreted the poem very differently. The sirens were created as an extension of the gorgons to deliver messages for them, right?"

Pango nodded, but Merrick looked at me like a suspicious bobcat ready to pounce.

"So wouldn't it make sense," I continued, "that the sirens would be our best bet at interpreting the poem correctly?"

Merrick put his hands on his hips. "Do you think the Violets didn't think of that? They asked for their interpretation as soon as the gate closed."

"And what did they say?" I asked.

Pango rocked his head side-to-side. "I believe it was something like, 'Drown in hell.'"

"They wouldn't help you?"

"Of course not," Merrick said. "They love it here. They don't get sick like we do. With the gate closed they don't have to spend their time regurgitating memories for the gorgons to consume. They don't want the gate to open."

The sirens knew the answer. I was sure of it. That's what my mother had tried to tell me. I had to see them. "My mother used to be one of them. Doesn't that give me some kind of family rights to their secrets?"

Merrick laughed, but Pango stared at me all seriously and contemplative. It was odd to see them reverse roles.

"The Violets will never agree to let you see them," Merrick said. "Nixie kidnapped you, for gods' sakes."

"He's right," Pango murmured. "The Violets won't allow it."

"All of this is ludicrous." Merrick stood behind Pango, rubbing his back. "We have to meet with the Violets tomorrow to update them on Yara. Is this what we want to tell them? That she is conjuring up a new plan with her dead mother?" He snickered. "I think not."

I sat forward. "Pango, you have to tell me what the selkies' plan is. Maybe it will help me figure out what my mother's message means."

Merrick bristled. "Not until you're feeling better."

Pango snapped his head around. "Merrick, I love you, but shut up. You're hovering behind me like a henpecking old biddy. Go whip up a pie or something."

"Don't tell me to shut up. If you don't want my help, just say so."

"So." Pango stood up and pushed Merrick out of the room. "I'm not saying I believe these spirit shenanigans, but I love a good story, and this one is a Moby Dick. So shoo." He waved him out the door and shut it. "Great gorgons, that man can frazzle my nerves."

Pango downed the glass of juice on my nightstand. "My how I wish that was a pomegranate martini. The good liquor lord knows I need one for what I'm about to tell you. We don't have much time, so I hope you're wearing your brave girl panties."

"I can handle it."

Pango crossed his hands over his heart. "The selkies' plan is to kill you."

"What?" I croaked.

"I know, right? Heartless hooligans."

"Rownan would never let them hurt me."

"Aww, it's sweet that you believe that, but in their screwball minds, Rownan is the only one who can take you to the gate. Anyone who isn't a gorgon—or at least part gorgon—and swims into the Catacombs will turn to stone."

I could feel the blood draining from my face. "This is why Rownan mysted me? He wanted me to trust him so he could take me to the Catacombs and turn me to stone?"

"No, Senorita Sunbeam. According to the gorgon curse, the *soul* has to be sacrificed. Selkies and merfolk have very different interpretations of what that means. Remember, they share their souls through blood."

I swallowed so hard I nearly choked. "Rownan wants my blood?"

"They believe your blood has to be spread over the tombs in the Catacombs—all of it. There's malarkey in the poem about sacrificing for all the lost souls so they can return—or some rigmarole that those brain-freezed morons deciphered incorrectly. A rumor surfaced that your bloodshed will resurrect the souls entombed down there."

"My—could that possibly—no, right? That's insane."

"Of course it's insane. When you're dead, you're dead. I

have friends entombed in the Catacombs that I would love to see rise from the ocean floor, but don't you think they might be peeved that they've been living the life of a rock for eighteen years? It's not logical."

I fidgeted with the tube attached to my arm. "You don't believe my mom talked to me, do you?"

He glanced at the door and lowered his voice. "I might. If she learned something from wherever she is, then maybe she's trying to teach you before it's too late. Currently our only two plans end all Romeo-and-Julietish. No mother would want that for her daughter."

My mother didn't care much about me while she was alive. Maybe she was trying to make up for it from the other side.

I itched at the tube in my arm. "Can you take this thing out? It's annoying."

"Sure." Pango stood up and started playing nurse. He let out a frustrated sigh when Merrick knocked. "In a minute, Mrs. Grundy!"

"Two minutes, Pango!" Merrick shouted through the locked door. "By then, if you two are still planning a séance, I'm calling in the Violets to perform an exorcism."

Pango looked at the door and stuck out his tongue. "He tries to make jokes, but it's just not his cup of tea. I'll tell you my plan, but I have to be quick about it. We don't have much time."

I nodded as he pressed a Band-Aid on my arm.

"If there is another way to open the gate, you have to figure it out. And you can't do it here on Solis. The Violets will ask us for the truth tomorrow and we can't lie. Merrick will spew out the details like Old Faithful, and the Violets would never be convinced another plan could be spelled out on a Ouija board. The sirens may be your best bet. Stay with them until you figure this thing out. Because unless you agree to our method and can swear to the Violets you'll drain Treygan of all his songs, they will be forced to give you to the selkies. None of us want that. So, my juristic jailbird, you have to fly this coop and go find your last-minute miracle."

"But what about Merrick?"

"Let me worry about him. Just follow my lead once we leave this room." Before turning the doorknob he paused and whispered, "Be careful with the sirens. If you suspect they're in cahoots with the selkies, get out of there fast."

Visit ... sirens ... blood ... die.

I silently prayed that I hadn't tragically misinterpreted my mother's message.

Rownan

I tripped on the first step and stumbled onto the porch, cursing under my breath. I pounded on the door, leaned against the railing and waited. A few minutes later the door creaked open and we sized each other up in the darkness.

"Can you at least turn on the porch light?" I grumbled.

"Are you drunk?" Lloyd asked.

The porch seemed to sway under me. "Why? You offering me a drink?"

"I'm not offering you anything, but I am wondering why the hell you're at my door in the middle of the night."

"Yara. Why else?"

He swung the door wide open. "Get in here, but leave that chip on your shoulder outside. I don't have the energy to fight with you."

We sat at the kitchen table in bitter silence. Lloyd wouldn't let me say a word until I ate something and drank some coffee.

"I hate coffee." My words came out semi-slurred. "It doesn't sober you up. That's a myth."

"It's to wake your ass up. You look like you're about to fall over. Not to mention you reek of liquor and are stinking up my home."

"Been a rough few days."

He grunted and watched me take a swig of my steaming, liquid manure. I fought the urge to spit it out.

"Okay," Lloyd said. "Get on with it."

"Your adopted niece is in love with Treygan."

"Well, lah-tee-dah."

I set my mug down. "I came here to ask for advice. Can you stop being a dick?"

"I'm sorry. Refresh my memory. When was the last time you and I sat down for a cozy chat? I can't recall us having any father-son moments in decades."

"Spare me the sarcasm. You knew where to find me if you wanted to see me."

"For a month you've paraded around this island—right outside my door, no less—and made yourself comfortable in one of *my* homes, yet hardly said a word to me. You think I didn't know what you were up to? You're lucky I didn't tell Yara who you were and what you planned to do."

"Look at you," I sneered. "The more you meddle the sicker you get. Jack knew you couldn't stop me. Look at what happened to your kidneys when you helped Vyron cast that spell. You're barely hanging on as it is. We're all shocked you aren't dead yet."

"No kidding," he grumbled. "I've had to watch my step every day. If I meddled again, Yara would have been left with no one. Do you have any idea how many times I wanted to smack some sense into you?"

"Trying to earn another Daddy of the Year award?"

"Dammit, Rownan, you're my son!" His palm slamming

the table made coffee splash over the rim of my mug. "I hate that you let Jack push you around and tell you what to do, even when you know it's wrong. But I still love you. Whether you believe that or not, I have always loved you."

"Bullshit! Look around this place. All your precious carvings of mermaids, sirens and gorgons, but there are no selkies, huh? Heaven forbid your illegitimate son's species be represented in your home."

He lowered his eyes and turned his balding head.

I gripped my mug and stared at the ring of coffee on the table. "You're the only father I'll ever have, and you hate *me* because of what my mother did."

"I forgave your mother a long time ago. Liora and I both forgave her."

"Ha! You think Liora didn't die resenting my mother for having your first child?"

"Liora gave me a child too."

"A child who killed her."

He slammed his hand on the table again. "Shut your mouth!"

"You'd prefer it were me, wouldn't you? Would you rather I volunteered to live as a gorgon? For Treygan—your good son—you would do anything. For me you couldn't care less."

"Your brother is cursed with the ability to turn people to stone. You think he considers himself my *good* son? Don't you realize all three of us are cursed with burdens and tragic flaws? Most days I hate myself for messing with nature. I greedily threw stones into the water, and look at the damaging ripples it caused." He took a deep breath. "But then I think about you boys, and Yara, and how much I love all of you. I would do it all over again."

I shook my head and stood up. "Yeah, right." Turning to Lloyd for help had been an epic mistake.

"Sit down. I'm not finished talking." He leaned forward, resting his ashy elbows on the table. "The past eighteen years have bordered on nightmarish. Lately, the only thing that made it bearable was Yara and Liora."

"Liora?"

He flicked his hand in the air. "She still hangs around. She assures me all of this hasn't been for nothing. Me helping Vyron and Cleo turn human, the broken promise, the gate closing, the war between the sea creatures, between my sons—all of it is for a reason. That's the only thing that keeps me going. Otherwise I would have told Yara the truth years ago and let the curse kill me. I couldn't leave her alone. I had to make things right."

"You've lost it, old man. You're claiming to talk to ghosts."

"One ghost. You can think I'm crazy. I don't give a damn. I know what's true, what's right, and what has to be done."

"You swore you would never take sides."

He shook a calloused finger at me. "And I've kept that promise."

"You let Treygan turn her into a mermaid."

"I wasn't here when that happened. I had nothing to do with it."

"They're in love! His emotions could turn her to stone in the blink of an eye."

"I couldn't change what he did. All I could do was make sure she had protection."

"Protection? She's not protected. I've seen them together. He looks at her with so much passion it's a miracle she's not a statue already."

"She has the necklace. She'll be fine."

I squinted at him, trying to figure out his twisted, senile mind. "What necklace?"

"I gave her a necklace containing my good gorgon blood. She's protected from being petrified."

"I've never seen her wearing any necklace."

His fuzzy, white eyebrows lifted. "What?"

"Yara hasn't been wearing a necklace the past few times I've seen her. Mermaid armband, plant hallmarks, wrinkled dresses, yes, but no necklace."

He stood up, bracing himself on the table. "Without the protection of that necklace they could slip up. One heated or intense moment and Treygan could kill her."

His nose and hands twitched a few times as he stared across the kitchen. It was the first time I had ever seen him scared. Then I had an epiphany. "You knew they would fall for each other. Why else would you give her a necklace with good gorgon blood in it?"

"They've loved each other for years. He was in the picture long before you showed up, ever since the night he saved her from drowning—she just never knew who he was."

"Legit? Treygan saved Yara's life?" How did I not know that?

"Do you know how many times I watched her stand in the surf, crying into the ocean? She may not have remembered him saving her, but her soul knew he was out there somewhere." Lloyd fiddled with a plastic hospital bracelet around his wrist. "They were already connected. There's no stopping the bond soul mates share once they've met. Look at you and Vienna."

The mention of Vienna melted my heart. "You really believe Treygan and Yara are soul mates?"

"I know it. But that doesn't mean her life isn't in danger by being with him unprotected."

"They aren't together. The Violets ordered them to be kept apart until the Triple Eighteen. They don't think Yara will go through with their plan now that she's in love with Treygan."

"What are they going to do?"

I leaned against the counter. I didn't want to tell him, but I had to. "Help us with our plan."

"No," Lloyd gasped.

"See, you are taking sides."

"Jack's plan is asinine. I don't understand how he could think killing her is the answer. He used to be much more intelligent."

"He thinks it's the only shot we've got at opening the gate."

Lloyd started limping around the kitchen. "I've got to find her."

"To warn her about us? It's a little too late for that, *Dad*. She's run out of options."

"Rownan, I'm going to need your help."

I laughed. The alcohol must have weakened my defenses. Time to tell the old man the truth. "I came here to ask you for *your* help."

"My help?"

He watched me suspiciously, but for the first time in almost two decades I thought I might say something to make my father proud. "I don't know if I can go through with it. I keep telling Jack I will, but when the time comes, when it's just me and Yara at the gate, I don't think I'll be able to hurt her."

His whole body seemed to relax. He rubbed a hand over his chin and hobbled toward the counter. "Well, then, I'll put another pot of coffee on. It seems we have a long night of planning ahead of us."

 Treygan The sun would be rising in a couple of hours. Delmar and I had been hiding behind some boulders overlooking Pango's house for almost an hour. Delmar insisted we had to wait for the changing of the guards, but I was antsy.

Everything felt wrong: being apart from Yara, Delmar risking his rank to help me, asking guards to look the other way, and the Violets considering the selkies' plan. To make things right within a week seemed impossible, but there had to be a way.

"There are Jalen and Enzo coming for their shift," Delmar said. "We'll be able to go in soon."

"What if they changed their minds?"

"Then we fight."

"Pango and Merrick really don't know we're coming?"

Delmar shook his head, keeping an eye on Jalen and Enzo. "They haven't been out of the house since sunset. I couldn't get a message to them without looking suspicious."

"What does Kimber think about all of this?"

He flashed me a sideways grin. "Who do you think has been watching the house all night?"

"Ugh. Delmar, I don't like her being involved."

"Aw, come on, it's like the good old days when all of us used to get into trouble together. Only now we're working against Rownan instead of with him."

"That was innocent kind of trouble. Who knows how the Violets will react if we get caught."

"Don't worry about that unless it happens." He motioned for me to follow him. "Time to go."

We hurried along the path, hiding in the shadows until we reached the house. Jalen walked away when he sensed us, acting like he needed to do a perimeter check, but Enzo stared at me as we approached him.

"Hit me," he said.

"What?" Delmar and I glanced at each other.

Enzo pointed to his face. "Hit me. And you better lay me out cold. If the Violets question me, I want to be able to say you knocked me out."

"Enzo," I started, "I don't think that's necessary for—"

Before I could finish my sentence Delmar hit Enzo so hard he flew backward, landing unconscious on the ground.

"Delmar, what the hell?"

He shrugged. "Now he can say he never saw it coming, and it won't be a lie."

"He's your friend."

"Right. That's why I did what he asked. Now go get your girl."

He pushed open Pango's front door, but neither one of us were prepared for what we saw: Merrick tied to a chair with a hand towel gagging his mouth and secured with duct tape.

"Well, that's unexpected," Delmar said, shutting the door behind us.

Pango came around the corner holding a martini and

wearing an apron that said, *Squeeze me, stomp me, make me wine.* "Hello, gentlemen. May I offer you a drink while the cinnamon buns finish baking?"

I walked over to Merrick who was trying to hop his chair toward us. "Why is Merrick gagged and tied up?"

Pango sipped his drink. "He was being difficult and had to be restrained."

"Difficult about what?"

"Helping you and Yara. He wanted to go to the Violets and tell them everything."

I had just pulled the towel out of Merrick's mouth, but shoved it back in before he could say a word. "Hand me the duct tape."

Merrick groaned and tried kicking me, but Pango had tied him up too tightly.

Delmar put his arm around Pango's broad neck and laughed. "Damn, you two are an entertaining couple."

"Is Yara resting?" I asked.

One of Pango's green eyebrows lifted. He took another sip of his martini and turned toward the kitchen. "Was that the timer dinging?"

"Pango." I drew out the 'o' until he turned around.

He set his glass down. "Fine. Truth be told, she isn't here."

"What do you mean she isn't here? Where is she?"

"She flew the coop."

"Did she go to see Lloyd again?" Delmar asked.

Pango glanced at the ceiling, rocking his head from side-to-side. "Not exactly. Maybe flew the coop wasn't the right choice of words. More like she fled to the nest."

"The sirens' nest!" I shot across the room, ready to throttle him.

Delmar stepped between us. "Hang on, let's hear why. Pango wouldn't tie Merrick up for no good reason."

"Of course I wouldn't. I'm the one who likes to be tied up." Pango blew a kiss at Merrick who grunted through his gag.

I backed away from everyone. My mind was already out the door and speeding through the ocean. I needed to find Yara. "Start explaining, Pango, and do it fast."

"Technically, you're my aunt," I told Otabia. "Aren't you obligated to help me? Bound by blood to your dead sister, or something?"

Otabia circled the sunken living room where Nixie and I sat together. Every ten seconds Otabia would let out an ear-piercing shriek. Her constant twitching made her black bangs swing over her fast blinking eyes. It was a little scary and a lot disturbing.

"Are you okay?" I asked her.

Nixie had her head in my lap, twirling the ends of my hair around her fingers. "She's hungry and mobbing you."

"Mobbing me?"

"This is her normal feeding time, and your unexpected visit has her on the defensive. It's her natural instinct to treat you like a predator. She wants you to leave our nest."

"But you're fine with me being here?"

"I think you being here is a good thing." Nixie's shimmering, red hair tickled my legs every time she moved her head. Her sisters intimidated me, but something about her comforted me.

"Why are you so nice to me, but she," I glanced up at Otabia, "seems to hate me."

Nixie's ruby eyes illuminated with joy. "I owe my life to your mother. No other water sprite in all of history has been promoted to a siren. I might have died like the rest of them if she hadn't chosen me as her replacement." The burgundy toenails of her bare foot pointed at Otabia. "She and Mariza have always been sirens. They're just bitter because Cleo chose to leave them and be human."

A white heron had been perched quietly on a windowsill, but squawked obnoxiously when Mariza flew into the room. Her brown wings flapped so hard my hair blew into my face.

Otabia let out another high-pitched shriek. "Useless harpy! I've been calling to you for an hour. Where have you been?"

"Call me a harpy again," Mariza threatened, "and I will pluck all of your feathers out."

Otabia continued circling. Mariza looked me up and down and started blinking fast too. She followed her sister at a slower pace around the room.

"I came here for help," I explained. "I just want answers."

"You want answers?" Otabia hissed. "Fine! I possess them, but you'll have to drink from me to learn the truth."

I swallowed hard.

"You should take her up on it," Nixie said, running her nails along my neck. "She might not offer again."

I promised Treygan I would never drink blood, but when I told the sirens I suspected the merfolk and selkies' plans were wrong, they didn't deny it. If Otabia was offering me a chance to save my life and Treygan's, then wouldn't it be worth drinking a little blood?

"Okay," I muttered.

The heron flew into the room. The torches burst into roaring flames. Nixie shot up from my lap. Mariza and Otabia moved so fast they were a blur of brown and black. Suddenly, all three sisters were within an inch of my face, pupils dilating and heads bobbing while they made clicking noises with their tongues.

Otabia strutted in place and spread her wings, snapping her teeth at Nixie and Mariza until they backed away. "Mine. She's mine, hags. Buzzard off!"

Otabia grabbed my wrists and yanked me to my feet. Her

fingers felt hard and crusty, and her thumb nail pierced my skin. I looked down. Her fingers were talons, curved, ugly and dangerous. Blood trickled down my arm.

Nixie and Mariza sang, their wings quivering. Why did I agree to this? I had a sickening feeling that I might be dead within minutes.

"First, I drink from you." Otabia licked her charcoal lips. "Otherwise I'll be too famished to share."

The other sisters laughed. I figured she was lying, but I was in no position to argue. The pain in my wrists got worse the longer she held onto me. "Fine."

Otabia's wings wrapped around us so fast I didn't have time to see Nixie and Mariza's reaction. We were enclosed in total darkness. The other sisters chirped frantically outside the wall of Otabia's wings, but I focused on her guttural breaths.

"You better share a dreadful memory," she purred. "Sadness, misery, that's what I want from you."

I couldn't see anything. Not her face, her eyes, nothing—only blackness. "How about the night my mother died?"

She loosened her grip on one of my wrists. Her wet tongue eased the burning sensation, but then her teeth sank into my flesh and I cried out in pain. My yelling faded away as she sucked warmth from my wrist and we spun through cold darkness.

I relived the night my mother died.

The stars weren't shining. I was sitting on the porch swing, kicking my small, bare feet back and forth so the swing would keep rocking. Crickets chirped frantically when a wind blew through the palm trees. A pinkish fog crawled closer to me, bending the grass in its path, causing the metal wind chimes to tinkle as the breeze reached the porch. I closed my eyes as it blew over my face, swirling my hair up into the air like it might carry me away. Then it whistled softly, continuing past me through the screen door and into the house.

"Pretty," I said.

The crickets fell silent. I could sense them crouched out in the grass, watching me with their tiny eyes, waiting. A sense of *wrongness* crept over me.

I slid off the swing as slowly as I could, trying not to disturb the eerie silence that had fallen over our yard. I tiptoed to the screen door and peered inside. When I pulled the handle the hinges squeaked so loudly my ears rang.

I held onto the banister and took the first step up the stairs, climbing one inch at a time, hoping if I moved slow enough my fears wouldn't come true. Even as an eight-year-old kid, I knew. Long before I cleared the last step and stared down our hallway to my mother's bedroom, I knew.

A firefly lit up outside the bedroom door. I wondered if the crickets asked it to fly in and watch me since they couldn't see me from the yard. I walked forward, moving at a snail's pace. If I looked behind me I was sure I would see a slimy trail of heartache smeared along the floor.

The firefly lit up again. It was in my mother's room. She would have yelled for me to get rid of it if she was awake, but my mother didn't yell. She didn't stir at all. I stood on the threshold of her room for six swallows. My mouth felt so dry I pretended each gulp contained the cherry Kool-Aid I had drank with dinner at Uncle Lloyd's house. The firefly twinkled. Outside, the crickets stayed silent. A floorboard creaked as I stepped into my mother's room.

She stared ahead, the same way she used to do every night on our back porch. Her eyes were always wide and unblinking, seeing something in the water that I could never see and mumbling about my father. I had asked her what she saw once and she answered, "Heaven."

My uncle had told me Heaven was where people went

when they died, so I figured my father was out in the ocean, in some part of it called Heaven. That's why my mom stared at it so much. Now she was staring at the ceiling the same way, but I knew my father wasn't up there.

My father had to be out in the water waiting for her. I sat on the floor beside her bed for hours, crying, picking at the scabs on my knees, and wondering how I could get my mother to Heaven. Then I had an idea.

I kissed my mother's cool hand, dragged her out of bed, down the steps and out the back door. Through my grunting, I apologized to her every time her legs or arms thwacked against a step or doorway. By the time we reached the old rowboat on the beach, I was dripping sweat and my muscles trembled. The old rowboat was perfect for taking her to see my father. Flowers even grew through the bottom of it.

I struggled for what felt like forever, rolling my mother up over the edge and into the boat. But then a strong wind blew and I was relieved at how easy it was to push the boat into the surf. At first the cold water made me shriek and gasp. There were no paddles, so I held onto the back of the boat and kicked, trusting my mother's word that somewhere out there was Heaven. I would keep swimming until we found it.

By the time I noticed the boat was sinking into the water, I was out too far to turn back. I kept kicking, even as saltwater waves crashed against my face and burned my throat and nose. My feet and hands eventually went numb as water rose over the rim of the boat. The rough wood slipped from my fingers. I clung to my mother's body, too tired to kick anymore. And together we sank below the dark water, hoping to find my father.

Tears were streaming down my cheeks when Otabia blurred back into my sight. She didn't have her wings wrapped around us anymore. Nixie and Mariza stood behind her. They all seemed much calmer and sad.

"Who did you love more," Otabia asked, "your mother or father?"

I sniffed and wiped my face. A lingering drop of blood ran down my arm. "I loved them both."

"Ah, come, child, no need to be so diplomatic with me. You felt a connection with one more than the other. You may have loved them both, but which one would you die for?"

"I don't know. My mother, I guess. If I could've traded places with her the night she died, I would have."

"I see. When your father died so tragically, did you feel the same instinct to protect him?"

"My father died when I was four. I don't remember it."

"He died in a fire. Lungs gave out. Did you know he was a fireman?"

I nodded.

"The occupation says something about his spirit, doesn't it? Brave, heroic, selfless and fearless that man was—your mother's first and one true love. Made me and Mariza sick seeing her so attached to a man. She succumbed to your father's every whim. Dreamed of mortal marriage, a house and children. Quite a debacle, those two were."

I wrapped my arms around myself. "She fell apart after he died because she missed him so much."

"Your mother would have done anything to make your father happy," Mariza said. "Her biggest fear was that someday her perfect hero of a man would see her for the average and weak human she had become. That he would leave her, or find someone he loved more than her."

Otabia swooped closer in one swift move. "Certain moments in time change our course forever. Do you want to know what your parents were truly like? I was there the day you were born. I stood by your mother's bed." She dug her talon into her arm and a line of black blood surfaced. "Drink and relive it for yourself. You'll find the answer you're looking for."

My hands trembled, but I held her arm tight. I thought, over and over, *I'm sorry, Treygan.*

Then my mouth closed over Otabia's bleeding gash.

Her blood tasted like licorice. I cringed after the first swallow, and then in I went, spiraling into Otabia's soul and reliving her memory.

We were in Uncle Lloyd's house. Otabia held my mother's sweaty hand while my uncle, Mariza and Nixie bustled around her. My mother was panting, her eyes looked tired but her face glowed. Sirens were emotionally connected, but besides feeling my mother's emotions, Otabia also knew her thoughts.

She was ecstatic that she was giving my father his dream, confident that having a baby would bond them forever, but relieved that she wouldn't have to keep the child. My father looked worried, pushing the wet hair from my mother's face and coaching her through breathing.

My mother gave one last push. Otabia, Nixie and Mariza all screamed in unison with her, all of them feeling the same pain. With my first cry, Mariza announced I was a girl. She laid me in my mother's arms. My father looked at me, his newborn, and joyful tears filled his eyes.

My mother sensed the change in him. She realized the slimy baby crying between them had become his most important reason for living. Her worst fear had come true.

My father had found someone he loved more than her.

Her jaw tightened, her nostrils flared. She handed me to my father, closed her eyes, and wished I had never been born.

I forced myself out of the memory and stumbled backward, away from Otabia. "Why would you show me that?" My eyes burned, trying to hold back my tears.

"You fool! There is more you must see." She raised her bleeding arm. "Drink."

"No. I don't want to know anymore."

My mother had never been loving, but I had convinced myself it was because of her sick heart, that she missed my father so much she had nothing left to give. My uncle made me believe she had loved me, she just didn't know how to show it. Now I had seen and felt the truth. My mother hated her own child.

Worse than that, the memory revealed another heartbreaking truth. I stared out the open window at the sun trying to peek through rain clouds over a distant island.

"Uncle Lloyd," I muttered, trying to fit all the pieces together. "In the memory, Mariza and Nixie had wings. You were all in siren form. My uncle knows about you. He knows about all of this, doesn't he?"

Nixie glided over to me with drooping wings. "Of course he knows, sweet Yara. Who do you think helped your parents transform into humans? Why else would your mother have brought you back to Eden's Hammock?"

I couldn't find any air to breathe. Rownan being a part of this and lying to me was bad enough, but Uncle Lloyd? The loving man who looked after me and raised me as his own daughter? He was a part of this? Which side had he schemed with? I thought of Rownan visiting the island. Uncle Lloyd never said much about him, but he never forbade me to see him or warned me to be careful of him.

My uncle must have sided with the selkies. Why else would he allow Rownan on his island? The sisters talked at me, but their words evaporated into the faraway clouds. I felt faint.

The only family I had, my uncle, had put on an act this entire time. The man I worried about and prayed for every night was nothing more than the grandmaster of a plan to bleed me dry and hand me over to the gorgons. My whole life everyone I loved had either hated me or deceived me.

Everyone except Treygan.

Wings flapped all around me. Torches roared around the room. I put my hands over my ears to drown out the sirens shrieking.

When I turned around and saw Treygan standing in front of me I almost collapsed. He wrapped his arms around me and I buried my face against his chest.

"Take me someplace safe," I begged him.

 Sunrises became more precious to me with each passing day.

For fourteen years my life had been one constant countdown. It never bothered me until Yara became my love rather than my obligation. At times like these, when her delicate soul leaked through the cracks in her stubborn outer shell, I wondered if I had always loved her. Perhaps my overwhelming instinct to keep her safe had been more than sympathy or an old promise to her mother.

Yara hadn't said a word since we left the nest. She went through the motions of swimming and eating. She even let me help her shower, but she never uttered a sound, never looked at me once. She only stared into the distance—into some world I couldn't currently be a part of. I let her be and didn't push her to tell me what happened.

For hours she had been lying almost comatose on the sofa. I grabbed a white sundress from the supplies Delmar had thoughtfully provided and sat beside her.

"Yara, you should sit outside and get some sun before it sets. It might help you feel better."

She sat up like a robot and stared straight ahead. I studied her stiff profile. She looked defeated, beaten by life or whatever the sirens had told her. Or maybe she thought I had let her down. We had been apart for days. Pango tried to recap important updates, but I could only imagine what must have gone through her head these past few days.

"I didn't want to be separated from you," I said. "It may feel like I abandoned you, but—"

"What?" She turned to look at me.

"I'm sorry. I don't know what thoughts have been torturing you all day, but if I caused any of your sadness, then I promise I'll try to make it up to you."

She blinked. For the first time since the nest it seemed to register that I was with her. "You? No." Her eyes darted to the wall of windows behind me. Then her gaze drifted over our surroundings, taking in the expensive furniture, antique floor vases, Italian marble floors, and the massive living room. "Where are we?"

"A secluded beach house. We can hide out here."

"House? Looks like a mansion."

I looked around too, appreciating the grandeur of the place for the first time. "Delmar likes to overdo things."

She glanced at her terrycloth robe, then at the dress in my hands. "I vaguely remember us showering together."

"You were crying. Hot showers are a comfort to humans. I thought it might help you feel better." Her cheeks blushed. Mine probably did too. "I tried to keep my eyes above your neck."

"Tried?" She ran her fingers through the ends of her hair, inhaled and smiled. "Shampoo."

"And conditioner. Once again, human comforts. I figured—"

She wrapped her arms around me and rested her head against my chest. For a few minutes we just sat there, holding each other.

"Does this mean you forgive me?" I asked.

"Forgive you? For what?" She pulled back to look at me, clutching her robe to her chest.

"Not coming to you sooner."

"There's nothing to forgive. You're here now, that's all that matters."

I ran my hand down her soft cheek, wishing to every god in the heavens that it could be different, that I had a long future ahead of me instead of rapidly dwindling days.

"Is that dress for me?" she asked.

I held it up against my chest. "What makes you think it's for you? Don't you think it would look good on me?"

She laughed, the light in her eyes and voice slowly returning. "I can't imagine you in a dress."

We were still laughing when she stood and dropped her robe to the floor. She raised her arms over her head while I fumbled with the dress, trying not to gawk at her beautiful, naked body. Vivid thoughts of what I wanted to do to her flashed through my mind, but I kept control of myself and slid the dress over her arms and head, pulling it down until it covered her. My hands lingered at her waist. I tugged at the fabric, pretending to smooth away invisible wrinkles.

"So, yellowish white must mean you're blushing," she said.

I felt my embarrassment intensify and her smile grew bigger. God, how I loved to see her smile; it was contagious. "We should get some sun before it's gone for the day."

"Okay."

"Shall we go up on the roof?"

"The roof?"

"When you were fifteen I checked on you and you were

sitting on the roof of your house. I asked Koraline to let me know if you did it again. You did. A lot."

Bewilderment flickered in her eyes. "I did? I don't remember that."

"I want to snap my fingers and return all of your memories to you." In time, most of them would return, but I would never be able to see her that way, whole and sure of herself and her past—or future.

"Right. The memory vacuum thing. Can't Delmar just give them back to me? Isn't there a reverse switch?"

"If it were possible he would have done it already."

"Okay then, to the roof. Maybe it will trigger something."

We walked through the pool room and Yara whistled. "Fancy-schmancy."

Delmar had thought of everything. Half of the pool was inside, but the floor-to-ceiling windows let in plenty of sunlight. We had a place to rest or swim without being spotted by high-flying spies. Not that I worried about the sirens looking for Yara. They were fed up with the situation. But when Jack found out we had run off together, he would come looking for us. If Rownan couldn't shadow me, Jack might myst a rich islander into searching by plane. But we still had a day or two before Jack would find out. No need to stay cooped up until it was necessary.

I stepped out onto the pool deck and Yara followed, searching the exterior of the house.

"Are there steps or a ladder or something?"

"Or something," I confirmed, waving my hand and stirring the water in the pool.

"Oh, right. Can I try operating the water elevator?"

I glanced up. "I don't know. That's a long way to fall if you don't keep it solid."

"You don't have faith in me?"

I sighed inwardly. "Let's go over some basics first."

She cracked her fingers and shook out her hands, preparing for her first lesson in making water bridges. I didn't need to warm up my hands, but I would have them ready in case her first time wasn't perfect.

Her first attempt was almost flawless. She hadn't noticed the gradual lean that would have eventually crashed sideways onto the patio, but when I pointed it out she straightened us quickly and took my directions without any stubbornness.

After a trip back down to get a blanket, then another to get food and drinks, she mastered it and no longer need my help.

"You were right. I do love it up here. The view is incredible." She rolled onto her stomach and rested her chin on my chest. "How come we don't get sunburned?"

"One of the perks of being mer." I lay there, one hand behind my head, the other tracing the vines on her shoulder, trying to ignore the somber sun sinking from the sky.

"I can't do it," she said. "I can't take your memories from you. You have to understand how impossible that would be for me."

I ran my fingers through her hair. "If you don't do it then the selkies will kill you."

"Not if they can't find me."

"Do you think they'll stop hunting us if that gate doesn't open? They'll kill both of us, and I wouldn't blame them at that point."

Her voice quivered. "You're all I have, Treygan. I can't lose you."

"You have friends—Pango, Delmar, Kimber. You have Lloyd."

"He's a liar. My entire life with him has been a lie."

"Who told you that?" She turned away from me, facing the setting sun. A new hallmark of copper wings had formed across her back—the hallmark of a siren. I sighed. "You drank siren blood."

"They promised to show me a way to fix all of this."

"And did they?"

"No. They lied. Just like you said they would."

I scooted forward and wrapped my arms around her. "I'm sorry. I should have been there sooner."

"It's not your fault. Everyone—my parents, the man I called my uncle, Rownan—they all lied to me. You are the one truth in my life, Treygan. You're the only soul in this world I fully trust, and you're telling me I have to help you forget me and leave me forever. How? How am I supposed to do that?"

"You have to be strong."

"You're the strong one."

"I'm strong because of you."

She leaned against me and I inhaled the sweet scent of apple blossoms. I didn't know what else to say. If the roles were reversed, I didn't know if I could do it. My job was the easy one. Yara would be left behind to suffer. I hated myself for putting her in that position.

"My—Lloyd," she said. "He's your father, isn't he? He's the gorgon turned human."

"Yes."

"I want to go see him. I want him to know that I know. I want to ask him how he could act like he loved me and then lie to me for fourteen years."

"He does love you. He stayed out of this battle. He vowed not to take sides. Rownan and I pleaded our cases and he refused us both. We're his sons, but he told us he would have nothing to do with our plans. You can trust him."

She remained quiet. I desperately wished I could hear her thoughts. "Will you go with me?" she asked.

"I'm not letting you out of my sight again until the end of this."

"Don't say that. The end. I hate the way it sounds."

I nodded. "Come on, let's give my father a chance to explain himself. He has earned it."

Seconds after we broke through the water, Lloyd stood at the back door frantically waving us into the house. "Hurry! Hurry!"

"What's wrong?" I asked.

"They've been passing by here searching for you two."

"The selkies?"

He pulled us inside the door and drew the curtains. "Selkies, merfolk, sirens. The only charmed place on the island is this house or within twenty feet of it. But if any merfolk are in the water nearby, they may have sensed you already."

Yara stared at him with her mouth agape. "Look at you. Finally decided to stop pretending you're clueless, huh? You could have protected me from all of this. You could have protected your own son!"

Uncle Lloyd looked hurt for a moment, but then glanced at the ceiling. "Yara, you and I need to talk upstairs. Treygan, you keep a lookout for anyone approaching the house."

"We can talk right here." Yara crossed her arms and sat on the couch.

Lloyd stood up straight. "Something tells me you have a few choice words for me, and I'd rather you say them in private, not in front of my son."

Yara glanced at me and I nodded. He knew Yara's temper. I didn't blame him for wanting to handle the conversation behind closed doors.

She stomped up the stairs and Lloyd followed. At first Yara's shouting was so loud I worried the sirens would be able to hear it from their nest, but after a few minutes the only sounds I heard were their footsteps on the floor above me.

I prayed she would forgive him. Soon they would need each other more than ever.

"**Y**ou can't expect me to believe that!" I shook my head, trying to clear the absurdity out of my mind.

"It's the truth, kiddo," Uncle Lloyd grumbled.

"You're telling me that your failing kidneys and my mother's bad heart were the result of you keeping me away from the gorgons?"

"And your father's lungs too. Stheno and Euryale sent a clear warning. Once we became human we weren't allowed to interfere with underwater politics. We interfered, so we had to face the consequences."

I sat at the foot of the bed beside him. "How could they— how is that possible?"

"The sisters have friends in high places. Poseidon is a god. He gave us life. He can easily take it away or make us suffer."

My anger slowly drained out of me, but more questions rose to the surface. "So, if you aren't on Rownan's side, then why did you let him hang around here? You knew the selkies planned to kill me."

He walked over to my dresser and opened the top drawer. "You're too damn lovable. I knew the closer he got to you, the harder it would be for him to go through with Jack's plan." He handed me my stone necklace. "Here, you dropped this. Found it on the road between our houses. Keep it with you at all times, you hear me?"

I opened the locket and looked at the faded photo of my parents. "You and my father put the eighteen year spell on me. I get why that was bad. But what did my mother do that was so horrible? She *wanted* me to live with the gorgons."

"Where in the worlds did you get that crazy notion? She would have done anything to keep you out of that grotto."

"She hated me. Otabia let me see my birth firsthand. She wished I was never born."

He harrumphed and rubbed his hands over his stubbly chin. "Look, I don't know what Otabia showed you, but Cleo did everything in her heartbroken power to keep you safe. It was her idea to run away from here and hide you. After your father passed, she was afraid she might die too and you would have no one. Then the gorgons would find you and take you anyway. She brought you back here and had Nixie send Indrea to advise her. They met with Treygan, asked him to be your guardian, and planned your transformation perfectly. She knew it was pushing the envelope way too far. She knew it would kill her, but she did it anyway, and she made sure that enough people vowed to look after you once she passed."

I couldn't speak. I just studied my parents smiling up at me from a tiny, faded photo, and wished their love for me wasn't such a faded memory in my heart.

Uncle Lloyd cleared his throat. "I wanted to tell you, but I couldn't. If I meddled, I could have died too. You would have been left alone. You were a child. We all wanted you to have a normal childhood. As normal as it could be, given the circumstances."

"I think she's been trying to tell me something."

"Your mother?"

I nodded. "I've seen and heard her twice since I've been turned."

Uncle Lloyd glanced at the corner of the room, then back at me. "You sure it was her?"

"Who else would it be?"

He scratched at the flaky skin on his arms. He looked worse than ever. "Could have been Liora. She's checked up on you several times. I needed to know you were okay."

248

"Can you talk to her any time you want?"

He grinned. "You used to be the one she communicated with all the time."

"What?" I gasped.

"Since you arrived on this island, she's been watching over you. When you were a kid, your mind was open to seeing and hearing her. She began teaching you, trying to prepare you for the Triple Eighteen hullabaloo. Your experiences with her were removed from your memory when they turned you, but who do you think made you a Yellow?"

My eyes bugged. "Liora made me a Yellow? How?"

"She was a Violet. A damn powerful one at that. Smart too. Blessed be, I loved that woman. She could predict my chess moves ten turns in advance." He glanced at the corner of the room again and smiled. "Liora was there when Delmar turned you. She wanted to make sure nothing went wrong. He couldn't see her, of course, and she was a bit offended that you didn't retain anything she taught you about merfolk, but by then she'd already granted you Yellow status."

"Why Yellow?"

"She knew you'd teach others a thing or two about love and loyalty."

I had so many questions, but I worried the answers would bring my uncle more pain. He was already rubbing his knees like they ached worse than usual. "Could you die for telling me all of this?"

"Maybe. But you're eighteen now. You have a home, a new family. You'll be fine. No matter what happens to me."

The thought of losing him—and the fact that he had been sick all these years because of me—bordered on soul-crushing. Too many people had sacrificed themselves for me. I wasn't worth all this pain and heartache. It had to stop. "Treygan can't take my place. I won't allow it. Tell me what I need to do to live with the gorgon sisters."

He laughed his big, full-belly laugh. "You won't allow it, huh?"

"No. I won't. And I don't understand how you ever could. He's your son."

"Yara, you're forgetting I used to be a gorgon. I know how they think. Treygan could never take Medusa's place. The trinity must consist of all females."

My breath caught in my throat. "Then why did you let Treygan believe it for all these years?"

"He never spoke to me about it. Not one word. He never asked me for my opinion or for help. Probably too worried what would happen if I meddled one more time. He, your mother and Indrea came up with that hogwash plan. Liora said it was the first time Treygan had ever felt like he had a purpose. He could finally help someone instead of hurt them. I stayed out of it so I could live long enough to raise you. Meanwhile, Liora prepared you for what needed to be done."

"But I have no idea what needs to be done."

"Yes you do. Deep down you do. You just took the first step, volunteering to take Medusa's place. That's the most important part of the sacrifice."

"What else do I have to do?" Again, his focus shifted to the corner. The room felt warmer and smaller, like there wasn't enough air for both of us. "Why do you keep looking over there?"

"Liora," he said, but it wasn't a reply. He was speaking to her. "I think now is as good a time as any."

I scanned the room frantically for any sign of light, an orb, anything, but it was just my bedroom. No signs of a spirit anywhere.

Uncle Lloyd stood up. "Come on, ladies, we've gotta do this in my room."

ᒣᒣᒣ

We stood in front of one of Uncle Lloyd's handcrafted wood panels, a mermaid similar to the one downstairs, carved in even more intricate detail. I had a jumbled flashback of talking to a woman in this same spot, but then it was gone.

"How did I never notice before?" I asked. "The mermaid in all your carvings is Liora."

"You don't remember much about these carvings, do you?"

I shook my head.

"Well, then," he coughed and wheezed, leaning against the portrait. "This might seem farfetched, but bear with us. In a minute she'll look very lifelike. Focus on her eyes." He spoke in a language I didn't recognize and seemed to be reciting a poem as he ran his fingers along the crests and ridges that were the mermaid's hair

"I would ask you if this was a joke, but based on the last couple weeks of my life, my gut says you're dead serious."

"You betcha. Liora is about to show you something that no living soul has ever seen. Remember all you can. Save it not just to your memory, but your soul. This is crucial for surviving the Triple Eighteen. I'll explain the rest when you get back. She's gettin' antsy." He said one final sentence in a choppy, foreign language then stepped away from the portrait.

I took a deep breath and stared at the carved, teak eyes in front of me.

When they turned bright amethyst I gasped. I had seen Uncle Lloyd's wife in photos hung throughout the house, but she looked human. Now she was a breathtaking Violet mermaid: blinking, moving and—if I didn't know better—living.

Clouds passed over her eyes, and my chest was tugged forward before I could deny what was happening.

I was Liora, standing in front of a waterfall. But unlike my

experiences with Treygan, I could separate myself from Liora, even though I was living the experience as her. Just like I did with Otabia.

A shimmering, multi-colored waterfall roared in front of me, the top lost from view. The water whispered poetry.

"All you have to do is pass through it," said an angelic voice.

As hard as it was to pull her focus away from the gorgeous falls, Liora turned to look at the speaker.

The woman glowed bright as the sun. She had flowering vines for hair. Her skin matched the shimmering waterfall with swirling shades of pink, lavender, periwinkle, chartreuse and goldenrod. She smiled, and Liora thought of a pale crescent moon on a summer evening—one of those rare occurrences when the sun and moon are visible in the sky at the same time.

Liora knew she had reached the place between life and death. She knew who the woman was, and what the iridescent wall of water was.

"It is glorious through there," Medusa said. "No pain, no hate, only love and beauty."

Liora looked behind us and saw an angry sky. Red lighting flashed over brown, muddy clouds. Moss-colored waves rose and crashed out of a threatening sea. A seagull shot out of the water, strangled by plastic six-pack rings. He flopped on the ground near her feet, eyes bulging, feathers slick with oil.

Liora's gaze drifted from the stricken bird to her silver belly covered with amethyst hallmarks. A barren feeling washed over her, but she wasn't sure why. Half of her body was mer, the other half human, separated vertically but blending together in a seamless way.

She picked up the seagull and lifted him into the waterfall. It parted like a curtain and the water sucked him through. On the other side his eyes instantly returned to normal and the plastic dissolved. He gave a joyful cry and flew off on strong, healthy wings.

"So simple," Liora said.

"So simple," Medusa repeated.

Standing at the waterfall, Liora didn't see her life flash before her eyes. The people she left behind didn't weigh heavily on her mind. Life and all the people she knew were like a tiny thread brushing against her cheek while the rest of her was wrapped in luxurious, warm blankets of peace, love and happiness. The tiny thread could have easily gone unnoticed, but she felt it, mentally grabbed the end of it and held on tight.

"My baby and husband," Liora said to Medusa. "I can't go yet."

"Others will look after them."

"My son turned me to stone. You cursed him to punish me. He will never live a normal life."

"I do not curse my children. You chose this path. You chose to love a gorgon."

"We have no control over who we love. You of all souls learned that to be true." Liora pointed at the waterfall. "That is your heaven. You had the love and foresight to create an afterlife for all of your children. Let me do my part in making sure my son will be alright."

They both glanced at the raging, angry storm behind us.

Medusa folded her hands in front of her. "I do not have the ability to send you back."

Defeated, Liora spun in circles, alternating visions of the luminous waterfall and the turbulent sea. Light, dark, then light again. She knew there had to be a way to communicate with Lloyd and protect Treygan.

"Angels," she murmured. "Humans have angels. Do we have that also?"

Medusa's crescent moon smile appeared on her glowing

face. She walked in front of Liora, turning her back to the waterfall. At first Liora searched Medusa's star-filled eyes, waiting for an answer, but then she saw something behind her. Subtle outlines of faces and bodies flitted through the water. Liora knew they were souls who hadn't entirely passed through to the other side.

"The Inbetween is much harder than life or death," Medusa warned.

"But they do it, don't they? They find a way to communicate and help the living."

"Some do."

"I choose to be an angel," Liora said firmly.

"Are you certain, Liora?"

"Yes. I will find a way to provide a good life for my son if it kills me." She laughed at her ironic last words as a wave swept us into the waterfall.

"Oh, my gosh," I gasped, stumbling on the floor of my uncle's bedroom. My skin felt heavy and foreign to me. The wood panel had returned to normal, but I couldn't stop staring at it.

"I can only imagine." Lloyd sat on his bed and sighed. "Yara, do you want to open the gate?"

"Of course," I said, still shocked by what I experienced.

"You're willing to take Medusa's place?"

Images of a dark grotto surrounded by a red, raging sea terrified me, but everyone would go home. Hundreds of lives would be spared. I nodded.

"If there was a way for you and Treygan to be together in the end, would you be willing to do anything—no matter how scary or crazy it seemed?"

My heart beat so hard it pulsed in my fingers and toes. Could Treygan and I really be together? "Yes. I'll do anything!"

He took a deep breath and looked at the empty space beside

him. "Was it enough? Are you sure she'll remember when the time comes?"

He was asking Liora. I couldn't hear her reply, but what did her memory have to do with me opening the gate?

"Alright, then," Uncle Lloyd said. "Listen carefully. Liora has a plan. We raised you to be strong, smart, and to fight for what you want. Let's hope we did a thorough job."

day 14

Treygan and I had been hiding out for three days.

At night we rested together in the pool. During the day we would talk, tell stories, laugh, watch movies, play games, practice my abilities and push the boundaries of physically enjoying each other.

Most of the time we only touched or caressed each other, but several times he let me kiss his neck, shoulders and chest. His lips were off limits, which made me crave them that much more. Twice I tried sneaking my mouth close to his, but he stayed in control—which drove me nuts because I never felt in control.

We played a game where we wrote words and messages on each other's skin with our fingers. Actually, it was my game. He just played along, sometimes rather reluctantly, until I made moaning noises. Then he would write out long sentences that started at my neck and ended at my toes. I never translated any of those. My mind was mush by the time he got halfway through.

I had never felt closer to anyone in all my life, but I wasn't allowed to tell Treygan about the plan. I couldn't even tell him what Uncle Lloyd and I had talked about because I worried sharing any details would lead to more questions. Questions that might reveal a truth I needed to keep hidden from him.

Treygan had asked several times—in a nonintrusive way—if it went well, if Lloyd explained himself, if I was still angry, if I trusted him again. Uncle Lloyd advised me to put everything in the form of a question since I couldn't lie.

"If I didn't trust him, why would I agree to let you cast his spell on the house?" I looked around the living room, but it didn't seem any different. "Do you think it worked?"

"No idea," Treygan shrugged. "I never had my father's flare for spells. Let's hope I did it right."

"You've known you had the ability to cast spells, but you never tried to use it?"

"My whole life I have fought using my gorgon abilities. If I could remove that part of my soul, I would."

"Is that possible?"

"No. Even Lloyd, who became a human, still has gorgon in him. It's in my veins, my muscles, my skin, and hidden away in my soul. There's no way to remove all of it." He paused. "We need to practice."

I groaned and looked away. We didn't need to practice, but I couldn't tell him that.

He lifted my chin. "Are you getting bored of my memories?"

"Of course not. I just hate that you still expect me to take them from you."

"You have to, Yara."

"You keep saying that." I shuddered. "But I can feel when it hurts you."

He wrapped his arms around me, purposefully breathing against my neck. "Afterward, I'll write on your body for as long as you want. An entire novel."

We had moved into our bartering stage. He could always

convince me to practice by making me melt physically. I wanted to say no, but he had a hypnotic effect on me that left me defenseless.

"Fine, but you know I hate this. After I've successfully taken one, I'm done until the Triple Eighteen."

"Deal."

He sat on the floor and I crawled onto his lap. It was my favorite part, the calm before the storm, the silent moment before his eyes clouded over. He knew it too, so each time he waited a little longer, holding me, staring at me. No noise between us except our breath. The urge to kiss him suffocated me. Every cell of my skin screamed for his lips, but my urges had to go unfulfilled. That was the worst part.

"Follow your desire until the end," Treygan said, "until your thirst is satisfied."

He and I had very different ideas about what I desired. "Mm-hmm. Just get on with it."

Silver and blue clouds passed over his eyes. Our souls became one.

It was the day that changed Kimber's life. She was a Red, and looked like she couldn't have been more than twelve. A lollipop stick stuck out from between her pink lips. If I hadn't been living the moment as Treygan, I would have laughed at everyone gathered around a spinning glass bottle. I had seen the game in a movie before. What a ridiculous way to get someone to kiss you.

Treygan thought so too. When the bottle pointed at him he didn't get nervous or excited. He felt sick. He glanced at Delmar, who looked cute and scrawny as a young kid with red hair.

Treygan got to his knees and crawled to the middle of the circle. The rest of the kids giggled or made teasing comments.

Kimber's skin flushed with blue as she pulled her pink lollipop out of her mouth and crawled toward Treygan.

For a split second I was back in my body, staring at the constellation of freckles on Treygan's cheek, but I dove back into the clouds in his eyes, remembering his promise. If I succeeded at taking this memory from him, I would never have to try again. This one made him sad. He would be better off not remembering it.

Treygan's lips pressed against Kimber's, but something felt off. I wasn't fully in the memory. I flashed back and forth between remembering the past as Treygan and me sitting in present-day Treygan's lap. Back and forth, over and over. It was so disorienting.

Jealousy and need swept through me like a tidal wave. I couldn't believe how hard it was to stay in control, or to even stay in Treygan's memory. As Treygan, I felt Kimber's lips turn to stone and heard a kid shouting. Then I was me again, feeling warmth against my lips and flesh between my teeth.

"Yara!" The panic in Treygan's voice snapped me fully back into my own body and I gasped, sliding my clenched teeth from his bottom lip. "Spit it out! Spit! Now!"

Blood and saliva spewed from my mouth onto the floor. Treygan wiped frantically at my lips. He had already thrown me off his lap and scrambled to his feet. "Keep spitting! *Do not* swallow. I'm getting you water."

He ran to the kitchen while I crawled to my hands and knees. My head spun. The gold veins in the marble tiles kept blurring. What made me bite into his lip like that? He had taught me how to consume mentally without drawing blood. Why did I bite him?

He forced me to sit up, holding a glass to my face. "Rinse

and spit. God, Yara, you can't swallow my blood. Please don't swallow any of it."

I did what he said, taking a sip and swishing it around my mouth. I looked around with my cheeks full of water.

"Just spit! We'll clean it up later."

I spit it into a nearby vase. After another rinse I spit again and looked at Treygan, my hands shaking. "What the hell was that?"

"Your thirst for blood kicked in too strongly. Sirens can drink gorgon blood without it hurting them, but I don't know how it would work with you being a mermaid. We can't risk it."

"Oh, my God, look what I did to you!" I had practically torn a hole through his lip. Blood was dripping down his chin.

"I'll be fine. Are you okay?" He held my face, examining me. "Open your mouth."

"Nothing happened. I would know if part of me turned to stone."

He looked in my mouth anyway, making me feel like a strep throat patient.

"I don't get it," he said. "My emotions were way too intense when you bit me. My blood and saliva were in your mouth. I don't understand how I didn't petrify any part of you."

"Maybe I'm immune like the sirens." I puckered my lips and batted my eyes. "Kiss me and we'll find out."

He rubbed his thumbs over my cheeks. "Don't joke about that."

Joking was all I could do. Not telling him the truth, hurting his lip and making him worry made me sick with guilt. "This consuming memories thing is never gonna happen."

"It has to." He dropped his hands from my face.

That simple action always stung. I had a few precious days left with him. Every time he stopped touching me—or looked away from me, or left a room—I got a sneak preview of the future. A future where we might not be together. What if Lloyd's absurd plan failed? I needed to know how Treygan felt about the ghost thing, but I had to word it right.

"Promise me something," I said.

"If I can."

"Promise me that if this insane plan kills you, you'll come back and haunt me. None of that walking toward the light, or moving on because you think it will be good for me. That's crap. I want you forever. Even if it's just your ghost."

"That's no way to live, Yara." He used a kitchen towel to wipe the blood off his face.

"What if it was reversed? Would you want me to stay here with you?"

"This is a pointless discussion. I'll be a gorgon, I won't be dead."

He wasn't taking the bait. I would have to ask outright. "What if I died? Would you want me to haunt you?"

"I don't think that's something we get to choose."

I wanted to tell him about his mother and Uncle Lloyd, and about the waterfall, but they made me promise not to. "I believe it's possible, so please, humor me and answer the question."

"What was the question?"

I shoved his shoulder. "Would you want me to haunt you?"

He pulled me onto his lap, raking his fingers through my hair and sending warm waves rippling over me. "I think your real question is do I want you forever. Yes, I do. If I could change all of this and you and I could be together, I would. But if you died, I don't know what I would want. Now that I know what it's like to have you, existing without you wouldn't be living." His hand glided to my shoulder, tracing the neckline of my dress. "I couldn't do *this* with your ghost."

His touch lit up my skin with flames of mind-numbing pleasure. I didn't ever want him to stop.

"You're my Yamabuki," he whispered. "You're tough. You'll survive this."

Strong, steel-willed, refused to take no for an answer: Uncle Lloyd said I naturally possessed those qualities, and because of that he believed our secret plan would work. If he was so certain, then why couldn't I tell Treygan? Why did I have to keep such vital information from him? I flexed my biceps like a bodybuilder. "Yeah, I'm tough. That's what Uncle Lloyd said."

Treygan kissed my arms. "You should listen to him. He knows what he's talking about."

I hoped with all my heart and soul that was true.

day 17

Rownan

I had spent the last few nights locked in the basement of the bar. Lack of moonlight would have been bad enough, but Jack meant business. Each day the torture got worse.

   The steel door swung open, waking me from an imaginary nightmare and throwing me back into my real one.

"You ready to start talking yet?" Jack asked.

I lowered my head, too weak to hold it up anymore. He yanked me to my feet and dragged me down the corridor, through the dark, empty bar, and up the stairs. He kicked open the door and shoved me out onto the roof. Out into the blazing sun. Same routine as yesterday.

I already knew what awaited me. Handcuffs dangled from a chain padlocked to the thick pipe connecting the main AC handler to the rest of the units. My coat was spread out over a metal box a few feet away from me.

Jack didn't need to tell me to sit. I collapsed to my knees. He pulled the chain to me and snapped the cuffs on my wrists. The heat bordered on sweltering. My thirst got worse with each passing minute, but Jack wouldn't push it so far as to kill me—least I hoped not—so I suffered.

He lit up a seag and bent down, blowing a cloud of cold smoke into my face. I tried to inhale whatever I could, but my lungs felt like they had melted out of my chest.

"Rownan, this is the stupidest thing you've ever done. Just tell me where they are."

I had stopped answering him yesterday when the sun fried my brain and my thoughts went all scrambled. I didn't even bother grunting anymore.

"You traitor. You're willing to die so that mongrel brother of yours can hide away and play house with that harpy?"

Mongrel. It must have slipped his mind that I was a mongrel too.

"Thought I taught you better than this," he spat. "I thought you were loyal to our kind."

I am. God dammit, I am.

Dina walked over with a frosted mug of blood and squatted down beside me. "Tell him where they are so you can drink it. I hate having to do this."

I leaned my head against the hot metal casing of the AC handler and closed my eyes. The first day my mouth watered so badly that I drooled all over myself. Today I had nothing left. My mouth was drier than the Mojave.

"Set it down over there," Jack said, as if Dina hadn't gone through this same drill numerous times yesterday. She knew she had to leave it out of my reach, and we both knew what came next. "Drink from him."

"Jack, he's white as a clam. I don't think—"

"Do it!"

She took my arm in her hands. I didn't open my eyes. "I'm sorry, Rownan."

Her claw tearing through my skin didn't hurt. My soul being shared with someone other than Vienna was the agonizing part. I don't know how long she drank from me. I tried to block out everything: the pain, the heat, the thirst. One more day. I only had to survive one more day.

Jack shouted threats and orders above me, but in my daze of half-consciousness none of it made sense. Dina held her bleeding arm in front of me, pressing the warm liquid to my lips. Part of me wanted to open my mouth, latch onto her and suck her dry, but I pictured Vienna's angelic smile and forced my teeth and lips to stay clenched together.

Eventually Jack mumbled something and they both walked away. I toppled over, face down on the hot concrete. The metal biting into my wrists didn't hurt as badly as yesterday. The whirling roar of the AC units kicking on and off, the rattling of steel casings and the screeching of fan belts all blended into a satanic lullaby. Fans blew warm air around me, strangling me and burning my lungs.

I refused to look at my coat. Thoughts of icy water, Vienna's cool and exhilarating kiss and our long future together in Rathe swirled through my cloudy mind. I focused on the sun until it burned my eyes. Finally, it faded from blazing orange to black, just like the end of a burning seagarette.

I woke up from my haze of horror to the fluttering of wings and thought maybe I was dead. An angel stood above me, wings extended high at her sides. Light formed a halo around her entire body.

"You stubborn bastard." Nope, not an angel. Just Nixie, silhouetted by the sun and looking down at me like I was some helpless creature at her boots. Which I was. "Why the hell are *you* protecting them?"

I couldn't tell anyone about the plan. I hardly understood it myself, but if it worked the way Lloyd swore it would then I could endure any amount of suffering. My spirit lifted a tad when I thought Nixie might be there to help me. She could uncuff me, give me my coat, and fly me to the water.

Ah, water. The thought of it stirred hope inside of me. But my luck wasn't that good.

Jack appeared behind her, smoking through his gap-toothed grin. "Nixie agrees with me. Your plan to give Treygan and Yara time together was idiotic, but you succeeded. Time's up. Where is she?"

I couldn't remember how many days had passed. Was their time up? Could the sun dissolving over the roofline be the Triple Eighteen? I tried to speak, but my mouth wouldn't open.

Jack bent down and flicked ashes on me. "I'm done with this game. Drink that blood and tell me where the girl is or Nixie will start snatching away your memories of Vienna one by one 'til there's nothing left."

The rest of my body had shut down, but my pulse pounded in every part of me. "No!" I barely gasped.

"Well, looky there," Jack laughed. "*That* got a reaction out of him. Wish I'd thought of that threat earlier."

"I still get a song, Jack. You promised." Nixie's high heeled boots clicked against the concrete and she squatted down in front of me. "Guess those panicked eyes mean you're agreeing to drink."

Did I imagine her words? Lloyd couldn't have predicted every step of this so accurately. Yet here we were, right on schedule, the players reciting their lines almost verbatim.

"Yeah, yeah," Jack said. "As soon as he's out of his vegetative state you can have your soul cocktail." Jack yanked me up by my hair and raised a glass to my mouth. I used what little strength I had to open my lips and catch the blood he poured. "Start talking."

As I sipped and gulped from the glass, Dina covered me with my coat. The blanket of cold had never felt so good.

"I didn't shadow him," I said in a weak whisper. "But I can. After I get my strength back."

"Tonight you'll sleep in the moonlight and recover. Tomorrow you track that worthless brother of yours, we take the girl, and we all go home."

I nodded and kept drinking.

"It didn't need to be this hard, Rownan." Jack used my neck to put out his seagarette. I grimaced at the searing pain as he flicked the butt into my mug. "Nixie, take him to the pool next door. It's frosted. Dunk him then take whatever memory you want."

Nixie grinned at me and licked her lips.

No, Nix, I thought. *I already have a song picked out for you; a long conversation between me and my father.*

Lloyd had been right. This plan could actually work.

 I had watched my last sunset.

I stood in the doorway to the back deck, gazing past the pool at the ocean. Yara moved slowly down the steps and tiptoed through the house. I sensed her movements, but had no idea why she was being so sneaky. I didn't bother turning around when she crept up behind me. I trusted her too much to suspect anything.

She whacked me over the back of the head.

I stumbled forward and turned around to see her giggling and holding a pillow in each hand.

"What was that for?" I rubbed the back of my neck—even though it didn't hurt.

"Let's fight." She tossed me one of the pillows.

"You want us to pillow fight? May I ask why?"

"My wings hallmark got me thinking about feathers. I

remembered one of my favorite scenes from an old movie, *Almost Angels*. Have you seen it?"

"No."

"There's this scene where a bunch of choir boys are getting ready to go to bed and one turns on a radio even though it's lights out and he knows they could get in trouble. The boys start dancing to the music, and then someone starts a pillow fight. They're all laughing and smacking each other with pillows while feathers fly everywhere. They know they could get caught and be punished, but they don't care. They just go crazy and have fun. After watching that I always wanted to pillow fight with someone, but I didn't have any friends and smacking my uncle with a pillow never seemed like a good idea."

"But smacking me with one does?"

She smiled like a mischievous dolphin and nodded.

"Seems a bit childish." I dropped the pillow at my feet and walked past her to the stairway.

"Come on. Don't be so serious all the time." I was halfway up the stairs when she called out behind me, "Just because you're twice my age doesn't mean you have to act like an old fuddy-duddy!"

"I'm a baby according to the sea monster aging scale," I shouted back.

When I came back downstairs she was in the pool room. I hit the power button on the stereo and lively jazz music hummed through the house. I tore a small hole in each of the pillows I had grabbed from upstairs and tossed two to her. Her pout changed into a dazzling grin.

"A *real* pillow fight requires at least two bundles of feathers each." I held my two pillows out at my sides. "This will get messy."

"The messier the better."

I let her take the first swing. Simultaneous hits on my hip

and shoulder caused a few feathers to fly through the air. She watched them, giggling like a child. She was looking up, so I didn't miss the opportunity to smack her in the stomach.

She must have had serious aggression bottled up, because she was relentless, smacking me nonstop. More feathers danced around us. I had never seen her laugh so hard, and it made me laugh too. It didn't take long for her pillows to become flat and droopy. My eyes lit up with playful revenge.

She half-screamed a "nooo" through her laughing fit and ran away.

"Payback time," I said, chasing her around the pool.

She turned and attempted to hit me with one of her limp pillowcases. Then she slowed down and dropped her weapons, putting her hands out in front of her. "You can't *really* hit me, I'm a girl."

I raised my pillows. "No, you're a relentless Yamabuki."

She pushed against my chest, keeping me at bay as she stepped backward. I kept moving forward, matching her step for step.

"Okay, okay, how about we make a deal?" she pleaded.

I shook my head and cocked my arm back to administer a severe pillow lashing. "No more deals. You're mine."

We were both so caught up in the moment that neither of us realized how close we had strayed to the pool. Yara took one last step backward. In that split second her eyes widened and her arms flew up. I tried to grab her, but it was too late. She splashed into the pool, feathers flying all around her.

She broke through the surface, coughing and spitting up water and laughing hysterically. She sifted wet feathers through her fingers. "A pillow fight in water. How appropriate for two sea monsters."

I ripped open one of my pillows and flung its feathers into the air. Yara twirled around, trying to catch them while I dove in.

My eyes stung from the chlorine. I expected to grab her

feet, but found her fins instead and pulled her back under. In an instant her tail transformed to legs and she wrapped them around me as we floated back to the surface.

"Thank you," I said, wiping water from her face.

She pulled herself closer and squeezed her thighs tight around my hips. "For what?"

"For the best times of my life."

"Thank you for granting my wish for a pillow fight."

"If it were up to me, I would grant every wish you ever made."

Her smile faded and her legs loosened. She threw her head back and stared at the dark sky.

"Hey," I said, squeezing her waist. "Where'd you go?"

She looked at me and sighed. "Why didn't you wish me anything?"

"What?"

"The day of my welcoming celebration, everyone but you gave me a gift and wished me something."

"I did give you a gift."

"No, you didn't."

I pulled her arm from around my neck and put it between us, nodding at her arm band.

"That's your gift to me?" She snorted. "What does it represent? A long life of C-weed smoking?"

"Did you look inside?"

"Yeah, three joints. Thanks."

I brushed my lips against her wrist. "You didn't find the real gift?"

She looked down at her armband. "There was something else?"

I flipped the top of the fabric down and unzipped the tiny, hidden compartment. "In there."

"I didn't know it had another pouch." She dug her fingers inside and pulled out the pearl. "Wow. It's … incredible."

"It's an agape pearl—the rarest in the worlds. I've only heard of one other in existence."

"It looks like a diamond, or a crystal mirror. Where did you find it?"

"In a strange-looking oyster at the gateway to our realm. When you hold it up to sunlight you'll see every color of the spectrum. Legend says Poseidon gave one to Medusa. It represents the highest form of love: pure, self-sacrificing, and eternal. Every time you look at it, I want you to know—" I looked away, focusing on the patio chairs around the pool. My emotions were too intense.

Over the past few days Yara had learned not to force me to look at her. I had to keep my feelings under control.

"Your skin is turning back to normal," she said. "It's okay."

I shifted my gaze to the wet feathers floating between us. "I want you to know I would do anything to keep you safe. That's my wish for you, that you live a long, happy life. Full of freedom, sunshine, laughter and love."

"You give me all that stuff."

A massive lump formed in my throat. "I want you to find love again … after I'm gone. You deserve kisses, a husband, kids if you want them and—"

"Stop it. I just want to enjoy this moment. This. Us. Right now. No thinking about the future. We still have tonight and tomorrow night to be together."

The realization hit me like a torpedo to my chest. How could I have forgotten to explain the lie about her birthday?

"What's wrong?" she asked. "I don't like the look on your face, or the green and blue covering your skin."

"Yara, your mother led everyone to believe your birthday was a day later than it actually is. She arranged it that way so I could turn you before the selkies."

She stared at me, unblinking, letting the information sink

in. Her jaw went slack. "You mean, *tonight* is our last night together?"

I tucked her head under my chin, hugging her close. "I'm so sorry."

She squeezed her legs and arms around me tighter than ever. We floated there in silence, clinging to each other. Clinging to an impossible hope that the night would never end.

day 18

I wanted to stop the sunlight from sneaking through the curtains. Forget controlling water, I needed the ability to freeze time. Treygan and I had moved into the master bedroom around three a.m. so we could curl up in bed together. Pretend for a while that it wasn't all coming to an end today.

Treygan spooned up against me. "For the first time in my life I'm sad to see sunlight."

I looked over my shoulder at him. "Do you really believe that by the time the sun sets today, we won't be together anymore?"

"Yes, but it doesn't change the fact that all of it happened." He nuzzled my neck. "If I could make it all end differently, I would."

"Do you think if we were normal, if you were *just* a merman and I was *just* a mermaid, that you would still love me?" The mattress bounced as he quietly laughed, so I reached around and pinched him. "What's so funny?"

"A few weeks ago you thought our kind were anything but normal. And it's a ridiculous question."

"What's so ridiculous about it?"

"Never mind." He brushed his dry, warm lips against my shoulder. "But yes, I would love you if you were 'normal.'"

I rolled over to face him. "What if you only feel that way because of what I represent? I'm the key that opens the gateway to your world. To you that's the most important thing. That's the *only* thing. You're feelings for me could be based on what I might be able to do, not who I am."

"You're right, you are the key." He ran his fingers along my cheek. "You've unlocked something in me I never thought I would feel. Something Delmar has described to me for decades. I never believed the emotions he talked about were real—until you. Now *you* are the most important thing to me. You opened something inside of *me*, not the gate."

I couldn't hold back my smile. "You said you weren't romantic."

"I'm not."

"That was romantic."

He blushed. "Yeah, well, you bring out all sorts of silliness in me."

Beams of sunlight spilled across his muscles and hallmarks. His messy hair was spiked up in sexy chaos. His constellation of freckles seemed to twinkle on his cheek. I couldn't imagine never looking at him again.

"What are you doing?" he asked.

"Memorizing you."

"I like it better when you memorize me with your lips."

I kissed each of his eyelids, his forehead and his nose. With my finger I wrote, *I love you,* starting under his anchor hallmark and ending just below his stomach. He propped himself up on one elbow and whispered to me to lie flat on my back. So I did.

He leaned toward the foot of the bed. Starting at my toes, with his fingertip he wrote, *Once upon a time,* up the entire length of my legs. Then he slowly unbuttoned the front of my sundress. I forgot about the Triple Eighteen, the gorgons, the gate and everything else. I almost forgot my own name as Treygan used my entire body to write out what he believed would be our last chapter.

Hours later, we were stretched out on the sofa together. Treygan told me stories about Rathe, his grandmother, what Delmar and Kimber were like as kids. He even told me stories about his father.

I ran my fingers through his hair. "Is it weird for you to hear me call him my uncle since we aren't related?"

"He's been there for you since you were born. I wouldn't be surprised if you called him Dad." He stared at the ceiling for a minute and smirked. "He would've loved walking you down the aisle."

"You would ask me to marry you?"

He pressed his forehead against mine. "Definitely. You would have made the most beautiful bride the worlds have ever seen."

Treygan's head snapped up. He cocked his head like he was listening for something. I could feel his heart pounding in his chest. He jumped to his feet.

"What?" I asked.

"Motorcycles. Lots of them."

My heart pulsed in my throat. The mansion we were staying in sat at the end of a five mile dirt road. Delmar said no one would ever find us here. "Do you think it's the homeowners?"

"No, Yara." His face tensed so tightly I thought it might crack. "It's the selkies."

My stomach plummeted to my feet. The knock at the door caused both of us to jump.

"Stay here," Treygan ordered.

I sensed my uncle as if he stood in the room with us. "It's Uncle Lloyd. He told me he was coming here today at five. It's a quarter of." Time had slipped away from me. I hadn't said everything I needed to say to Treygan.

He glanced down the hallway leading to the front door. "Better yet, stay directly behind me. Just in case."

"In case what?"

He pulled me to my feet. "Please, just trust me."

When we got to the door Treygan looked through the peephole and swore under his breath.

"Treygan," Uncle Lloyd shouted through the door. "Let us in. Rownan is here to help."

"Sharkshit," Treygan yelled back. "You led them here!"

"I swear on Vienna's soul, we didn't," Rownan said. "We don't have much time. Jack and the rest of them will be here in minutes."

Treygan threw the door open and Lloyd and Rownan rushed inside. For the few seconds the door was ajar, I heard the rumbling of motorcycles in the distance.

Rownan secured the deadbolt. "I know it's hard to believe me, but I swear I've kept them away as long as I could. I met with Delmar and told him you needed back-up. I turned on my own kind to help with this plan."

"What plan?" Treygan asked through grinding teeth.

Uncle Lloyd limped to my side and held my hand. "Treygan, we don't have much time. Rownan told Jack he'd come here, get you to trust him, and then drug you. They wanted you unconscious so you couldn't turn anyone to stone when they came to take Yara away."

Treygan pulled me away from my uncle and began to say something, but Uncle Lloyd raised his hand. "Of course none of that is going to happen, but we need to act quickly. The sirens are on their way here. They'll fly you to the gate."

I could imagine the bewilderment on my face. That wasn't

part of the plan we discussed. Rownan half-winked at me. Did Lloyd really trust Rownan? Could *I* really trust Rownan? Should I have even trusted Uncle Lloyd?

"Sirens don't want the gate opened," I argued. "What if they don't show up?"

"They'll show," Uncle Lloyd said.

Treygan's arm tightened around my waist His ears perked up again, but this time he almost looked relieved. "They're coming, Yara. Can you hear it?"

He pulled me through the living room and threw open the patio doors. The motorcycles were louder, but somewhere in the distance was the faint humming of jet skis. Goosebumps spread up my arms. I searched the far-reaching ocean but saw nothing except the whitecaps of waves. Treygan held me tight, his heart pounding against my back as we squinted at the horizon.

The first few merfolk broke through the pink and orange mist. They stretched across the water, growing in numbers and coming closer by the second. The sound of engines got louder as more and more appeared. There had to be dozens of them.

I choked up. "They came."

"I told you," Rownan said, standing beside us.

The motorcycles were pulling into the driveway. One by one we heard each engine shut off. Any hope I had evaporated.

Sweat dripped down my back. "They're already here. The merfolk won't make it."

"They'll make it," Treygan promised, letting go of me.

He walked out onto the deck. With open palms, he lifted his hands at his sides. His shoulders expanded as he took a massively deep breath. The ocean quivered like an earthquake shook beneath it. Treygan's back muscles rippled and veins bulged in his neck. He groaned, deep and loud, throwing his arms forward. The foamy surf ebbed back into the ocean, leaving nothing but miles of wet sand in its wake. Treygan lifted his arms higher. In the distance, enormous waves crested behind the mob of jet skiing merfolk. His groaning turned into a roar as he threw his arms backward. The waves rushed forward, pushing the merfolk toward the coastline so much faster than they had traveled just seconds before.

I envied his power, but I was so proud and grateful to have his love.

He dropped his hands and pressed his damp forehead against mine. "Nixie will be here soon to take us to the gate."

I wiped the sweat from his face. "But you said to never trust the sirens."

The jet skis poured onto the beach. I watched Pango, Merrick, Delmar, Kimber and many more merfolk raise individual waves from the ocean, surfing barefoot all the way onto the pool deck. Some ran into the house, others circled the perimeter. No one said a word. A dozen ran inside, spreading throughout the house and standing guard at every window and door.

Delmar circled back through the kitchen and smiled at us. "A few were against this plan, but we still outnumber the selkies by twenty or more." He kissed my hand before running toward the front door. "Consider us invincible."

Treygan's grip on me relaxed. Invincible. Uncle Lloyd always said there was no such thing, to never let your guard down.

"Yara, where's your necklace?" Uncle Lloyd asked.

"In my arm band."

"Give it to me."

"What necklace?" Treygan glanced between us. "What's going on?"

I handed the stone locket to Uncle Lloyd and he shoved it in his pocket.

"I gave her a necklace with good gorgon blood in it. In case you slipped up."

My mouth dropped open. The red veins in the pendant were blood?

"Why didn't you tell me she has been protected this whole time?" Treygan's eyes wandered suspiciously between me, Uncle Lloyd and Rownan. "Why are you taking it back?"

Nixie landed outside by the pool. Her boots clicked against the tile as she strolled inside. "All these adoring fans, and no one laid out a red carpet for me?" She grabbed my hips and pulled me against her. "Oh, that's right. This is *your* big premier. Isn't it thrilling? All these people fighting for you?"

"Not really." I tried pushing her away, but her strength was inhuman.

Mariza and Otabia fluttered onto the deck, crouching in the doorway and clicking their tongues.

Nixie assessed Rownan and Treygan standing together. "Rownan," Nixie purred, "don't you and I need to switch places?"

Treygan glanced around in a moment of confusion. From the corner of my eye, I saw my uncle nod.

It all happened so fast.

Nixie blurred across the room, grabbing Treygan from behind. Rownan did the same to me, pinning my arms behind me.

Treygan thrashed, yanking against Nixie's grip. "No! Get off of her!"

Uncle Lloyd looked concerned but not surprised, so I didn't struggle. This had to be part of the plan. He turned his back to us, pulling a small, metal case from his back pocket. Treygan kept shouting, threatening everyone, yelling my name, calling for Delmar.

"Calm down, son," Uncle Lloyd said gruffly. "You can't turn me or Rownan to stone, and the sirens are protected too. You're only risking Yara's safety by letting your temper rage." He opened his case and the silver tip of a needle glistened in the light. The blue liquid filling the syringe almost looked black.

He plunged the needle into my chest so fast I never saw it coming.

"Nooo!" Treygan's scream echoed through the high ceilings.

Fire ripped through my heart, spreading through every vein and capillary. I screamed, long and loud, until my throat felt like it had had been sliced with razor blades and my voice finally gave out.

Uncle Lloyd kissed the top of my head. "I'm sorry, kiddo. I hate that it had to be this way." He kept speaking in a hushed voice. "I thought we'd have more time. I couldn't risk it. Not with the selkies pounding down the door."

The room became tinted in shades of blue, then red. My eyes blazed. The flashing colors sent me into a dry-heaving fit. Treygan's screaming and the high-pitched squawking of the sirens made my ears feel like they were bleeding. My knees felt like icicles melting out from under me. Rownan released his grip and I slumped to the floor.

Uncle Lloyd knelt beside me and held my hand. "Yara, look at me. Remember what Liora said. When you reach the waterfall, you'll be tempted. You'll almost forget everything here, but you have to fight. You've got to remember your purpose."

That part I knew about. The needle to the heart was the shocker.

He said he would have to inject me with evil gorgon blood, but we planned on a slow-drip IV. He said it would be worse than any pain I could imagine, but I agreed to it. If it kept Treygan safe, I would have agreed to anything.

I couldn't remember the rest of the plan. Details blurred. I tried to ignore the deepfreeze spreading through my body. I gasped in agony. "How?"

"Cling to important memories. You said you still have our first day with the worms. What did you do with the worms?"

"Worms?"

Treygan screaming threats at everyone made it hard to focus. I hated hurting him like this. Would he think I betrayed him?

"Yara!" Uncle Lloyd shook me. "What did you believe about the worms?"

I squinted through the blue haze covering my eyes, concentrating on Uncle Lloyd's face. "They—I wanted them to cross the sidewalk."

"Why?"

"Because … I didn't want them to die."

"Right. You believed they should make it to safety. Just like the sea creatures. Remember your beliefs, Yara. Whatever happens, hold strong to your beliefs."

I squeezed his hand, shivering and buckling over in agony. "I'm scared," I whimpered.

"Fear is natural." He rubbed my fingers between his hands. "It's what you do with that fear that changes your fate. You can save all of them. You're strong enough. Stay true to your heart, even in your darkest hour."

"Treygan," I whispered. He was pulling and rearing against Nixie, trying to get to me.

Uncle Lloyd looked over his shoulder. "Let him go."

In a flash, Treygan threw Uncle Lloyd across the room, letting out the angriest roar I had ever heard. Uncle Lloyd landed on a floor vase, shattering it before rolling across the tile and finally stopping against a wall. The sirens screeched and wings flapped all around me.

Treygan was above me, his fingers lacing with mine.

"No," he begged. "For the love of Poseidon, no, no, no." He cradled my head while his eyes swept over me. "How could you do this to her?" he yelled. "That was blue gorgon blood. Evil blood. It will kill her!"

The pain grew sharper, but so did my vision. Everything

looked clear and crisp. Red blood dripped from Uncle Lloyd's fingers and forehead as Rownan helped him to his feet.

I found Treygan's cobalt eyes again. My voice came out strangled. "This was my decision. Everyone has always made decisions for me. This time I got to decide."

"No," he pleaded.

"She's part siren, selkie, and mer," Uncle Lloyd panted. "Turning her to stone will take much longer than anyone else. You have time to get her to the gate before it happens."

A white heron flew into the room, landing near me on the floor. I stared at it, realizing it was the same bird I had seen many times since being turned.

The eyes didn't look like a normal heron's. They were sad, familiar and haunting. They were the eyes of my mother.

Rownan

Treygan glared at our father. "How could you do this?" He glowered at me, his jaw muscles flexing. "I will never forgive either of you for this. Never."

Lloyd spoke to the sirens as if nothing had happened. "Get them to the gate before the sun sets."

Before I knew it, Mariza had her arms around me. Otabia had Treygan, and Nixie flew off the back deck in front of us, carrying Yara into the sky.

The sisters flew in a wide triangle. Nixie took the lead position. Otabia glided through the sky to the far right of me and Mariza. Treygan occasionally kicked and squirmed and shouted at her, but I couldn't make out what he said. He was too far away and the rushing wind drowned out his words.

"Mmm, do you smell it?" Mariza sniffed the air. "Despair, anger, fear, time ticking away. It's so tantalizing."

The old man's plan had to work. If it didn't, the selkies would shun me, or kill me—if Treygan didn't kill me first. What if the sirens didn't take us to the gate? How could Lloyd trust them?

"Why did you agree to this?" I asked Mariza. "You and your sisters don't want the gate opened."

Her cinnamon eyes glinted and she flicked her head. "We are obligated."

"Obligated? To whom?"

She nodded at the white heron flying beside Nixie. "Cleo, the meddling twat. She couldn't die and leave us in peace. Had to hang about and order us around."

I stared at the heron flying ahead of us. "Holy shit."

The spirit of Yara's mother was communicating through a bird? What the hell was this world coming to? How many people—or ghosts—did Lloyd have working on this plan?

Nixie stopped. Her wings flapped as she hovered above a dark circle of water. The gateway was below us.

"Which one of you boys wants her?" Nixie asked. Yara hung limp in Nixie's arms.

Treygan practically growled. "Nixie, if you give her to Rownan, so help me gods, I will make your existence hell."

"Ooh." Nixie licked her lips. "We've progressed to threats, have we?" She looked at each of us and scrunched her shoulders to her ears. "Oops," she sang, lifting her empty arms above her head. "I dropped her."

Yara splashed into the water. Otabia released Treygan and he dove in after her. Nixie, Otabia, and the creepy heron I was still trying to believe was Cleo all stared at me, wide-eyed.

"Listen to Yara," Nixie commanded me in a harsh voice. "Whatever she asks, you do it."

Before I could say a word I fell through the air, plunging feet first into the water. My coat instantly changed into my seal skin.

I wasn't sure how many selkies Jack had taken with him to the house, but at least fifteen were gathered at the entrance to the Catacombs, along with thirty or so merfolk. Selks and mer, separated like two gangs ready to attack at the first signal.

I swam past the crowd, not making eye contact with anyone. Treygan had Yara cradled in his arms. He and the Violets were deep in conversation. Yara barely turned her head, but her face twisted with pain. Her eyes stopped searching when she saw me.

Do it, she thought to me.

Do what?

Drain me of my blood over the tombs.

What the hell? Lloyd didn't tell me that part of the plan. I told him I didn't want to hurt her. Nixie said I had to do what Yara asked, but that couldn't be what she meant.

Rownan! Yara mentally shouted. *You have to, before it's too late.*

I turned around, scanning the crowd of selkies. Dina and Eve hovered near the front, watching me intently like everyone else. I extended my sight so everyone could hear me. Thankfully, they couldn't hear my heart pounding.

Someone has to distract the Violets and Treygan while I take Yara away from him. I only need a couple seconds. Enough time to get her into the Catacombs.

No one but me, Treygan, and Yara could safely swim into the Catacombs. They all knew that. No merfolk would attempt to follow me. *Do whatever it takes to keep Treygan away from me.*

Eve turned to Dina and a few others. After a minute they all nodded, and Eve looked at me again. *You better be right behind us. They'll know we're up to something.*

Eve, Dina and four other selkies swam toward Treygan

and the Violets. Indrea turned first, her body tensing like she expected a fight. Eve took off her wristband, holding it out in front of her. I had no idea what she said, but Indrea's suspicious glare softened.

I circled high, acting like I was swimming past everyone into the Catacombs, then u-turned and swam full speed at Treygan's back.

Merfolk screamed and poured forward, but I was too far ahead of them. I rammed Treygan with one powerful blow. Eve and the others had each grabbed a Violet. In Treygan's moment of distraction, Dina pried Yara from Treygan's arms. I snatched Yara from her, swimming as hard as I could into the Catacombs while Dina and another group of selkies tried to restrain Treygan.

Yara dug her fingers into my chest. *Do it,* she urged. *While they can still see. Cut me.*

I didn't want to, but in the craziness of my adrenaline pumping and with the chaos behind us I didn't hesitate. I sliced open her arm from shoulder to wrist. Blood flowed into the water around us.

Thank you, she thought.

A red and dark blue cloud trailed from her limp arm. The evil gorgon blood was already so much a part of her that she was bleeding both colors. Lloyd was right. It hadn't killed her, but what if the blood loss did? I weaved through tombs, passing blurred stone faces.

The gate was just ahead, but the sun had almost set. No gorgons were there, no light shined through. It wasn't opening.

Yara touched my chin. She felt like a block of ice in my arms. *See, you can tell them you tried. My blood didn't bring the lost souls back to life. You were loyal to your kind.* Her eyes rolled backward and her lids fluttered closed.

Even underwater my eyes burned. After all I had done, all I had put her through, she still cared about me. Lloyd said she would be in more pain than any of us could imagine, yet she pushed through the pain to help me appear loyal to a group of monsters who wanted to kill her.

I'm sorry, I said to her. *I'm so sorry.*

But what good were my words if she couldn't hear them?

Treygan crashed into my back like a wrecking ball.

Yara flew out of my arms and I smashed face-first into a stone statue. Pain exploded through my skull. For a second I thought I was blind. A few blurry blinks later I saw pieces of shattered tomb sinking to the ocean floor. I sank too, rattled and numb from the hit.

Treygan grabbed me by the hair, yanking me upward. I locked one hand around his throat, squeezing as hard as I could. His veins bulged, but he didn't flinch. I extended the claws of my other hand and slashed open the skin on his chest. His fingers closed over my wrists. *I'm going to break every bone in your spineless body.*

I managed to wiggle my right arm out of his grasp, but he snapped my left wrist like it was a piece of coral.

I howled in agony and tried to swim away, but he yanked me back.

You heartless bastard, he said. *I'll see you in hell.*

One of his hands clenched my jaw, the other wrapped around the top of my head. He would break my neck and it would all be over. He had more than enough strength to do it, and I deserved it. The gate wasn't opening. I would never see Vienna again. My brother hated me. My father was ashamed of me. I had nothing to live for.

This is my hell. Go ahead, I urged.

A soft, deep moan resonated through the water. The fury disappeared from Treygan's eyes. He loosened his grip and turned away from me, looking at Yara. She hung onto the arm of a stone merman. She was so pale she almost looked like one of the tombs, but with yellow hair. Treygan released me and swam to her.

My sight had returned, but my head throbbed. Was I imagining a snake slithering over Yara's shoulder? I swam over to apologize, and to make sure I imagined the snake.

But the snake in her hair was real. Worse than that, Yara's fins had turned to stone. Treygan's worst fears were coming true. I didn't want to see it go down like this.

Treygan's tail changed into legs. Every one of his hallmarks swirled. His skin pulsed between dark blue and gray. He sat on the ocean floor with Yara in his lap, pushing the snake and her floating hair from her face over and over again.

I sank down on the other side of her.

The crackling was the worst sound I had ever heard. Stone formed inch by inch, moving up her tail, leaving nothing but rock where life used to be.

Yara's eyes were open. She and Treygan stared at each other, but I didn't try listening to what they were saying. Treygan shook his head. Yara reached up and touched his cheek.

When he leaned down to kiss her I looked away. My brother kissed his soul mate a first and final goodbye. Life had never been fair to him.

Yara's other arm floated upward, brushing against my stomach, but she didn't look at me. She was still gazing at Treygan. The stone had only spread to her stomach, but her lips were hard rock.

She pressed two fingers over her chest then placed them against her eyes. She reached for Treygan as her shoulders and arms crackled, hardening into stone. By the time her fingers touched his face they were gray rock.

I didn't need to hear Yara to know her last words to him. Her heart, her soul, she shares with him. He taught me that pledge when we were kids.

Treygan let out a deep bellow that shook the water around us.

I had never seen my brother cry. His tears turned to stone as they poured out of him. He held the statue of Yara in his arms, rocking back and forth, his forehead pressed against lifeless rock.

I looked around at all the tombs, some reaching upward, some wide-eyed, one half-shattered. What had we done? This wasn't how it was supposed to end.

Treygan looked up, glaring at me. *You and Lloyd did this to her.*

I had no idea. He said she asked to be transformed into a gorgon. I didn't know it would kill her.

And what good did it do? The sun has set. The gate didn't open!

I glanced at the dark, sealed gate, knowing Vienna was somewhere on the other side. Every breath was a struggle. Every time I blinked I saw Vienna's face—a face I would never touch or kiss again. *I'm sorry, Treygan. Now you know what it's like to be in love. If it was Yara on the other side of that gate, and you had one shot to return to her, wouldn't you try anything to make it open?*

He didn't reply. He just hung his head, clinging to Yara's tomb, unable to let go of the inevitable. All of us had blown it. We would never return home.

I'm not sure how long I stared at the waterfall. The colors were mesmerizing, but a boom of thunder shook me from my daze and I turned to see a luminous woman with flowers for hair standing beside me.

"Hello," she said.

"Hi."

Another clap of thunder rattled through me and I looked to

my left, watching an angry storm rip and tear its way through the dark space beside us.

"I love storms," I confessed. Something moved in the waterfall, diverting my attention. "But the light and all those colors are so beautiful."

A slimy Koi fish the color of vomit flopped out of the stormy surf and landed at my feet. Its eyes bugged, a hook hung from its bloody mouth and its scales were peeling.

"Can we save it?" I asked.

The woman nodded to the waterfall. I picked up the fish and lifted it toward the ever-changing wall of color. A hole opened and the fish swam through. The hook vanished, the Koi's eyes returned to normal, its scales changed to a healthy, golden glow.

"Just like that," I said.

"So simple," she agreed. "You may also go."

Why would I need to climb through the waterfall? I looked down at my body. My legs were stone, crumbling steadily into pieces. I stared at the waterfall again and the outline of a tail appeared in the ridges of the water. Something tugged at my memory.

"Through there," she held back part of the waterfall like a curtain. "You'll be free from pain."

I peeked inside as a heron flew past me, landing on the branch of a pink tree. The bird morphed into a woman. My mother. Giant, white wings spread out behind her, the curve of each feather gleaming with hints of pink and gold. She was smiling. I had forgotten how pretty she looked when she smiled. Her eyes motioned at something behind me.

I turned around and watched the storm. "What if I don't go through the waterfall?"

"You would rather weather the storm?" the beautiful woman asked.

"I like storms. Someone told me that after the clouds clear, the sky is a blank page waiting to be filled with sunbeam songs, moonlit poetry, and stories written in the stars."

Who taught me that? An old man's face flashed in front of me, but quickly faded to a blur of yellow.

"Sometimes beauty is hidden under a veil of tragedy," the glowing woman said.

A poem. Medusa. A tiny thread brushed against my mind and I grabbed onto it. The fabric of my life raveled back together. Faint memories weaved their way back to me.

The lightning and thunder stopped. Blue and silver clouds disintegrated, leaving a constellation of teal stars twinkling in the sky. Two blue moons shone above them. Something seemed familiar about them. I could almost see a wide nose forming beside the group of stars that made up the Canis Major constellation. The faint outline of a body appeared below a ghostly face. A blue tail formed in the sky. Its iridescent scales shimmered with possibilities of my future.

"Treygan," I whispered.

I looked back and forth between the two of them: my mother, the siren, a breathtaking angel; and Treygan, the merman, my true love.

Medusa stepped closer to me. "You must choose."

"I choose to be a mermaid."

Her laughter shook the waterfall and starry sky until everything blurred around us.

"I meant choose between being an angel or retiring in peace. You do not get to return to life. You died."

"So?"

"So?" She smiled.

"I know who you are. You created a new world with three new species of creatures."

"More than three," she corrected. "You have not seen the other realms."

"See, you did all of that, but you're telling me you can't send me back?"

"That is not how the rules work."

"Then make new rules, Medusa."

She glanced at the waterfall like she might be considering it. I kept pleading my case while I had the chance.

"You wanted me as your replacement. Well, here I am. *You* need *me*. Your sisters need me. I'm the only human-monster mix that's female. I'll do it. Send me back."

She laughed again. "You are a unique conglomerate containing too many types of blood. Your instincts would be in constant battle with each other: warm, cold, light, dark."

"They would balance each other out," I argued, remembering Uncle Lloyd's theory. "I'm perfect for the job. Once a human, now a gorgon, just like you. You created the sirens, selkies, and merfolk. I'm a mixture of all of them. I have a vested interest in all sides."

She glowed brighter—if that was possible. "You are giving up the chance to enter paradise, only to return to a life of darkness as a gorgon?"

I felt powerful and wise. More so than I had ever felt while I was alive. "I'm still part mermaid, I would need the sun." She flinched and I held up my hands. "The only gorgons sentenced to the grotto were you and your sisters. You and Poseidon have children who can roam the land and waters in the other realm, correct?"

She nodded.

"So the curse wouldn't apply to me. I wouldn't need to live in the grotto, but I would agree to visit as much as Stheno and Euryale needed me to. Power would be restored to the trinity in exchange for life restored to me. It's a heck of a deal."

She grinned again. The woman smiled or laughed at everything. "You are only doing this for love."

I smiled too. "Isn't that how all of this started? You and

Poseidon broke and bent rules and created new ones, all because of love."

The flowering vines in her hair slithered around her head and some of the petals closed or fluttered to her feet. "You should know I had nothing to do with the curse. Seeing my children suffering, trapped outside of their home, it bemoans my soul. My sisters have grown angry and vengeful over the centuries. I cannot control their actions."

"Then send me back. If they get their third they'll be happy and open the gateway. Everyone wins."

"You make it sound so simple."

"Come on, Medusa. Sending me into an eternal waterfall of peace and healing is simple, but figuring out how to put my soul back in my body is impossible? I doubt it."

Her pearly eyebrows lifted. "You remind me of myself when I was young. Stubborn, fiery, would do anything for love. It was love that helped me achieve greatness. My sisters, Poseidon, my children, they gave my existence meaning."

"Then send me back. Give me a chance to do something great. In the name of love."

"I do not have that power."

I looked at the sky where the celestial form of Treygan once shined. Nothing but black sky was visible. The waterfall had disappeared. We floated alone in an infinite sea of darkness. Medusa glowed brighter than the sun, but she couldn't give me my life back.

According to Uncle Lloyd and Liora, Medusa should have agreed to the deal by now. But I couldn't give up. I refused to take no for an answer. I had to be overlooking something important.

A momentary sparkle of light caught my attention. In the hollow of Medusa's throat, a tiny sphere was embedded in her luminous skin.

"My pearl," I gasped.

She lowered her head and rested her fingers over it. "No, *my* pearl."

Treygan had said Poseidon gave an agape pearl to Medusa. It represented eternal love—just like mine and Treygan's. I had a revelation and prayed that I was right. None of this would have been possible without Treygan. I would have never been turned, never learned to love all the merfolk, never found my soul mate. Treygan was my Poseidon. He said I made him stronger, but he gave me strength and love I never imagined possible. Together, we could do anything.

"Fortunately, you know someone who *does* have the power to send me back." I stepped toward Medusa. "I want to talk to Poseidon … please."

She batted her star-filled eyes. Beams of colored light shot out of the crystal pearl at her neck and blew me backward.

A huge man three times the size of Pango appeared at Medusa's side. He was translucent, ethereal. He spoke in a voice so deep it shook the rainbow-colored sky and water around us. "Yes, my love."

Medusa leaned against his broad shoulder and stroked his beard. The flowers in her hair bloomed again. "Poseidon, this child wants to achieve greatness and help our worlds. Will you help me send her back?"

To say he was intimidating would be an understatement. He studied me with ominous, silver eyes. White-capped waves churned across them each time he blinked. "Why would you want to return to such a tumultuous place? Those worlds have become tragic stories."

My voice trembled. "I want to help write a better version."

He and Medusa glanced at each other and she smiled. Poseidon raised his glowing trident above my head, but I threw my hands up.

"Wait!" I shouted. "If you are sending me back, I would like to make a few requests."

Treygan My teeth ached from being clenched so tightly.

I failed to keep Yara safe. I failed as a guardian. I failed my people.

Rownan swam away, holding his broken wrist. How could I face the others? How could I face them? How could I tell them we were never going home? Let Rownan tell them. I had nothing left to say. Nothing left to give.

I might as well have turned to stone too. All I could do was cling to Yara, hoping it was all a nightmare. Her vapid, rocky eyes stared back at me. My jaw trembled uncontrollably as my stony tears sank in the water around us. I wrote out the words, *I love you*, across her stone chest. Each breath I took tore the hole in my heart wider.

My own father had done this. Yara had been right, we shouldn't have trusted him. Why did I believe in him? Why did I let him and Rownan through the door of that house? I stayed away from them for years. I should have never let them back into my life. I should have run away with Yara. I should have done a million things differently.

I should have been the one to sacrifice myself.

I leaned down and rested my forehead against hers. The first crack was so quiet I thought I had imagined it.

A second crack zigzagged down her forehead, splitting down the middle of her nose like a porcelain mask. I stopped breathing when I saw flesh inside the seam.

Her hands crackled, bits of rock shooting up into the water. I started tearing away layers of stone from her face, not believing my own eyes. Her skin. More and more of her skin appeared as I picked away crumbling handfuls of rock.

I was sure I was dreaming or hallucinating until her eyelids opened. I carefully brushed away the debris in her eyelashes, revealing long, amber sunbeams. *Yara?*

She smiled. I scrambled to my knees and tore away the rock from her chest and stomach. My heart pounded like a jackhammer as she tried moving her limbs. Every crackle and pop made it more real. She wasn't dead. I didn't know how, but she was alive.

She sat up, watching me break apart the hard shell over her tail.

Are you okay? I asked.

Um, she glanced around, lifting her arms, trying to brush the white and gray residue off of her. *I think so.*

I stared at her. *Do you remember what happened? Do you know who you are?*

Her lips slowly lifted into a smile. *I am Medusa, and I have returned to destroy the Earth.*

I have no idea what face I must have made—shock, horror, disbelief. But Yara laughed and threw a chunk of stone at me. *Of course I remember, Treygan. I'm your Yamabuki, and we need to open the gate.*

I tackled her like a dog happy to see its best friend. She floated backward, clinging tightly to me. *Wait,* I said. *You just lied. How is that possible?*

Can you stop asking so many questions?

I squeezed her so hard the remaining rock on her back shattered. *I thought I lost you.*

The ground started quaking, churning the water in the Catacombs. The current grew stronger, pushing us backward along the ocean floor and stirring up sand. Weeds blew off the tombs, swirling past us.

A thin line of white light appeared, like massive elevator doors struggling to open. Then it expanded, fast and wide. The gateway home was finally open. It was so bright that Yara and I shielded our eyes from the glare. The Catacombs had been such a dreary place for the last eighteen years that I had almost forgotten how sublime it was with the gate open.

One of the gorgons, Talus, swam toward us. His serpent tail propelled him faster than even I could swim. Dozens of snakes slithered and hissed around his head. His fiery eyes never met mine, he only looked at Yara.

"No!" I shouted positioning myself between them. My shout was muffled by the water. I tightened my grip on Yara. She reached up and turned my face to hers.

Treygan, it's okay, she said. *You have to let me go.*

I kept one arm locked around her, staying between her and Talus, pushing him away. *Take me! I will take Medusa's place.*

Talus flashed his jagged fangs, his snakes snapped at my face. *Release her. She belongs to the sisters.*

Merfolk and selkies were rushing past us, passing through the bright light of the gate and returning home. Several stopped and hovered around us, watching the scene we were making, or maybe shocked by the sight of Talus. None of us had seen a gorgon for eighteen years. I sensed the Violets swim up behind me as I argued with Talus. Yara pulled away from me, trying to wiggle out of my arms.

I kept my focus on Talus's flaming eyes, pleading my case. *I'm monster and human. I know more than her. I'm stronger. Take me instead!*

Caspian turned my chin toward him. *Treygan, let her go. What's done is done.*

My emotions calmed. I glared at Indrea, struggling to stay angry. *NO!* I screamed.

Talus ripped Yara away from me, dragging her behind him, swimming so fast through the gate I didn't have time to see her face one last time. I lurched forward, trying to go after them, but Caspian and Sixel had a firm grip on my arms.

I have to talk to her! He can't just steal her away for eternity.

Indrea cradled my face in her hands. *This was her destiny,*

Treygan. It was decided before she was born. You have to accept that now.

My jaw quivered again. My hands felt cold and empty. They had just been holding her, holding onto my miracle, the only girl brave enough to love me. The only girl I ever loved. How did I let something so precious slip through my fingers?

I didn't even get to say goodbye, I said to Indrea.

She gently smoothed my hair back. *Goodbye would have made it much harder.*

day 20

Treygan I had memorized every crack, line, curve and color variation in the rock wall before me. Thirty eight hours sitting in front of the entrance to the gorgons' grotto left me a lot of time to study rocks.

I had never imagined returning to our realm. For over a decade I had planned to take Yara's place inside the grotto after the Triple Eighteen—or die trying. I tried finding an entrance numerous times—underwater and on land—but found nothing. I screamed for Stheno and Euryale until my throat was raw. I begged the gorgon kin to ask the sisters to let me in. Nothing worked.

Delmar popped through the water at the edge of the rocky slope. He didn't say anything, just hoisted himself onto the flat ground and sat with his back to me—exactly like he had done yesterday. I walked over and stood above him, looking out at the divided ocean. The selkies' half was dark and cold, ours so light and warm; both shimmering and filled with life.

"How long do you plan on staying here?" Delmar asked.

"As long as it takes. I'm still her guardian."

He swung his indigo tail side-to-side through the water. "She's taken her place. There's nothing left to guard."

I watched sprites dance across the top of the water like the fireflies of Earth.

Delmar let out a deep sigh. "You've refused higher rank for years, Treygan. The Violets are insisting you become an Indigo. They've arranged a celebration in your honor."

"My honor? Tell them to honor Yara, or Lloyd, or even Rownan if they want. I didn't do anything except stand by while Yara was sentenced to an eternity of cold, secluded darkness."

Delmar stood and faced me. "You kept us all alive. Without C-weed we would have died within weeks of the gate closing."

"Great. And now what's my purpose? For years it's been harvesting the crops, protecting Yara, making sure everyone I cared about was healthy and safe. We don't need weed anymore. Everyone is back in our realm. I failed to protect Yara, so what purpose do I serve?

"How about your friends? Do we mean nothing to you?"

"Del, don't you get it? As crowded as the worlds are, my entire life I have felt alone. I accepted I would never be able to have a relationship like you and Kimber. I knew I could never have a girlfriend, or a wife, or share myself with someone in the way you say is so amazing. I accepted my fate. Then Yara changed everything. She loved me—even the evil, scary parts of me. I want that back. Is that so greedy? To know she's in there," I pointed at the grotto, "and to want to be in there with her, is that so much to ask?"

Delmar's eyes widened. "You would choose a life in the grotto over freedom?"

"To be with Yara, yes."

"You're crazy."

He turned away, but I grabbed his arm. "What if it was Kimber in there? Would you flit around out here, going on with your life, acting like it's okay that she's been banished from sunlight, beauty and freedom?"

His eyes narrowed. He glanced at the towering boulders of the grotto. "No, I would probably dynamite the place until I broke through."

"Exactly. And don't think I haven't thought of that already."

He put his hand on my shoulder. "But she's one of them now. She wouldn't be the Yara you fell in love with. She's probably a viperous monster."

I gave an exasperated laugh. "I have always been a viperous monster, but she loved me anyway."

He bowed his head, his long hair curtaining his face. "You're my best friend. I support you in whatever insane choice you make. But if they do let you in, I will miss the hell out of you."

I nodded and he dove into the water, resurfacing quickly. "I'll come back every day to see if you need anything. Maybe one day you won't be here anymore. For whichever reason."

"Wouldn't that be nice," I said.

I watched him swim away, a blur of indigo beneath the water. I sat down, leaned against a rock, and stared up at the three suns in the merfolk sky, counting the multi-colored stars around them.

A faint but steady whirring sound grew louder. I looked down to see something tiny roll against the side of my foot. It sparkled in the sunlight. My breath caught in my throat. I picked it up and squeezed my eyes shut. *Please don't let me be dreaming. Please.*

I opened my eyes. The agape pearl was still there, twinkling in the palm of my hand. I held my breath and looked at the grotto.

Yara.

I got up slowly, afraid if I made any sudden moves she would disappear like a mirage. I walked toward her, afraid to blink. The closer I came to her, the more changes I noticed. Her hair was white and diamond-like. Her irises were dark with glints of silver in them.

For a few precious minutes we just stood there, staring at each other. I took her face in my hands, thanking the gods I could see her, touch her and still smell apple blossoms wafting over me.

"Why are you looking at me like that?" she asked. Her voice still sounded like harp music.

"You're—you've changed."

She nodded. "I'm a motley monster."

"You're beautiful," I whispered. "You put Medusa to shame."

"Shhh, Stheno and Euryale are very protective of their sister."

She lifted a section of her shimmering hair and a silver snake coiled out from behind her neck, flicking its tongue. She raised her eyes and sighed. "It's the only one, but I'm mad at myself for not specifying no snakes in my hair during our negotiations."

"Negotiations?"

"Yeah, with Medusa and Poseidon."

My eyes bugged. "Beg your pardon?"

She waved her hand dismissively. "Long story. I'll explain later."

"You talked to—and negotiated with—the creators of this realm, and you're brushing it off like it's not a big deal."

Large, pearly wings exploded behind her.

"Holy Poseidon," I gasped. "You have wings too. What happened in there?"

She glanced over her shoulder at the grotto. "They said they couldn't change who I was. My blood is a mixture of human, mer, selk, siren, and gorgon. I have to live and adjust accordingly."

I circled around her, examining all of her changes. She had some new hallmarks, and her original ones had changed somewhat. Flowers grew on her twisting vines. A pale blue moon had formed at the base of her spine, opposite her rainbow-colored sun. She had a serpent hallmark almost identical to mine running between them. Her real snake appeared to be sleeping on her shoulder. She hadn't retracted her wings, but sirens could any time they wanted. I wondered if her new pet snake worked the same way.

My smile was uncontrollable. "You're no longer a Yamabuki. You're the triumphant water dragon who conquered the Eternal Falls, just like in the legend."

"Oddly enough, there was a waterfall, but I resisted the urge to jump into the mist, so you can still call me Yamabuki."

"I don't know." I wrapped my arms around her waist. "Depends what color your tail is."

Her eyes lit up. "Wait until you see it!"

We walked to the water's edge. She dove in and lifted her tail above the water. Diamond-like scales matched her hair, glimmering with every color of our realm's rainbow.

"We might need to think of a new nickname for you," I teased.

She changed her tail to legs and climbed out of the water.

I took her hands and pulled her close to me.

She smiled when I started swaying back and forth. "What are you doing?"

"You were a horrible dancer before. Let's hope you inherited some new moves as your selkie ability."

Sadness flashed in her eyes, but her voice sounded hopeful. "Rownan. Did he—?"

I rested my forehead against hers. "One of the first through the gate. He and Vienna are probably making up for lost time as we speak."

She squeezed me tighter. "Good. What about Koraline?"

"She woke up a few hours after they carried her through the gate. She's recovering with her family."

Yara let out a relieved sigh. I could almost see the guilt dripping off her shoulders. "And where is your father?"

"Who gives a damn?"

Her eyebrows arched high. "Treygan, we're both alive and together because of him. I demanded to take your place with the gorgons. He told me your plan wouldn't work, that he's been preparing me my whole life for what I needed to do. He swore Medusa was reasonable and would compromise, but I had to die to see her and make a deal. He swore she would send me back if I didn't take no for an answer."

It seemed impossible to believe, but everything about the past few days—weeks—felt that way. My father had protected me and Yara at any cost. "I guess I need to pay him a serious thank-you visit."

"Definitely. Do you know how hard it was to believe him when he told me death didn't have to mean the end?"

I tucked a white strand of hair behind her ear. "He was right. I wouldn't have believed it. I'm still afraid I'm dreaming right now."

"Mermen don't dream," she said mockingly.

"Touché." The grotto towered ominously behind her. "How long do we have?" I asked. "I want to ask Stheno and Euryale if I can live in there with you."

She cocked her head to the side. "Aww, how cruel of me. I haven't told you yet."

"Told me what?"

"I'm not sentenced to the grotto like them. It's part of the deal. We still have some ground rules to iron out, but I get to roam freely—come and go between the worlds as often as I want."

My hallmarks swirled joyfully. I was filled with so much hope and happiness I couldn't speak.

Yara laughed. "Treygan, your skin is so bright it's almost blinding."

"We can be together? Here? Beyond the grotto?"

"Yes, we can be together. No restrictions." The glow of her smile made me dizzy, but something mischievous lingered behind it.

"*No* restrictions?" I asked. "You don't mean—"

She flapped her wings once before curling them around us. She lifted her chin, leaning closer to me. "I'm part gorgon now. Your petrifying power is useless against me."

For the first time ever I didn't suppress the passion I felt for her. I didn't pull away, or try to change my train of thought. I caressed her face, pausing for a few moments so she could have the calm before the storm that she enjoyed so much. I waited for her shaky inhalation and pressed my mouth to hers. My lips found heaven.

She shivered and I pulled back, still scared I might hurt her, but she smiled and drew me back to her. She ran her fingers gently over my eyes, then down my cheek, muttering something about a constellation. She whispered, "Kiss me again."

When our lips met there was nothing soft about it. We devoured each other. The simple act of our breath and tongues tangling together was more incredible than anything I had ever felt. I lifted her up and she wrapped her legs around me. Even as we splashed into the water, I couldn't stop kissing her.

For over a decade I had planned on the Triple Eighteen being the end of me. Instead, it was a new chapter in a story of endless possibilities. I silently thanked Medusa and Poseidon for giving me a feisty, beautiful, loving and stubborn mermonster to swim beside me for the rest of my very long life.

day 21

The thin lines of moss above Stheno's eyes narrowed as I finished proposing my idea.

Even in the dim glow of the fire-lit grotto, I could see the disapproval on Euryale's leathery face. For a long time the only sound was the dripping of stalactites. The sisters took forever to think about everything. I had learned to be quiet and wait patiently for one of them to answer, otherwise it just turned into another argument.

We heard the call of the sirens and Euryale's fangs slid over her lip. The pictures in the history books had it wrong. Their fangs came out of their bottom teeth, and they were jagged, not smooth.

"Well," I said. "Sounds like your breakfast has arrived. We will discuss this later."

The water of the cave pool stirred. I stood at the edge, waiting for Mariza and Otabia to appear. The black and brown birds burst through the surface, shaking the water from their wings. Then they each morphed into their siren forms.

"Yara," Otabia nodded, slicking the water off her arms.

"Good morning, Otabia."

Mariza wiped blood from her chocolate lips with the back of her hand. I prepared to dive into the water, but paused. "Mariza, you didn't kill anyone last night, did you?"

"Only Stheno gets to know that answer," she cackled, crouching in front of the gorgon.

Otabia made her sickening, gagging sounds that meant she was about to regurgitate. I shook my head, transformed into bird form and dove into the pool. Twisting and turning through the narrow, water-filled tunnels of the grotto, I thought about my mother. She had lived this life. She had traveled these caves and flew around this realm. I never thought we had much in common. Turns out we were more alike than I could have ever imagined.

Daylight appeared at the small opening ahead and I shot through it, transforming into monster form in midair. Nixie sat atop the highest rock of the grotto. I flew over to her and sat beside her, both of our legs dangling over the side.

"I hate that your wings are bigger and prettier than mine," she snapped.

I retracted them. The puff of wind sent our hair whooshing over our faces. My snake disappeared too, which meant I wouldn't be able to think as clearly, but visits with Nixie didn't require excessive brainpower. "There, I'm back to normal. You have no competition."

She snickered, but seemed sad. "You are far from normal."

"What's wrong? You haven't been yourself the past couple days."

She glanced at me then stared down at the oceans below us. "I think she's gone."

"Who?"

"Your mother."

Nixie hadn't mentioned my mother since she carried me to the gateway on the Triple Eighteen. I hadn't stopped thinking about her, but I didn't realize Nixie thought about her too.

"She is gone," I said. "I saw her cross over into the Eternal Falls."

Nixie's wings drooped, resting on the ground behind us. "That means she'll never come back. She doesn't need me anymore."

I turned to fully face her. "You said she bossed you around and made you do things you didn't want to do. I figured you would be happy to be free of her."

She picked at her red nails as if actual polish would come off. "I know, but now I feel sort of lost, like I serve no purpose. I don't even get to regurgitate memories like Otabia and Mariza because you refuse to drink blood."

I tried not to laugh. "Is that what you want? To spend your life throwing up stolen human memories for me?"

She shrugged. "At least it would give me something to do."

"Nix, you're still my siren, assigned to help me. We have some major changes in the works. When the time comes, I'm going to need your help and your abilities. I can't do it alone."

Her eyes twinkled. "You promise?"

"Yes, I promise."

She gently swung her knee-high boots against the rock wall below us. "It's hard losing her twice, isn't it?"

"What?"

"Your mother," she said. "It mangled my heart when she died the first time, but then her spirit stayed for all those years. Now, it's like she died all over again. I miss her."

"It was different this time. She looked peaceful and happy crossing through the waterfall. It wasn't anything like finding her lifeless in bed."

"I agree. That was awful."

My head snapped up. "How do you know it was awful?"

"I was there. She knew death was coming, so she called to me and I held her while she died."

"No, she was alone in her bedroom. You weren't there."

Nixie smiled. "I disguised myself as the wind so you wouldn't see me. You were sitting on the porch swing. I flew right past you."

I grabbed Nixie's arm, my mouth hanging open. "*You* were the pretty pink wind?"

She nodded and flexed her lean muscles. "Who do you think helped you get her into the boat?"

My eyes bugged so wide I thought my brows would fly off my forehead. "Why did you let me put her in that boat? You must have known it would sink."

"We—my sisters and I—vowed not to show ourselves to you until you were eighteen. Your mother explained what you were doing." She twirled her ruby hair around her finger. "It was cute that you thought you were taking her to be with your father. Your mother liked the idea of her body disappearing into the ocean. She would have preferred evaporating into the sky, but that wasn't possible, was it?"

It all clicked into place as Nixie talked. "That night, were you the one who told Treygan where I was? That's how he knew I was drowning?"

"Guilty. Well, your mother made me tell him. She chose him as your guardian because he was the fastest of all merfolk. And good thing, because even he barely made it to you in time."

"How could I have been so clueless about everything?"

"Your mother was an expert at keeping secrets."

"No kidding," I grunted. "My whole life it was a secret that she cared about me at all."

Nixie took my hands in hers. Her talons dug into my skin. "She sucked at being human. She hated it. Imagine knowing what you know now about our existence, then returning to a human life. No powers, no flying, no sharing your soul with someone. Then imagine your soul mate dying."

My heart skipped a beat and I choked on my breath.

"Exactly," Nixie said. "Your mother was devastated when Vyron died. She blamed herself for everything: for making a deal with the gorgons so they could be human, promising you to that dark life in the grotto, making Vyron and herself so sick that it killed him and would eventually kill her and Lloyd. She hated herself and what she'd become."

"She hated me too. Otabia let me feel that for myself."

"Oh, Yara. Don't be a dimwit. If you had held on a little longer you would have seen that it was your mother who asked Lloyd to help them protect you. Your father agreed, of course. He loved you just as much as she did, but your mother asked for the spell to be cast. It was her idea to run away and protect you. Then more tragedy followed. The gate closing, Lloyd's kidneys shutting down, and Vyron dying in that fire. She couldn't take anymore. She thought she was doomed. She believed any action she took would make things worse."

"But she wished I was never born."

"She wished that because she never thought she would love you as much as she did. When she agreed to hand you over to the gorgons, she didn't know how strong the bond between a mother and a child could be. She knew she could never give you up. And that meant she and Vyron would have to die to protect you. It was a no-win situation for her. Until …."

"Until what?" I prodded.

"Until she died and found out she could be your angel. Watch you live your life, help keep you safe, and make sure everything turned out okay. She and Liora were a team."

"You know about Liora?"

"Cleo told me years ago. Lloyd even hung their portraits side by side in his house."

The angel wall panel. I could picture the white-washed wings clearly. I always thought she resembled my mother. But in my memories my mother was sick, skinny, with sunken eyes and hating life. The angel looked healthy, strong, bright-eyed and joyful—just like she did after she crossed through the falls. "My mother is the angel wood portrait."

Nixie smiled and poked the wings hallmark on my back. "The *siren* portrait, but yes, angel is also appropriate."

My mother did love me. So did my father, Lloyd and Treygan. Even a twisted, sultry siren helped keep me safe. I had a whole secret team of supernatural creatures looking out for my wellbeing and I never knew it. At least, not that I could fully remember.

"She really loved me," I whispered.

Nixie put her arm around me and kissed my cheek. "She had to choose between giving herself the life she dreamed of, or giving you the life of your dreams. She chose you, Yara."

Tears streamed down my face. Happy tears. Through their rainbow blur I saw a streak of midnight blue in the water below. Treygan popped through the surface, smiling up at us. I waved, kissed Nixie's forehead, and stood up.

"You're coming to the celebration, right?" I asked.

She stood and put one hand on her hip. "It's the first time all the sea creatures have partied together in almost two decades. I wouldn't miss it."

Nixie spread her wings and flew off the cliff while I did a swan dive into the ocean and swam to Treygan.

"You ready?" he asked, giving me a long and passionate kiss before I could answer.

"Yes," I finally managed.

"I can't believe Lloyd agreed to throw the party at his place."

I laughed and ran my fingers through Treygan's nearly-black hair. "He wanted to celebrate his son reaching Indigo status."

"I could have been an Indigo a long time ago."

"I know, but you stayed a Blue to protect me."

He smiled his sexy, cocky grin. "That's right, so don't forget it."

We kissed again then I tugged his arm. "Come on, I can't wait to see everyone, especially Koraline and Rownan. And you better not ignore me like you did at the last party."

Treygan wrapped his arms around my waist. "Nothing and no one could ever separate us now."

When we swam through the gateway I expected to see others on their way to the party, but the Catacombs were empty. They weren't even catacombs anymore. All of the tombs had been taken back to Rathe and given to the family members of the lost souls. Only sand remained, and the remnants of forgotten plants.

Where is everyone, I asked Treygan.

The party started at sunrise. As Pango says, we're fashionably late.

We were nearing Eden's Hammock when Treygan dipped under me and swam backward facing me.

I laughed. *What are you doing?*

Memorizing you.

Between those words and *that* look he had in his eyes, I melted.

He pulled me on top of him and we floated upward, locked in a kiss. When his lips traveled down to my neck I lost control of all rational thought. I pulled his hair, moaning and making little sighs of pleasure. We broke through the surface just as his tongue grazed the ridge of my ear.

"I love you, Yamabuki," he whispered.

Fire spread through every part of me. My fingers raked down his chest and he gasped. He tried pulling away, which only made me want him more, so I dug in tighter and kissed him again.

"Claws," he grunted as I sucked on his bottom lip.

I let go and looked at my hands, shocked to see deadly, pearly claws. "Oh, my gosh! I'm so sorry."

I had reopened his wounds from Rownan's attack, but Treygan shrugged it off.

"Guess I know what your selkie trait is," he chuckled.

I instantly changed into human form.

"Oh, wow." He beamed.

"What?"

"You're back to being a brunette."

"Yes!" I threw my head back, grinning triumphantly. "I hoped that would happen. I didn't look right as a blonde."

"Does this mean you'll never be a Green, or any of the other ranks?"

"I'm a White. Medusa said that will never change."

Treygan's hair and tail were darker because of his new Indigo rank, but thankfully his eyes remained the same cobalt blue I loved staring into. "Treygan, no matter what rank we are, or how we might change, will you promise me something?"

"If I can."

"You'll always be my guardian?"

He smiled, pulling me close again. "We'll guard each other."

"I like the sound of that." I snaked my body against his, leaning in for another kiss.

He shot me a questioning glance. "Careful, human skin is much more sensitive." He looked me up and down with more love in his eyes than I had ever seen, and more lust than any siren had ever shown.

I nibbled his ear and breathed heavily. "We've earned the right to lose control." He changed into human form, kissing my neck between his words. "We're going to be really late."

"They're good at waiting," I said breathlessly. "They had eighteen years of practice."

We bobbed in the water, two bodies and souls tangled up as one.

Delmar had told Treygan the truth. There was no better feeling than being in love. And I could now attest to Koraline's motto firsthand. We *should* love until it kills us, because there truly is nothing better worth dying for.

THE END

KAREN AMANDA HOOPER

Born and bred in Baltimore, Karen has been making up stories for as long as she can remember. In high school she discovered her passion for putting her thoughts onto paper, but it wasn't until her late twenties that she wrote her first novel. Due to her strong Disney upbringing, she still believes in fairytales and will forever sprinkle magic throughout all of her novels.

Karen is currently sunning and splashing around Florida with her two adorable dogs.

To learn more about Karen and her writing, visit her website at www.KarenAmandaHooper.com. You can also find her at www.YAconfidential.blogspot.com where she has teamed up with a stellar group of Young Adult authors and created a teen-focused blog for writers and readers.

CPSIA information can be obtained at www.ICGtesting.com
Printed in the USA
LVOW091550290312

275320LV00010B/15/P